I0717272

Parlatheas Press Titles:

<u>The Cayn Trilogy:</u>

Son of Cayn
City of Cayn
Blood of Cayn

<u>Chronicles of Damage Inc.:</u>

Phantoms of Ruthaer
Mask of the Vampire

<u>Adventures of Roger V:</u>

A Thief on King Street
Message for the Devil

Message for the Devil

A ROGER V ADVENTURE

Jason McDonald
Stormy McDonald

Parlatheas Press, LLC
Hollywood, SC

Note: This is a work of fiction. Names, characters, places, and incidents are either a product of the authors' imaginations or are used fictitiously. All situations and events in this publication are fictitious and any resemblance to actual persons, living or dead, or to businesses, companies, events, institutions, or locales is purely coincidental.

Cover Image & Design:	C. Jason McDonald
Title Page Design:	MJ Youmans-McDonald
Title Page Border:	Rebecca Read from www.pixabay.com

ISBN: 978-1958315149 (paperback)

DEDICATION

To my father: You have been and always will be my inspiration.

Jason

To Kevin and Lacy, who never back down from life's battles, meeting every challenge with strength and humor. You're my heroes.

Stormy

"My past is an armor I cannot take off, no matter how many times you tell me the war is over."

– Jessica Katoff

"You never really understand a person until you consider things from his point of view... until you climb into his skin and walk around in it."

– Atticus Finch
To Kill a Mockingbird

CHAPTER 1
THIRTY GOLD PIECES

Tuesday, April 1, 1969

*H*ands stretched toward the ceiling and her feet bound, Queen Ambrose Battenberg hung in the middle of an iron plated room. Blood dripped from her ripped skin and ran along the floor into a drain.

Roger Vaughn reached for her. A thick rope wrapped itself around his neck, stopping him. He gasped out her name, but she didn't respond.

"It was you who did this," said a sepulchral voice. The words echoed inside his mind. "If you hadn't exposed her to the dærganfae, none of this would have happened."

The floor gave way beneath him. Roger's stomach slammed into his chest, stealing his breath. For the briefest of moments, his body floated. Then, he fell.

The noose constricted, and his body jerked.

Heavy drops of water pattered against the second story balcony door, and Roger took an involuntary step back as he blinked the nightmare — no, *daymare* — from his vision. He still felt the burn of the rope on his neck.

Diagonal sheets of rain scoured pollen from his tiny balcony's wrought-iron rail. The historic buildings and streets of his neighborhood glistened.

Despite knowing his friends and Queen Ambrose had escaped Terra, he didn't know if they had survived the return journey to their shared home-world of Gaia, and the uncertainty haunted him, especially visions of the young queen. Her torment by the ghostly executioner in Charleston's Old City Gaol had become more frequent over the past few days, and it was taking a toll on his sanity.

Trying to calm his racing heart, he leaned his shoulder against the doorjamb and watched yellow-streaked water sluice down a granite curb along Church Street and enter a grated inlet, where it would eventually make its way into Charleston Harbor.

He needed a diversion, something to take his mind off the events at the Old Gaol. Back home on Gaia, there seemed to be an adventure around every corner. Here, they hid themselves like thieves. A part of him felt they were playing hide and seek, another part felt he was asking for trouble.

Roger glimpsed his reflection in a pane of wavy glass. Skillfully applied powders and creams softened his few Islander features — traits handed down to him by his great grandmother. During his service to the Highlord of Gallowen, he'd learned to mask his height and wiry build through posture and disguises so there would be nothing remarkable about him. He was everyone; he was no one. Not even his family had seen his true self in the past ten years.

Perhaps it was the weather, but he felt cooped up, trapped. He turned from the balcony door. In keeping with the colonial architecture of the three-story building that housed his office, pale plaster and maple wainscotting ran along three sides of the room. The fourth side held his bookshelves and the door to the foyer.

Even though his office had electricity, all the lights were switched off. The faint electrical buzz from the walls and fixtures had set his teeth on edge. Wan daylight seeped through the windows that flanked the balcony and cast shadows across the heart pine floor. The wood's heavy grain and random knots made the surface appear uneven.

Picking up a leatherbound tome from his desk, Roger returned it to the shelf, then selected the next volume from his set of encyclopedias. He sank into his desk chair with a world-weary sigh and lit the beeswax candle. After only a few minutes of reading, he was up again. Pacing back to the window, he glared at the empty street.

There was a gentle rap at his office door.

Turning away from the rain and thoughts of home, Roger moved behind the scarred mahogany desk. "Come in," he said.

Wearing black frockcoats, woolen breeches, and low-heeled riding boots, the two gaunt men who entered looked like no one Roger had met thus far during his brief time on Terra. Both paused just inside the doorway, scanning the room's layout before turning their attention to the bookshelves between them and the desk.

Orderly rows of bottles and jars filled with multi-colored fluids and powders occupied the space above his books.

Centered on a shelf near the top were glass beakers set in metal frames, glass stirring rods, a mortar and pestle, and a neat stack of trivets.

At the far end, a low shelf within easy reach of Roger's chair held a two-inch wide leather belt with an assortment of pouches along its length. Fastened tightly by rawhide loops were a half dozen terracotta grenades. Bulbed at each end, intricate runes worked their way around the pipe-like shafts.

Roger watched his visitors' eyes linger on the top shelf.

In a position of honor sat a wooden placard bearing a haint-blue hand with its fingers splayed. A single eye with a red iris stared out from the center of the palm.

The knock-kneed man in front hobbled across the room. He extended a bony, gnarled hand in greeting. "Roger Vaughn, I presume. My name is John Fisher. This is my companion, Joseph Roberts."

Roger shook John's hand. He had a firm grip, but not the callused one of a laborer — a merchant, perhaps. "Please take a seat, Mister Fisher," he said, gesturing to the wooden chair in front of his desk.

Turning to the other gentleman, he nodded toward four metal-framed chairs that surrounded a round table made from white plastic, a housewarming gift from Nate. "Would you be kind enough to drag one over from the table for yourself?"

"Much obliged," Joseph Roberts replied, remaining next to John. "We plan t'not tarry."

Noticing Joseph was missing part of his ear, Roger hid his frown and took a seat.

After handing his coat to his companion, John Fisher maintained a tight-lipped smile as he gripped the chair. When he finally managed to sit, he let out a deep sigh, and his whole body relaxed.

"What can I do for you?" Roger asked.

"Mister Vaughn, my wife's missing. I want you to find her."

Roger leaned back. "Mister Fisher, I believe you came to the wrong place. I don't find people."

"You must," John said. His eyes took on a feverish gleam, and his hands clenched the arms of his chair.

"It's not that I don't want to help, but I've lived here less than a month and wouldn't even know where to start. Have you tried the local constabulary?"

"Mister Vaughn, you're the only one who can aid me."

Suspicion flared inside Roger's mind as he studied the two men. He'd been pining about home when they entered and failed to note their out-of-place accents. That, and there wasn't a drop of rainwater on them.

"How did you get my name?" asked Roger.

"We have a mutual acquaintance. A *blumkinde* named Junopsis. He said you could find her."

Roger fought to keep his reaction neutral. A former slave of the Dark One, Junopsis was a humanoid creature Roger and his Gaian friends had set free while searching for the missing Queen Ambrose. He'd neither seen nor heard from Junopsis since one of the Sha'iry — the Dark One's priests — tried to kill all of them. Roger was relieved to know the blumkinde had survived, but it also alarmed him that Junopsis had sent these two men.

"I take it, she's been missing since March fifteenth," Roger said.

"Yes."

"Just over two weeks," Roger said, dreading the reply.

"Yes."

Roger struggled against his memories of the events at the Old City Gaol and its ghost tower. Captured by its Executioner, he had been subjected to visions of his friends being tortured and executed. Unable to differentiate between reality and the aethereal, he lay helpless until Sir Cerdic's voice had cut through his despair and brought him back. The memories fed a deep-seated fear of the Gaol's inherent evil, and he'd made a point of staying away from that side of the city.

"Mister Fisher, if Junopsis sent you, then you know my situation. I'm not from Charleston, and I only agreed to open a consulting business to help the local constabulary on an as-needed basis."

A look of desperation entered Mister Fisher's eyes as he raised his clasped hands. "Please. You must help me — help us. The Jack Ketch is out there, and if he finds her before we do, he'll take her back to the Gaol." Unless John was an exceptional actor, he sincerely believed his wife was in danger.

With a sinking feeling this would lead him back to that

infernal place, Roger pushed aside his book and a day-old newspaper and retrieved a notepad and pencil from the top desk drawer. "Mister Fisher, I'll try to help, but understand my resources are limited."

"I have every confidence you will find her," John replied, setting a canvas bag on the newspaper. It tipped over and several gold coins spilled out. "There's thirty pieces of gold in that pouch. It's all I have. Feel free to count them if you want."

Roger eyed the money. Based on his limited experience, he knew gold coins weren't used in Terra like they were in Gaia, his home. In fact, he hadn't seen any of the locals spend a gold piece — only silver pieces.

"What's your wife's name?" he asked.

"Lavinia."

"Age?"

"Twenty-eight."

"Can you describe her?"

"Black hair. Velvety eyes. Tan skin. Beautiful..." John's voice broke. He lowered his head and convulsed with a stifled sob.

"Mister Fisher, I apologize for these questions, but I have to ask."

"I understand," John replied, still trying to get himself under control.

"How did you meet?" Roger asked.

Joseph gave John's shoulder a reassuring pat and said, "The two grew up on his uncle's farm in Rowan County, North Carolina. Lavinia was one of the slaves, a mulatto. Colonel Fisher didn't approve of the attention John gave her. Said she had a drop of the devil's blood in her. To separate the two, his uncle's lawyer sold her to a doctor here in Charleston."

John straightened in his chair and calmed himself before saying, "I gave up my home to search for Lavinia. It took four years, but I found her working as a houseslave for Doctor Glover. I pleaded with the doctor and, after much convincing, bartered two horses and all their gear for her. From there, we happened upon what we thought was a bit of fortune. Mister John Ball needed someone to keep Six Mile House for him. We agreed." John turned away and said in a quiet voice, "How could we know that decision would prove our undoing?"

"When did the two of you marry?"

"We didn't," John replied, eyes downcast, his hands once more in his lap. "At least, not in the church. We lived together for five years. It was a common law marriage."

"I see," Roger said, jotting down notes. "What was she wearing when you last saw her?"

Again, John Fisher broke down with tears trailing from his eyes.

"I need to know," Roger insisted.

"A white gown. The same one..."

"Mister Fisher, what happened when you escaped the Gaol? Why didn't you move on? That's what most of the prisoners did."

"That's just it. We were supposed to. I saw the Light, but I don't think Lavinia did. In our haste, we became separated. Joseph here found me, and we've been searching for her ever since."

"Where would she go? Did she have any friends in town?"

"Her sister, Sally. She was part of Doctor Glover's household for a time, but that was the first place we checked. Neither Lavinia nor Sally were there."

"What was the doctor's full name?"

"Joseph Glover."

"You said you became separated. How did that happen?"

John took a moment before he answered, "When we left the Gaol, she became agitated. She wouldn't say why. All the time looking back over her shoulder, as if someone was following her. I think it was the Jack Ketch. She pushed me away and ran. She wanted to save me."

"Jack Ketch?"

"The Executioner."

"But he was dead," said Roger, trying to convince himself. "I saw his body."

"Mister Vaughn, you and your friends released the prisoners, but the spirit of that place is not so easily defeated." Joseph stared out the window as he spoke. "It calls to us. It wants us back. It seeks to punish us — all of us."

"Why don't you leave Charleston? Get as far away from that thing as you can," Roger said.

"I will not leave without Lavinia!" John Fisher replied with a sudden burst of strength. "Even if it means returning to the Gaol."

Outside, a car door slammed.

John Fisher tugged on Joseph's sleeve and, with help, rose from his seat.

"Is there anything else you can tell me?" asked Roger.

Leaning forward, John placed both his hands flat on the desk. "She's out there, Mister Vaughn. When you find her, tell her I won't leave without her. Tell her that schooner for Cuba will be there waiting."

"What about you? Where can I find you?" asked Roger as he stood.

"Bring my wife back to me. Bring her back to the Six Mile House, where Dorchester Road intersects Goose Creek Road near Ashley Ferry."

John took his coat from his friend, and the two headed toward the door. Before leaving, John turned and said, "Be vigilant, Mister Vaughn. The Jack Ketch is out there, too. If the Gaol finds out you are aiding us, it may call upon you as well."

Frantic footsteps pounded on a metal stair, and the reception area's exterior door burst open. "Mister Vaughn, sorry I'm late!" a female voice called out. "The streets were flooded, and traffic got backed up."

In his office, Roger stared down at the gold pieces. He plucked one using just his thumb and forefinger. About an inch in diameter, the coin's reeded edge was worn nearly smooth. Under the silhouette of an eagle with its wings splayed was the sum 5D. On the opposite side was the silhouette of a woman's capped bust over the date, 1818.

Roger raced into the waiting area. A walnut desk guarded his office door. The secretary's chair sat empty. On the far wall was a velvet chair, a table, and a short lamp. A loveseat took up the back wall. Hanging above it was an encaustic painting of concentric blue and yellow circles on a field of red. All were leftovers from the previous tenant.

"Miss Tyler, did you see anyone leave?"

"No," she replied from the hallway that led to his living quarters.

He threw open the front door and searched the parking

lot below. Except for a two-tone, seafoam green and white Nash Metropolitan pelted by rain, there was nothing there. His guests had vanished.

"Who would be out in this mess?" Brie asked. She stood half-in, half-out of the bathroom doorway, toweling off her hair.

"Yes, who would be out in this mess," Roger repeated.

Brie turned off the bathroom light and joined him at the door. "You okay?"

Roger handed her the coin still gripped in his hand. "We have our first case."

Brie held it up and said, "Wow! I've never seen a gold coin before. Who's our client?"

"John Fisher."

"Do we get to kill someone?" Her sapphire-colored eyes sparkled with a mixture of excitement and mischief.

"No, Miss Tyler," Roger said. "We do not get to kill someone." His breath caught briefly as he took in her saturated floral dress. It clung to her like a second skin, and his heart skipped a beat. Tall and slender with golden-brown hair, Miss Tyler carried herself with the confidence and free spirit of a roaming troubadour.

"Maybe next time," she said with a sigh. "So, what are we doing?"

"*I'm* searching for a missing wife."

"Mister Vaughn, that was not our deal. I'm supposed to help you, remember? Besides, you're stuck here without me, unless you plan to walk everywhere."

It was true. Roger had found he had an aversion to certain elements of Terran technology. It could have all been in his head, but something about the refined oils and items made with what Miss Tyler called *fossil fuels* made him sick to his stomach. They, along with radio waves and electricity, seemed to have a debilitating effect on him. He was fine with magic and alchemy, but Terran technology, not so much. That's why the office was devoid of phones, television, and radio. He refused to use the plastic conference table. He even tried to cut off the power, but Miss Tyler had put her foot down. It was also why he didn't pilot those four-wheeled chariots. He'd much rather have a good horse.

"You know you can call me Roger," he said.

Brie's forehead clouded and her eyebrows drew down on

him. "No, *Mister Vaughn*, it wouldn't be proper. I mean, you saved my life at the lighthouse and all, but I'm your secretary. We work together. It's important to people, especially my parents, that we maintain a professional relationship."

It was Roger's turn to give her a skeptical look. "Since when did you start doing what your parents tell you?"

"Since now," Brie replied primly, handing him back the coin. "Who's the wife?"

Roger went into his office and scanned his notebook. "Her name is Lavinia. She went missing a couple of weeks ago."

Brie crossed her arms and cocked her head. "Two weeks ago. You mean when Ambrose was here, you and your friends rescued us from the Old City Jail, and then you missed your opportunity to go home."

The fact that he'd chosen Brie — a woman he'd only just met that day — over his family, friends, and job remained unspoken between them.

"Yes."

"Was this Lavinia imprisoned there, like me?"

"I suspect so. Although from the coins, I'd say she'd been there much longer."

Brie stepped into his office and held out her hand. "Let me see that coin again."

"There's a pouch full. Pick one," Roger said. He absently tapped a pencil against his notes and wished he'd thought to ask for Doctor Glover's address.

Out of the corner of his eye, he watched Brie select a coin and let out a slight gasp.

"1811... We're not looking for Lavinia Fisher, are we?"

"Why? What's wrong?" asked Roger.

She looked up at him and narrowed her eyes. "You don't know, do you?"

"Know what?"

"John and Lavinia Fisher aren't some poor lost souls. Back in the early 1800s, they kept a tavern outside Charleston, where they spent years murdering and robbing. People travelling the road nearby would disappear, never to be heard from again. After they were caught, the police dug up two bodies on the property and found even more in the cellar. Some say Lavinia Fisher was the first female mass murderer ever hanged in America — definitely the first in South Carolina."

Roger studied the young woman who'd ensconced herself in his outer office as his secretary-cum-guide to all things Terran. She was scooping the coins back into their pouch as if they carried a curse. He realized she was genuinely alarmed.

"At the City Jail, did we set those cutthroats free?" she asked.

"I suspect so. All the more reason to take the case. We can't let murderous ghosts run amok."

"And if we do find her?"

"We send her and her husband out of the mortal realm to their final judgement."

Brie sighed. "Fine. Where do we start?"

"Did the tavern they ran have a name?"

She scrunched her nose as she thought and said, "I think they called it the Six Mile Inn or House."

"Do you know where it was?" Roger asked.

"North of town somewhere. It burned down a long time ago."

"Could it be near the intersection of Dorchester Road and Goose Creek Road?"

"Maybe. I know where Dorchester is, but I haven't heard of Goose Creek Road. Wait, I have your map at my desk," Brie said. She ran off and returned with a large street map with creases allowing it to be folded and tucked away in a car's glovebox. She laid it out on Roger's desk and traced a line with her finger. "Here's Dorchester. It turns at the railroad tracks and ends at Rivers Avenue."

"Could Rivers be another name for Goose Creek Road?" Roger asked, leaning over the desk.

"Maybe. It does lead to Goose Creek and Moncks Corner beyond that."

"What's there now?" he asked.

"I'm not sure. I know the Navy Base where my father works extends to Rivers Avenue, but I don't know if this intersection is considered part of it or not. We'd have to drive out there and see." Brie eyed Roger and asked, "Do you think the stories about them are true?"

That was the exact question Roger asked himself. His initial impression of John Fisher was not that of a killer.

Maybe his companion, but not John. John Fisher came across as a man deeply devoted to his wife. Yet this couple had been accused of horrible murders, and he assumed tried, convicted, and then punished. They got what they deserved, didn't they? But then again, the Executioner had held the Fishers prisoner for almost a hundred and fifty years, keeping their spirits from the Eternal Father's judgement. One thing Roger did know: the John Fisher he had met was not the person Brie had described. Something didn't add up.

Roger examined the map, realizing how out of his depth he really was. Back on Gaia, he had the resources of the Highlord to help him. Here, he had Brie and Nate Stone.

After putting three of the coins in his pocket, he dropped the heavy pouch into the lowest desk drawer. He stared at it for a moment, thinking he was being paranoid. Deciding to err on the side of caution, he slipped a rounded lodestone into the pouch, cinched it tight, and locked the drawer.

Roger collected his leather belt with its numerous pouches and moved to the hall closet, where he grabbed his oilskin duster and the trilby Brie had given him.

"Mister Fisher said we're supposed to take her to Six Mile. Put on a raincoat and bring the map. Let's check out their story. It may be nothing, but there's only one way to be sure."

CHAPTER 2
SIX MILE HOUSE
Tuesday, April 1, 1969

*R*ain dripping from his trilby, Roger locked the office door and followed Brie down the metal steps and across the parking lot.

Trimmed in shiny steel, water beaded and trailed down the hood of the two-tone Metropolitan. Brie went around to the car's helm while Roger slid into its passenger seat.

The engine purred to life.

Coming from a world without cars, Roger clutched the edge of the fabric bench with his left hand, while his right held the door handle in a death grip.

Brie backed the car out of its parking space and pulled up to Church Street. With windshield wipers sliding across the glass, Brie peered left, right, and left again before turning north. Water splashed the sidewalk as they drove through puddle after puddle. She passed Saint Philip's Church with its lofty steeple, navigating her way through the maze of narrow streets.

"So, how do you find a ghost?" Brie asked, shifting the lever at the steering column. The hum from the Metropolitan's engine deepened, and the compact car sped forward.

Roger folded the map so he could follow their route. "It depends."

"Depends on what?"

"How they died, where they died, and why they're still here."

"Did you chase ghosts back on Gaia?"

"No."

Brie looked askance at Roger. "So, what exactly did you do?"

"I was part of the Highlord's Confrérie des Freux or, roughly translated, Guild of the Rooks."

"Rook? Like the chess piece?"

"More like the bird, but, yes, sometimes like the chess piece."

"I'm not sure I understand."

"We gathered information for the Highlord."

"You mean you were a spy?"

"Yes," Roger answered, giving her his most disarming smile.

"Uh-huh," Brie said, clearly not impressed. "And that makes you qualified to hunt ghosts?"

"Not exactly."

"Then what, exactly?"

"Miss Tyler, I'm a problem solver."

"*That* makes you sound like an assassin."

"No, I'm not an assassin. Unfortunately, in my world kill or be killed situations tend to arise more often than one would like. Ideally, I observe people, and can tell a lot about them by just noticing the details. Call it my special power."

"So, these ghosts, they were just people?"

Roger looked up from the map. "They acted like it. They had human problems. The complication, of course, is they're dead and travel the aether."

"Which is why we don't see them every day."

"Yes."

Keeping both eyes on the road, Brie gripped the steering wheel with her hands at two and ten o'clock. Stress lines formed at the edges of her mouth. "Okay. What's the plan?"

"First, I want to see about this Six Mile House. Learn what I can about it and John and Lavinia Fisher. The more we know, the faster we can find his wife. Second, we research Doctor Joseph Glover and see if he has descendants who still live here. Lavinia may be searching for her sister."

"She had a sister?"

"A Miss Sally. Apparently, they were both slaves brought here from North Carolina. Assuming Mister Fisher and his friend weren't lying."

"I never knew Lavinia Fisher was a slave."

"My guess is they kept it a secret, especially with she and John living together like they were."

Brie shifted in her seat and said, "Change of subject. What are you going to do with those gold coins?"

"Each one's worth five dollars. I guess I'll pay the rent."

"What!" Brie's head jerked toward Roger, and the car veered wildly before she got it back under control. "You have to know they're worth a lot more than five dollars. Plus, I don't think Vie will want anything to do with ghost coins. She's given up on hoodoo and stuff."

"Why wouldn't she take it?" asked Roger. "It is an American coin, isn't it? At least, that's what it says."

"I know, but the gold alone is worth a lot more than its face value."

Roger took one from his pocket and hefted it. "I didn't think about that. Back home, a gold piece is a gold piece."

"Not here. Especially one that old. You may even find a collector who's willing to pay a decent price."

"How much do you think its worth?"

"No idea, but I can ask some of my professors. One of them may know how to find out."

"Is that safe?"

Brie shrugged. "You have a better idea?"

"The shop where I bought my alchemy equipment carried a lot more than glass vials and beakers," replied Roger. "If the owner isn't a coin collector himself, he probably knows someone who is. We can go there before we head back — if his store is open."

They came to Columbus Terminal, where cranes lifted containers off a massive ship. According to Brie, it took several days to empty one ship onto railcars that went across the country. Beyond it, two steel trussed bridges, one recently opened, spanned the Cooper River. They rose two hundred and fifty feet into the air and, with Charleston's flat terrain, had sweeping views of the ocean on one side and the lush landscape on the other.

Brie had taken Roger over them. Once. The trip across the newer Pearman bridge to Mount Pleasant hadn't been too bad, though he had asked Brie to keep in the lane farthest from oncoming traffic. Coming back... he vowed never to return. The older, two-lane Grace bridge dipped and swayed with the movement of the many vehicles traversing it, as if about to collapse. Even more horrifying were the glimpses of grey harbor water through gaps in the deck. He had never feared heights. However, even from a distance, the sight of the bridge caused an uneasy twitch in his gut.

Ahead, water completely covered East Bay Street. Brie followed a line of cars onto Columbus Street, then Meeting Street. At Morrison, she turned onto King and entered the Neck, a neglected no-man's land that bore industrial scars.

Serving as the gatekeeper, a twelve-story apartment building seemed out of place amongst the rail lines, sprawling cemeteries, and metal silos. They passed a whitewashed tavern with no windows. Painted on the wall, a canted gold crown encircled the body of a goat. Over it were the faded letters, "King Billy's." Roger noted the penciled circle already on his map. Two things about travelling through Charleston: it was easy to get lost, and every one-way street went in the wrong direction.

Separated by a narrow band of grass to their right, King Street ran alongside railroad tracks with spurs that shot off to the east. In the distance, glimmers of azure sky broke through the grey clouds, and the rain slowed to a drizzle. Roger unbuttoned his duster and shifted objects from its pockets to the pouches at his waist.

"Are you ever afraid that utility belt of yours will explode?" Brie asked with a smile.

"Sometimes."

Her smile vanishing, she shot him a concerned look, and he could tell she was trying to decide whether or not he was joking.

The serpentine overpass known as I-26 approached from the left, paralleled the road for a distance, and gradually turned northwest. Sprawling industrial buildings surrounded by asphalt parking lots filled the triangular gap.

At the intersection of King and Discher Streets, Roger jerked his head to the right. "Turn here," he said.

"What?"

"Just do it."

Tires sliding on the wet pavement, Brie rotated the steering wheel one way, then the other. The Metropolitan groaned in protest but straightened when they came to a stop at Meeting Street.

"Over there," Roger said, checking his map and pointing. "That's Four Mile Lane. Looks like the House is still there, just beyond it."

Turning right, Brie eased the car across a rail spur and passed a brick church. On the left, an unmarked gravel road led to a dilapidated two-story house supported by a six-foot tall brick foundation wall and a pair of masonry chimneys. Weathered clapboard siding bore evidence of termites and carpenter ants between patches of colorful fungi and lichen.

Shattered remnants of shutters clung like parasites beside boarded-over windows. Facing the road, the side of parapeted front porch stairs framed a dark archway that led to what Roger assumed was an aboveground cellar. He could just make out a number "4" painted above the apex of the arch. To the left of the archway were faded letters spelling "MILE," and on the right, "HOUSE." Knee-high weeds and flowering brambles filled the opening, as if trying to prevent anyone access to the area under the old house. Bright yellow tape barricaded the stairs.

They parked in front of a sign posted in the yard. Across the top, bold letters warned, "KEEP OUT — DANGER!"

"I thought you said we were going to Six Mile House," Brie said.

"I did," Roger answered, stepping out of the car, "but you said it burned down. How long do you think Four Mile House has been here?"

Brie studied the building as she rounded the car. "Looks to be as old as those coins in your pocket. I'd say at least a hundred years."

Off to the right, thick brambles and a mass of vines with broad, dark green leaves formed a rough, barn-like shape. Roger wondered if the abandoned building supported the greenery, or if the plants prevented the building's collapse.

"They plan to tear it down in October," Brie said, reading the fine print at the bottom of the sign.

"Could you imagine being a weary traveler and stopping here for the night?" Roger asked, gesturing toward the two buildings and abandoned yard. "Picture it. You've been riding on a wagon for most of the day, seeking a place to sell your goods. Probably heading to the market downtown. You can't see the road, and every noise sets your nerves on edge. Exhausted from the trip, you see a twinkling light through the trees, and with it comes the promise of a fire and some ale. It's not so different in Gaia."

"You'd probably get the latest gossip," Brie added. "Is the road clear, or are there rumors of highway bandits?"

"Four Miles," Roger mused. "Four miles from what?"

"City Hall. You know, at the four-corners of law, where you can get married, taxed, divorced, and go to jail all at the same intersection and on the same day. I'd bet we're four miles from there, as the crow flies."

Roger nodded, then said, "Let's investigate Six Mile."

The two slid into the Metropolitan, crossed Meeting and the railroad tracks, and turned north. After traveling over the Five-Mile Viaduct bridge, King Street widened to five lanes and became Rivers Avenue. As if they had crossed some invisible border, the neighborhood turned mercantile. Wide driveways and concrete parking lots led to squat buildings. Islands of brown grass tried to break the monotony, but they couldn't compete with all the glass and steel. At irregular intervals along the side of the road, signs directed travelers to various gates entering the Navy Base.

When they came to the post office at the corner of Cherokee Lane, the sun broke through the clouds. Steam began rising from the asphalt. They cracked open their windows and let the flow of air cool them.

Roger marveled at the various types of cars and trucks braving the weather. Armored with painted metal and chrome, each bore a proud heraldic mark on the hood. This one was of clan Ford; that of clan Chevrolet. Their hungry engines growled as they raced by, each with its own distinctive tone, drowning out the hum of the Metropolitan.

On the other side of Cosgrove Avenue and across from Dorchester Road, they slowed when they came to a series of single-family homes. The repetition of construction from one to the next reminded Roger of the brown brick apartments near the Old City Gaol. It must have been more government housing. A property sign confirmed his suspicions: "Tom McMillan Homes — U.S.H.A. Defense Housing Project — Navy Yard."

"Is that where Six Mile House is supposed to be?" Brie asked, eyeing the housing.

Roger consulted his map, then surveyed the signs around them. With businesses that catered to the military, the buildings along this stretch of Rivers Avenue appeared newer.

"Looks like it," he answered.

Driving farther down the road, they came across another housing development, this one called, "Ben Tillman Homes."

"What do you want me to do?" asked Brie.

"Turn around. Let's stop at that library," Roger answered, nodding his head toward the building at the corner of Rivers and Dorchester.

"You think they may know something?"
"Only one way to find out."

Roger stepped in front of Brie and opened the door for her. She had removed her raincoat, and the conditioned air from inside the library gave her skin goosebumps.

The musty smell of old pages almost hid the mechanical odor blowing from the vents. Roger swallowed. The chemicals they used made the back of his mouth taste metallic.

Thankful for the lack of people, he approached the desk where an elderly woman wearing bifocals with a silver chain looped behind her neck replaced the checkout card in the back of a book. In the cart beside her, more books sat with their spines facing outward.

"Excuse us, Ms. Simmons," Brie said after reading the walnut desk plate. "We were wondering if you had a section on local history."

The librarian looked over the rim of her glasses and replied, "We have a whole section dedicated to Sherman's March to the Sea and the War of Northern Aggression. How local were you wanting?"

"Actually, we were hoping for information on Six Mile."

Suddenly, Ms. Simmons beamed at them, and she said, "Most of our information is at the State Archives, but we do have copies of a few plats that may be of interest. I'm afraid they're all black and white though. The new photostat machines have color copies, but..." Ms. Simmons' voice trailed off as she disappeared into a back room. She returned with a manila folder, labeled "History of Six Mile," and laid it on the desktop. The first page was part of plat 6881, showing Dorchester Road intersecting with State Road.

"That's it," Brie said, pointing to where the two streets met, and the surveyor had written 6 Mile House in cursive.

"Oh yes," said the librarian. "The infamous den of iniquity."

"What happened there?" Brie asked.

Warming to a favorite subject, Ms. Simmons took off her glasses and said, "Late one evening in February of 1819, a man named John Peeples arrived at the inn with a wagonload of furs and asked to be put up for the night. The tavern keepers, John and Lavinia Fisher, were welcoming, but something about them seemed off to him — overly friendly, if you get my meaning. Instead of falling asleep, Peeples took his bedclothes and pillow and made a dummy under the sheets. He blew out the lantern and sat down behind a stand in the corner and waited, expecting the worst.

"Sometime past midnight, he overheard the Fishers planning ways to assassinate him and dispose of his body. Scared, but keeping his wits, he remained quiet and slipped out the window. Leaving his wagon behind, he saddled his horse and galloped to the city, where he notified the local police.

"Already alert because of the recent robberies of two stage lines by highwaymen, a large police force went to the House. As you might expect, the Fishers and their gang of ruffians had prepared for them. They barricaded the doors and windows and refused to surrender. The sheriff sent for the military, and a bombardment commenced.

"Many shots were fired, but the people inside yielded only after the house was set ablaze. Using the smoke and confusion for cover, most of the gang made their escape. But not John and Lavinia Fisher. The police arrested the two gang leaders along with five of their accomplices and carted them off to jail."

Ms. Simmons leaned across her desk conspiratorially. "They said Lavinia was a witch. She lured guests with her beauty and, having fed them a hearty meal, poisoned them with oleander in their tea. During their trial, investigators searched the burned-out house. Under the remains of a trapdoor in the floor, they made a ghastly discovery: a pit filled with bones. Human bones! Skeletons of other wayfarers. John and Lavinia Fisher were hung a year later. She in her wedding gown, no less.

"At the hanging, her last words to the minister and the gathered audience were, 'Cease! I will have none of it. Save your words for others who want them. But if you have a message for the devil, give it to me; I'll carry it.' And with that, the 'Trapdoor Murderess' leapt off the platform, hanging herself and stealing the privilege from the executioner.

"A lot of people say it was those words that doomed her. God wanted to pardon her, but she refused it, and the devil didn't want to hear her message."

Roger coughed to clear his throat and noticed Brie glancing at him out of the corner of her eye.

"Lavinia Fisher is buried in the Unitarian Church's cemetery. If you want to read more, you can check out a copy of Ms. Martin's book, <u>Charleston Ghosts</u>, over there in our nonfiction section. It includes a short piece on the Fishers."

"We will, thank you," Brie said.

"Who ended up getting the land where the inn stood?" Roger asked.

Ms. Simmons furrowed her brow as she dug through the file. "Six Mile tract was part of Marshlands Plantation, purchased by John Ball in 1810. He died seven years later, and Nathaniel Heyward, Sr., bought it at an auction. However, there was a dispute over the land, all 371 acres, which included the Houses at Five- and Six Mile. Interestingly enough, John Fisher's uncle, Colonel George Fisher, filed a claim on the land. Then there was Patrick Duncan, who said the land had been transferred to him by the former owner, John Wragg, a loyalist. Those claims never bore out, and the land went to Elizabeth Manigault and her husband Charles. In 1880, their descendants sold it to Ms. Cecelia Lawton, who sold it to the government. Ten years later, Charleston was awarded the contract for the naval yard."

As she spoke, the librarian pulled out two surveys with mostly illegible writing denoting various property boundaries. The older one showed the land belonging to the heirs of John Wragg. The other had the land belonging to Nathaniel Heyward, Sr. The last document she produced was a hand drawn map of Chicora Park. In the upper right near the Cooper River, Cecelia Lawton's name was visible.

"Nathaniel Heyward? Who's that?" Brie asked.

Ms. Simmons stared down at the tiny writing and replied, "Nathaniel, senior, was the wealthiest rice planter in South Carolina and Elizabeth Manigault's father."

Inside the folder were other documents, including more maps of the area and newspaper announcements, but the one that stood out was a color rendering of a proposed ten-story hospital. Listed at the bottom as benefits to the region were 500 beds, 375,000 square feet of floor space, modern features such as central heat and air, two intensive care units, and seven operating rooms.

The librarian pointed to the rendering and said, "Groundbreaking is planned for February 14, next year. They've already moved everyone out of the housing across the street and should start demolishing the homes shortly. That's if the government sticks to the schedule."

"That's going across the street?" asked Brie.

"Oh yes. Everyone here is looking forward to it."

"It's going to be built over the old Six Mile site?" asked Roger.

Ms. Simmons laughed. "Bless me, no. What made you think that?"

"I thought Six Mile House was at the end of Dorchester."

"It was, technically," the librarian answered, closing the folder. She reached for a cardboard tube with "USGS Charleston – 1919" written on a label at the end, slid out the map inside, and unrolled it. "You see, all this land, even where this building stands, was mostly marsh and creeks. Dorchester originally stopped at Meeting Street Road. Back that way." She pointed west toward the interstate. "That is, until they redirected it when they put in the railroad. With Charleston built on top of itself like it is, no one really knows where the original house stood, I'm afraid. If you want more information, you can talk to Professor Mike Hollingsworth, the archivist at Towell Library. He has a collection of newspaper articles from that time, and an original eyewitness account of the hanging."

"Thank you very much for your time," Roger said, stepping back from the desk. "You were very informative."

"Let me check out that book you mentioned," Brie told Ms. Simmons, "and we'll get out of your hair."

CHAPTER 3
PAPER TRAILS

Tuesday, April 1, 1969

*C*rossing the library parking lot, Roger asked, "Did you get all that?"

"I think so," Brie said. She held up a thin green book. "Hopefully, this will remind us of anything we forget."

They stopped on either side of her car, each staring across the street. Roger tried to envision the new hospital. Despite the apartment houses slated for demolition, he wondered if the construction crew would discover skeletons like those under the Six Mile House. If they did, what would they do?

On his home-world of Gaia, the matter would be handled by local priests, and the dead laid to rest in a nearby graveyard. Word likely wouldn't reach beyond the local community. But, then again, the new hospital was a military project. When it came to strategic matters, the Highlord and other monarchs only doled out specific bits of knowledge. The last thing they wanted was a panicked or enraged public, especially with the ongoing war against the Dark One's minions.

Here on Terra, the line between right and wrong seemed blurred. Roger had read the newspaper articles about Vietnam. America faced its own war with the Dark One. The reported number of casualties was staggering. It left him wondering: if they did find long-buried corpses across the street, would anyone even care?

"What are you thinking about?" Brie asked him.

Roger blinked and replied, "What would happen if the construction workers found bones?"

"They'd have to stop work. Police would get involved, and if they're human remains, they'd bring in archeologists to study the site."

"Would they really do that? Delays of any nature would be expensive for the workers and the owner."

"Of course, they would. Who would want to build over an old grave site? That'd really stir up the dead."

"Maybe so."

"One thing's for sure," Brie said with a smile. "If they did build over old bones, we'd have job security, especially if we find Lavinia."

"Are you sure you want to be part of this investigation?"

Brie opened her car door as she replied, "Witches, ghosts, and mass murder. Let's just say my curiosity's piqued."

"As a future anthropologist you mean," Roger added. "That is what you're studying at school, isn't it?"

"Yes, but it's more than that. There's something about digging up history in your own backyard. It makes it more real."

"Makes sense, I guess." Sliding into his seat, Roger asked, "Do you think the constabulary kept the information on the Fishers' arrest at Six Mile?"

"Maybe. We can find out."

"I still want to see if we can find where the Six Mile House stood."

"You heard Ms. Simmons. No one knows."

"Humor me," Roger said.

Brie shifted the Metropolitan into gear, exited the parking lot, and turned west on Dorchester. Sidewalks lined the road, broken by driveways that led to people's homes. When they came to the intersection with Meeting Street Road, Roger motioned south. With a curt nod, Brie waited for the traffic light to change, then turned.

A patch of grass bordered train tracks to their right. To their left was a vacant corner lot. Next to it was a fenced in yard with an open gate and parked cars. Bulk construction materials piled against the fence created a narrow drive aisle that circled a squat building with metal siding.

With his map folded so he could see where they were, Roger said, "If you draw a straight line from where Dorchester turns to cross the railroad tracks, it should intersect Meeting right about here."

Brie slowed as the road curved.

"My guess is Six Mile House was there, near that building," he said, "assuming this road was the property boundary, and the Houses were all built on the east side."

"What do you want me to do? I don't think we can go inside the fence unless we have business there."

"Pull over," Roger said, pointing to a narrow patch of gravel between the road and the rail lines.

Brie stopped the car and looked over her shoulder, clearly frustrated. "There's nothing here. No house of horror; no den of inequity. Nothing. For all we know, they paved over it when they redirected Dorchester."

Roger laughed. "It's never simple, is it?"

A large truck rumbled down the road. Its engine thrummed, spewing exhaust.

"I've seen enough," Roger said, noting the irritation in Brie's eyes. "Let's talk with Nate."

Brie shot down Meeting and merged onto King Street. Passing under the interstate, they entered the more genteel neighborhoods that surrounded Hampton Park. They drove with the windows open, and when Brie stopped at an intersection, they heard a loud roar in the distance.

"What was that?" Roger asked.

"The zoo," Brie answered. "It's been there for as long as I can remember. Not many people go there anymore. It's really just a lot of chain link fences."

"But that was a lion, wasn't it?"

"His name is Leo."

"Oh. And they keep this Leo in a fence?"

"Him and the other animals."

Roger frowned, imagining a Parlathean lion in a cage. He'd actually encountered one during his travels across Detchia. It had been early in the morning when the mists were thick. The wind shifted, and through the swirling fog he spotted the lion on the far bank of the White River. Staring into those eyes had been one of the few times in his life he felt true, primal fear. Bowing his head toward the lion, he had faced down that fear. Now, he felt a flutter of shame at the thought of one of those majestic beasts chained and put on display.

"Do you think King Street's still flooded?" Brie asked.

"What?"

"The street, do you think it's still flooded? If it is, we'll have to go around."

"Your call," he answered.

Brie made a face, then aimed the Metropolitan south toward the Crosstown and drove under the ramps leading to the interstate and Cooper River bridges.

Water still lay on the road, but the level had receded enough to allow cars to pass. Miniature waves slapped against Roger's door as they drove within the wake of the car in front of them. He had to fight the urge to lift his feet.

Brie kept them moving as they slowly gained higher ground. Once past the Crosstown, she navigated the maze of narrow streets leading onto the peninsula.

The gable ends of rectangular two- and three-story clapboard residences lined both sides of the street. Commonly referred to as Charleston Singles, their front doors were located on the end of long, colonnaded piazzas that made the buildings look sideways. Dating back to the years before what the librarian had called "the War of Northern Aggression," many suffered from lack of attention and needed repair. The fortunate ones had been converted into student housing for the College, but the majority were abandoned fire hazards.

As they neared the intersection of St Philip and Vanderhorst, Roger recognized the three-story shrievalty by its crenellated parapet. Rising high above the street corner, a tiny turret, complete with an arrow loop, grew out of a larger corner tower. The building's scored limestone veneer resembled a castle wall, making Roger feel homesick. Brie turned into the visitor parking lot.

When she stopped the car, Brie asked him, "You okay? You've been awfully quiet."

Staring at the dashboard, Roger couldn't shake the overwhelming feeling he was trapped, like the lion. "Just thinking about home," he said finally.

Brie squeezed his hand and said, "I can't imagine what you're going through, but know that I'm here."

He gave her a gentle squeeze back before reaching for the door handle. "Let's see what the CPD has for us."

Inside, the sergeant at the front desk stopped them with a cold stare. "Can I help you?"

"Yes, we're here to see Nathan Stone," Brie replied.

"Your names?"

"Brie Tyler and this is Roger Vaughn. We're friends."

"Miss Tyler, Mistuh Vaughn, wuh brings oonuh here," Tee said in his deep baritone voice. A Gullah sea-islander,

Corporal Tecumseh Middleton stood over six feet tall and had a broad nose set under sharp eyes.

In jest, Roger had mentioned to Brie that he thought the man had Nephilim somewhere in his lineage. She told him that Tee had served more than a decade on the police force, and he was still trying to make sergeant. Determined like John Henry hammering rock for the railroad, Tee kept chipping away at the social barriers. He already served as Nate's training officer. Who knew, maybe he would make captain someday.

Tee gave them a wide smile that came across more intimidating than friendly and extended his large hand.

Roger returned the gesture and felt the thick calluses that covered Tee's fingers and the pads of his palm. He had a firm grip, but its power extended beyond the physical.

As he stepped away, Roger clasped his hands together and surreptitiously rubbed a thumb across the sharp tingling in his palm. There was a duality about Tecumseh Middleton that was apparent when he spoke — the man he displayed for his peers, and the man steeped in the tradition of his home and community. Roger suspected Tee could be a powerful root doctor if he ever chose to follow that path.

"Brie, what brings you here?" Officer Nathan Stone asked from the doorway. Dressed in a crisp uniform, he carried himself with authority. Brie ploughed through it and gave him a fierce hug.

"Tee, Nate, it's good to see you again," Roger said, taking Nate's hand.

"We have our first case," Brie said excitedly.

"A case? What do you mean a case?" Nate asked. It was clear all kinds of alarms had gone off in his head.

"Missing persons," Roger said. "A man visited my office earlier today. He's looking for his wife."

Nate's expression turned from alarmed to puzzled. "He came to *you*?"

"Yes."

"Maybe we should meet in the conference room. I can have Lieutenant Bell join us."

"That's not necessary," replied Roger. "We just need to see an old case file."

"How old?"

"1819, maybe 1820," Roger said, looking to Brie for

confirmation.

Brie nodded in agreement. "Yeah, 1819 probably."

Suspicion narrowed Nate's eyes. "You've got that 'nothing to see here' look."

Tee crossed his arms. "Uh smell trouble."

"This isn't like last time, is it?" Nate asked. "You know, when you and your friends tore up half the city."

"It wasn't half," Roger said defensively. "And it wasn't us who did the tearing up."

"I know, but you're the only one left to blame. The captain was not happy we let you and your friends go. Lieutenant Bell took some serious heat for you."

"This is nothing like that," Roger said, and then added quickly, "although it may be related."

Nate stepped aside and said, "I've heard enough. Let's talk to the Lieutenant."

The conference room hadn't changed since the last time Roger was there. Ruefully, he remembered the expression on Lieutenant Richard Bell's face when the Highlord explained where they were from and what was happening to his city.

They didn't have to wait long. The watch commander entered the conference room with Nate a step behind him. The senior officer's receding hairline gave him a tonsured appearance. However, his face held a few more wrinkles than Roger remembered.

Tee closed the door and stood guard in front of it.

"I promise, this is not like last time," Roger said.

The three constables did not relax. They kept staring at him as if expecting him to grow a second head and sprout wings or something.

"Mister Vaughn," Lieutenant Bell said, "forgive our caution, but you being here is like scratching a raw scab. Stone, here, says you would like access to an old case file, is that right?"

"Yes, sir. We're investigating the Six Mile House."

"I thought you said you were looking for someone."

"We are," Roger answered. "Lavinia Fisher."

The three constables gave a collective gasp.

"The witch?" Lieutenant Bell asked.

"Yes, sir. John Fisher, along with a friend of his, visited

my office earlier today. He hired us to find her."

"You're crazy," Lieutenant Bell spluttered. "She's dead. He's dead."

Roger pursed his lips, trying to think of the best way to explain. "Lieutenant, they're ghosts, and they haven't moved on. I think they were set free when we killed the Executioner at the Old City Gaol."

The Lieutenant wiped his hand down his face. "Was he a ghost, too?"

"He was, but he'd become something much more powerful."

"After your friends left town, we searched the jail — we found no bodies."

"But that doesn't mean it was empty."

"I really hate it when you talk like that."

"Sorry, sir."

"So, what do you need from us?"

"The Fisher case file."

"From 1819?"

"Yes, sir. According to your Constitution and the Bill of Rights, the Fishers should have been accused of a crime, gaoled, convicted by a trial, and sentenced. I'm certain you would have a paper trail."

"If they're ghosts, why would they care? What difference does it make for them now?"

"Lieutenant, it makes all the difference. Trapped ghosts seek to resolve their human issues — something they left unfinished or gaining revenge for a wrong done to them. I'm hoping we can discover what that is in order to find Lavinia."

"Couldn' oonuh dig up she'own body and ketch her sperrit in a jug or bottle?" Tee asked. His Gullah accent had grown more pronounced. "Doctuh Wampus could'uh done it."

"Maybe, although I'm not familiar with that method," Roger said. "Lavinia's husband wants me to find her so that they can pass on to the next life together. I think he's sincere. I do know that he will not leave without her. If we trap her, I'm not sure what would happen."

"Okay," Lieutenant Bell said after a pause. "I'll put in a request to the State Archives. Might take a few days."

"Any help you could give us would be greatly appreciated."

A knock at the door interrupted them.

"Watch Commander, you're needed," a constable said when Tee opened the door.

"What is it, Sullivan?"

"Dispatch sent Chapman and Tucker to investigate a report of a body in front of the Calhoun Monument."

"Do what?"

"The person who called it in said he thought the man was asleep or praying or something. He was about to walk on when he saw a trail of rope leading away from the statue. Turns out it was the dead man's intestines. With the rain and all, it'll be a muddy mess. I was about to notify Forensics."

"Go ahead," Lieutenant Bell replied. "I'll be along shortly."

"Yes, sir, but that's not the worst of it. Chapman said it looks as though the man walked out there alone. The rain washed away most of the blood, but his footprints are plain enough. They're right beside his guts. Chapman and Tucker are still looking for a weapon." As he closed the door, Officer Sullivan muttered, "Why does it always have to get weird on my shift?"

The watch commander studied Roger through a narrow-eyed glare. "Does this have anything to do with your so-called case?"

Roger shrugged. "I don't see how it could."

"I don't believe in coincidences."

"What do you want me to say, sir? The little I know about ghosts indicates the majority of their interactions with the physical world are limited to lights and sounds, with the rare occasion of slammed doors or thrown objects. If the man in the park had been scared to death or pushed down a flight of stairs, though, that would be a different story."

"Fine," Bell sighed. "We'll let you know when those records you requested are available. Stone, escort them to the door."

"Thank you, sir," Roger said, barely catching himself before he started to bow.

Outside, Brie clapped her hands together. She spun around and walked backwards. "Did you hear that? They found someone dead. Eviscerated at the base of old man

Calhoun!"

Roger gave her a wry smile and said, "You have problems, don't you?"

"No. It's just that I've never been part of a mystery like this. A man trailing his guts. Can you believe that? Could it have been suicide? Like Hari-kari? Or do you think someone did it? I think someone did it." Her words came out in a rush.

"Miss Tyler, death is not entertainment."

Brie poked out her lower lip. "That's not what I meant. How could someone do that in broad daylight? Why there? Marion Square is a busy park, surrounded by busy streets; someone had to see something."

"I remind you it was a hard rain."

"Not that hard."

Roger eyed his assistant over the top of the car. She was right, of course, but he didn't want to feed her morbid curiosity. News of the dead man, while alarming, shouldn't have anything to do with them. Yet he agreed with Lieutenant Bell regarding coincidences. Roger had a sinking feeling the dead man was tied to the Fishers, but he couldn't tell that to the watch commander. "All right," he said to Brie. "We can drive by for a quick look. That's it, though. We aren't stopping."

Flashing him a smile, Brie jumped in the car, and had it cranked before he took his seat. They followed Saint Philip to Calhoun where Brie turned left.

Bounded by streets on three sides, Marion Square was a six-and-a-half-acre greenspace located downtown. Centered along the southern edge rose a tall, slender monument. Atop was the statue of a man with his cloak draped over one shoulder. Holding a scroll in his hand, he looked down on the city. The plaque at the monument's base read, "Truth, Justice, and the Constitution."

At the moment, patrolmen worked around the stair-stepped pedestal, keeping spectators behind the barricade tape.

A black station wagon drove past them. With constables directing traffic, it did a U-turn and pulled up onto the sidewalk. Two men in white lab coats exited the vehicle, opened the back, and slid out a gurney.

Brie continued slowly down Calhoun. Roger caught sight

of the dead man slumped on the ground. It looked as though he had fallen to his knees. Next to the body, a man wearing a suit and tie wielded a boxy camera. Spatters of blood on the monument base stood out in stark relief with each flash. Something may have been written there, but the rain had left the graffiti streaked and impossible to read from a moving vehicle. Behind the cameraman, another man in a suit stuck small, triangular flags in the ground, apparently marking the dead man's trail.

"Turn right at Meeting," Roger said.

"How long do you think he's been there?" Brie asked while they waited to turn.

"No telling," replied Roger. "He could have died while it was raining or early this morning, perhaps before the sun rose."

There was a gap in the traffic. Brie goosed the gas, and the Metropolitan shot around the corner. Roger slid toward the helm and barely managed to stop himself by gripping the door. "This must be what it's like to fly one of those jet fighters."

"Funny," Brie sniped. "Where to?"

"Let's stop at the Unitarian Church."

"You want to see Lavinia's grave?"

"Let's just say I want to test a theory."

"You don't think she's there, do you," Brie declared.

"No, I don't. If Lavinia had turned away from the Eternal Father like Ms. Simmons said, why would the church accept her into their graveyard?"

At Horlbeck Alley, Brie turned right and zipped down the narrow lane. The brick wall beside his window blurred past too close for his comfort, and Roger shifted in his seat, trying not to look beyond the car's hood. When they came to the intersection with Archdale, a cold shiver trailed down his spine. Magazine Street lay straight ahead. It was where he had fought the Archer, the dærganfae assassin who had nearly killed him. It was also the location of the Charleston Gaol, where they had been held captive by the Executioner. Brie hadn't talked much about that experience, and he hadn't pushed.

When Brie turned left, Roger recognized the bell tower. Backed by blue skies, the yellow Unitarian Church stood tall and proud, supported by its flying buttresses. This was where he and his Gaian friends had fled from the Sha'iry and their sclábhaí. They had rushed through the garden-like graveyard during the middle of the night and jumped the wall abutting the gothic church.

The wrought-iron gate stood open. Brie parked along the curb, and they began their search.

They followed a narrow, cobblestone pathway that led under the canopy of palm trees, magnolias, and gnarled oaks. To either side, vines and leafy shrubs ran wild over the gravestones. Four steps into it, Roger felt he had left civilization and entered a secret tropical jungle. Thick, winding roots had knocked several of the markers askew, giving them a disheveled appearance. An hour passed as the pair searched the graveyard paths and worked up a sweat, but neither Brie nor Roger recognized any of the names.

A young man stepped from the church and watched them move from stone to stone. "Can I help you?"

Brie stretched before responding, "Yes. Maybe you can. We're looking for someone."

"Who?" the man said as he approached.

"Lavinia Fisher."

The man stopped and gave them both a deep frown. "I fail to understand why anyone thinks that witch was buried in our churchyard." He put his hands on his hips and said, "Please pass the word to anyone who cares to listen. Lavinia Fisher is not buried here. And before you ask, Annabel Lee is not here either."

CHAPTER 4
DARK ALLEYS
Tuesday, April 1, 1969

C *ome in a Stranger, Leave a Friend.*
        Roger contemplated the message over the front entrance before grabbing the door handle and stepping inside the two-story, burgundy brick tavern. In the evenings after Brie returned home, he'd been experimenting with the various restaurants around town. His last waiter had recommended this place. It definitely wasn't as stuffy looking as some of the places he'd tried.

A glossy bar dominated the left side of the long, narrow room. Along the right-hand wall, wooden benches flanked narrow tables where patrons faced one another under the dim glow of red and gold fixtures. The couple closest to him drank beer straight from bottles and shared a plate of fries coated in cheese sauce. A dirty ashtray sat between them with cigarettes propped on the corrugated edge. Smoke curled from the glowing tips and added to the haze clinging to the ceiling. The smell rankled his nose. Smoking wasn't common in Gaia, and those who did used pipes whose tobacco carried the aroma of herbs and exotic spices.

Above the booths, glowing beer and liquor advertisements laid siege to black and white photos displaying revelers. At the far end of the room, an American flag hung vertical from the brick chimney. He stared at it and wondered if the stars should be replaced with an eagle holding cigarettes in one claw and a whiskey bottle in the other.

Music played, but Roger couldn't tell where it originated. Slow, almost like religious music, a deep-voiced singer crooned, "Don't take your guns to town."

Claiming one of the red leather seats at the bar, Roger nodded to the barkeep.

"What'll you have?"

"How about a beer and..." Roger thought a moment before saying, "a cheeseburger with everything on it."

"Sure thing," the barkeep replied as he reached under

the counter and pulled out a frosty, long-necked bottle with a red label. He popped off the metal top and slid the bottle in front of Roger before heading to the kitchen.

Roger took a swallow, relishing the bitter taste of the hops. The tavern was almost empty. However, with it being Tuesday, he suspected the owner was happy just to have customers. Come the weekend, the place would probably be standing room only.

More people entered, including a broad-shouldered ruffian in a dusty leather vest and chaps. Tattooed flames ran the length of his forearms. Partially covered by a black leather cap, his bald head seemed small and out of proportion. Leaving an empty seat between him and Roger, he sat down and motioned to the barkeep.

"Be with you in a moment," the bartender said as he set down Roger's plate of food.

"Anything else?"

"Another beer."

Roger stared at the cheeseburger. He recognized the cheese, the grilled onions, lettuce, and tomatoes, but there were other items on it he didn't — the meat being one of them. He inhaled, taking in the aroma. Instantly, his mouth started to water, and he took it as a good sign. Grabbing the sandwich with both hands, he bit into it. Warm juices dribbled down his chin and squeezed between his fingers.

Roger took another bite before sitting it back on the plate. Using up his napkin to wipe his face, he motioned to the barkeep. "Can I have another napkin? Or maybe a towel."

"Here, use this one. It's fresh," the barkeep said, handing him the towel from his shoulder. "You like the cheeseburger?"

"Very good," Roger mumbled, sopping his chin, and wiping his hands, "but it's messy."

After taking another swallow of beer, Roger eyed the burger and chose a better angle of attack.

If nothing else, the day had been interesting. Too late to visit the antique store, he and Brie had gone back to the office and read the short account by Ms. Margaret Rhett Martin. Written from John Peeples' perspective, "The Wayfarer at Six Mile House," provided a brief summary of the events that fateful night in 1819 when he had stopped at the inn before going the rest of the way into Charleston. While the story captured the air of mystery, the librarian's retelling had provided the most pertinent details from the book's narrative, leaving both Roger and Brie wanting to know more. Sadly, the book provided no reference material, and its introduction stated that 'the account does not follow public records,' but it was 'the true legend.' Roger took those statements to mean that, like the minstrels of Gaia, the author had taken a grain of truth and added embellishments.

Before Brie left for the day, she'd made him promise not to go to the antique store without her. The memory elicited a smile which faded as he thought about the case. What did he know? The end of Ms. Martin's tale said that the rest of the story had been suppressed. He wondered why. Had the truth been so horrible, or was something even more nefarious at work?

Roger gave himself a mental shake and steeled his mind against forming premature conclusions. Facts must be discovered; not made up.

Fact 1: John Fisher had hired him to find his wife, Lavinia.

Fact 2: Both had been detained by the local constabulary, held at the Old City Gaol, and executed. Their spirits remained trapped there until Ambrose Battenberg killed the Executioner — probably — Roger amended.

Fact 3: Joseph Roberts was bound to John. Despite being free, he had helped John. Was it friendship or something more? He had not passed on like the other ghostly inmates.

Fact 4: The Six Mile House had burned down, hiding whatever evidence had been inside.

Fact 5: If you followed the money, Marshlands Plantation had gone to Nathaniel Heyward, Senior, and his daughter Elizabeth Manigault.

Fact 6: Their descendants sold it to a Ms. Lawton, who eventually sold it to the government. Based on the survey, the naval base was built on those lands.

Did any of this have anything to do with why Lavinia had not moved on or where she was now?

Roger pushed away his empty plate and ordered a third beer. After wiping his hands and mouth on the towel, he stared ahead, only vaguely aware of the half-filled bottles of liquor lining the shelves in front of him, and tried to piece together the facts into a reasonable image.

Conversations grew louder. The bar had become crowded, and the pall of smoke deeper. He found the noise, smoke, and press of strangers distracting. It was like the two tales about the velvety-eyed Lavinia, dressed in her wedding clothes, and the counternarrative of her as a witch. Either may or may not be true, but the rumors added a level of complication to the mystery; rumors that may be just a distraction.

He swallowed the last of his beer and reached into his pouch to pay for his meal. When he did, one of the gold coins fell out and landed on the floor. Roger leaned down, but before he could grab it, the burly man with tattooed arms picked it up and laid it on the bar in front of him.

"You dropped this," he said. He spoke with an odd high-pitched voice that was incongruous with his build.

Straightening, Roger slid the coin back into his pouch and replied, "Thank you."

"Nice piece of treasure you've got there."

"It was a gift."

Not wanting to get trapped in a conversation, Roger paid the bartender with the last of his cash and stepped outside. He took in a deep breath of fresh night air and let his mind clear. A ten-minute walk lay ahead of him. Fortunately, the clouds had moved on. The stars were supposed to be out, but he couldn't see them for all the streetlights.

Turning down East Bay, he passed the empty stalls of the downtown market. Across the street, construction scaffolding partially hid the U.S. Customs House with its wide steps. An elaborate pediment, supported by two-story limestone columns, peeked above the metal framework and hinted at the detailed architecture of the entablature.

Continuing down the historic street, Roger felt the weight of someone watching him. He paused and studied the others on the street while pretending to peer at the display in one of the shop windows. Most of the people seemed to have destinations, but a little over half a block back, the man from the bar ducked into a doorway. Roger smiled to himself and continued toward home.

He crossed Queen Street and passed a grocery store with arched windows. In their reflection, he spotted two men on the other side of the street shadowing him. Adrenaline rushing, he slowed as he approached the worn pavers of Unity Alley. To either side of the entrance, abandoned three-story buildings stood like silent sphinxes.

Hands in their pockets, the two men pursuing him crossed the street in his direction.

Roger was about to challenge them when he felt something pressed against his right shoulder. It felt like a pistol, but he couldn't be sure. It definitely didn't have the sharp point of a knife.

"Down the alley," the tattooed man from the bar whispered in his ear just as his two compatriots stepped onto the sidewalk.

A grim smile on his lips, Roger kept his hands at his sides and did as the man said. Infrequent wall sconces lit the dark alley and created deep pools of shadow between them. He kept a steady pace, calculating the best place to rob someone.

Up ahead, another man waited where the shadows grew thickest. When they joined their fellow conspirator, the tattooed man pressed his weapon to Roger's back.

"Stop here."

Three men circled in front of Roger.

"Give us the gold coin," said the tattooed man from behind him.

"Sure," Roger replied with a purposeful quiver in his voice. "I don't want any trouble."

He reached into his pouch where three of John Fisher's coins lay. He pretended to fumble as he deftly plucked a single gold piece from its brethren without allowing them to clink together. With a false tremble, he let the coin drop to the pavers. Metal on stone rang in the darkness.

When the tattooed man let up the pressure, Roger lowered his left shoulder and whipped around counterclockwise. Moving out of the line of gunfire, he let the man's extended forearm slide across his back, the gun now pointing safely behind him. He brought up his left arm, trapped his assailant's gun hand, and held it tight against his body. With his right, Roger drew a knife and plunged the three-inch blade into the man's throat.

Drowning in his own blood, the tattooed man slumped with a loud gurgle. Roger used the man's body as a shield as he threw his knife at the man to his left and snatched another from within the folds of his clothes.

Behind him, a siren wailed. Blue lights flashed from the East Bay end of the alley and reflected off the shocked faces of the two remaining men. Covered in blood and wearing a sardonic grin, Roger figured he must have looked like the devil himself. He took a step back, letting the tattooed man fall.

The other two men ran.

A bright spotlight illuminated the alley, and a dark silhouette yelled, "Police! Freeze!"

The constable charged forward, aiming his pistol at Roger. His nametag read, "Bradley."

Roger considered his options. Making his decision, he sheathed his unused knife and raised his hands. "Evening, constable. Can I help you?"

A second constable eased past his partner. His eyes narrowed when he caught sight of the tattooed man at Roger's feet and the handgun lying next to the gold coin. He knelt and checked the body for a pulse. "This one's dead."

"Against the wall!" Bradley ordered.

Roger complied, letting the officer pat down his clothing. "Constable, if you don't mind, that's my money. Those men tried to rob me."

"Thompson, I have a concealed weapon, and I smell alcohol," Bradley announced as he slid a knife from a wrist sheath and held it up for his partner to see. Continuing his search, he pulled out another blade and another.

"Actually, I have two daggers and three knives," Roger added, hoping the constable would appreciate him being helpful. "The fourth knife is in that ruffian over there."

While his partner checked the other dead man and radioed dispatch, Bradley slid the various blades under his own belt and took possession of Roger's utility belt. He made a cursory search of the numerous pouches, finding an odd assortment of bottles and jars, whalebone spectacles, a hand mirror mounted on a telescoping rod, flint and tinder, a ball of string, bits of leather, a miniature hammer and prybar, locksmith's tools, a small sewing kit, several rings, and a handful of gems.

"What *is* all this stuff?" he asked, opening yet another pouch to find two more gold coins.

"Tools of the trade," Roger answered.

Not finding any identification, Bradley asked, "What's your name?"

"Roger Vaughn."

"Well Mr. Vaughn, you're under arrest on suspicion of murder and armed robbery," Officer Bradley said and pulled out a pair of handcuffs. As he grabbed Roger's wrist and cuffed him, he warned, "You have the right to remain silent. Anything you say can and will be used against you in a court of law. You have the right to talk to a lawyer and have him present with you while you are being questioned. If you cannot afford to hire a lawyer, one will be appointed to represent you before any questioning, if you wish one. Do you understand each of these rights I have just explained to you?"

Roger answered, "I assure you, constable; I will cooperate any way I can."

CHAPTER 5
ARRESTED

Tuesday, April 1, 1969

Sitting in the back of the patrol car, Roger watched two men from the low-slung ambulance haul out a gurney. The metal legs extended, and they wheeled it down the alley. He thought about escaping, but the idea of being on the run didn't appeal to him. Instead, he pictured the look on Lieutenant Bell's face when they arrived at the shrievalty, assuming the senior officer was still on duty.

Two other patrol cars arrived and blocked off East Bay. Their rotating blue lights seemed anachronistic when compared to the surrounding buildings. Roger's thoughts drifted, and he wondered what had become of his weapons, belt, and sundry possessions.

Officer Bradley slid behind the wheel and cranked the patrol car. Thompson, his partner, entered from the other side and picked up the CB receiver. "1-Echo-8 here. Have suspect in custody. En route to Central."

"10-4, 1-Echo-8," the dispatcher replied.

Aiming south, Bradley eased the car past the police barricade and turned down Broad Street.

With his hands cuffed behind his back, Roger sat forward on his seat, shifting from one side to the next to see out the window. Fronted by granite curbs, bluestone sidewalks, and palm trees, the sheer faces of limestone and brick buildings flowed past. Beyond the "Four Corners of Law," Officer Bradley turned north onto a one-way street called Logan. Parked cars crowded both sides with narrow-faced Charleston Singles towering behind them. Roger jerked up and drew closer to the window.

"What is it?" Thompson asked, turning his head.

"I just noticed all your piazzas face south."

"What are you, an architect?"

"No. It's a habit of mine. I notice the details."

"You sound funny. Where are you from?"

Roger leaned back as best he could and replied, "You wouldn't believe me if I told you."

"Try me."

"I'm from Gallowen. My father is Earl Wolverton. I used to live at Blaiðwyn Hall, near Tydway, but now I reside in a room off Church Street."

"Gallowen? Is that in England?"

"No, it's a country on the eastern coast of Parlatheas."

"Look, wiseass. You're already deep in it. Don't make it worse."

"Told you, you wouldn't believe me."

"Let it go, Thompson," Bradley said. "He'll talk at the station."

Muttering under his breath, Thompson faced forward, a hint of red coloring his ears.

At Magazine Street, Roger caught a glimpse of the Old City Gaol. He really hoped this mystery wouldn't lead back there again. On the other side of Magazine, the two-story, brown brick housing development brought back memories of his fight with the sclábhaí. As big as Charleston seemed, it really was a small town.

Bradley veered onto Coming Street and continued north, passing more Charleston Singles. A block to the east, the austere buildings of the College of Charleston peeked from between the houses and down alleyways. Roger's thoughts turned to Brie. He suspected she would be angry, but he couldn't decide if it would be because he'd been in danger or because she'd missed the adventure.

They crossed Calhoun Street and turned right onto Vanderhorst, coming at the crenellated shrievalty from the west side. In the sally port, Bradley waited for the security gate to close behind them before walking around the car to let Roger out. Thompson stood back with his hand on the butt of his pistol.

They marched Roger through the vestibule and stopped at the counter on the other side. The sergeant manning the intake area checked his clipboard and said, "Room #3. The watch commander wants to talk with him."

"What?" Thompson became red in the face. "This jerk's not going to be processed? He killed two people."

The constable shrugged and replied, "Don't ask me. I just work here."

Bradley nodded to Thompson and said, "Why don't you go sign us in. I'll get this guy cleaned up and escort him to interrogation."

Before leaving, Thompson eyed Roger, clearly trying to send a message of violence if he tried anything.

Gripping Roger by the upper arm, Bradley led him through another vestibule, across a busy hallway, and down a short corridor to the restroom. Roger opened the tap, wet a paper towel, and used it to wipe away the dried blood. Checking himself in the mirror, he straightened his shirt.

"Ready when you are, Officer."

Bradley opened the door for him and motioned toward four doors marked with numbered plates. Door number 3 held a small room with stark white walls. In the middle was a square table with two metal chairs opposite each other.

"Have a seat," Bradley said. "The watch commander will be with you shortly." With that, he stepped outside and locked the door.

The overhead lights made a faint buzzing noise that lurked at the edge of his hearing. It was like having ants crawl across his skin. Roger inhaled, catching the odor of disinfectant and coffee. To take his mind off the electrical current, he took out a lockpick hidden within the seam of his breeches and began working on his restraints. He was leaning against the wall rubbing his wrists when Lieutenant Bell entered, carrying a thick manila file folder in the crook of his arm.

"You sure made a mess of things, didn't you?" the lieutenant said, eyeing the empty handcuffs on the tabletop.

Roger shrugged and replied, "Those men tried to rob me. What was I supposed to do?"

"For one thing, you weren't supposed to kill them. Fortunately for you, the two men had criminal records a mile long, which means the D.A. will decline to prosecute." Bell reached into his pocket and sat the gold coin on the table. "Yours, I take it?"

"Yes, sir," Roger said with a nod. "I was at a bar when it fell out of my money pouch. That's when those men began following me."

"You should have found a callbox and reported them," Bell said. "It would have saved everyone a lot of trouble, especially you."

"I can take care of myself," Roger replied, giving the watch commander a pointed look.

Bell let out a derisive snort. "I see how you take care of yourself."

"No offense, but where I'm from, this type of thing is normal. Sure, we have constables and shrievalties, but we also take care of ourselves. It makes the thieves think twice before picking your pocket."

Bell slapped his hand on the table. "That's not what we do here. People have rights — even criminals. That means you don't go around killing them. What you did wasn't self-defense. It was intentional. I know your type. You could have avoided the whole situation. Now, the solicitor is breathing down my neck, wanting to know more about you. What do I tell him?"

"The truth, I guess."

Taking a kerchief from his pocket, Bell wiped his forehead. "Sit."

Roger got a sinking feeling as the lieutenant opened the manila folder and pulled out a stack of glossy black and white photos showing the crime scene at Marion Square. On top of the photos was a copy of a mostly illegible handwritten document. "The State of South Carolina," stood out proudly in the upper left-hand corner. At the lower right-hand corner was the name Robert Y. Hayne, Attorney General.

"What's this?" asked Roger.

"That is the Attorney General's indictment for crimes against David Ross. John and Lavinia Fisher, along with William Hayward and James McElroy, were indicted for assault with intent to murder. It says the four wielded, pointed, and fired a loaded weapon at David Ross with the intent to kill him. It does not say who held the weapon and pulled the trigger. But it does say that Ross was beaten, wounded, and had great fear for his life.

"After you left, I met with Professor Hollingsworth at the College of Charleston. He said the Fishers' case had gone before a jury, and they passed what's called a true bill, stating sufficient probable cause existed to place them on trial for their crimes."

Roger scanned the document. "This is the first I've heard of David Ross. Who is he?"

"I don't know. The tales I've heard only mention their attack on John Peeples," Bell answered as he slid out a list of typed names and rotated the paper so Roger could read them. The name at the top had been circled in red.

William Hart – Foreman
Luke Bowes   William Mathews
William Brisbane   William Owens
John Davis   J.S. Packer
James Fogartie   Joseph Tyler
Peter Gaillard   Caleb Walker
I. Gespeale   William Wheelen
David Murray   Maj. John Wilson

"This is the list of jurors who heard the Fishers' case," Bell said. He took out a photograph and placed it on top of the stack.

Roger studied the man in the black and white image. His milky eyes stared out in glossy surrealism. The photo captured the precise slice across his gut. Bloody entrails lay on the ground behind him. Bell slid out another photo. It showed the granite stone base of the Calhoun Monument. Dark smears formed rough letters and numbers. Streaked by the rain, one part was still legible.

"Ezekiel 22:3," Roger read aloud. "Is that code for something?"

The lieutenant gave Roger an odd look. "It's a verse from the bible. *...and give her this message from the Sovereign LORD: O city of murderers, doomed and damned — city of idols, filthy and foul. You are guilty of the blood you have shed, and you are defiled by the idols you have made.*"

Roger stared intently into the dead man's eyes. "Who is he?"

"According to his driver's license, you are looking at William Hart of Charlotte, North Carolina," Bell answered. "A bank vice-president, he was here visiting the plantations with his wife, Lauren, and their son, Bill, Jr."

"That name can't be right," Roger said, glancing at the juror list then back at the photo. The shock of what he was seeing started to sink in. "It has to be a coincidence."

Lieutenant Bell fidgeted with a typed form on Medical College Hospital letterhead. "I thought that too, until I received Hart's preliminary autopsy report."

Roger's throat went dry. On the subject line, it read, "CAUSE OF DEATH – UNKNOWN." Underneath, the coroner wrote, "Time of death has not been determined. Normal procedures such as body temperature and lividity were inconclusive. Preliminary estimates put T.o.D. anywhere from twelve to eighteen hours *prior* to discovery by police. Penetrating trauma was caused by an extremely sharp instrument such as a knife or scalpel. Drug testing confirms large amounts of prednisone, dapsone, nalidixic acid, and PCP (Angel Dust) were present in his system. Trace amounts of Scopolamine and Oleander were also noted."

"Twelve to eighteen hours? Are they sure?" Roger asked. He looked at a photo of a fresh footprint beside a triangular flag. "Hart couldn't have been out there that long. Someone would have seen him."

"The coroner at the medical college is good. I doubt he made a mistake."

"It has to be — unless Terra has necromancers who can make the dead walk. Barring the arcane, Hart had to have been alive when he entered the park."

"That's why you're here," Bell said as he leaned back in his chair, watching Roger intently.

Roger narrowed his eyes at the watch commander. "You think I had something to do with this?"

Bell shook his head. "No, not really, but some here do. The events of two weeks ago are still fresh in our minds. Good people were hurt that day at the City Marina, some died. And, while on the surface this death appears to be different, it has the same smell. At the very least, I think you know something. You have to admit there's a real possibility your missing witch and William Hart's death are related. The fact his name just happens to be on a list from 1819 — information you requested — confirms it."

"Lieutenant Bell, I was hired to find Lavinia Fisher and that's what I'm going to do."

An uncomfortable expression came over Bell's face as he said, "The ghost of a dead witch — sounds like a bedtime story to me." He leaned forward. "I've never believed in ghosts, and I'm not about to start now. If Mr. Hart was murdered, it had to be a living, breathing person who did it. Somehow, you're connected to this man's death."

"You can't be serious," Roger said.

"It's all I have unless you give me something, Mister Vaughn. A dead man walking the streets of Charleston doesn't fall within the purview of the police manual."

With his eyes fixed on the report, Roger stood. "Nate mentioned a task force you've created for unusual crimes. Let me help you. Put me on your payroll as a consultant."

"The captain advised against it, but he's left it in my hands." Bell smiled. "You start tonight."

Roger ran a hand through his hair, his mind racing. "I want Nate and Tee. I also need information: reports, access to Hart's crime scene, everything you have."

"You got it. As long as you get results."

Turning toward Bell, Roger said, "You're risking a lot on me, aren't you?"

"Do you remember when we first met? You were in our conference room, hardly able to walk on your own. Your friends helped you, but it was your determination that got you moving. Some people would have given up, but not you. I admired that. Yes, I'm risking a lot on you. Don't let me down."

CHAPTER 6
PIECES OF HOME
Wednesday, April 2, 1969

"*M*ister Vaughn, it's me," Brie announced.

Roger blinked at the sunlight streaming through the windows. He lifted his head from his desk, and a photo stuck to his cheek. He peeled it off and collected the numerous typed forms and glossy images covering the wooden surface into neat stacks.

Before he could deposit them in the half-filled box by his feet, his office door opened, and Brie entered, carrying a steaming cup of coffee. Tight jeans and a thick V-neck sweater clung to her curves. "It's freezing outside. That rain yesterday must have brought a cold front behind it." She eyed the stacks on his desk as she handed him the paper cup. "You've been busy. Were you up all night?"

Standing to stretch, Roger took a sip and replied, "Most of it. I had an impromptu meeting with Lieutenant Bell. He wants us to help with a case."

"What about Lavinia Fisher? Can we handle two cases at the same time?"

Roger took another sip. "May not be two cases." He watched as Brie spotted the photo of the dead man from Marion Square.

"Is that our case?"

Roger handed her the preliminary autopsy report. Her eyes widened when she read the short paragraph from the coroner. "Twelve to eighteen hours! How's that possible? People drive by that square all the time."

"If we were in Gaia, I'd say he was a zombie, and we have a rogue necromancer on the loose."

"A zombie?" Brie asked, her face full of confusion.

It always amazed Roger when he introduced what he thought was a common term to this world. He explained, "A corpse that's been brought back to life using dark magic. The soul's gone, but the body remains. I've seen necromancers animate whole armies on a battlefield and turn what had been a victory into utter defeat."

Her eyes wide, she asked, "That's who killed this guy on the square?"

"Maybe not directly, but all that I'm seeing is pointing in that direction."

"What's our first step?"

"Well, Miss Tyler, I say we get rid of some of these gold pieces," Roger replied as he opened the bottom drawer of his desk and pulled out the pouch. "Then we meet with Nate and Tee."

Eyes alight with excitement, Brie sped down Queen Street. At King Street, she turned left and found a vacant parking space.

"Now don't stare, and whatever you do, don't make any sudden moves. Scott Silva is a little... twitchy."

"Twitchy?"

"You'll see," said Roger as he stepped out onto the sidewalk.

Shutting the car door behind him, he faced a rundown two-story building on the southwest corner of King and Queen Streets.

Supported by granite columns, a solid stone lintel spanned over the glass storefront and single lime green door. Sparkling gold paint on the window spelled out "ANTIQUES" in ornate calligraphy. Behind the storefront, stacked boxes, statues, bicycles, and an odd assortment of furniture fought for breathing room. Patches of faded peach stucco adhered to the building like spackled make-up. Along the roof, limestone cornices adorned the parapet, remnants of a grander time, now long past. Curtains behind the upper windows blocked any view of what might lie beyond.

"This is where you found your alchemy equipment?" Brie asked with an arched eyebrow.

Roger nodded as he pushed open the front door. At its top, a brass bell clanged loudly. "Scott, it's Roger! I brought a friend."

Suspended from a high ceiling decorated with embossed tin tiles, a bare bulb illuminated the foyer and the narrow pathway between mountains of old newspapers, books, and magazines piled atop mildewed furniture — all giving off the pungent odor of rot.

Brie covered her mouth with her hand but quickly

dropped it. Roger gave her an encouraging smile as he trekked deeper into the building. "Scott!"

After several twists and turns, the piles of paper gave way to glass curio cabinets filled with statuettes, charms, jars, and cobalt blue bottles. Oil paintings in gilded frames leaned against them.

"Is that a human skull?" Brie whispered.

"Yes, my dear. That is a human skull," a wrinkled man answered. "Poor Yorick, I knew him well."

Short compared to Roger, with long silver hair pulled back in a queue, Scott wore black pants and a black vest over a black tee shirt. Contrasting with his clothes, a large silver buckle clasped the two ends of a leather belt that carried an ornate leather pouch attached to a chain. He stood slightly hunched and squinted at Brie with his right eye. The left side of his face drooped, nearly closing his other eye.

"Where are your jokes now? Your pranks? Your songs?" Brie responded, staring at the skull.

Scott's lips quirked into a lopsided smile. "Roger, you brought a literate skirt to my den."

"Don't get any ideas. She's under my protection."

"I dig it," he replied, his eye developing a nervous twitch. "What can I do for you?"

Roger held up the Fishers' pouch and opened it so Scott could see the gold pieces inside. "I need to swap some of these for cash. Can you help?"

"May I?" Scott asked.

"Sure." Tilting the pouch, Roger retrieved a coin and handed it to him.

Scott licked his lips as he eyed the coin. He brought it to his nose and inhaled. "This has the smell of the undead, Roger."

"I didn't steal it. It's for services rendered, freely given."

"As long as they don't want it back," Scott said as he turned and motioned for them to follow.

Bare bulbs lighting the way, Roger and Brie hurried to catch up with Scott, who kept a constant hand on the various items lining the path. As if caught in the minotaur's labyrinth, they wound their way through clutter-filled aisles until they came to the sales counter. It stood like a barricade separating the public from the back-of-house: a ten-foot-wide cleared area in front of a plaster wall with three closed doors. The door on the far right had a plaque that read "OFFICE."

Scott lifted a hinged section of the counter, stepped behind it, and then lowered it back in place. Setting the gold coin on the micarta, he knelt and came back up with a set of scales and a large magnifying glass. After weighing and studying it, he said, "I'll give you fifteen dollars for each one. That will cover the melt value."

"No way," Brie blurted. "They're worth at least two hundred apiece."

Scott eyed her as he said, "I admit they're noteworthy collectibles, but they're not cherry. This one has been worn smooth, and if I had to grade it, I'd say it's Fine, tops. You can't expect top dollar."

"No, but we can expect a fair price," Brie said, her back stiff.

"Who's protecting who here, Roger?" Scott asked.

Roger shrugged and replied, "It's mutual. We protect each other."

"Damn right. The name's Brie, by the way."

"Well met, young lady." Scott gave her a slight bow and started laughing. "You two deserve each other, that's for sure. How about a hundred?"

Roger turned to Brie, who gave him a curt nod. "Sounds good. Let's start with these four." Roger took the three from his own pouch and added them to the one already on the countertop. Scooping them up in one hand, Scott disappeared into the office.

"That's four hundred dollars," Brie whispered out of the corner of her mouth.

"Will that be enough?" he asked her.

"More than enough."

When he returned, Scott counted out three one-hundred-dollar bills and then five twenty-dollar bills. "Look about right?"

"Thanks, Scott," Roger said as he folded the paper currency and slipped it into a pouch. Keeping out one of the hundred-dollar bills, he handed it to Brie. "This one's for you."

"Anything else?" Scott asked.

After returning the bag of coins to his belt, Roger tapped the counter with his fingers. "Have you heard any rumors about a necromancer being in the city?"

Lightning flashed in Scott's eye. "No. A mage wouldn't show his face around here. If they did..." He gripped the edge of the counter as if he meant to rip it apart. "I'd eat 'em."

"Scott, it'll be alright," Roger said, seeing he had stepped on a nerve.

"What is it?" Brie asked.

Scott snapped, "I don't like mages."

"I'm sure they don't like you either," said Roger, trying to be funny. "Probably teased you when you were a kid. What happened? Did one cast a spell on you?"

A distant look came over Scott. Still holding the counter, he slowly rocked back and forth. "When we are born, we cry that we are come to this great stage of fools." He stared past them, eyes unfocused. "It were a delicate stratagem, to shoe a troop of horse with felt. I'll put 't in proof, and when I have stol'n upon these sons-in-law—" Seemingly trapped in his own cluttered mind, Scott rocked faster and yelled, "Then, kill, kill, kill, kill, kill, kill!"

"Scott, it's okay," Brie said. She reached out, but Roger grabbed her wrist and pulled her behind him.

"Let him be," he warned.

"But he's upset."

"You have no sense of self-preservation, do you?" asked Roger. "You could lose a finger... possibly your hand."

"Don't be ridiculous. Mr. Silva isn't going to bite me."

"Better safe than sorry." Roger waved a hand in front of Scott. Not getting a reaction, he said, "I think we broke him."

Alarmed, Brie darted around Roger, raised the counter, and wrapped Scott in a hug. Even though he continued rocking back and forth, he stopped yelling. He looked at her, his good eye still unfocused, and said, "They kill us for their sport."

"What's he talking about?"

"Come on, Brie, let's go."

"We can't leave him like this." It was clear she felt helpless. She looked at Roger and said, "You're so smart. Do something."

Roger sighed. He didn't like getting involved on a personal level. Professional friendships were easy. You knew where you stood. He studied Scott's face, every wrinkle, every age spot, searching for a sign.

On a hunch, he retrieved two objects from a belt pouch and laid them on the counter: one a sparkling ruby, the other a torn piece of leathery, patina-stained hide. "These are for you. Add them to your hoard," said Roger. "They're pieces of home."

Scott froze, and Brie let him go. His hand trembling, he picked up the hide and brought it close. Some of the patina broke away, revealing tiny fan-shaped scales that had an iridescent sheen. As he held it, a tear trailed from the corner of his good eye. He rubbed his fingers over its surface and smelled it. He pressed it to his cheek.

"It's spoils from a fight," Roger said. "I know it's not what you're looking for, but maybe it's a start."

Gripping the bit of hide with both hands, Scott disappeared into his office and shut the door.

Brie started to follow, but Roger waved her back. "Let him go."

"Do you want your ruby?" Brie asked, seeing it still on the counter.

"Leave it," Roger replied as he retraced their steps toward the exit.

"What just happened?"

"I'm not entirely sure."

"Come on. You gotta know something."

Roger stopped and looked at the piles lining the aisle. "Did you see how he ignored the ruby? He chose the scaly scrap of leather instead. I think he's... lost his true self. Now, he's old and alone."

"But you called them pieces of home. Is he from Gaia too?"

Roger gave her a quick nod. "I believe so."

Brie's mouth formed a large O, and she seemed to be on the verge of a thousand questions.

Not trusting himself to tell her what he really thought, Roger held up his hand. "I don't know what brought him here. Was it by choice or was he banished? Who can say? What I do know is that, whatever it was, it broke his mind." He motioned toward the mountains of clutter. "You see all this? I think he's been trying to fill a void but, you see, everything here is Terran. He needs items from Gaia — pieces of home."

He continued toward the door.

"How is it possible for Scott to be here?" asked Brie.

"Magic, I presume," answered Roger. "Though I couldn't tell you if it was a spell or something else."

"You think a wizard cast a spell on him?"

"The way he reacted, that's my guess."

"Could a wizard send him back? Could they send you back?"

They had reached the front door. Roger turned and gripped Brie by the shoulders. "Travel to Gaia is not that simple. It took special magic for me to come here. I suspect the same would be true for Scott. Brie, be careful around him. All he knows is that he wants something that's always outside of his reach. It's quite tragic."

"But you helped him."

Doubt gnawing inside his gut, Roger looked over Brie's shoulder and down the lit path. "Did I?"

CHAPTER 7
RED SHIRTS

Wednesday, April 2, 1969

*A*rms crossed, Nate stood by the desk in Roger's office. The half-filled evidence box sat at his feet. "It's about time," he said. "Where have you two been?"

Tee turned away from admiring the sparkling glass vials and bulbed beakers of Roger's alchemy equipment. They still wore their police uniforms.

Roger kept the smile from his face as he thought about what his neighbors might think. He'd met the artist who owned the gallery downstairs, but not the occupant of the third floor. The reputation of Doctor Wampus — the root doctor who previously owned the office — had kept them at bay, but with the constabulary frequenting Roger's office, he suspected his reputation would only get worse. Or better, depending on your point of view.

"I needed some local currency," Roger answered.

"Look, Roger, we don't appreciate being kept in the dark. What's going on?" Nate asked. "Lieutenant Bell didn't tell us anything other than to get our butts over here."

"At least you had your key," Brie said.

Nate glared at her then took a step toward Roger. "How did you get this box of evidence? It's police business."

Roger replied, "Lieutenant Bell put me on the payroll. I'm a consultant now."

"When did that happen?"

"Last night, after I was arrested."

Brie gasped, and Roger held up a hand to forestall whatever outburst she was preparing to make. The quiet in the office became palpable. The stern expression on Nate's face conveyed the same intense disappointment Roger often received from his father and elder brother in recent years.

"Never mind why I was at the shrievalty," said Roger. "What's important is I'm pulling together a team, and I want you, Tee, and Brie to be a part of it."

Nate and Tee shared a quick glance. "A team?" Tee asked.

"Call it what you want, but Lieutenant Bell said you could work with me. I'm not going to lie to you. It'll be dangerous. I believe Mister Hart was under the influence of a necromancer, or at least the Terran version of it, and I'm going after them."

Nate and Tee stood shoulder to shoulder. While Nate's confusion was clear, Tee's countenance grew more serious, and he made a sign against evil. "Uh conjuh-man wuh calls de dead is serious bidness, Mistuh Vaughn. Wuh mek yuh fuh sho'?"

Brie grabbed Hart's autopsy report and handed it to Tee. "Here. Read this."

The two policemen held the document so they could read it together. Nate's eyebrows crawled up his forehead when he began reading.

"A necromancer," Nate said as if mulling the word over.

"It may not be a necromancer in the strictest sense," said Roger, "but it is someone who can keep a man on his feet even after his heart's stopped beating. It could be magic, or it might even be through alchemy. It's not unheard of."

"Think Frankenstein's monster," Brie added.

"You're nuts!" Nate exclaimed.

"How do you explain that report?" Brie asked.

"I can't," Nate replied. "But until we've exhausted all other explanations, I will not believe there's some mad scientist out there raising the dead."

"What about someone using magic to turn a corpse into a puppet, more or less?" asked Roger.

Nate shook his head. "Not magic, either."

"Even after what you saw — the Archer and the sclábhaí?" Roger asked.

Nate straightened and said in a grim voice, "Even after what I saw."

"What about all that stuff you watch — Twilight Zone, Outer Limits, Star Trek? Somewhere deep down, you believe in magic or, at least, the possibility of it," Brie added.

"Those are just television shows, Brie. Entertainment. It's science *fiction*; it's not real."

Roger gave him a broad smile and gripped his arm. "That's exactly why I want you to be part of my team."

The confused look returned to Nate's face. "What?"

"I look at this world through the lens of my experiences.

We all do," Roger explained. "We look at William Hart's death, and we see different things. I see a necromancer, Tee sees a shaman, and you... you see a man who was by himself. You want it to be deliberate self-murder. Anything else would stretch the boundaries of your world."

"What do I see?" Brie asked.

"To use sports vernacular, you're the referee. Untainted by the weight of experience, you see the truth."

A slight smile formed at the edges of Brie's mouth before she dipped her head, and her hair hid her face.

"Can oonuh ketch dis conjuh-man?" Tee asked.

"Yes."

"How?" Nate asked.

"Like Lieutenant Bell, I don't believe in coincidences," Roger answered as he walked to his desk and dug out the list of jurors. He stared at it briefly before handing it to Nate.

"What's this?" Nate asked.

"That's the list of jurors from John and Lavinia Fisher's trial. Lieutenant Bell met with the archivist at the College of Charleston, and he gave him this list along with the Attorney General's indictment."

"William Hart — the foreman? But the man at the square was from Charlotte," Nate said, throwing him a quizzical look.

"All we have to go on is the victim's name and that list."

Handing the list to Tee, Nate said to Roger, "I think you're reaching. Even if they are related, how does that help us if the man committed suicide?"

"For one thing: the timing. It's been two weeks since we freed the aethereal prisoners from the Old City Gaol. The other thing: Hart was killed the same day John Fisher hired me to find his wife."

"But that means Lavinia could be the killer," Brie said. "We have to stop her."

"De witch is free," Tee stated. His deep baritone voice resonated in the room.

Nate took back the list from Tee. After rereading the names, he looked up at Roger and asked, "Revenge?"

"It's a real human motive," Roger said.

"But for a hundred and fifty-year-old crime."

"Imprisoned in that place, would she think of anything else?" Roger asked. "And I remind you, Lavinia Fisher did not move on. She's still here in Charleston."

"Does that mean Brie and her family are in danger?" asked Nate.

"Why would we be in danger?" Brie demanded.

Nate handed her the list of jurors.

Frowning as she read it, Brie said, "As far as I know, we aren't related to this Joseph Tyler. My father's from Syracuse, New York, not Charleston. Still, I think you're jumping to conclusions about the revenge angle."

"Miss Tyler's right," Tee said, "but duh only way we gwine know f'certain is if anudduh person dies."

"Unless we find Lavinia first," Roger countered.

"I don't know about this." Nate ran his fingers through his hair. "I feel like you're asking us to wear red shirts."

Unsure about the reference, Roger said, "I'm not asking you to join a cult or commune with the dead using a spirit board or anything. Do what you are trained to do: look for clues and report back to me."

Nate gave Tee a slight nod.

"We'll help," Tee said, "but if we light out, we gwine uh see it t'ru to de end."

"Agreed," Roger replied.

"Wuh's de fus' step?" Tee asked.

"Change out of your uniforms into street clothes. It will allow us to move more freely. When you're ready, meet up with Brie and me at Marion Square." Roger walked to the shelves and handed each of them a leather pouch. "Carry these on you at all times. If you come across a ghost, sprinkle the contents on the ground around you, forming a complete circle. The iron filings will disrupt the ghost's connection to the material world. They won't be able to cross it."

"What if it's flesh and bone?" asked Nate.

"We use our guns," Tee said with a smile.

Standing on the bluestone sidewalk along Calhoun Street, Roger opened one of the hardened leather pouches at his belt and retrieved a metal vial and ivory box.

"Hold this," Roger said, handing Brie the box.

He removed the stopper from the vial and inhaled its contents. *One... two...* On three, he let out a giant sneeze that rocked him to the soles of his feet.

"Bless you," Brie said. "You alright?"

Still not able to speak, he nodded as he replaced the stopper and stuck the vial back in its pouch. Brie held up the ivory box, and Roger took out a pair of whalebone spectacles joined by a brass rivet. He adjusted them to fit his face and pushed them back on his nose with a finger.

"What are those things?" Brie asked with a smile on her face. "They make your eyes look huge."

Blinking back the tears, he scanned the area cordoned off by the barricade tape. A hundred feet from the road, the statue of John C. Calhoun loomed over them.

"Thanks," Roger said as he took back the ivory box and tucked it away.   "The glasses, in combination with the powder, allow me to see magical auras."

"You can *see* magic?"

"The aura. Back on Gaia, I could tell you the school and sometimes the name of the mage who cast the spell. Here, with all the electrical fields, I'm lucky if I catch a whiff."

Roger scanned the stone pavers of the sidewalk, then moved onto the grassed lawn leading to the base of the statue. Stepping past the barricade tape, he followed the small flags marking Mister Hart's path.

"I'm not seeing anything."

He knelt beside a flag and ran a finger along the edge of a shallow impression of a shoe. Beside it was the slithering trail left behind by Hart's intestines. The report listed the estimated death as twelve to eighteen hours prior to time of discovery. The tracks appeared to have been made early Tuesday morning, during the rain and not before it. Doing the math in his head, Roger realized that would put Hart walking toward the statue no more than six hours prior to the police finding his body.

He removed his glasses and put them back on. It didn't make sense. The tracks didn't glow. Even necromantic magic had an aura.

Roger slipped a knife from its sheath. The intricate scrollwork etched into the blade glowed bright red, typical of battle magic. The glasses were working. He returned the weapon to its sheath and took off the glasses. "Nothing. Not a bloody thing."

"Let me try," Brie said.

"Sure," Roger replied, rising.

He held out the vial. "One sniff should be enough."

"It's not a drug, is it?"

Roger pursed his lips and thought about it. "It's an alchemical compound of dried plants and powdered mushrooms that open your senses to magic."

"Yeah, that sounds like a drug."

Roger shrugged. "The effects don't last long. The worst part is the dizziness... and the nausea."

Brie wrinkled her nose, eyed the vial warily, then sniffed its contents. A violent sneeze tore from her. Tears dampened her cheeks and her jaw clenched.

Roger counted silently. Five seconds passed before Brie opened her eyes. He handed her the spectacles.

She set them on her nose and froze. "Your eyes are glowing," she said softly.

"What color?" Roger asked.

"Gold."

"Good. All divination auras glow gold. Remember that." Roger took out his knife and asked, "Now what do you see?"

"*Oooh*, that's pretty," she said. "It's red."

"Fire — one of the four elemental magics."

"How many types of magic are there?"

"Mages are a bit cagey when it comes to explaining things, but as I understand it, the Korellan system classifies magic into Astral, Charms, Divination, Elemental, Illusion, Protection, and Necromancy. They use the *effect* to name the seven schools, but that's a bit misleading."

"Seems simple enough. Why do you say it's misleading?"

Roger made a face and said, "Well, take Elemental magic as an example. Earth, Air, Fire, and Water are all Elemental, but they each have their own properties — their own distinctive color so to speak."

As he spoke, Brie became distracted. She reached out her hand, palm down, and whispered, "Fanérosi." Each of the victim's footprints darkened as if small clouds blocked out the sun. Just as quickly, the shadows vanished.

"How did you..." Roger's mind reeled. She shouldn't have been able to do that. "You just cast a detection spell."

"I don't know. It just felt right," Brie replied, staring at her hand. "Same thing happened when I first met Ambrose."

"That's incredible," Roger said, stunned.

"Mister Vaughn, what is magic?" Brie asked in a voice

that reflected fear and awe, as if she had both contracted a terminal disease and witnessed a miracle.

"Now you are going to get me in trouble," Roger said with an easy grin.

"Why is that?"

"If you ask a hundred different mages that question, you'll get a hundred different answers."

"You must have a theory," she said, handing him back the glasses.

"Put them back on," Roger said as he drew closer to her. "Feel the breeze. Concentrate on it. You can't see it, but it's there, made from particles so small they're invisible to the naked eye."

Beads of sweat formed along her brow, and she leaned forward. Finally, Brie said, "I see something." She reached out as if to touch it.

Roger didn't know how to feel. She had just passed one of the tests of magic given at the Academia. Recalling one of his first lectures, he said, "What you see is the primordial ocean from which we are all created. But it doesn't just form the air. It makes up the fundamental building blocks of the world, including all its solid shapes, fluids, and gases. It also forms you and me.   It flows through us, connecting everything together, and it can be manipulated — if you know how."

Brie gave him back the glasses and wiped a hand across her forehead.

Gazing intently into her eyes, Roger said, "The textbook answer is that magic is the willpower we use to manipulate the elements or create something out of nothing, even if it's just an illusion. But you can't create something out of nothing. There's always a price."

"Did you find anything?" Nate asked as he and Tee walked up.

Roger glanced at them, then did a doubletake. Nate wore a snug tan suit with a brown tie and matching fedora. He carried it like a suit of armor that reminded Roger of his friend Cerdic, a paladin back on Gaia. Beside Nate, Tee had on high-waisted, burgundy, bell-bottomed slacks and a buttoned up, long sleeve shirt with a wide flaring collar. Overlapping black and red hearts wrapped around his massive torso.

Shaking his head, Roger was at a loss for words. Finally, he asked, "Are those your street clothes?"

Nate inspected himself before replying, "Yes."

"Of co'se," answered Tee.

"What's wrong with them?" asked Nate.

"For one thing, Tee looks like he's going to a bacchanal," Roger said.

"I prefer de term festive," Tee rumbled.

"Next time wear something that won't attract attention."

Nate replied, "You didn't say anything about going undercover."

Tee gestured toward his clothes. "Dis is what I wear. Dey an extension of my personality."

Roger turned to Brie for support.

"Welcome to the modern world," she said. "It's 1969. Did it ever occur to you that *you* may be the one who stands out?"

Feeling as if he had been blindsided, Roger's mouth dropped open. He shut it as he turned to face each of them.

Giving Roger one of his intimidating smiles, Tee laid an arm around his shoulders and said, "It's all good. We can get yuh some proper threads later."

"I think we should start," Nate said, turning toward the statue.

"Right," Roger said and pointed to the ground. "We searched the area leading to the base. There was a faint magical residue, but it vanished before I could get a good look at it." He thought about asking Brie to try again but decided against it. Magic was tricky on Gaia, and he suspected it would be the same on Terra, maybe even more so.

Nate paralleled the flags as he walked toward the statue. "The forensic report said they didn't find a lot of Hart's blood. Just what was on the pedestal and the trail left behind by the intestines."

"From the timing, Hart had to be a zombie before he got here," said Tee.

"I'm still not buying that," Nate argued.

"Do you have an alternate explanation?" Brie asked.

"Couldn't the drugs they found in his system have slowed his heart rate, reducing the amount of blood loss?" asked Nate.

Kneeling beside the bloodied base, Roger scratched his

chin. "Oleander can do that, but I'm not familiar with the others."

"Angel Dust is diff'unt. It's nasty bidness," Tee said. "It makes yuh see things dat ain't dey. Had a cuz'n dat took it. Crashed him car and lost him'own arm. Awake de whole time, en' he didn't feel a t'ing."

"Tee, could you ask Vie?" Brie asked. "She may know something. Probably knows more than the coroner."

Tee frowned. "I'll akx, but don't get yo hopes up. She's still mo'nful 'bout losing her father."

Nate considered the dark stains for a while and said, "Ezekiel 22:3. That's a little ominous."

Beside him, Roger looked back toward the street. People walked up and down the sidewalk. Some were curious, but most kept their eyes averted and walked faster. "Someone wanted to send a message," he said.

"Public place with lots of pedestrians and a lot of traffic," Nate said, rising. "It makes sense."

"Who's Hart's message for?" Roger asked. "Is it a warning for all of Charleston as the verse suggests? And if so, why now?"

A grim expression on his face, Nate replied, "Let's go through the evidence box and see if we can find out."

CHAPTER 8
A GLIMPSE OF THE PAST
Thursday, April 3, 1969

*R*oger hunched over the desk in his office, notes from the meeting with John Fisher spread out before him. He flipped through the pages with a frown. It seemed the deeper they went into this investigation the more questions he had.

After returning from Marion Square with Brie, Nate, and Tee, they had spent the rest of yesterday going through photos and statements from Hart's evidence box. Nothing jumped out at them. It was decided that Tee and Nate would talk with Lauren Hart this morning. After that, they planned to visit the coroner and see if they could gain any insight on the cause and time of William Hart's death.

Roger stood and collected his gear. Lieutenant Bell had set up an appointment for him and Brie with Professor Hollingsworth, the archivist at the College of Charleston. It was a twenty-minute walk, and he wanted to catch up with Brie after her class. She had asked him to meet her at the Cistern. From there, she said, it would be a short walk to the Towell Library and the conservation room.

Early yet, the day promised to be warmer than yesterday, so he chose a pale dress shirt with a long linen blazer and no necktie. He still hadn't figured out how to wear his belt with a jacket and not look like a misplaced cowboy. One day soon, he'd have to come up with something different to carry his tools and alchemy potions.

After making sure the office door was locked, he adjusted his trilby and moved down the metal stairs. Keeping to the sidewalks, his route took him past St Philip's Church, the City Market, and up St Philips Street. He crossed George Street and followed the short perimeter wall of the Cistern Yard until he found an open gate.

Brie had mentioned the school enrolled five hundred students, but waiting at the raised oval cistern, Roger was surprised to see them stream from the buildings all at once.

He felt conspicuous and tried to blend by not remaining in one place. As he walked, he found his gaze wandering to the live oaks trailing bearded moss from their thick branches.   They gave the campus a feeling of solemn antiquity.

Brie bounded down the steps of Randolph Hall, wearing a bright red jacket over a rainbow-flowered sundress and carrying a bundle of books within the crook of her arm. After spotting him, she hurried across the yard and gave him a tight one-armed hug. "You made it."

As they pulled apart, Roger asked, "Want me to carry your books?"

"You're sweet, but no thanks. I got them."

"So, where's this Towell Library?"

"There," she answered, nodding toward a raised two-story building with arched windows.

Instead of heading toward the double doors at its center, Brie aimed for a set of concrete steps that led down to the half-basement. She grasped the doorknob and entered.

A wave of cool air washed over them. Roger shut the door behind him, wishing he had brought his duster.

"We're here to see Professor Hollingsworth," Brie said to a seated young lady with her hair piled in a beehive.

"He's waiting for you through there," she replied as she rose from her desk and motioned toward an open door. "In case you haven't been warned, you will not be allowed to take anything into or out of the conservation room. So, no pencils, pens, paper, cameras. If you have any items in your pockets, please deposit them here with the rest of your things." She laid a plastic tray on her desktop.

"May I leave my books with you?" Brie asked as she placed her purse onto the tray.

"Certainly," the secretary replied.

Roger frowned at the shiny plastic tray. "You want everything?"

"It's for the protection of the documents," the lady explained. "Some are quite old and fragile."

"Just give her your utility belt," Brie urged. "You wouldn't want it to blow up while we're meeting with the professor anyways."

The secretary stepped back with a gasp.

Roger undid the wide belt at his waist and dropped it onto the tray. "Be careful with that."

Eyeing it as if it were a coiled snake, the secretary said,

"I promise, no one will touch it."

"Thank you," Brie said, taking Roger by the arm.

The professor waited for them inside a low-ceilinged room with rows of wide bookshelves that ran from one end to the other. Appearing as though he was about to give a lecture, he stood erect at the head of a wooden table, wearing rimless glasses and a tweed coat with leather patches at the elbows. Beside him, a metal cart on castors carried several heavy-duty accordion file boxes.

Offering his hand, he said, "I'm Professor Michael Hollingsworth, but you can call me Professor Mike or just Mike, as you like." He shook Brie's hand and then Roger's.

"Brie Tyler."

"Roger Vaughn."

"Please have a seat. I have the files Lieutenant Bell requested. What, specifically, are you looking for?"

"Ms. Simmons, the librarian on Rivers Avenue, mentioned you might have an eyewitness account of John and Lavinia Fisher's hanging, as well as a collection of newspaper articles from that time period," Roger answered.

Mike opened the first box and said, "In 1834, an attorney, John Blake White, wrote an essay on capital punishment in which he described his observations of that fateful day." He slid out a manilla folder and sat it on the table. Inside was a yellowed manuscript with brittle edges.

The title flowed across the sheet, and Roger began to have misgivings that he and Brie would be able to read it.

"Here. I have a photocopy. It's easier to handle," Mike said, taking out another folder. "Please try to keep them in order. The page number is penciled in at the top. You have the room reserved for one hour."

Roger scanned the first page, looking for a word he recognized. The writing was similar to his native Glaxon, but the verbiage was different enough to make him feel he was deciphering a code. After he finished the page, he passed it to Brie, who checked behind him. On the thirteenth page, he stopped. "Here it is."

Brie leaned closer, and they began reading:

> *We were called to the prison on professional*
> *business the evening previous to the execution. At*
> *the insistence of the gaoler, we went down with*

him to the ground cells of the prison where he unlocked a door, which opened into an extensive apartment. The furniture of this chamber, illuminated only by the lantern our guide carried, consisted of several coffins, a gibbet, whose disjointed parts lay lumbering against the wall, some fragments of rope, a spade, a pickaxe, and a few like implements of death and the grave.

Two proper sized coffins being selected and delivered over to another attendant, we followed the gaoler to another cell at a remote corner of the building. After repeated calls, a voice at length answered from within as from a sepulcher. The door being unbarred and opened, we beheld stretched upon the floor a being that appeared to be anything rather than human. Haggard, pale, emaciated, it began slowly to rise from the floor, growling like some glutted hyena at being roused from his lair. It stood at length erect before us resembling more an anatomical preparation than a true and living man.

"Thus am I served (growled he) whenever you want my work. But give me something to drink. I must have drink and I will be contented!!"

This was the Executioner! We stood in the awful presence of a Minister of Justice. We shrunk with reverential horror at his glance!

This solitary, this mysterious Being lived alone in Creation. Neither wife, nor child, nor kinsfolk had he, and he acknowledged no human tie to this world. He was a pensioner upon the Sheriff for mere food and scanty raiment, and had been so, for a long time upon the bounty of many a predecessor. Here then stood before us in unsophisticated reality, a Murderer of State, a pensioned cutthroat, a day laborer of death who did his work for pay with fidelity and skill and all by virtue of law and under the sacred sanction of Justice!

This miserable man, being extremely intemperate, it became necessary to confine close by, when his services were about to be required.

Again and again, he entreated to be supplied with liquor, which was positively refused, though with assurance that, after the execution, if well performed, he should command as much to drink as he desired. A transient but ghastly smile flickered for an instant on his cheek when the door of his cell was again closed and bolted.

"Oh my God! Is that him? Is that the Executioner from the Old City Jail?" Brie asked. Pushing up from the table, she stalked to its far end. A haunted look crept into her eyes as she confessed, "I have nightmares about him. Nightmares from when he imprisoned me. He..."

Roger rose and took her hands. He gazed deep into her eyes, trying to exude strength and confidence. "I do too. Phantom images that send my heart racing. But the Executioner is dead. Cerdic and Queen Ambrose killed him."

"Are you sure? I mean, how can anyone kill a man who lived and died a hundred and fifty years ago?"

"Would it help if I finished reading it by myself?"

Her jaw set, Brie let go of Roger and said, "No, we'll finish it together. Maybe we'll discover some clue about him and the Fishers."

Sitting back down, they continued reading the events of the next day:

In the lobby, silently awaited the Sheriff and his attendants. At the furthest end of the gallery stood the Executioner, arranging with professional skill, the slipknot and the noose and stretching to their utmost length, the fatal cords.

The hour at length arrived and the order was given to prepare the convicts. The door was thrown open and what a scene was exhibited! The miserable man, Fisher, and his wife were both before us. Two finer forms, the sculptors fancy has seldom sketched: tall, graceful, we might almost add majestic, but alas! Fallen, helpless, degraded to the very dust! As the door opened, the eyes of this hapless woman fell upon the ghost like apparition of the Executioner when she sent forth a shriek, that chilled every heart with horror! After long parley and much difficulty and even resistance on her part, the Jack Ketch adjusted the cords and pinioned his victims which he performed with indifference the most cold and with skill the most perfect. To depict with justice the horrors of this scene would require the pen of a master, a Byron or a Scott. It was made up of a thousand minute incidents, too much so, to note, yet, which essentially tended to fill up the whole picture, with most terrible and affecting interest.

The prisoners had provided themselves at their private expense with loose white garments which they put on over their clothes. They threw themselves once more into each other's arms and bade each other an eternal adieu.

"Well!" Brie exclaimed. "So much for the legend of Lavinia being hung in her wedding gown."

"They weren't married," Roger said. "John Fisher said they were something called 'common law.'"

"That means they lived together for several years and presented themselves as married during that time. These days, I think the required time is seven years. After that, a couple is considered married in the eyes of the law." She sighed, then said, "Makes me wonder how much more of the legend is made up or exaggerated."

Roger gestured at the document. "I guess we'll find out."

From this moment, the Executioner appeared to take possession of this devoted pair and henceforth to claim them as his own. He left them never for an instant but stood forth a conspicuous figure in this melancholy group. It may be considered presumptuous to dive into this human heart and to pretend to scour its secret mysterious operations, but in contemplating this extraordinary individual (whom to behold once, was never to forget) it was impossible to consider him but as one of the most debased and abandoned of the human race.

The unhappy victims descended the stairs, arm in arm, to a coach in waiting at the prison door and the cavalcade slowly moved forward, flanked by a company of cavalry.

Arriving within sight of the gibbet which was erected a little way out of the City we even now remember the horrible picture of despair exhibited on the countenance of Fisher, when he first beheld the frightful reality. His cheek assumed a livid pallor, his eyes involuntarily closed, a tremor shook his frame. He drew his wife to him in a convulsive grasp to his bosom and in a few seconds he looked up, nerved for the execution.

The coach reached the spot. The culprits and the Jack Ketch descended. Fisher mounted the scaffold and cast his eyes, mournfully around at the immense multitude. Not so his wife, she positively refused to go up. Neither persuasion nor threats could prevail. The constables were at length constrained to resort to bodily force and she was almost dragged to the stand. This unhappy woman could not believe it possible that she was destined to die. She called upon the multitude to rescue her and stretched forth her trembling arms, imploring pity. At one moment she would rant and blaspheme and stamp and rave with incoherent wildness and now with execrations the most shocking she would imprecate perdition on the Executive who would consign a woman to an end so ignominious.

Silence like that of death hung over this vast assembly broken only by the shrieks of this very maniac upon the verge of Eternity! Nothing could be more appalling! She was totally unprepared to die.

It was truly pitiable, it was heart rending, to behold this unhappy husband, himself just about to perish and needing every moment for his own soul, bending, with interest the most intense toward his panicked wife, and in tenderest accents, conjuring her to make peace with Heaven.

All was unheeded. Her whole mind was engrossed by the one absorbing thought, the hope of pardon.

The Sheriff in a sober and impressive voice

assured her that her expectations were wholly groundless — that her moments were few and numbered and that she must assuredly die!

No human tongue can adequately describe the intense interest of this moment. Happily, the words of the Sheriff were electric. She seemed to pierce with her eyes into his very soul. For a moment she was mute. Her execrations were hushed, and now, with frantic gesticulations, she called upon Heaven to have mercy upon her and to save her soul alive! Brief exclamations, hurried ejaculations half uttered, but glowing words, flowed from her lips with rapidity quicker than thought. She felt she had delayed too long to make her account with Heaven and now the dreadful messenger of death tugged at her despairing heart! Her prayers though late, we fervently trust ascended to the Throne of Grace and pleaded trumpet tongued in her behalf for mercy.

While these agonizing scenes were passing, the Executioner was beheld, mounted aloft on a ladder, hovering like a Vampire over these devoted beings, engaged in making fast the cords, and adjusting the caps over their faces. One more thrilling pause ensued! This ill-fated pair stood trembling upon the narrow isthmus between time and eternity!

A private signal passed from the Sheriff. The platform gave way — they fell — all was hushed and still. Their loose white garments, only, floated on the breeze!

CHAPTER 9
THE LETTER

Thursday, April 3, 1969

*R*oger stared at those last few words of White's account. The essay continued for another two and a half pages, giving White's opinion on capital punishment, but he couldn't bring himself to read it. He didn't know how to feel; he didn't know what to say.

Next to him, Brie sat back, a hand over her mouth, as she stared wide-eyed at the page.

"The hour is come, Farewell, Sir, Farewell," Professor Mike recited with a dramatic flair. "At two o'clock, February 18, 1820, John and Lavinia Fisher embraced each other for the last time. The newspaper reported that she died without a struggle or a groan, but it was some time before John ceased to struggle. Their bodies were taken down and carried to Potter's Field, where they were buried.

"John Fisher wrote a letter the day of his execution. It proclaimed his innocence, but it also let the public know he had been railroaded." As the professor spoke, he slid out a news article from the accordion file and handed it to Roger.

Charleston Gaol, Feb. 18, 1820
Rev. and Dear Sir,

The appointed day has arrived — the moment soon to come, which will finish my earthly career; and it behooves me, for the last time, to address you and the Rev. Gentlemen associated in your pious care.

For your exertions in explaining the mysteries of our Holy Religion and the merits of our dear Redeemer; for pious sympathy, and benevolent regards as concerns our immortal souls, accept Sir, for yourself, and them, the last benediction of the unfortunate — God, in his infinite mercy, reward you all.

In a few moments, and the world to me shall have passed away — before the Throne of the

Eternal Majesty of Heaven I must stand — shall then, at this dreadful hour, my convulsed agitated lips, still proclaim a falsehood? No! Then by that Awful Majesty I swear, I am innocent. May the Redeemer of the World plead for those who have sworn away my life.

To the unfortunate, the voice of condolence is sweet — the language of commiseration delightful — these feelings I have experienced in the society of Mr. ______________; a stranger, he rejected not our prayer; unknown, he shut not his ear to our supplication; he has alleviated our sorrows — May God bless him. He has wept with us — May Angels rejoice with him at a Throne of Glory.

Enclosed, Sir, is a key that secretes my little all — Give it to him, and say for me, as he deserted me not while living, I hope he will discharge my last request. How my property is to be disposed of, he will find explained in a paper within my trunk, to which is attached a Schedule of the whole. I only wish him to see it removed to a place of safety, until to whom it is given shall call for it. The hour is come!

Farewell, Sir, Farewell!
John Fisher

"Who was this written to? The name is blank," said Roger.

"No one knows. Nor does anyone know what John Fisher left behind."

"Do you know who attended him?" Brie asked.

"I don't have it here, but an article, circulated in 1897, mentioned the unhappy couple were visited by many ministers while confined. However, it only named two people: Dr. Richard Furman, pastor of the First Baptist Church, and Reverend Galluchat, of the Methodist Church.

"I'm not one who is prone to speculation, but if I had to guess, I'd say John Fisher wrote his letter to Dr. Furman."

"Furman — as in Furman University?" asked Brie.

"The same."

Pointing to a passage, Roger asked, "Who is Mister Fisher accusing here where it says, 'May the Redeemer of the World plead for those who have sworn away my life'?"

Mike steepled his fingers and asked, "How much do you know about the Fishers' arrest?"

"Just what we read in the indictment you gave Lieutenant Bell."

"And the short story by Ms. Martin," added Brie.

"I take it you've already noticed the discrepancies," said Mike.

"You mean like how they were accused of assault, but Ms. Martin said they had been condemned for being mass murderers," Brie said.

Mike nodded.

"And how it was John Peeples in her story, but the accuser's name was David Ross in the indictment," said Roger.

"Correct—"

The lady from the front desk poked her head into the room. "Professor Mike, you have fifteen minutes."

"Thank you, Ms. Bailey." He paused for a moment as if to collect his thoughts, then said, "President James Monroe planned to visit Charleston in the spring of 1819. It was part of his Southern tour to inspect coastal defenses. As you can imagine, it sent local officials scrambling, from the governor to the sheriffs. The economy had slowed for South Carolina, and the President's visit could bring a lot of federal money. We wanted a naval base in Charleston. However, we were in competition with other port cities such as Savannah and Norfolk. Coastlines had to be surveyed, and the city prepared.

"During this time, highwaymen were taking their toll on trade and travel. Many of the citizens didn't feel safe, and rightly so. The wagon trade, for its part, had been diverted to younger and smaller towns to sell their wares. The merchants of Charleston were starving.

"In February of 1819, the citizenry had had enough, and a lynch mob set out for Five Mile House, then operated by William Hayward. Apparently, a gang of these highwaymen prowled the area of Ashley Ferry, and the mob sought to root them out. What's interesting about this is that they set out to drive away a group they couldn't identify.

"When they arrived at Five Mile, they ordered everyone to leave. The people there, including Mister Hayward, protested and began to resist. The lynch mob burned it down — all of it. The House was completely destroyed.

"The lynch mob then moved on to Six Mile House. They gave the same order to leave. Probably aware of the events at Five Mile, John and Lavinia ushered everyone out, abandoning their home. Once everyone vacated the site, the mob left behind a single man to watch over the House. His name was David Ross.

"The mob returned to Charleston, a success in their minds.

"John and Lavinia came back to find David Ross had taken possession of their house. As you can expect, they attacked him, and he ran off into the woods.

"Two hours after Ross fled, John Peeples shows up at Six Mile House. He is beset upon by nine or ten armed persons and robbed. He escapes to Charleston and informs the sheriff. In his statement, Mister Peeples says that he didn't know the names of the people who beat and robbed him, but he believed that among them were John Fisher and his wife Lavinia Fisher, William Hayward, Joseph Roberts, William Andrews, Seth Young, James McElroy, John Smith, and James Sterrett — the Six Mile Housemen as they were called.

"These were the two crimes that condemn John and Lavinia Fisher: assault on David Ross and highway robbery of John Peeples. I've read the news articles written during that time, and there's no mention of mass graves, witchcraft or anything else that has permeated our more popular retellings of this tale.

"The High Sheriff of Charleston District set out with a party of gentlemen and surrounded Six Mile House. John and Lavinia and the other members of the supposed Six Mile gang surrendered without a fight. They were loaded into a paddy wagon and taken to the City Jail on Magazine Street.

"The sheriff's group set fire to the House, razing it, and all the outbuildings around it, like they did at Five Mile House."

"Didn't the indictment say John and Lavinia were to be tried for assault?" Brie asked.

"Yes, but this is where things get murky," replied Professor Mike. "They were tried and convicted of assault. However, on January 18, 1820, the City Gazette reported that they had been convicted of highway robbery at the last

Court of Sessions and were to be hanged. As far as I can tell, they were never formally charged with crimes against John Peeples. And remember, John Peeples didn't know the people who beat and robbed him. I'm guessing that there was a lineup, but who knows what really happened? What I do know is the sheriff arrested six people on February 20, 1819, and only three were officially charged with crimes and hung: William Hayward and John and Lavinia Fisher — the operators of Five- and Six Mile Houses. With the proprietor of Marshlands plantation, John Ball, already dead, the sheriff had effectively seized the land needed for the navy base.

"I'm not given to wild conspiracy theories, but this blew my mind when I first read what had happened. It also makes you wonder why the state engineer, Major John Wilson, was on that jury. Was it pure coincidence?"

Roger and Brie looked at each other and back down at the eyewitness account by John Blake White.

"The execution was originally scheduled for February 4, 1820, but a petition from John and Lavinia, several clergy members, and a number of citizens asked for more time. Governor Geddes granted the respite, and their execution was delayed until February 18 — one year after their arrest.

"Public opinion at that time leaned toward the Fishers being innocent. They wanted them exonerated. There was even a communication on January 31, 1820, signed by Joseph Roberts confessing to the highway robbery. All this was ignored."

"No wonder Lavinia's pissed," Brie said.

Roger gave her a sharp look before turning back to Professor Mike. "What happened to William Hayward?"

"He was hung on August 11. That same year."

"And the other members of the Six Mile gang were set free?" asked Roger.

"More or less. As far as I can tell, they all had criminal records. Joseph Roberts had had his ear cropped. James Sterrett was branded for larceny. None of them faced the gallows. The sheriff was focused on the three tavern keepers. There was even a proclamation by the governor offering a five-hundred-dollar reward for John Fisher when he and Joseph Roberts escaped the jail. The authorities found them the day after they escaped, hiding under an overturned boat, and they were rearrested."

"He didn't want to leave Lavinia," Brie said in a hushed voice.

"It's possible," Professor Mike said. "He and Roberts had plenty of time to get away."

"You mentioned they interred the Fishers' bodies at someplace called Potter's Field," said Roger. "Do you know where it is?"

Professor Mike replied, "I don't. There's speculation that construction workers found it last year when they dug the foundations for the new Basic Science Building at the medical college.

"I heard a lunch-time story from the engineer in charge describing how skeletons popped out of the ground when they started excavating. They stopped construction, and during the delay it rained, of course, and bodies floated to the surface. He told me the ones he saw were well preserved — not surprising, given the highly tannic water table there. Some of the coffin lids still bore a red dot, signifying those who had died of a contagious disease."

"I read about that," Brie said. "The news said they found over a hundred corpses." A dawning horror crept over Brie's face. "That's where they buried John and Lavinia? They could have been the ones who popped out of the ground."

"*Maybe*," Professor Mike stressed. "These cemeteries were filled to capacity with human bodies. If the superintendent adhered to the city ordinance of 1801, the one under the medical college may have held as many as ten thousand people."

"That's crazy!" Brie blurted.

"That's Charleston," Professor Mike replied.

Roger frowned. Finding Lavinia's grave had been part of his plan. With her remains, he could have called Lavinia Fisher to him. But now, knowing that her body might have been disturbed and reinterred someplace else, he felt as if he had hit a brick wall.

"Based on his description of the executioner, I'm not surprised John Blake White was against capital punishment," Brie said with a shiver.

The professor smiled at her and nodded. "White was controversial for his time. Not only did he speak out against capital punishment, but he also allied himself with opponents of nullification." Seeing their confusion, he explained, "Nullification is when a state refuses to enforce a federal law it believes is unconstitutional. One of the seeds of the Civil War, it pitted state's rights against federal sovereignty. The debate went all the way to Washington and included proponents like Vice-President John C. Calhoun, Senator Robert Hayne, who wrote the Fisher's indictment, and even our governor at the time, John Geddes. Although, I suspect our governor was more focused on his personal honor. His son, John Geddes, Jr., acquired the Charleston City *Gazette*, which tried to stifle the voices of people like John Blake White. Despite Geddes' efforts, he still managed to write dramas that addressed American issues like anti-dueling and sanctioned murder."

Professor Mike stood up. "I'm afraid that's all the time I have today. Leave everything on the table. Ms. Bailey will see that the documents are returned to their proper place." He shook their hands.

At the door, he asked, "Mister Vaughn, what's the police's interest in this matter?"

"I'm afraid we can't answer that, Professor Mike," Brie said before Roger could speak. "It's part of an active investigation."

CHAPTER 10
THE MAN IN THE GREEN SUIT
Thursday, April 3, 1969

*L*eaving Towell Library and heading toward the parking lot, Roger asked, "Why did you say that about it being a police investigation?"

"Something I saw on the boob tube," Brie replied. "Police never answer questions that may compromise an investigation."

Roger thought about that for a moment. "You did right, Miss Tyler. The last thing we want is for Professor Mike to think we're ghost hunters."

"Ghost Hunters," Brie repeated with a mischievous smile. "Can we call ourselves that?"

"No."

"How about the Wraith Wranglers?"

"No."

"Or—"

"Brie!" a female voice shouted.

Roger turned and spotted Brie's identical twin sister, Cam, coming towards them.

Even though they looked similar, the two were very different. Where Brie was carefree and colorful, Cam was trim and neat in a pair of no-nonsense grey slacks and beige blouse. She wore her golden-brown hair wrapped in a coordinating grey chiffon scarf, making her look older than Brie.

After the two hugged, Cam gave Roger a firm handshake. There was a hint of disapproval in her eyes, and Roger wondered how much Nate, her fiancé, had told her about their case.

"Looking to enroll?" Cam asked.

"No," Roger replied. "We had a meeting with Professor Hollingsworth."

"Police business?"

"Yes," Brie answered. "It's amazing how much history is here. You never know when you might step on someone's grave."

Cam made a disgusted face and said, "You're awful."

"It's true. We were just talking about those coffins they unearthed near Bee Street."

Back stiff, Cam said to Roger, "Has Brie mentioned you're invited to supper?"

Roger replied, "No. But we have been a bit preoccupied."

"We're observing Good Friday tomorrow. After the service, Nate and his family are having supper with us. Mom told Brie she could invite you," Cam explained. "Brie, you were going to invite him, weren't you?"

A touch of red blossomed on Brie's cheeks. "Of course," she snapped.

"It's not a date," the two sisters said, suddenly facing Roger.

Cam added, "Liturgy of the Word will be at three, so plan to arrive at two-thirty. Mister Vaughn, can you make it?"

"I'd be honored," Roger answered. "If Nate's going to be there, could you ask him to pick me up?"

"I forgot. You don't drive, do you?"

Brie glared at her sister. "Cam, I got this," she said. "You don't have to schedule our day for us."

"I just thought, since we're together and all, it may be a good idea to talk it through."

"No, you're being controlling again," Brie said. "I was going to invite Mister Vaughn once we returned to the office. And I'll make sure he has a ride."

"That's all well and good, but I know how you are. It'll be lunchtime tomorrow before you get around to asking him. Some people like to have a little advance warning."

Feeling uncomfortable, Roger edged toward the Metropolitan. The thing was, Cam was right. They both would have gotten distracted. However, Cam being right didn't make them arguing about him any easier.

"I'm sorry, Brie," Cam said. "Nate's told me about this case you're working. It's not what he said, but what he didn't say that makes me nervous."

Brie relaxed and hugged her sister tight. "It's alright."

"I don't want you to get hurt," Cam whispered. "Last time, you had us all worried you weren't coming back. I think it's why mom's been so clingy."

"I can take care of myself," Brie said, "and I have the bravest men in Charleston protecting me."

Cam let Brie go. She turned and gave Roger a hard stare. "Promise you'll take care of my sister, Mister Vaughn."

Momentarily startled by the power and authority Cam exuded, Roger placed a clenched fist over his heart and held her gaze. "You have my word as a gentleman, Miss Tyler. I'll do everything in my power to keep Brie safe."

Inside the car, Brie leaned over and plucked a tissue from the glovebox. Wiping her eyes, she said, "I don't know why Cam gets so worked up."

"She's worried about you. Probably worried about Nate, too."

Brie started the car and headed toward the office. Roger noticed she drove slowly, and when the light turned green at an intersection, she was still pressing the brake.

"Still thinking about Cam?" he asked.

"Maybe a little," Brie replied, shifting the car into gear. "It's a lot to take in."

"You mean our meeting with the archivist?"

"Yes. It's awful what happened to the Fishers."

Roger's brow clouded in thought as he looked out the window. The buildings went by, but he didn't see them.

"You were hoping to find out where she was buried," Brie said.

"Yes. There's a ritual I know that will summon a ghost if you have the body — or skeleton in this case. I wanted Vie or Tee to try it, but now I guess we'll have to do it the hard way."

"What's the hard way?"

"Find out what Lavinia wants."

"Like talk to her?"

"I wish it were that easy."

"Talk to me then. What aren't *you* saying?" Brie asked.

"After reading the eyewitness report and John's letter, then listening to Professor Mike, I'm getting mixed signals. Mister Fisher is devoted to his wife. I think that part holds true, but what about Lavinia? Was she as devoted to him? What does she want? Revenge, or something more complex? And if it is revenge, revenge on who? All the people who put her in gaol are dead."

Brie's lips pressed together, and Roger could almost see the wheels turning inside her head.

"Till death do us part," she said.

"What?" asked Roger.

"I know you told me they had a common law marriage, but I was imagining if they had been married in a church and exchanged wedding vows. They inhabited the same prison cell, they were hung as husband and wife, and they were buried as husband and wife. No children, no growing old together. And to learn they may have been falsely accused... it makes my blood boil."

Brie turned down Church Street and into their parking lot.

At the foot of the stairs, a man with long silver hair watched as they pulled up. He wore a plaid forest-green suit that looked as if it had been buried under a pile of books and recently reclaimed.

"That's Scott from the antique store," Brie exclaimed.

Roger opened the car door, keeping his hand near the hilt of a knife. He scanned the lot for others, but it appeared the collector had come alone.

"Scott, I'm surprised to see you away from your store. What brings you to my part of town?" Roger asked, slowly walking toward him.

"Afternoon, Ms. Tyler, Mr. Vaughn. Can we talk inside?" Scott asked.

"Sure," Roger answered, noticing that Scott had shed his hippie accent.

Taking off his belt and trilby, Roger set them on their low shelf before moving behind his desk.

"Have a seat," Roger said, motioning to the visitor's chair.

Scott glanced about the room, looking everywhere but at Roger. His eyes stopped and focused on the wooden placard.

With a flash of green fabric, he leapt toward Roger and thrust forth the patina-stained hide. "This piece, this tiny scrap holds a meaning I cannot divine, and it drives me mad. You did this to me!" he roared.

Knocking back his chair, Roger pressed the tip of his knife against Scott's throat. "Back. Off."

Scott swallowed, casting his eyes down at the silver blade. "Come, shepherd, let us make an honorable retreat," he said, and stepped away.

"You took the time to put on a suit, comb your hair, and

walk to Roger's office," Brie said from behind Scott. "You didn't come here to hurt anyone. So why are you here?"

Scott faced her and said, "I bear a charmed life, milady. One in which I have, on multiple occasions, contemplated falling on my own sword, but you give me purpose once again. Tell me the origin of this leathered skin."

Sheathing his weapon, Roger let out a long sigh. He righted his chair and sat back down. "It's from Gaia, a mirror world of Terra. A world where magic prevails — not technology."

Taking a seat, Scott asked, "Are you from this Gaia, too?"

"Yes," Roger answered.

"But not Miss Tyler?"

"No, I'm a native Charlestonian," Brie said as she leaned her hip against Roger's desk.

"Then where am I from?" Scott asked. "Am I from this Gaia as well?"

"What's your first memory of this place?" asked Brie. "Do you remember how you got here?"

Scott stared at his hands in his lap. "I remember the day the Cusabo found me naked, lying on the sandy shores of Morris Island — before the time of the Spanish conquistadors. A derelict washed up from the sea, they nursed me to health and allowed me to live among them. We hunted, we loved, and we fought to protect the tribe. I learned from them what it means to be a man.

"But time continued its relentless march, and those who rescued me became old while I remained just as they had found me. It spooked the medicine man, who began to speak out against me, saying I brought bad luck to their people, and they cast me out.

"I found solace amongst the inland tribes, and when the aggressive Westo moved to the banks of the Savannah and began raiding the local villages, the Cusabo accepted me back. That was 1670 — the same year the English established Charles Towne. You see me here, you gods, a poor old man. As full of grief as age, wretched in both."

Pushing away from the desk with a frown, Brie asked, "How old are you?"

"I am as you see me, milady. I suffer the ravages of time like a lonely mountain, eroding one piece at a time until nothing is left but a pile of rubble."

Brie laid a hand on his trembling shoulder and gave him a sorrowful smile.

Roger retrieved his whalebone spectacles from their pouch and studied the man in front of him. Even without inhaling the mushroom powder to amplify their magic, he could see that Scott cast off a shimmering aura that revealed none of the intricacies hidden beneath the surface. It did, however, reveal two things: the magic was Gaian, and it had the markings of a powerful transformation spell.

Laying his spectacles on the desk, Roger said, "You're the victim of an incantation."

"Can you get rid of it?"

"No. It takes a mage to get rid of a mage's spell."

Red crept up Scott's neck, and he struck Roger's desk with a fist. "Mages!"

Keeping a firm grip on his shoulder, Brie said, "What did the Cusabo call you?"

Noticeably calming, Scott replied, "Eto-v'lkē Es-hóyvtes. It roughly translates to *one taken from the forest*."

"But you were found at the beach," said Brie.

"Their medicine man gave me that name. Told the village he saw it in a vision. I always took it to mean that he was calling me a fish out of water. Or something like that."

"Have you lived here the whole time?" Brie asked.

Something in her voice made Roger begin to worry. The question had more weight than casual curiosity.

"Yes," Scott answered. "I watched Charleston grow from a simple toehold in a strange land to become the city it is today."

"You're familiar with its history?"

"Yes," Scott said with a nod.

"Brie, where are you going with this?" Roger asked.

Facing Roger, Brie said, "We can use his help. He knows things — he's been there, literally."

Roger was about to shake his head when Nate called out, "You'll never believe what we discovered."

Nate and Tee stopped when they spotted Scott.

"Sorry, I didn't realize you had company," said Nate.

Scott licked his lips and rose from the chair. "That's okay. I gotta split anyways."

"Stay," Brie said, giving Roger a pointed look.

Feeling outmaneuvered, Roger inhaled through his nose

and exhaled slowly. Brie had already made up her mind about Scott. Would she feel the same way if she knew what he was — what he really was?

An old saying came to mind, *"Keep your friends close but your enemies closer."* He wondered if that adage applied to this case. Making up his mind, Roger said, "Scott, you're welcome to stay. However, after you hear what we discuss, you may decide to go your own way. If you do, no hard feelings."

"If you're going after a mage, I want in."

"I don't know that there is an actual mage," explained Roger, "but the recent death at Marion Square certainly bears the hallmarks of necromancy. The victim, Mr. Hart, shares his name with a long-dead man tied to the conviction and execution of Lavinia Fisher. The same day he was killed, I was hired to find Mrs. Fisher, whose ghost appears to be at large in the city. I have a feeling that, to solve my case, we'll have to also solve the mystery behind Mr. Hart's death."

"You're searching for Lavinia Fisher?" asked Scott.

"Yes, we are."

"I can help," Scott replied. "Let me be part of your hunt."

CHAPTER 11
FLOWERS IN APRIL
Thursday, April 3, 1969

Clearly unsettled by Roger inviting a stranger into their investigation, Nate said, "May I remind you that this *is* police business."

Roger held up his hand. "It's alright. Scott, here, may have insight into this case that could prove beneficial."

"What is he, some sort of history buff?" Nate asked.

"Something like that," Brie answered with a sparkle in her eyes.

Nate studied the newcomer before stepping forward and extending his hand. "Nate Stone, CPD."

Scott rose and shook hands. "Scott Silva, antiques dealer."

Tee loomed over Scott and said, "Tecumseh Middleton, but eb'rybody calls me Tee." The large man gripped Scott's hand, and a strange, almost fearful, expression came over his face. "Oonuh have yo'own shop at the cawnuh of King and Queen Streets?" asked Tee, his Gullah accent becoming thick.

Nodding, Scott replied, "Been there a long time."

Tee backed away, giving Roger a worried look.

"What's the matter?" Brie asked.

"Doctuh Wampus say tek'care if I ebbuh got reason to wisit him'own store. Dat he dainjus."

"This won't be a problem, will it?" Roger asked.

"No," answered Scott.

"Not fuh me," Tee answered, "long as de man hyuh be helping us."

"Good," Roger replied.

The two men slowly moved to opposite sides of the room, more focused on each other than the investigation.

Raising his voice to get their attention, Roger said, "Now that everyone is acquainted, tell me what you discovered."

Nate handed him the official autopsy report and said, "Turns out William Hart died of a heart attack, despite the gut wound. Something about the mix of drugs in his system slowed his metabolic rate so he wouldn't bleed out, but the PCP kept him moving. The coroner said he suffered from a rare mycobacterial infection."

"A rare what?" Roger asked.

"The doctors think it's a type of leprosy," Nate replied. "All his symptoms were internal, which is why they didn't diagnose it at first."

"Leprosy, are you sure?" Brie asked. "I thought that died out with the Middle Ages."

"Naw, it's still hyuh. Jis' treatable," Tee replied. "De man bin tekin' steroids en' antibiotics, but'um not enough. De coroner say he born wid'um. De nerve damage was so bad yuh could'uh cut him head clean off, and he'd not feel a t'ing over de burn he feelin' inside. Like when yo arm fall asleep. Lavinia done put de root on'um."

"Hell is empty," muttered Scott, "and all the devils are here."

Roger cleared his throat and asked, "Who has access to the drugs they found in his system?"

"We asked that question," Nate answered and began reading from a pocket notebook. "The coroner told us the steroids and antibiotics were prescribed by one Joseph Glover, M.D., a professor at the medical college.

"As for the other drugs, they're mostly local. Oleander is a plant native to the east coast as far north as Virginia Beach, so you could get that pretty much anywhere. Scopolamine is used to treat seasickness. It's part of the nightshade family and also freely available. PCP, or angel dust, was used in the 50s as a general anesthetic. They discontinued its use a few years ago because of the side effects. Now, it's a popular recreational drug. It's not legal, but you can still get it."

"Do you know anyone who sells PCP?" asked Roger.

"I'll akx Vice. Dey'll know someone," Tee replied.

"What about this Doctor Glover? Could the medical college still have some stashed away?" Brie asked.

"It's possible," said Nate, "but once it became known how dangerous it was, I'm sure they destroyed most of their supply."

"It's a place to start," Roger said. "What about the Harts? Why were they getting treated here instead of in Charlotte?"

"Miss Lauren Hart say dem went tuh odduh doctuhs, got

dey opinions. Best dey could offuh were palliative relief," Tee answered. "When we talked wid de coroner, he say dem never seen nuttin' like'um. Leprosy's supposed tuh be treatable, but it wut'n' in Mistuh Hart's case."

Tee got a sad look on his face and said, "Now, Hart's son has it. Dat's why dey hyuh. Dey come tuh consult wid Doctuh Glover and start treatments. Dey hoping newer drugs could beat it dis time. So, Hart akx'd fo' de days off, got approval, and de t'ree arrived Sunday ebenin'. Dey saw de doctuh Monday mawnin' and spent de rest of de time tryin' tuh relax."

"Relax?" Brie asked.

Nate flipped through his notes and said, "After meeting with the doctor, they ate lunch and visited Magnolia Gardens out on Highway 61. Mrs. Hart said her husband began to feel sick during their tour of the gardens, so they cut the sightseeing short. They returned to the hotel. Mister Hart told his wife he was going to the lobby and see if he could find some cold medicine. He never came back. That was between six and seven Monday night. We met with Ms. Mindy Kaiser, the attendant in the lobby. She told us that she'd sent him to a nearby drug store. Tee and I checked. No one at the drug store remembered seeing Mister Hart."

Roger read the last line of the autopsy report and had to read it again. *Mr. Hart's clothes smelled of petrichor.*

Rising from his chair, he walked to the window. A niggling thought came to him as he recalled the discussion with John Fisher. "I don't like coincidences."

"Roger, what is it?" Brie asked.

"When I talked with John Fisher, he mentioned we had a mutual acquaintance: a *blumkinde* named Junopsis. Junopsis told him where to find me. That means they met in a place John knew, and I'd bet anything *blumkindes* gravitate toward the fanciest gardens they can find — like a pig to slop. How fancy is Magnolia Gardens?"

"It's pretty fancy," replied Brie. "Do you think Junopsis saw both John Fisher and Mr. Hart there?"

"I want to find out."

"What do you want us to do?" Nate asked.

"Talk with Doctor Glover," Roger said. "Find out if he treats anyone else, and if he's related to the Joseph Glover of John and Lavinia's time."

"What about me?" asked Scott.

"I saw a lot of old newspapers at your place. How far back do they go?"

"As far as you want."

Roger turned away from the window and faced him. "I want you to find out as much as you can about Lavinia Fisher and where they buried her body."

"If I remember correctly, the Potter's Field near what's now Bee Street was in use at the time," said Scott. "However, to find a specific body there now would be akin to discovering the proverbial needle in a haystack.

"The hanging was a spectacle, to be sure, but the papers cared little for the burial of commoners and criminals. In the Potter's Field, graves were marked with temporary crosses, if they were marked at all. We also have to consider the activity of resurrectionists — vile knaves who robbed graves of their occupants and sold the corpses."

Roger hadn't thought about that. It seemed stealing bodies wasn't exclusive to Gaia. He fought against the doubt. "Search anyway," he said finally. "Pull together anything you can find on John and Lavinia Fisher, particularly regarding their graves."

Scott rubbed his chin. "That'll take some digging."

"Mister Silva, do you have a library card?" Brie asked.

"No, why?"

"I've seen your store. Those piles of newspapers are staggering. It'd be easier to search the card catalog."

Scott gave her a panicked look.

"That's the case," Roger said. "Take it or leave it."

"Cowards die many times before their deaths; the valiant never taste of death but once," Scott answered. "Farewell. To my task will I."

Roger settled into the Metropolitan. He wore his utility belt over his linen blazer and carried his four knives with him, but he had decided to leave the two longer daggers in the office.

Brie drove west on Broad Street and followed Lockwood. As they crossed the Ashley River Bridge, the sun crept toward the horizon. Roger figured they'd have an hour or so to search the plantation before it closed at dark.

"Can you hurry it up?" Roger asked. He rolled down his

window, and let the wind distract him from the fumy smell coming from the engine.

"I told you it's a thirty-minute drive. Sit back and enjoy the ride."

Forehead creased with concentration, Roger opened his map and compared it to what he saw outside. They followed Highway 61 west through Saint Andrews where the neighborhoods were new, and garish signs attracted your eyes to retail centers. Adjusting the folds of the map, Roger traced their route with his finger as it paralleled the Ashley River. A bolt of panic hit him when he came to the edge of the paper. He flipped it over, turning it this way and that.

"You okay?" Brie asked.

He gave Brie a nervous laugh and said, "Here, there be monsters."

She threw a quizzical look his way, focusing briefly on the map. "Relax. It's a straight shot from here. I won't get lost."

Folding the paper until it was a thin rectangle, Roger slid it back in the glovebox and tried to do as she said. He let the purr of the engine and rush of wind lull him into a sense of peace and closed his eyes.

All at once, he felt as if he were falling, the noose tightening about his neck. He jerked upright with a gasp and looked around. The Metropolitan continued its course with Brie at the steering wheel. He wiped a hand down his face, trying to dislodge the vision.

Giving up on relaxing, Roger said, "Your sister mentioned tomorrow is Good Friday. What's that?"

"Do you celebrate Lent and Easter where you're from?" Brie asked. Seeing his blank look, she continued, "It's our way of commemorating the forty days Christ spent fasting in the desert. It ends this Sunday on Easter or as some call it, the Day of Resurrection."

Straightening in his seat, Roger realized just how close the traditions of their worlds were. "The period of bright sadness. Yes, we celebrate something similar on Gaia. We call it Pascha."

"Tomorrow, we celebrate the Passion of the Lord."

"I see," Roger said. "We normally fast that day."

"We do too, except we're allowed one meal with no meat. Daddy and Mr. Stone plan to fry fish this year. On Sunday, we always attend Sunrise Mass at Blessed Sacrament."

Roger thought about the implications. In the strictest sense, he wasn't religious, despite having attended church, listened to the priest's sermons, celebrated holidays, and worked with several people who shined under the Eternal Father's divine blessing. During the war with the Dark One and his Sha'iry, Roger had always travelled in shadow. He had come to face the fact that he was a spy and a thief — occupations officially frowned upon by the church.

It seemed certain truths were common to all the realms. With that thought came the solace of knowing. He knew the Eternal Father was real. He had witnessed miracles. For Terra to adhere to the same traditions based solely on faith gave him hope.

Outside his window, the landscape west of the Ashley River turned rural. Ancient trees bordered the narrow lane with overlapping boughs forming a bearded canopy. Underneath, the air carried a chill, and deep shadows streaked the pavement.

"What did you see when you looked at Scott?" Brie asked. When Roger didn't answer, she said, "Back at the office before Nate and Tee arrived, you saw something. What was it?"

His eyes focused on the road ahead, Roger answered, "Transformation magic."

"Transformation. You mean a magic spell changed him?"

"Yes, and the magic was Gaian." Roger thought back to the bit of scaly hide. "Yesterday, Scott chose a scrap of leathery hide over a ruby. That was dragon scale."

"Dragon? As in Saint George and the Dragon type dragon?"

"This may come as a shock to you, Miss Tyler, but we have dragons where I come from. It's rare, but you come across a piece of scale or tooth or claw from time to time. We have other monsters as well — creatures that terrorize towns, searching for food or just plain mischief." He shifted in his seat, watching the play of expressions on Brie's face as he spoke.

"His longevity, his hoarding — Scott is definitely more than he appears. Did he stumble through a magical portal, did he come here by choice, or was he banished? If someone banished him, then why? There are too many questions and not enough answers.

"To muddle things further, the magic used upon him altered more than his physical form. It changed him mentally, making him forget his past. It broke his mind. I suspect that all that clutter at his shop is his attempt to replace what he lost, but it's not enough. It'll never be enough." Roger laid a hand on Brie's shoulder and said, "Be careful around him. If I'm right, there's no telling what he might do. He's insane."

Stress lines formed at the edge of her mouth, and Roger could tell she was working her way through what he had just told her.

Finally, Brie said, "At old man Calhoun's statue, you saw what I did. Do you think I could cast magic powerful enough to make someone forget who they were?" She shook her head. "No, I would never do that."

"Where I'm from," Roger said, "there are creatures that prey on the weak. Some feed on them; others demand tribute. If a town hired a mage to ward off such a creature, a transformation spell would have done the trick. Banished to a new place, it would have been like starting over."

"You're assuming Scott was one of these creatures," said Brie.

"True. Because of the spell used on him, I couldn't see his true form; I could only get a sense of it. The real question you should ask yourself is: is evil passed down from father to son, or is it learned?"

"What?"

"The creatures that prey on the weak are typically evil creatures, or at least perceived that way by most of the civilized world. What if this curse or spell, call it what you will, gave Scott a chance to start over?"

"But you said it yourself, it's made him mad."

Roger shrugged. "He knows right from wrong, and he's been living among Terrans for a long time. Yes, I think he's mad, but thankfully his madness has made him civilized. Imagine what would happen if he started to remember."

"You come from a scary world, Mister Vaughn."

"Compared to your world, I guess I do," he replied.

"So, all your talk about a necromancer — that was real?"

"Yes. Necromancers come in many varieties. Who knows, maybe Terra has a few I haven't heard about. Like these root doctors."

Eyes fixed on the road, she asked, "How do you know so much about magic? Did someone teach you?"

"I was a student at the Academia de Artes Magicae in Tydway," answered Roger with a laugh. "At least until I was expelled."

"Expelled?"

"Long story." He was beginning to feel Brie had taken a wrong turn or they had already passed the plantation when he saw the entrance for Drayton Hall. Just beyond it, a road sign indicated the next plantation was just ahead. He pointed at the sign.

"No, you're going to answer me, even if I have to stop the car," she said.

Roger chuffed and opened his mouth to make a joke, but the determined set of Brie's jaw made him realize she wasn't joking. With a resigned sigh, he decided to give her the bare basics of what happened. "It started as a harmless bet. A few of my classmates didn't think I could create fire. Using acid and iron filings, I captured inflammable air in sheep intestines and hid them along the edge of the main hallway leading to the dining hall. It was one of the few places in the school with bare stone walls. No one was around, and it seemed harmless enough.

"Anyways, it all went as planned. I invited my classmates to see my new spell. With a little sleight of hand, I ignited the fuse while waving my arms, recited a few words I happened across in the library, and poof. Fire engulfed the hallway. Unfortunately, it was larger than expected." Roger remembered feeling the heat as he leapt to avoid the fireball. "Who knew the headmaster was going to enter the hall at that exact moment? Furious, he grabbed me by the ear, and we marched to his office. You see, I already had a reputation for pulling pranks, and the headmaster had finally had enough, especially since he lost his eyebrows."

"What happened?" she asked, a smile on her face.

"He informed my parents what I had done and expelled me," Roger answered.

"Oh, no."

"It worked out for the best. The Highlord heard about my exploits and recruited me into his cadre of spies. I was never suited for academia, anyways." He didn't tell her that his parents had almost disowned him. To this day, they still thought he was a no-good lay-about.

Flanked by brick piers and white fences, the entrance to the plantation's gardens came up quicker than expected. Brie downshifted and the engine growled. With a slight shimmy, the Metropolitan slowed, and Brie turned down a dirt driveway dappled with afternoon sunlight.

It was hard to imagine anything historic being out this way, let alone a plantation. There seemed to be nothing but trees. Just as the thought crossed his mind, the trees along the right side gave way to a cypress swamp. An alligator, sunning on a partially submerged log, eyed them as they passed.

Ahead, verdant grass and ancient oaks marked the edge of the swamp, and beyond, Roger caught glimpses of sunlit lawns.

Brie drove through an open gate and pulled up beside a clapboard booth. A distinguished gentleman wearing a pith helmet leaned out the small window.

"Two tickets to the gardens please," Brie said, holding up cash.

Taking the money, he handed Brie a paper map with arrows marking the different trails and numbered circles denoting places of interest.

"We close in an hour," the man informed them. "The gates will be shut, but don't worry, we'll have someone standing by to open them when you leave."

"Thank you," Brie said.

"What's in bloom?" Roger asked, studying the map.

"Snapdragons, dogwoods, several varieties of azaleas, some of our roses, foxgloves, pansies, wisteria, and there's more. Those are the ones I remember right off the top of my head." The man pointed to their map and said, "The path starts to the right of the main house. It'll take you straight to the gardens. Follow the numbers in order, and you should have time to see everything if you don't dawdle."

Roger gave the man an appreciative nod.

Ahead of them, the road forked, and a sign directed them to the left. Live Oaks lined both sides of the road like gnarled sentries. Behind the trees to the right, split-rail fencing bordered a sunny horse pasture. A peacock screamed in the distance.

Brie rounded a curve as it led in front of a gabled, two-story house with a wide veranda supported by white columns.   A square turret rose from the roof with a weathervane mounted at its peak.   On the lawn opposite, several couples lounged on blankets while children ran about, trying to entice sheep and miniature horses to the split-rail fence.

Beyond a walled petting zoo was the tree-shrouded, half-empty parking lot. Brie picked a space closest to the house and driveway. Several spaces down, two elderly couples stood outside their cars, planning where to eat for dinner. In the row behind them, an olive-colored coupe with a long hood and a fastback roofline backed into a parking spot. Cigarette smoke curled out the open window.

"How many times have you been here?" Roger asked, stretching his legs and eyeing the activity.

"When Cam and I were young, our parents brought us every spring." Brie closed her car door and looked over the top of the cabin at him. "We're here, Mister Vaughn. Now what?"

"How big is this place?" Roger asked, feeling a little overwhelmed.

"How would I know?" Brie responded, giving him a weird look.   "I'd guess it's hundreds of acres, especially if you include the swamp and rice fields, but the gardens are only a part of it. They probably take up twenty-five acres or so."

"Twenty-five acres? Where are they?"

"This way," Brie answered.

He and Brie walked past the petting zoo and aimed toward a gravel path that cut through a hedgerow. It was marked number one on their map. A small, corresponding wooden sign with an arrow pointing along the trail directed them to the next point of interest. Shaded by magnolia trees, azalea blossoms dotted the garden floor. Flowering plants of all shapes and colors became a tunnel as they proceeded from one number to the next. Along the way, they pointed out the different plants to each other, relishing the quiet of the garden. Occasional encounters with others intent on enjoying every available minute in the gardens reminded them they weren't alone.

Afternoon shadows deepened, and the temperature

cooled. The meandering path followed the Ashley River, with numerous side paths leading back toward the main house. Brie smiled and nodded to a man in red corduroy bell-bottoms and a dark plaid shirt as he passed them a fifth time. Roger fought the urge to glare, reminding himself that there were limited paths in the garden, and they had encountered several people multiple times.

Moss laden oak trees leaned out from the bank. Brie stepped off the trail and found a seat in the crook of a low hanging tree branch. "I could stay here forever," she said, dangling her feet over the black water.

"I doubt it. You don't like the cold."

She made a face at him and said, "That's not what I meant."

Standing beside her, Roger focused his gaze on the flowing river. "It's nice, even peaceful." As he said it, he knew he could never settle here. Like the current, he felt the constant need to keep moving — to always think two steps ahead. That was the only way to stay alive.

"Why don't you sit?" Brie asked, patting the thick bough.

"No, we need to find Junopsis."

Brie let out a loud sigh and pushed away from the tree. "We're between numbers six and seven, and there's twenty-five of those circles. Are you certain he's here?"

"No. Just a hunch."

"Well, lead on, Macduff," Brie said, gesturing with her arm.

From the tone of her voice, she seemed mad, and Roger couldn't understand her sudden mood change. Glancing at the map, he got his bearings and strode toward the next intersection. The crunch of gravel let him know Brie was behind him.

The map led them away from the river, back toward the plantation house. Roger took in another deep breath of untainted air. It smelled like the earth after a rainstorm. He stopped and sniffed again.

"What are you doing?" Brie asked. Hands on her hips, she scanned the path for anyone who might be watching.

He held up a finger and turned in a circle, letting his nose be the guide. "Petrichor."

"Petri- what? It's a garden. Of course, they have..." She drew closer and whispered, "What am I looking for?"

He handed her the map as he aimed in what he thought was the correct direction. It was an older path, not marked and clearly meant for the staff. Stone steps, worn smooth, wound their way toward a small lake. Vibrant colored flowers abounded on either side. Well maintained, the azaleas here showed no sign of fading blossoms.

Walking single file, the two crept through the leafy garden. Roger sniffed again. With all the flowers, it was almost impossible to follow the petrichor undercurrent. He tried to pierce the gloom, even as the sun dropped lower. A flash of blue-violet amongst the red and pink blooms caught his eye.

Whipping out one of his knives, Roger crashed through the azaleas, causing an explosion of petals. He reached out with his left hand, grabbing the slender humanoid plant by the back of its fibrous, green neck, and shoved it face-first against the bole of a magnolia tree.

"Afternoon, Mister Vaughn," the creature said in a conversational tone.

"Afternoon, Junopsis."

The *blumkinde's* normally vibrant blue-violet tones became a muted yellow, and a heady scent, eliciting memories of a forest glade after a summer rain, filled the air.

"Stop that," Roger ordered.

"I can't. It happens when I get excited or upset."

Relaxing his grip, Roger let Junopsis turn around even as he kept the tip of his silver blade close to its throat.

Two moist, solid black eyes peered out between thick layers of iris petals. Beneath them, a thin line marked its mouth.

"What can I do for you?" Junopsis asked.

"Tell me you're not working for the Dark One again."

"I'm not. I swear," replied Junopsis. He gestured to either side with viny arms. "I work here now, tending the flowers."

Junopsis pointed to his green ankle. There was a discoloration where the Dark One's shackle had been removed. "I remember all too well what it was like being a sclábhaí. Do you think I'd be foolish enough to jeopardize this? I love it here."

"Then why did you send John Fisher and Joseph Roberts to me?"

"I didn't want to get involved, but Mister Fisher needed help, and I thought of you."

Roger couldn't read the *blumkinde's* eyes, but he noticed the iris petals were slowly regaining their color. "Why should I believe you?"

"It's the truth."

A slight gasp distracted them both.

"That's Junopsis?" Brie asked. "He was one of the sclábhaí who attacked us at the marina?"

"No, milady," Junopsis answered. "I was saved by Mister Vaughn and his friends."

Guilt swept through Roger as he thought back to that day in the abandoned building. If it had been up to him, Junopsis would be dead. He could have chalked it up to following orders, but in his heart, he knew he had already decided Junopsis' fate before the Highlord even spoke. It was Cerdic alone who saved him.

Releasing the *blumkinde,* Roger stepped back and sheathed his weapon.

CHAPTER 12
SINS OF THE FATHER
Thursday, April 3, 1969

*F*ollowing a game trail hidden amongst the trees and shrubbery, Junopsis led Roger and Brie back toward the river. He crouched low, stopping whenever someone passed along one of the nearby paths.

In a tiny glade overshadowed by a copse of young pines and redbuds, he knelt behind a thick bush. Beyond it, flagstone pavers wrapped around an elaborate brick and marble tomb. Built on a high bluff, the ancient memorial overlooked the Ashley River.

"I was tending the plants at the base of the tomb when Mister Fisher and his companion found me. I nearly went into shock." Junopsis placed a hand on his chest, reliving the experience. "You see, we are a quiet species and get caught up in our work. I was afraid the gardeners had found me, but when I realized the two men were ghosts, I became curious."

"What were they doing here?" asked Roger.

"Waiting for Mister Fisher's wife," Junopsis replied. "When she never showed up, the two men broke out into an argument. Mister Fisher accused his companion, the one with the cropped ear, of betraying him. However, the other man assured Mister Fisher he had done as requested. He had told Sally that the reverend would have their trunk. She knew what to do. She knew it had to stay hidden. That's when Mister Fisher asked if I knew someone who could help find his wife. I heard you had an office downtown, so I sent them your way."

"Did they do anything else while they were here?" Roger asked.

"No, but they were worried. Somehow they knew John Fisher's trunk was missing."

Through a gap in the thick bush, Roger studied the marble cherubs on the side of the tomb. A large crack marred its surface. The man in red bell-bottoms wandered up from the riverside path. Roger watched the newcomer read the various inscriptions before moving farther down the trail.

"What about Mister Hart?" Brie whispered.

"Who?"

Roger jerked his attention back to the *blumkinde.* "On Monday, you met Mister Hart here in the gardens," he murmured.

The scent of petrichor wafted through the air, and Junopsis became still.

"Do you want to keep working here?" Roger asked. He kept his voice low, but the implied threat was unmistakable.

Junopsis' vibrant colors faded, and he took a frightened step away from Roger.

"Tell me."

"Yes, he was here. I watched him from behind that magnolia," Junopsis answered, gesturing toward the other side of the tomb. "He, too, was interested in the trunk. I had it in my head he was looking for a way inside the vault, but the burial chamber is subterranean. What you see on the surface is decoration. Something had him scared. He kept looking over his shoulder and muttering to himself."

"Did you hear what he said?"

"He mentioned his son — Bill, I think his name was — and that he must find the cure. Something he thought was inside." Junopsis pointed to the plaque at the base of the tomb. "He went crazy when he read that it had been opened in 1916, and the family discovered the great earthquake of 1886 had collapsed the ceiling, completely destroying everything inside except the lead coffin of the original owner. There's even a photo showing the tomb in ruins."

The petals surrounding Junopsis' face turned beet red. "He thrashed about like a wild animal and began digging with his bare hands, ripping my plants out of the dirt. My plants! I didn't know what else to do. I wrestled him to the ground and kept him from doing any more harm. When he saw me, saw what I was, he froze. It was horrible. His eyes went wide, and he began crying uncontrollably. I could smell his desperation. People were coming, so I let him go."

"Were you worried he'd rat you out?" Brie asked.

"No," Junopsis said in a sad voice. "He rambled on about his family, saying he shouldn't have to pay for the sins of his father. The look he gave me before he ran off, it was like one condemned to death. I moved deeper into the garden before anyone could spot me and didn't see what became of him."

"You didn't follow him out?" asked Roger.

"No. Why would I want to?"

Footsteps crunched on the gravel, and Roger caught sight of a pith helmet amongst the branches.

"We have to go."

"Time already?" Brie asked.

Roger answered with a curt nod.

"Your flowers are very pretty," Brie whispered to Junopsis, laying a hand on his arm. "The prettiest around."

Junopsis' blue-violet coloring turned vibrant, and the earthy scent of rain filled the air.

"Junopsis," Roger said, "stay humble."

"I will, Mister Vaughn."

"What was that last part about?" Brie asked, as the two exited the garden and aimed toward the Metropolitan.

"From what Junopsis told us, his people made a bargain with the Dark One. I don't know the particulars, but when we first found him, Junopsis was shackled to 'vanity' — his sin. I presume that's what made him a sclábhaí."

"That's terrible," Brie replied. "Are they all like that?"

"I expect so."

Roger closed his door, and Brie cranked the car. Shifting it into gear, she backed out of the space. Absent of other vehicles, the parking lot had an abandoned feel. She drove back down the driveway toward Highway 61. They were the last visitors to leave, and the person manning the plantation gate locked up after them.

A half-hour before sunset, the tree-lined road ahead was already dark. Brie pulled a knob, turning on the headlamps.

"Is it the trunk from John's letter?" Brie asked.

"It has to be," Roger answered. "John Fisher mentioned a key, a trunk, and instructions detailing how it was to be disposed of.

"I don't know anything about the family who owns that plantation, but given the time frame, I suspect they knew the good reverend. I'm thinking the trunk was meant to be buried and forgotten."

"But why there?" asked Brie. "Why didn't Reverend Furman bury it at his church?"

"No idea. Maybe he didn't want to be associated with it."

"Okay, here's another one. If John Fisher's trunk was meant to be hidden away, how did Mister Hart know about it?"

"Good question," replied Roger. "The logical answer is that someone told him."

Light reflected off the rearview mirror onto Brie's face. It grew brighter, filling the interior.

Roger threw a hand over the back of the seat and looked over his shoulder. Tears filled his eyes as he tried to see past the glare. Blinking them away, he said, "Speed up."

"What is it?"

"Just do it."

With a look of determination, Brie shifted the lever on the steering wheel and stomped the gas pedal. The Metropolitan responded with a growl as it shot forward, lurched when Brie shifted gear, and then shot forward again.

The intense light separated into two dots, and Roger realized it was another car. The two dots grew brighter as it gained ground.

"Can this vehicle go any faster?"

Brie threw him a panicked look when the Metropolitan's engine began to make a whining noise.

Not being able to look directly at the car behind them made it impossible to tell how close it was — that was, until it struck their rear bumper.

"Bloody hell," Roger griped as he stiff armed the dashboard, bracing himself.

The car behind them struck again.

Sliding off the pavement, the Metropolitan bounced and jostled. With a tight grip on the steering wheel, Brie righted the car and forced it back on the road. She swerved into the lefthand lane with a squeal of tires and smell of burnt rubber.

A deep thrum came up beside them, and Roger saw the other car closing. It was a two-door model with a powerful engine, but no heraldic emblem. He recognized the olive-painted coupe from the plantation and, at the helm, the man he noticed in the gardens.

"Hold on!" he yelled.

Sparks flew when the car slammed into their side. It veered away, preparing for another sideswipe.

Roger reached to his belt and slipped loose one of the

terracotta grenades. He cracked the bulbed end against the dashboard and slung it through the other car's half-open window.   It exploded, and a thick, reddish-orange haze enveloped the cabin. The car jerked and skidded off the road, slamming nose first against an ancient oak.

"Stop the car!" Roger said.

"Are you crazy?"

"Do it!"

Brie stomped the brake, turning the wheel in the process.

Before the Metropolitan came to a complete stop, Roger threw open his door and charged down the road, a knife in each hand.

Steam poured from under the car's crumpled hood, and he heard a faint crackling sound. Before his eyes, rust ate at the helm, enlarging the rough hole made by the grenade's contents.

Using the crook of his elbow to cover his mouth, he pulled a glossy stone from one of his pouches and said, "iljós." Light streamed out, and he shined it about the cabin.

The unconscious helmsman lay draped over the warped navigation wheel.   Blood from a wound on his forehead bubbled and hissed, burning its way down his face. Grimacing, Roger backed away and made a mental note to avoid ever working with rust powder while bearing an open wound.

The car's corroded floor panel gave an ominous groan.

"Oh my God! What did you do to him?" Brie asked.

"No worse than what he was trying to do to us."

"He's... he's melted," Brie said, moving toward the car with a horrified expression on her face. It was as if she couldn't stop herself.

"He's not melted, just covered in rust powder. Don't get too close. I've never seen it react so... vigorously with blood."

"You have to do something! He could be dying."

"Calm down. The powder is self-neutralizing. It will have run its course in another minute."

"But you *just* said you've never seen that kind of reaction. You don't know what will happen." Brie turned toward her car. "I have a jug of water in the trunk. We can at least rinse him off."

Roger stood aside and let Brie pour water on the man's

face and hands, revealing angry red streaks and tiny blisters. "Interesting," he said. "It cauterized the wounds."

"I saw him on the garden paths," said Brie. "Why did he attack us?"

Roger shrugged. "I've never seen him before today. He was very interested in that tomb where John Fisher's trunk was supposed to be hidden, though."

Brie nervously glanced up and down the deserted road. "Maybe we should get out of here," she suggested.

Going around to the car's other side, Roger opened the door and looked inside the glovebox. The registration card read "J.S. Packer."

"Damn," Roger swore.

"What is it?"

"Packer. That's one of the names from our juror list."

Trembling, Brie hugged herself and walked about as if in a daze. She stopped when she saw her car. "Father's going to kill me."

"I wouldn't worry about him," Roger said, as he joined her and realized she was in no shape to drive.

"What do you mean?"

"We'll talk with the constables first. Explain what happened. I'm sure they'll understand it was self-defense."

"We're going to jail," she said in a rush.

"Not us," Roger said with a grim smile.

Brie faced him with fear and worry deep in her eyes.

"He's the one who has a lot of explaining to do." As Roger spoke, the navigator's body fell forward when the steering wheel gave way.

"I'm going to be sick."

Wrapping an arm around her shoulders and holding her tight, Roger felt her shake despite his efforts to calm her. She jerked away from him and ran to the side of the road where she fell to her knees. Roger knelt beside her and held her hair while she vomited. When she finished, he helped her stand and handed her a kerchief.

"You used up all your water, but you can chew on these to get the taste out," Roger said, giving her a handful of colorful jellybeans. He took his time as he guided her back to the Metropolitan. Battered and bruised, the tough car hummed with life.

"Brie, I didn't mean to put you in danger," Roger said. "I

really thought seeing Junopsis would be a safe trip... and give you a glimpse into my world." The last part came out in a low whisper.

Gazing into his eyes, Brie squeezed his hand, and Roger could tell she was trying to put up a brave front.

"It's not your fault. I volunteered to be your girl Friday, remember?"

CHAPTER 13
SHERIFF CLEARY

Thursday, April 3, 1969

*H*eadlights lit the two-lane road as an older model sedan headed away from town. The shoebox on wheels slowed, and a man leaned out the window. "Y'all, awright?" In the backseat, two kids pressed their faces to the glass. The man swatted at them. "Get back!"

"We are, but he needs a doctor," Roger answered, gesturing toward the man in the rusted car. Standing beside the Metropolitan, he kept a hand near one of his knives.

Barely giving Roger and Brie a parting glance, the driver said, "We live nearby. I'll call the police and get you some help."

"We're in your debt," Roger called out as the car sped off. He watched the red brake lights get farther and farther away. "Will he call like he said he would?"

Sitting in the front seat of her car and munching on jellybeans, Brie answered, "You can count on it."

Two patrol cars arrived fifteen minutes later, their blue emergency lights casting odd shadows on the trees. The first car eased past Roger and Brie and parked sideways to block the road.

The second patrol car stopped in front of the Metropolitan. From the helm, a spotlight flared to life, and Roger raised his hand to shield his eyes. He spotted the silhouette of a constable exiting the copilot's side and heading his way.

Another spotlight lit the road behind Roger. He cast a quick glance over his shoulder as a second constable switched on a flashlight and peered inside the rusted vehicle.

"Sheriff Cleary, you're not going to believe this!" the officer said.

"Mason, keep your mind on what you're doing. I want the five W's: who, what, where, how, and why," the sheriff responded.

Roger suppressed a snicker. He wondered if the sheriff

was aware that he only had four 'W's' — unless you counted the one at the end of how.

"Yes, sir," Mason responded.

"Is the driver alive?"

"Yes, sir. But I'm not sure we can move him. I've never seen anything like it."

"Gault, where's that ambulance?"

"They're five minutes out, sheriff," replied the pilot of the patrol car facing the Metropolitan.

Sheriff Cleary stepped where Roger could see him. He was a bull-necked man built like a chiseled piece of granite. Clean-shaven, the rugged facial features and pronounced cleft in his chin seemed part of his starched uniform.

Tipping his hat toward Brie, Cleary asked Roger, "Mind telling me what happened?"

Brie stood and replied, "That man tried to run us off the road."

"Start at the beginning, ma'am. Who was driving?"

Brie took a calming breath before she replied, "I was. Bryony Tyler, sir, but my friends call me Brie." She flashed him a quick smile. "We had just left touring Magnolia Gardens. Here's our tickets and my driver's license." She handed the sheriff the stubs and a laminated card. "I saw the other car pull up behind me in my rearview mirror. He struck our bumper and ran us off the road. When I tried to get away, he rammed us in the side."

"Where were you, Mister...?" Cleary asked Roger.

"Vaughn. Roger Vaughn. I was in the passenger seat, urging her to go faster," Roger answered.

"It's true," Brie added. "My Metropolitan isn't built for speed, but she's a good car." She laid an affectionate hand on the hood.

"Do you have any identification, Mister Vaughn?"

"No, sir."

Cleary frowned as he eyed the pouches on Roger's belt. He seemed to be considering their story. In the distance, a third constable lined the asphalt lane with bright flares while Gault spoke into his two-way radio before taking a position next to the Metropolitan. Whether it was to direct nonexistent traffic or stop them from running, Roger wasn't sure.

"Sheriff!" Mason called out. "You should see this. It

looks like a bomb went off."

"Don't go anywhere," Cleary ordered.

A bad feeling blossomed in Roger's gut as he watched Sheriff Cleary lean inside the rusted coupe and inspect the corroded edges of the metal.

Drawing closer, Brie whispered, "Is that safe?"

"Should be," Roger replied.

Mason opened the glovebox and handed the car's registration to the sheriff.

"Sonuvabitch," Cleary swore, clenching the paper in his fist. With a nod toward Roger and Brie, Cleary and Mason returned with their hands on the butts of their pistols.

"Mister Vaughn, you stated you were in the passenger seat," Cleary said. It came across as an accusation.

"Yes, sir."

"Then tell me what happened to that car. You did something to it."

"Yes, sir. I threw rust dust at it," Roger replied, hoping honesty was still the best policy. At least, it always worked for his paladin friend, Cerdic.

"Rust dust?"

"Yes, Sheriff."

"What does rust dust do?" Cleary asked.

Roger gestured toward the car. "It eats iron."

"Do you think we're stupid?" Mason demanded. "Rust doesn't do that to people." He pointed at Roger's belt. "What all are you carrying in that fancy utility belt?"

The sheriff bent his head as if to ask another question, then punched Roger in the gut, knocking the wind out of him. "Explain the chemical burns on Mister Packer."

"You know him," Roger gasped. He thought back to the list of juror names in the trial of the Fishers. Cleary was not one of them.

"I don't see how that's relevant, Mister Vaughn. You admit to using a destructive device — this rust dust. Sounds like a chemical bomb to me."

"He was trying to kill us," Roger argued.

"I've heard enough. Mister Vaughn, you're under arrest. Confiscate his belt and search him. If he gives you any lip, add resisting arrest to the list of charges."

"But..." Roger started.

Gripping his shoulders, Gault slammed Roger against

the Metropolitan. "Arms out, legs apart!"

Brie looked at Roger for direction, uncertainty writ across her face. He gave a quick shake of his head even as Gault snatched away his belt and went through his clothes. Having a sense of déjà vu, Roger subtly shifted to make the search easier.

"Mason, grab me an evidence bag," Gault said, pulling out one knife after another.

"Got it," Mason said as he opened the trunk of the patrol car. He returned with a nylon sack and began filling it with Roger's possessions.

Moving to Brie, Cleary said, "Your turn, Miss Tyler."

"She hasn't done anything!" Roger yelled.

Gault punched him in the kidney. "Quiet," he hissed.

Roger forced himself to watch the sheriff slide his hands over Brie's dress. "Spread your legs wider." Cleary kicked her ankle. "Wider." Her face red, she bit her lip when he touched the inside of her thigh.

Spinning, Roger struck Gault's head with his elbow and took a step toward the sheriff, his other hand poised to strike.

"Roger, no!" Brie said. "Don't make this any worse."

Cleary gave him a sly smile. "Smart girl. She just saved your life, boy."

His eye already swelling, Gault seized Roger's arms and cuffed him so that the shackles pinched his skin. It was petty, but Roger was thankful the constable didn't do anything more. In the distance, a siren wailed.

"Ambulance's here," Mason stated, cinching the evidence bag.

"About time," Cleary said as he finished searching Brie. Not finding anything, he took Roger by the upper arm and pushed him toward the patrol car. "Gault and I are taking Mister Vaughn to the CDC. Have Miss Tyler wait in the other car until the third unit arrives."

"Come on," Mason said to Brie, reaching out.

She jerked away even as she followed him. "Don't touch me. I've had enough of that for one day."

Cleary leaned in close to Roger and said, "Behave yourself, boy. You try anything at all, and I promise you, Miss Tyler will be the one who suffers for it. Got that?"

Roger looked over his shoulder, making brief eye contact with Brie. His heart lurched when he saw tears streaming down her face. He wanted to tell her not to worry, that everything would be alright. Instead, he replied to Cleary through gritted teeth. "Yes, sir."

CHAPTER 14
DETENTION

Thursday, April 3, 1969

*G*azing out the window, Roger worried the entire way back into town. His worry turned into anxiety when they crossed the Ashley River and turned north. *Here, there really were monsters.*

They arrived at the dull grey county detention center. The main entrance protruded from the center of its face like a boil. Taking a side road, Gault drove around back and entered a sally port.

"Process him and take him to interrogation," Cleary said, once he stepped out of the patrol car. "I'll meet you there."

"Will do," Gault replied. Opening the rear car door, he motioned, and Roger butt-walked off the seat.

"Come on, this way."

Gault gripped Roger's upper arm like a vice and led him through the vestibule. Inside the intake area, a middle-aged woman with short blonde hair waited behind a desk, smoking a cigarette. A metal chair with mustard colored padding waited for him.

"Pam, got a special case."

Adjusting the document in the typewriter at her side, she asked, "Name?"

"Roger Vaughn, second son of the Earl of Wolverton."

"Address?"

"Church Street, Charleston, South Carolina."

"Charge?"

"Being surrounded by idiots," Roger said.

Gault smacked the back of his head and said, "Book him for striking an officer, resisting arrest, possession of explosives, and attempted murder."

"I beg your pardon," Roger said. "If I had wanted to kill him, I would have."

After smacking him again, Gault said, "Fine. Pam, put down assault and battery of a high and aggravated nature."

"You sound European, Mister Vaughn. Are you originally from Charleston?" Pam asked. The lit cigarette bobbed as she spoke.

"Actually, I'm from Gallowen. My family's estate is Blaiðwyn Hall, near Tydway."

"Are you a prince or something?"

Roger gave her his best smile. "Several generations removed on my mother's side, but being the son of an earl grants me more privileges."

Pam seemed confused as she stared at her typewriter.

"What is it?" Gault asked.

"He may have immunity," she answered.

"He may have what?"

"Sovereign immunity. It's like diplomatic immunity, but it encompasses royalty. We'd need to send his records to the Feds."

"That's not going to happen," Gault said. "Trust me, the sheriff wants to keep this one."

Frowning, Pam pulled the document from the typewriter and handed it to the deputy. "Be careful, Andy. If Cleary gets caught, he'll drag you down with him."

"The Sheriff knows what he's doing."

"I sure hope so, for your sake."

Gault gave the hallway a thoughtful look before saying, "Call over to CPD and S.L.E.D. Find out if the Duke of Earl, here, has any outstanding warrants."

Lifting Roger by the armpit, Gault pushed him into a room, where he was measured, weighed, fingerprinted, and photographed. Once finished, they moved back out into the hallway and entered a dressing room. A turkey-turd-tan shirt and matching pants lay on a chair. Across the front and back were the bold black letters, CCDC.

Removing the handcuffs, Gault ordered, "Put those on."

After rubbing his wrists to get the blood circulating again, Roger took off his linen blazer and handed it to Gault, who dropped it into another evidence bag.

Roger handled the prisoner uniform, feeling the texture. It was scratchy, and its chemical smell churned his stomach.

"Hurry up."

Standing there naked, Roger knew the experience was supposed to be degrading. His thoughts went to Brie, and he sent out a prayer for her to be safe. He hoped the sheriff would keep his dealings with her civil. If not... The thought sent a spike of fury through him.

He forced himself to relax and took his time putting on the shirt and pants. They were a little baggy, but otherwise serviceable.

"Quit modeling, princess, and come on," Gault said with a smirk and replaced the handcuffs. This time, Roger's hands were secured in front.

Their next stop was a square room with a metal table affixed at its center. Two chairs had been pushed in underneath. A mirror stretched the length of one wall. Unlike the room downtown where he met with Lieutenant Bell, this one held a fine bouquet of piss and vomit under the thick layer of disinfectant.

Gault shoved Roger inside and slammed the door behind him, locking it.

The buzz from harsh overhead lights set Roger's teeth on edge. He walked around the table, studying the room. When he came to the mirror, he sensed he wasn't alone. It lacked the finesse of a scrying spell, but he was certain somebody was on the other side.

Trying to not let his concern for Brie show, Roger took a seat and propped his elbows on the tabletop. Thoughts of Leo in his cage came to mind. He stood, needing to work off the excess energy, and paced the room. He hated waiting.

Roger was sitting at the table when Sheriff Cleary burst through the door. Thick of neck and broad chested, he looked like a minotaur. He just lacked the horns. Roger fought back a smile as he pictured the flush-faced sheriff with a ring through his nose.

"What's so funny, Mister Vaughn?" Cleary asked.

"Nothing, sheriff," Roger replied.

"You seem awfully calm for a man in your position. We have you dead to rights. The only thing in your favor is Mister Packer will live."

"I told you," Roger said.

"Boy, you need to smarten up." Cleary jabbed a finger in Roger's direction. "I could have you working the county farm tomorrow."

"I'm tired, and it's late," said Roger. "What do you want?"

"What were you and Miss Tyler doing at Magnolia Gardens?"

"Taking in the flowers."

"Kind of late, wasn't it? According to your ticket, you arrived an hour before they closed."

"It was spur of the moment," Roger replied with a shrug.

"Was it?" Cleary asked, taking the seat opposite Roger. "Did you see Mister Packer while at the gardens? Did you two argue?"

"He was there, and no, we did not argue. I've never seen him before today."

"Or were you two racing, and your girlfriend lost control?"

"That's not what happened. He struck us."

"Why?" Cleary demanded, slamming the table with his fist.

"I don't know."

Cleary sat back and said, "Your utility belt is a piece of work. Is it some new anarchist kit from Europe? There was even a pouch for your glasses. Our expert went through your jars and vials, including the one stank of cat piss. He's never seen anything like it. What was in that chemical bomb, anyway?"

Roger stared the sheriff in the eyes. "Plant food, along with some diatomaceous earth and blood meal."

"Do you think I'm a damn fool?" Cleary said, his eyes darting to the mirror. Sweat beaded on his brow. "The stuff that hit Packer and his car was not plant food. Did you know the steel frame ripped apart when we tried to tow it? We had to call for a rollback with a forklift to reopen the road."

"What can I say? Some plant food is corrosive."

Cleary rubbed a hand down his face. "You confessed to using a chemical bomb against Mister Packer, injuring him and destroying personal property. I know who, what, where, and how, but I don't know why."

"Do you really know how?" Roger asked, leaning forward.

The question stumped Cleary.

"I mean, if you have an expert who doesn't know what's in my rust dust, who's to say it isn't plant food?"

"Drugs, then. Whatever."

"Is it drugs, or is it explosives? I'm not an expert, but I distinctly heard Gault say you were charging me with carrying explosives."

"I'll change the charge if I want, Mister Vaughn!"

"Is that what happened to the Fishers?" Roger asked.

"What the hell are you talking about?" Cleary scowled, and again, his eyes darted to the mirror.

"You know Mister Packer, that's clear. But did you know Mister Hart?" The question wasn't a giant leap in logic. Considering recent events, it seemed likely he was dealing with a group of conspirators. Roger's next question, though, was a blind stab. "Was Packer a leper like Mister Hart? Like Mister Hart's son?"

Cleary jumped up, knocking over his chair and the table. He grabbed the front of Roger's shirt and threw him against the wall. "Who are you?"

"Roger Vaughn. I thought we had discussed that."

"No, you idiot!" Cleary pressed his forearm to Roger's throat. The edges of Roger's vision blackened as he struggled to breathe.

The door opened, and Gault pulled Cleary away from Roger. "Sheriff, you'll kill him."

"What the fuck do I care! I'll dump his ass in the swamp and let the alligators have at him."

"You can't," Gault said. "Remember that hard ass, Lieutenant Bell, from downtown?"

"Yeah, what of it?"

"He knows we arrested Vaughn. He's requested we release him into CPD custody."

Roger straightened his shirt and ran his fingers through his hair to hide his shaking. Sore from bruising, he cleared his throat and said, "I was hired to find Lavinia Fisher."

"What?" Cleary asked, distancing himself from Roger. "That's not possible."

"Who's he talking about?" Gault asked.

"No one," Cleary said.

Roger studied the mirror and asked Gault, "Who's behind the glass?"

Cleary gave his deputy a sharp look.

Gault swallowed. He started to answer, but then must have changed his mind. Instead, he said, "You can't hold them. We have no evidence."

"What are you talking about? He struck you. The pouches, the rust on the car, the confession..."

"Paul from the bomb squad went through every pouch, every terracotta cannister. He found acid, yes, and some crude black powder and iron filings, but the majority of what's there — the dust and liquids — he just didn't recognize. The contents of several containers evaporated when we opened them. He thinks it's voodoo shit from New Orleans."

Cleary looked from Gault to Roger, his confusion plain. "What about the black powder and iron? That's a bomb isn't it, complete with shrapnel?"

"Paul said it wasn't strong enough to blow your nose. And the stuff he does recognize is just stuff," Gault continued. "Vaughn had a pair of antique glasses, some candy, a pouch full of glossy rocks, a small stash of uncut gems, and some cash. Face it, it might be weird, but none of it is illegal or been reported stolen. We booked him on a felony charge. We can confiscate his weapons and his belt with its pouches, but that's it."

"What about the rust dust?"

"Whatever it was must have stopped working. The lab guys took samples from the car, put it on some scrap metal, and nothing happened. Try explaining that to the judge."

"You sayin' I should let him go?"

"The girl's already gone. Her father picked her up a few minutes ago."

Cleary had the look of a cornered animal. "You went behind my back and authorized her release?"

"Yes," Gault answered, talking quickly. "And there's an officer in the lobby waiting for Vaughn. Bell sent him. Face it, this is getting way out of hand. Let CPD deal with him. We'll press charges for assaulting an officer, so he's not going anywhere, but everything else, I guarantee a defense attorney would have a field day with it. There is no motive, no drugs, and no evidence to suggest this guy is a bomb maker."

Despite the deputy saying it, Roger knew he and Brie never would have made it to a trial. The sheriff wanted them buried. He eyed the deputy, trying to figure out his angle.

"This isn't over, Vaughn," Cleary said with a loud snort.

Roger could have left it alone. A voice inside his head even told him to keep quiet and let Gault escort him out the front door — unharmed.

"Cleary," Roger said with a grim smile on his lips. "You know Lavinia's out there. You heard what she did to Hart. She'll go after Packer next, and when she's done with him, she'll come after you. You're a dead man."

With a roar, Cleary charged into Roger, murder flashing in his eyes.

"Sheriff!" Gault said. He grabbed Cleary from behind in a makeshift bear hug. Another deputy rushed in from the corridor, snatched Roger by the arm, and pulled him out of the interrogation room.

Roger let the deputy lead him out. He leaned far over, trying to get a view of the adjacent room. The door was open, but he only caught a glimpse of the person inside — tall, blond hair, horn-rimmed glasses, and a dark, tailored suit that gave him a devilish air.

"Sheriff, stop! He's trying to get under your skin." Straining, Gault faced Roger. "And you, keep your trap shut!"

"I've got him," said the deputy holding Roger. "What do you want me to do with him?"

Gault replied, "I want him out of this building."

It was early Friday morning by the time Roger met Nate Stone in the front lobby. Standing there at the door with his hands deep in his pockets, the young officer didn't speak. He simply wore a frown. It was enough to let Roger know his situation with the Tyler family was tenuous at best.

Roger put on his linen jacket, now wrinkled, and followed Nate to his tan four-door sedan waiting in the parking lot. He half expected to see Brie, but the car was empty.

"Care to talk about it?" Nate asked as they pulled out onto the street.

"Not really," Roger said, rubbing his throat.

He shifted in his seat, missing the comfortable weight of his belt and knives. It left him feeling hollow, and he realized how much those pieces of home meant to him. A cold dread seeped into his gut as he thought of Scott and his antique store. *Was he destined to the same fate if he remained stranded on Terra long enough?*

Nate turned right onto Azalea Drive. Fog from the Ashley River blanketed the empty street.

"They have Brie's car," Nate said. "I expect Mister Tyler and I will be back to pick it up from the impound when they're finished with it."

"How's Brie?"

"Pretty shaken up. That Cleary... I swear."

"He's scared," Roger said. "He knew Mister Packer, the owner of the car that ran into us, and by the way he acted, he knew Mister Hart, too — I'm sure of it."

"Doesn't matter much now. We're off the case."

Roger jerked in his seat. "What!"

"When Lieutenant Bell heard what happened, he called me and Tee. We've been reassigned to a beat car."

"Two days and we're already being told to piss in a wicker basket. That has to be a record."

Nate slapped the steering wheel. "I get it. You're from another world; you have different ways; but a chemical bomb? It's a wonder they let you go."

"I didn't kill Mister Packer," Roger said defensively.

"*Humph.* That's what Lieutenant Bell said. I think he was actually proud of you," Nate replied. "But don't you see, you endangered Brie."

Nate turned right onto the North Bridge, and Roger gazed out the window as they crossed the Ashely River. A break in the fog revealed black waters that were as smooth as glass... or a mirror.

"You have to understand, I don't want Brie hurt," said Roger. "If I could, I'd lock her away in a tower, but like you, she's been exposed to my world. The dærganfae and the Executioner, they've marked her. The best way to protect her now is knowledge. Same goes for you. Burying your head in the sand will not make it go away."

"Explain that to her father."

"I know." Roger asked, "Any suggestions?"

Nate laughed. "I gotta know. Are you wanting to take her out on a date or have her still work with you? I have two different answers."

"Date? What do you mean?"

"Dinner and a movie, walks in the park, that sort of thing. My grandma calls it courting."

Roger thought for a moment. "Both, I guess."

"First off, you need to know what you want. Mister Tyler is a direct person, and he expects it from the people he meets," Nate replied.

They merged onto Highway 61, heading toward town.

"If you want to date her, she can't work with you. The Tylers are very traditional when it comes to that sort of thing. But you already knew that."

"If I date her, I won't see her as much," Roger said.

"True. She is spending a great deal of time with you. Mister Tyler knows that. The next few days are going to be interesting. I do know one thing. Brie's spirited enough to leave the house if her father puts his foot down."

Roger frowned. "What would you do, if this were Cam?"

"Ha! I fit the Tylers' mold of an acceptable suitor. I'm Catholic. They know my parents. Heck, I practically grew up at their house. Mister Tyler had me figured out a long time ago. He knows where I've been and where I'm going."

"I don't see me in that picture," Roger said.

"Which is probably why Brie likes you."

Nate followed Lockwood around to Broad Street, back to the land of stately mansions and colonial buildings. When Nate stopped at a red light, Roger asked, "Would it be a mistake if I showed up to dinner at the Tylers'?"

"Now you *are* trying to get me in trouble."

Roger stared out the window again, finding courage on those empty streets. "I don't want to stop seeing her," he said finally.

Nate didn't respond, and Roger wondered if he had heard him. At the next turn, they arrived in front of Roger's office. He let out a deep sigh and opened the car door.

"Thanks for the ride, Nate."

"Sure." Nate leaned over and said, "I plan to see Cam this evening, and I'm sure her parents will have a million questions for me. When your name comes up, I'll put in a good word. You just stay out of trouble."

"No promises," Roger said, shutting the door. He stepped up on the sidewalk and watched the car until it disappeared around a corner.

He inhaled the crisp morning air and trudged upstairs. The day was catching up to him, and he felt like a zombie as he moved through his office to his bedroom. Not bothering to undress, he crashed face first onto his bed and fell asleep.

CHAPTER 15
TIME TO EAT CROW

Friday, April 4, 1969

"*R*oger, wake up!"

Fighting his way back to the conscious world, Roger's first thought was Brie had returned. He opened one bleary eye and tried to focus on the smudged figure in blue at his bedroom door. His vision cleared, and the smudge became an attractive woman with lustrous black hair and startling cobalt-colored eyes. Her short-sleeved dress flowed around generous curves and stopped just below her knees, leaving arms and calves the color of warm honey exposed to the world.

"You really should get a phone," Vie said. Daughter of the late Doctor Wampus, she gave him a warm smile, revealing a perfect set of pearly white teeth that contrasted with the coppery red of her lips.

"Don't want one," Roger mumbled. Rolling over and shifting to a seated position, he held his head in his hands. "What time is it?"

"Eleven. Almost lunchtime." She eyed him critically. "You look like you were ridden hard and put away wet. Try not to sleep on your stomach. It's bad for your health."

Roger looked down at the state of his clothes. *He really was becoming Scott.*

"Not that I'm unhappy to see you, but what are you doing here? My rent's paid for the month."

Vie answered, "Get a shower. We'll talk while you get cleaned up."

"There's been another death, hasn't there?" asked Roger. He stood and removed his jacket.

"Yes."

"Packer?"

"I didn't ask, and Tee didn't say."

Roger swore to himself. Ever since her father died, Vie had turned her back on root work and anything to do with Doctor Wampus' lucrative business. Moving past her, he entered the bathroom, closed the door behind him, and started the shower to let the water warm.

"I like what you've done with the place," Vie said through the door.

"Thanks," replied Roger. "It's home."

"My father's sign on your shelves is a nice touch."

"Seemed the right thing to do, especially since you and he saved my life," said Roger. Letting the spray fall across his back, he closed his eyes and lathered a clear shampoo through his hair. It was the only brand he could find that didn't leave a chemical smell.

"I know this isn't a courtesy call," said Roger. "Why are you here?"

"Lieutenant Bell wants to meet you at one-thirty," she replied. "Be thankful I keep a key to your office. Otherwise, you'd have slept the day away."

"That was my plan," he grumbled.

"What was that?" Vie asked. "I couldn't hear you over the water."

"Nothing," he replied.

Roger quickly scrubbed away the last of the gaol funk, letting it rinse down the drain, and shut off the water. Toweling off the fog on the mirror, he stared at a man who had spent most of his twenty-seven years hiding. Gone were his powders and creams. He took in the shape of his leonine colored eyes and lightly tanned skin.

"You done yet?" Vie asked.

Wrapped in a plush robe, he opened the door and edged past Vie in search of clean clothes.

"Are mulattos stigmatized where you're from, too?" she asked, back pressed to the wall.

"Mulattos? That's the second time I've heard that word," he replied. "What does it mean?"

"Someone whose parents are different races, like me," she replied.

Roger glanced over and caught her studying his features. The scrutiny made him uncomfortable. Few people had seen his true face in recent years.

"Huh," Vie said. "From the looks of it, you're mixed too. You could pass for French Creole."

Roger quirked an eyebrow. "One of my great-grandmothers was an island princess from the Karukera Sea who married a Francescan nobleman. I've always assumed

I favored her."

Closing the bedroom door, he spotted two identical silver reales lying atop his bureau. Each bore the symbol of a cross with diagonally opposing lions and castles in each quadrant. They were one pair of eight twins created by Antonio de Erqueta, the esteemed assayer. Rumor had it there was some kind of bond between the twins. Something that wouldn't allow them to be separated. Queen Ambrose had proven it true.

Through the door, Vie asked, "Does that happen a lot where you're from?"

"Does what happen?" asked Roger as he retrieved a fresh tunic and a pair of breeches. Moving to the top drawer of his dresser, Roger retrieved his remaining two long-bladed daggers with sheathes and strapped them on before dressing.

"Interracial marriages," answered Vie.

"Sure. We have half-elves, half-orcs, even half-dwarves, though I've never seen one."

"That isn't what I meant," she said. "We don't have elves and such here... Well, not usually. If you don't catch hell for your skin color, why do you hide behind make-up?"

"Force of habit from my job. It helps me be forgettable."

"That's not likely," Vie replied with a scoff.

"But to answer your earlier question about being stigmatized, people everywhere are suspicious of anything and anyone different. In my world, it's usually along cultural lines, but it can be racial, too. For example, most humans have an automatic and deep-seated fear of orcs, and most orcs seem to see humans as lunch."

"I can see how that would be a problem."

With his hand on the doorknob, Roger eyed the coins for a moment, then stuck them in his pocket before stepping out of his bedroom.

"Thank you for the reales," he said.

Vie gave him a slight shrug. "I didn't want them."

Grabbing his trilby, he headed toward the front door.

Downstairs, a chauffeur stood beside the rear door of a sleek, black Cadillac. The tailored uniform, stretched across his muscular frame, gave him the appearance of a sophisticated gladiator.

"I'm paying you too much," Roger quipped from the metal stairs.

Vie threw him another warm smile. "Just keep it coming."

"Have you thought about taking up your father's mantle?"

The smile vanished. "I'm done with Hoodoo."

Roger laid a hand on her shoulder, stopping her march to the car. "Hoodoo didn't kill your father. Dærganfae did. Don't forget that."

Vie's face clouded, and her cobalt eyes bore into his. "How could I forget? I'm reminded every night, every time I fall asleep." She drew up her shoulders and said, "If my father hadn't gotten involved with your Ambrose, he'd still be alive."

His lips pressed together, Roger looked away, then turned back to her. "We all lost something that day, but we gained something, too."

"Tell me. What did I gain?"

Roger flashed her one of his best smiles and replied, "A friend."

She opened her mouth as if she were going to say something, then closed it. Instead, she wiped her eyes with the back of her hand. "Some friend you are. Making me come into town just because you don't have a stupid phone," she griped.

"And I appreciate it," Roger replied.

"Ms. Violet," the chauffeur said as he opened the car door. His face remained neutral, though Roger thought he detected a trace of disapproval. Seemed he rubbed everyone the wrong way at first.

"Have you met my driver, Dennis?" Vie asked.

"No, I haven't," Roger answered.

"Dennis, this is Roger Vaughn, a... friend."

"Nice to meet you, sir," Dennis replied. After seating Vie, he motioned toward the other side of the car with his hand and said, "If I may."

The Cadillac had a deep backseat that made Roger feel like he was floating on a cloud. He kept his eyes on Dennis, fascinated by the meticulous way he drove. The smooth stops and starts, the gliding turns. It was vastly different from Brie and her Metropolitan.

"Where are we going?" asked Roger. He resisted the urge to ask for a map.

"Not far."

Dennis looked into the rearview mirror and said, "I think someone's following us."

"Are you sure?" Vie asked.

"Red LTD with a white top. Pulled out at State Street just after we did and followed us onto East Bay. They're staying a few cars back. Might be on purpose."

"Let's be sure. Take a few turns and see if they keep up."

"Yes, Ms. Violet."

The effortless way Dennis steered the Cadillac through traffic was impressive. Roger wanted to look out the rear window. Instead, he followed Vie's example and tried to remain calm. Being chased on horseback was one thing, but having a car trail him was a new experience — one he didn't care for, especially after what happened leaving the gardens.

At the next intersection, Dennis put on his left blinker.

Vie faced Roger. "What kind of trouble have you gotten into?" There was a touch of panic in her voice, and Roger knew she was thinking about what happened to her and her father at the Queen Bee salon.

"It's not dærganfae," Roger assured her.

"I didn't say it was."

Not knowing exactly where to start, Roger said, "Three days ago, John Fisher hired me to find his wife, Lavinia."

Vie bolted upright in her seat. "Do what?"

"I know it sounds crazy, but I swear it's the truth. We must have released them when we freed Brie and Ambrose from the Old City Gaol."

"Keep talking."

"In an effort to figure out where Lavinia's spirit might be, we've spent the past few days trying to learn as much as we can about her and John — what actually happened to them and, in turn, where she's buried. If I can't find her, I'll try a summoning."

Dennis peered into the rearview mirror. "I don't see the LTD anymore," he stated. "Must have been my imagination."

"Well, keep your eyes open anyways." Vie pursed her lips, then asked, "How do a pair of ghosts from the early 1800s tie to Lieutenant Bell?"

"On Tuesday, when we visited with the lieutenant at the station, there was also a horrible death."

Vie's eyes went wide. "The man at Marion Square."

"Yes. His name matched one of the jurors for Lavinia Fisher's trial. The man I asked about earlier, Packer — his name was also on the list, and he attacked Brie and me after following us to Magnolia Gardens. When the county sheriff recognized Packer, his attitude toward me changed. You might think I'm paranoid, but I smell a conspiracy."

"I bet you have Brie, Nate, and Tecumseh all tangled up in this mess."

"They volunteered," Roger offered.

"*Humph*, I'm sure they did."

"Where are we supposed to meet Lieutenant Bell?"

"*You* are supposed to meet him at the pyramid in Magnolia Cemetery," Vie said.

"Why not the shrievalty?"

"Don't ask me. We're just providing the taxi service."

Roger scratched his chin. Lieutenant Bell wasn't one to ask for a casual meeting, especially in a cemetery. He must have learned something that had him spooked. Finally, he asked, "Are you sure that LTD wasn't following us?"

"Dennis?" Vie asked.

"No, Ms. Violet," Dennis replied.

Her brow furrowed, Vie said, "Let's make sure."

"Yes, Ms. Violet."

Roger watched as the chauffeur slid on leather driving gloves, all the time keeping the car on the straight and narrow.

"Hold on!" Dennis said.

When they came to the intersection at Calhoun Street, he stomped the gas and steered the Cadillac east. Horns blared from all sides as everyone slammed on their brakes. Roger grabbed his seat as they swerved and dodged around the cars ahead of them. With a screech of tires, the Cadillac cut across the opposing lane of traffic and shot down a narrow street that entered the deteriorated neighborhood of Wraggborough.

Taking a chance, Roger looked back. There were no cars behind them. The road was clear.

Dennis answered his unspoken question. "I feel confident we jammed the intersection." He slowed the

Cadillac and turned down a side street. "East Bay's coming up," he announced. "What do you want me to do?"

Something didn't feel right. Roger said, "Stop here."

"You gonna be sick, take it outside. I just had the upholstery cleaned," Vie said.

"No, it's not that," Roger replied. "It doesn't make sense. When you follow a person, you don't ride a horse in brightly colored barding."

Pulling into a parallel space behind a contractor's truck, Dennis shifted the gear into park and let the engine idle. Shaded by a blossoming dogwood, they waited within sight of the intersection ahead.

Roger studied the Charleston Single outside his window. A Fogartie Construction sign stood in the front yard, and he glimpsed men moving from one room to another. A two-story apartment house with a wide piazza across the front occupied the opposite side of the street.

"Why would anyone be following you?" Vie asked.

"No idea. Except..." Roger replied.

"Go on."

"Sheriff Cleary was overly belligerent. He threatened to feed me to the alligators."

"But that LTD wasn't the police."

"It could be the sheriff or one of his deputies in their personal car. A poor disguise, in my opinion," Roger replied. He stared out the window, thinking about Sheriff Cleary.

Vie faced him, her expression an odd mix of suspicion and curiosity. "I'm worried about you."

"There's the LTD," Dennis said.

In the distance, Roger caught a flash of red as it crossed.

"What now?" Vie asked.

"Follow it," said Roger, leaning forward in his seat.

Dennis eased out and turned north onto East Bay. They had just passed in front of the Cigar Factory when the LTD slowed and turned left.

"Roger, you still want us to follow it?" Vie asked.

"Forget it," he replied, feeling a little silly. "Let's go see the lieutenant."

They passed under the approaches to the Cooper River bridges. Traffic lightened, and Dennis kept the Cadillac moving at a steady pace. At Brigade Street, they turned right. Powerlines crisscrossed overhead and fed into several buildings that fronted lumber yards. Dennis slowed when he came to a railroad crossing and looked both ways.

"There's another car behind us," Dennis said before they came to the intersection at Huguenin Avenue.

"The LTD?" Vie asked.

"No. A blue Chevelle."

"Damn," Roger swore. "Could they use two-way radios?"

"Maybe," Dennis answered.

Roger looked out the rear window. "Did you see the LTD?"

"No."

"It could be a coincidence," Vie said. "People do live down this road. There's no reason why it isn't heading home."

"Miss Violet, it's a new model with a honky driver."

"Where's the cemetery?" Roger asked.

"A half mile that way," Vie replied, gesturing north.

"Is there any way to get there without being followed or causing a scene?" asked Roger.

Vie looked down at her hands. After taking a deep breath, she raised her head and said, "Dennis, continue down this road. Let's see what they do."

"This is a bad idea, Ms. Violet," Dennis said, his voice gaining an edge of tension.

"Just do it," Vie said, her jaw set.

Dennis pressed the gas pedal. They passed through a scrap metal yard and entered a no-man's land of marsh and thicket. On the other side, a wooden sign welcomed them to Porter Manor. Beyond it, a chain link fence wrapped the property.

Despite all the new construction, there was an uneasy air about the place, like no other Roger had visited in Charleston. Over twenty apartment buildings had been crammed together, forming random patterns. Identical in every way, the whitewashed structures seemed sterile and unforgiving. People hung out in shadowed breezeways and stared at them as they drove past. There were no children, no toys scattered about, and no playgrounds — only adults.

"Who lives here?" Roger asked.

"Families relocated from when they built the interstate and Crosstown," answered Vie. "They're the victims of eminent domain."

Dennis cast a quick glance in the rearview mirror. "The

Chevelle's turning around."

"Good," Vie replied.

Sandwiched between the buildings, mostly empty parking lots branched off to either side. Midways down the end of one, an elderly lady rose from her lawn chair.

When they passed a sign directing visitors to the leasing office, Dennis slowed.

In front of them, a line of men and women had started to form up. They wore hostile glares like war paint, daring them to go any farther. Many of the men carried bludgeons. One held the butt of a handgun that poked out from his waistband. His pants were the same brown as those Roger wore at the County Detention.

The men crowded forward.

Dennis looked over his shoulder. "*Uh-oh.*"

Roger twisted around. The elderly lady hobbled toward them, assisted by two men.

"Stop the car," Vie said. Her hand shook as she gripped the armrest.

Roger asked, "What's happening?"

Vie gave him a wan smile and said, "Time to eat crow."

Dennis opened Vie's door. She stepped out with grace that rivaled the royalty of Gaia.

The elderly woman pushed past the angry crowd. Deep wrinkles etched her face — each one telling a story of struggle. Hunched by the weight of time, she wore an orange, yellow, and green headwrap and a simple dress that covered her feet. Her features stern and unwelcoming, she gazed at Vie with piercing, black eyes.

"Gramma Huger," Vie said with a slight dip of her head.

"Wadduh yuh want, Miss Violet?" the lady asked. Her voice held a vitality that belied her age, and it was easy to believe the old woman could live another hundred years.

"I need your help," Vie said.

The old woman cackled. "Why on eart' would oonuh need Gramma Huger's help? Oonuh got yo'own fancy cyaa', handsome driver, and a big house outside town. Oonuh live de buckruh's dream, eat de buckruhbittle."

"You're wrong Gramma Huger," Vie said, her face flushed. "I live my own life."

"Oonuh tu'n yo back on yo'own life. Now, yuh libbin' in

someone else's skin." Gramma Huger pointed her crooked finger at Vie's chest. "Oonuh like de boo hag."

Fist clenched at her sides, Vie said, "Gramma, you don't understand."

A young woman stepped forward and said, "Vie, it's been two weeks since yuh farruh's de't'. When you didn't come see us, it hurt eb'ry one of us. Gramma Huger's right. You've become one of de buckruh."

Roger eased out of the car to stand beside Vie. He saw the tears brimming and realized what it had cost her to come here.

"I apologize for interrupting, but I'm the reason Vie's here," Roger said.

The crowd shifted and several men reached toward their weapons.

Vie held up her hand. "I didn't come here to fight. I want your permission to let my friend use the back way into the cemetery."

Gramma Huger turned her intense gaze on Roger, looking him up and down. "Wuh's yo name, buckruh?"

"My name is Roger Vaughn."

"Wuh yo bidness wid Miss Violet?" she asked.

The question seemed to imply more than what was spoken, so Roger answered, "Vie and her father saved my life."

"Oonuh know'um Doctuh Wampus?" Gramma Huger asked.

"No," Roger said. "I was unconscious when he was at the hospital."

"Wuffuh would the Doctuh save yo'own life?" she asked, her eyes wide from surprise. "A strange buckruh."

"He made a deal," Vie said. She shuffled her feet, and Roger could tell this was uncomfortable territory.

"He made a deal with Cerdic, didn't he?" Roger asked.

Vie swallowed and nodded her head. There was a haunted expression on her face, and Roger realized that she not only hadn't come to terms with the loss of her father, but she also hadn't come to terms with the Eternal Father healing her third-degree burns.

A mischievous expression crossed Gramma Huger's face, and she said, "If oonuh want my leave, then mek a deal wid me."

"What do you want?" Vie asked.

Gramma Huger took Vie's hand and began walking toward an apartment building.

"Gramma Huger, I don't have time for this," Vie said.

"You'll mek time," Gramma Huger said.

Roger followed as they entered one of the apartments. He remained in the breezeway with the crowd, staring into that dark room. After several long minutes, Vie stormed out. In her hands she held a list. "That woman's impossible."

"What happened?" Roger asked.

"I bought you passage," Vie said, not looking at him. She nodded toward a young man standing beside Dennis. "RC will take you to the fence. The rest is up to you."

"I understand," Roger replied.

"Do you? Do you really?"

"I know you didn't have to do this. We could have found another way."

She turned her head toward Roger as they walked and whispered, "I owe a soul debt to your knight friend and to my father. Now they're gone. I figure the only thing left for me to do is buy it back."

They arrived at the Cadillac and Vie handed the list to Dennis. "Go into town and purchase these items." She removed the gold bangle from her wrist and gave it to him. "I also need my father's bag."

"Yes, ma'am."

Before Vie could walk away, Roger took her by the arm. "Soul debts don't work that way. You can't purchase your way out of them. It's like forgiveness. You must forgive yourself before any healing can start. Look, I wasn't there. I was unconscious with a tube shoved down my throat. However, I know Cerdic, and you owe him no debt. Your debt, if there is any, is with the Eternal Father. He's the one that brought you back. It's him you need to deal with... and he's everywhere. My suggestion: be true to yourself. That's where you'll find the path to filling the hole in your heart."

Vie took in a deep, shuddering breath. "They want me to be their root doctor." In a softer voice, she said, "I can't do it."

"Why not? You have the gift."

"I swore I wouldn't become my father," replied Vie.

"Then don't be Doctor Wampus," Roger replied. "Be

Doctor... Skink."

Vie gave him a fleeting smile. It reflected in her cobalt-blue eyes and broke the sadness on her face. "Remarks like that are a quick way to get hexed."

CHAPTER 16
CHARLESTON PYRAMIDS
Friday, April 4, 1969

*R*C travelled fast, steadily aiming toward the line of trees to the north, and Roger pushed to keep up. "Men'e pace, buckruh," the skinny youth said with a wave of his arm.

They passed row after row of apartments, sometimes cutting through the breezeways. When they came to the fence, Roger noticed the opening cut in the links — one large enough for a person. On the other side, a path led through the dense thicket.

"Oonuh on yo'own frum hyuh," RC said.

Roger gave him a quick nod of thanks. He ducked through the rent fence and moved down the tunnel-like path toward the sunlight marking its exit. At the edge of the thicket, he knelt on one knee. Ahead of him was an expansive garden cemetery with ornate mausoleums, tall obelisks, and statuary. Bearded oaks with sprawling branches shrouded well-trod paths that wound between family plots and meandered along the marsh laden shores of a tidal creek. Beyond the marsh and creek, the grey waters of the Cooper River sparkled.

He'd visited the cemetery once, retracing Queen Ambrose's steps, and had a rough idea where the pyramid was located. He headed in that direction. Keeping the thicket on his right, he followed a gravel path shaded by a cluster of trees. Slowing his pace, he assumed the persona of a tombstone tourist.

Bordered by family plots with worn markers, the gravel path widened as it turned north and paralleled the marsh bank. Behind the gravestones, a blue heron stalked the tall cordgrass. Pretending to watch it, he scanned the area to see if anyone took note of his presence. He was alone, but it didn't stop the niggling suspicion he was walking into a trap.

Keeping close to the marsh, he continued down the broad path. When it turned back west, he decided to keep going straight and entered an oak grove. Maneuvering between the many markers and graves, Roger stepped out onto a meandering dirt road that cut across thick roots. In the distance, he could see the capstone of the grey pyramid north of him.

When he came to the edge of the grove, the dirt road forked. The lefthand route led toward the backside of the pyramid. Even though it was more direct, it afforded little cover. To the right, the road kept to the trees and made a wide circle that bordered the marsh before turning back toward the pyramid.

Caution getting the better of him, Roger took the longer route. It gave him time to wonder why all the secrecy. Cars following him, someone trying to run them off the road, a sheriff who feared the mere mention of Lavinia's name. At least they weren't actively trying to kill him yet, despite the sheriff's threat.

He passed several mausoleums, including one with an open doorway. Leaning closer to get a better view, he noticed the floor slab had been removed and brackish water partially filled the subterranean crypt. Half expecting decomposed bodies, he was surprised to see vacant stone shelves.

Roger returned to the dirt path. There was no one about, and he began to doubt Lieutenant Bell would be waiting for him. He reached the pyramid and climbed the short flight of steps. Shading his eyes with his hand, he made a show of reading the name over the recessed entrance.

Out of the corner of his eye, Roger spotted Lieutenant Bell standing with his back to a tall magnolia. With his receding hairline and dark suit and tie, he almost mistook him for a priest.

The worried expression on Bell's face deepened. "What took you so long?"

"We thought we were followed. Mean anything to you?"

Bell stared off into the distance. "You sure kicked over a hornet's nest."

"Me? I didn't do anything," Roger said. "That thing last night was self-defense."

"I'm not talking about that," Bell replied. "S.L.E.D. has taken over my office. They called me last night. Wanted you shut down and Nate and Tee back on the beat. Said we were wasting our time. Agents from Columbia showed up this morning, and one's been shadowing me all day. Oh, and that request for John and Lavinia's case file — rejected."

"Why?" asked Roger.

"How should I know?"

"How can a case from 1820 cause all this?"

"All I know is you've gotten someone's attention," said Bell. "Someone who can pull some serious strings. And get this: the head agent from Columbia's name is John Wilson. Major John Wilson."

"Figures," Roger said more to himself. "Did J.S. Packer die?"

"How'd you know?"

"Lucky guess."

"Heart attack, just like Hart. He was at the hospital, hooked up to all their monitors. They still couldn't save him." Bell shook his head in a short, sharp motion as if trying to dislodge an unwelcome memory. "Somehow, he managed to carve JER 21:14 into his own chest before the staff could stop him. In case you hadn't guessed, it's another Bible verse. *I will punish you as your deeds deserve, declares the Lord. I will kindle a fire in your forests that will consume everything around you.*"

"Ominous but appropriate, I suppose, if he suffered the same condition as Mr. Hart. Did he have any family?"

"No. At least none that claimed him."

Roger peered past the patina-stained gate into the shadowed confines of the pyramid. A colorful stained-glass window on the opposite wall glowed in the afternoon sunlight. "Sheriff Cleary knew both Packer and Hart."

Lieutenant Bell gave him a sharp look. "Are you sure?"

"Yes. He went mad when I mentioned their names."

"What else do you know?"

"I have guesses but nothing definite."

"Like what?"

"I think each of the men on the juror list for the Fishers' trial was cursed. They've had a root cast on them or something. Hart's autopsy confirmed he had a previously unknown form of leprosy. Despite living in Charlotte, he was being treated by a doctor here at the medical college. The same doctor is going to treat his son. Based on Cleary's reaction, Packer had it, too. I wouldn't be surprised if all fifteen jurors suffered from the same thing and passed it down to their descendants."

Bell wiped a hand down his face. "You really think these people are cursed?"

"Yes. It keeps them tied to Charleston."

"What's Cleary's connection?" Bell asked.

"No idea." Turning away from the pyramid, Roger walked back down the steps. "Lieutenant Bell, I believe John and Lavinia were victims of a grander scheme. Somebody high up the chain of command wanted their land. The Fishers were in the wrong place at the wrong time.

"Lavinia's sister, Sally, was supposed to have received a trunk and hidden it inside the tomb at Magnolia Gardens. Hart was there trying to dig it up before he was run off. However, the tomb's ceiling collapsed years ago, destroying everything inside, at least according to the plaque. What if that trunk held a spell book or something that bound those fifteen jurors to it?"

"If you're right, this chain of events started a hundred and fifty years ago," Bell said as he joined him, "but the two murders this week happened on my watch. Someone killed them; someone who's running loose on the streets." Looking as though he had swallowed something sour, Bell asked, "Do you think Lavinia is our killer?"

Roger's brow furrowed as he thought about Lieutenant Bell's question. "The timing makes sense. She's free of the Gaol, and revenge is a powerful motive."

"What troubles you?" Bell asked.

"This curse, if that's what it is, had to be cast after Lavinia was hung. There's no way John and Lavinia could have gotten to the jurors. Maybe John planned their revenge when he and Joseph escaped, but they were recaptured a day later. The curse had to be cast by someone with the time to track down each juror and collect something personal."

Bell let out a nervous laugh. "You think this witchdoctor is still around?"

"No, but knowledge of the curse may have gotten out. Obviously, the jurors' descendants know about it; they deal with it every day. What if someone is using the curse against them?"

"You mean blackmail?"

Roger nodded. "If Lavinia isn't the killer, then someone doesn't want the curse broken and is killing anyone who attempts it. Either way, my missing person case and your murder investigation are tangled together," he said. "Doctor Glover's the key. He must know something. I need to talk to him."

"Since S.L.E.D. arrived, they've had me running around in circuses. I'm afraid you're on your own. The police cannot help you."

"I just need you to stay out of my way," Roger said.

"Roger," Bell warned, his voice carrying the weight of his authority.

"A hundred and fifty years ago, the jurors may have been corrupt — who knows?" said Roger. "Regardless, Mister Hart's son deserves a chance at a normal life. Not suffering an inherited curse or a life embroiled in conspiracy. I plan to root them out one by one, and in the process, find Lavinia and stop her if she's the one behind these killings."

"You may be right, but these people have kept their illness secret for a very long time," Bell replied. "They'll resist."

"That's what I'm counting on."

There was a muffled *pop,* and Lieutenant Bell fell backwards.

Roger dropped to the ground and rolled in front of the pyramid for cover.

This wasn't the deafening gunfire he had experienced in the parking lot in front of the hospital two weeks ago. This shot was quiet, intended to not attract attention. Assassins.

Ducking as he went, Roger retreated to the pyramid's recessed entrance. Another *pop* chased after him, and a stone chalice flanking the steps exploded.

Flat on his back, Bell raised his pistol with a bloodied hand. He fired again and again, filling the air with the smell of gunpowder.

Roger heard a grunt from the other side of the pyramid, and the thud of a body hitting the ground.

"There's another gunman," Bell gasped. Pain filled his voice and blood soaked his jacket.

Retrieving two lockpicks from the folds of his tunic, Roger unlocked the pyramid's gate. Sunlight streamed through the stained-glass window and cast a rainbow hue on the floor. He stayed low to the ground as he peeked around the corner, a dagger in each hand.

A man's shadow stretched across Bell's unmoving body.

His eyes fixed on the pyramid's entrance, the assassin aimed his pistol at Lieutenant Bell's head. In his other hand, he pointed a second pistol at the tomb. His leather gloves matched his jacket. "Come out, or I'll kill him," he said.

"You're going to kill him anyways," replied Roger, his voice echoing.

"It didn't have to come to this," the assassin said. "If you had minded your own business, none of this would have been necessary."

Roger needed to do something quick; otherwise, the Lieutenant would bleed out. Taking in the assassin's flushed face a scary thought occurred to Roger. "Which one are you?"

The man's lips drew back into a cold smile. "Davis."

"Angel Dust?"

"What?" Mr. Davis replied, his head tilted slightly.

"You're taking Angel Dust for the pain."

The smile faded, and he stepped forward. "How do you know that?"

"I also know you're cursed. Your father was too."

Mr. Davis advanced another step. Uncertainty and anger replaced the confidence that was there just moments before.

"You don't know anything!" he shouted.

"I know you're impervious to pain, which means the only way to stop you is to kill you."

Mr. Davis raised both his guns and aimed them at the pyramid. "I'm going to count to three. One... Two..."

Roger surged out of the pyramid, flinging his trilby and then both blades as he dove to the side.

Continuously adjusting his aim, Mr. Davis fired. *Pop... pop... pop.*

Bullets bit into the stonework above Roger's head.

Rolling past the edge of the pyramid, Roger spotted the assassin Bell had shot. He ducked around the corner even as more gunfire dug into the landscape.

Perspiration dotting his forehead, Roger searched the ground and found the fallen assassin's weapon. A vision of the Dark One's symbol, a forked cross, flashed before his eyes. He fought the rising bile and nausea as he took up the cursed pistol and aimed it, two handed.

"Get out of here," Roger said through gritted teeth.

"I can't do that," Mr. Davis replied as he ejected the spent magazines.

Mr. Davis did not appear to feel the knives protruding from his leg and chest. He finished reloading and started toward Roger.

Shaking, Roger leaned against the stone wall and pulled the trigger. The shot went wild.

"Want me to stand still?" Mr. Davis asked, laughing.

Roger took a deep breath, held it, and aimed again.

Mr. Davis stepped up onto the grass. He stopped in front of Roger with his arms raised to each side. "Here. I'll make it easy for you."

Roger fired.

"My turn," Mr. Davis said.

Shutting his eyes, Roger focused all his effort on not being sick.

The gunshot rang out, and Roger felt something wet spatter his skin. He smelled blood and cracked open an eye. Mr. Davis lay face down, his foot twitching.

Pushing away the image of the forked cross, Roger tossed away the pistol then rubbed a hand down his face. It came away red. The sight of gore, while not unfamiliar, seemed odd until he began to notice bits of grey matter. He dropped to his knees and checked Mr. Davis to make sure he was dead. Blood streamed from the man's forehead where the bullet had exited. Yanking out his daggers, Roger wiped the blades and sheathed them.

Lieutenant Bell lay motionless in the now muddy path, and Roger rushed to his side.

"You alive?"

He reached down to feel for a sign of life but stopped when he realized the lieutenant's unseeing eyes stared off into the distance. In his hand, the lieutenant held his pistol tight across his chest, his finger still on the trigger.

Bowing his head, Roger closed Lieutenant Bell's eyes and said a silent prayer.

CHAPTER 17
GOOD FRIDAY, BAD FRIDAY

Friday, April 4, 1969

The crunch of gravel preceded a man's shout. "The gunshots came from over there!"

Roger jerked upright, his eyes scanning the cemetery. Three men headed his way. By the sound of it, more were behind them. Pistols drawn, they spread out, forming a rough cordon.

Staying low, he crabbed to the nearest patch of trees. Roger didn't hesitate. He kept to the shadows, using gravestones, tree trunks, anything he could find to stay hidden. He had no choice but to escape the way he came in.

The line of men surrounded the pyramid. When one came across Lieutenant Bell's body, he yelled, "Agent Murray, it's the lieutenant. He's dead."

"Davis is too," another person said, "and so is his partner."

"Roger Vaughn?" asked their stocky commander. He had a close-cropped widow's peak that fed into wide sideburns.

"Not here, sir."

"Search the area. I want that cop-killer found."

Roger crawled past the edge of the vacant mausoleum. From the opposite direction, two men rushed down the dirt road carrying pistols. Lean and hungry, they had the look of loping jackals.

Not knowing if he'd been spotted, Roger crept inside the crypt with no floor and climbed down the stone shelves into the black water. It felt oddly warm and held a marshy stench. With a grimace, he laid flat on his back and floated under the bottom shelf. Once concealed, he braced himself against the underside of the stone. His every movement caused a ripple, and it took all his self-control to relax. He counted silently, using the pattern to calm his breathing, and slowly submerged until only his nose, mouth, and hands were clear.

A sudden splash sent water lapping against the stone.

He held his breath, hoping someone hadn't jumped down in the crypt. Another splash, and he fought to keep from panicking. He resumed counting and waited. *If they were going to catch him, it wouldn't be because he gave himself away. They'd have to come in after him.*

The water calmed, and he chanced a quick gulp of air. Everything became still. A picture of the men watching the mausoleum firmly set in his head, he didn't dare move.

Agent Murray's words echoed in his ears. *They're going to blame me for the lieutenant's death.* A dawning horror overtook him. Davis and Murray were on the juror list. The conspirators were painting him as an outlaw, just like the Fishers one-hundred-fifty years before.

Roger didn't know how long he had remained inside the crypt. He lost count when he realized the water was rising with the tide. With barely enough space to breathe, he kept his cheek pressed against the underside of the stone as he drifted toward the edge of the shelf. Opening his eyes, he noted the mausoleum held an evening glow. He pushed himself up and peeked outside.

The croak of frogs competed with the singing cicadas and crickets. It gave him a certain amount of comfort, but he knew the cemetery would be watched and decided to wait until dark.

Wet and stiff, Roger exited the crypt and removed his boots to empty them of water. Someone had set up a lantern near the pyramid. The radius of light didn't reach far, and he spotted the bob of electric torches as teams searched the cemetery. He needed a way out. Nate, Tee, and Brie could all be in danger. With that thought, he placed the mausoleum between himself and the lantern and struck out along the edge of the marsh, back toward the apartments.

Thankful the moon hadn't risen, he moved from tree to tree, hunched low to minimize his profile. He toed through the grass, using feel to stay on firm ground.

When he came within sight of Porter Manor, his heart sank. Blue lights flashed, casting odd colors on the tree line. *Vie's Gramma Huger was going to kill him for bringing trouble to her doorstep.* He ducked into the thicket and watched.

Two rows of apartments and a greenspace were between

him and a dead-end parking lot lit by street lamps. A patrol car eased into view. It stopped, and its spotlight lanced between the buildings toward the trees. Low to the ground, Roger kept still. The spotlight snapped off, and after a few moments, the car pulled into an empty stall to turn around.

Backing away, Roger crept east toward the marsh. When he'd almost reached the cordgrass border, he heard the long blare of a horn and the jangle of a bell. A single light appeared in the marsh. It didn't bob up and down like a will-o'-the-wisp, nor sweep side to side like a search beacon. As it drew closer, the low rumble of an engine and rhythmic clang of metal on metal echoed in the air, and he realized it was the front end of a long train heading into town. He could just make out the steel rails raised on an earthen mound two hundred feet away. He made toward the railroad tracks, then stopped before stepping onto the viscous morass.

Brie had called the saltmarshes around Charleston pluff mud. Worse than quicksand, it pulled you down, and once you were in it, there was no getting out without help. She had told him about a deer that tried. People ended up having to lay sheets of plywood end-to-end just to rescue the trapped animal. He shook his head and opted to parallel the tracks in the hope that there'd be a cut through.

Turning south, he followed the fence line so that the apartments were to his right and the rails to his left. He moved fast, using the trees for cover when he could. After a few minutes, he came across a clearing with a narrow land bridge that led to the tracks.

A police spotlight blazed behind him.

Ground shaking, the train let out a deafening blast from its horn. The side of the different railcars came into view. There were flatbeds, cylindrical tank cars, and boxcars. White smoke from the engine hung just above their roofs. The train moved slow enough that he could make out each bolt on its wheels.

Roger charged down the path and caught up with a boxcar that had its cargo door open. With a burst of speed, he reached out, grabbed the door frame, and hauled himself inside. Wind rushed past him. A grim smile played across his lips. *This must be what it's like to ride a dragon.*

A miasmic whiff of sweat, body odor, and urine cut through the marsh smell. Roger stepped away from the cargo door, seeking the source. Shadows clung to the interior of the wooden boxcar, and it took time for his eyes to adjust. There on the floor was a bearded man in unkempt jungle fatigues. He sat up with his back to the wall.

Looking as if he had just woken, the man struck a match and lit a cigarette. "Where am I?" he asked. His eyes appeared glazed in the meager light.

"Charleston," answered Roger.

"What?" he said, getting to his feet. "Damn, I slept too long. Is that the station?"

Ahead, the steel rails merged with another line and turned southwest toward Columbus Terminal. Roger remembered seeing the cargo ship and railyard earlier that week.

"What happens at the station?" asked Roger.

"Who knows, maybe we'll luck up, and there won't be any bulls." With a leap, he grabbed the eave above the door using both hands and kicked with one foot against the door latch. Pushing up, he scrambled on top of the car.

Bulls?

Following the man's example, Roger grabbed the eave and stepped up on the latch. His foot slipped.

Dangling at the door opening, he looked down at the pluff mud rushing past. Roger tightened his grip and swung side to side. His foot made contact, and with a heave, he levered himself up and over the edge.

Aligned down the ridge, the man in fatigues lay flat on running boards, a wild smile lighting his eyes. "Makes you feel alive, don't it?"

Roger had to agree. The rush coursing through his veins made him feel invulnerable. Positioning himself behind the other man, he laid with his head turned toward the city.

The strip of pluff mud between them and the mainland ended when the train crossed a moat-like creek and entered a gate through chain-link fencing topped with barbed wire. A series of blasts from the horn echoed off the underside of the Cooper River bridges spanning above them.

They approached a series of railroad switches, and the train slowed. Lit by pools of light radiating from pole mounted lamps, Roger counted over twenty sets of tracks, with most of them clustered near East Bay Street where freight cars waited. It was a crowded space, and from what

Roger could tell, there was barely room to walk between them.

On his other side, warehouses lined the docks, filled with cargo ready to be transferred to the various railcars. Instead of moving toward them, they switched tracks again and aimed for the freight station.

A column of freight cars came along beside them. The man in fatigues sprang to his feet and leapt across the gap. Not looking back, he jumped atop the next car then disappeared over the side.

Roger was on his knees when they switched tracks and diverted away from the line of railcars. Grimacing at his missed opportunity, he laid back flat as they came alongside a grassy sludge pond with fewer lights. It wasn't much, but at least it afforded him some shadows.

Separated from the other freight lines, railmen armed with flashlights began inspecting the cars.

With a squeal of metal on metal, the train lurched to a stop. Roger scuttled toward the back and climbed down the ladder. Hidden between two boxcars, he peeked around the side and spotted a man wearing denim overalls and a striped cap. He had bent down to shine his flashlight into the undercarriage of the adjacent car. The radio in his other hand announced, "We found him! He's headed toward the Columbus Street exit."

As the railman stood and turned toward Columbus Street, Roger crept under the "cleared" car and crouched between the wheels. He looked in the same direction as the railman and spotted the flash of blue lights.

Bringing the radio up, the man asked, "JD, this is Rick. What do you want us to do?"

"Keep searching. There may be more."

"10-4."

Weighing his options, Roger decided there was too much light to dash across the yard. Instead, he followed the railman, using the darkness of the undercarriages to his advantage. He moved silently around the axles and couplers, and Rick, the railman, outdistanced him. He looked back as much as forward and noticed how the train curved. Near the engine was a squat building with an elevated platform that allowed the engineer and his men to detrain. A crowd had gathered under its canopy, many of them smoking cigarettes.

On the opposite side of the train from the station, Roger counted at least a half dozen sets of tracks. They branched, some slanting toward a waterfront warehouse. The others converged. Curving behind the station, they ended beside a maze of double and triple stacked cargo containers.

Down on all fours, he peeked out from under the train at the men on the platform.

"Everyone quiet!" said Rick, radio pressed to his ear. He nodded, and then turned to the men. "They caught him, but it's the wrong guy. Come on. The one CPD wants is still out there." The men on the platform rushed out, snapping on their flashlights. "Gus, take the top. Holler if you see anything."

Roger ducked back under, watching them come toward him. *How did he get himself into situations like this?*

The railmen split into two groups. One group searched the cluster of freight cars near East Bay. The other stuck with his train, checking it again.

Climbing the ladder, Roger waited. The man called Gus walked toward him along the running boards. Like a trapdoor spider, Roger surged up, grabbed the man's legs, and heaved him over the side. He flailed and shouted as he fell, landing flat on his back in the dirt.

Satisfied the workman would live, Roger jumped up and raced across the cars.

The men on the ground clustered around their fallen comrade. One pulled a pistol from a pocket in his overalls. He aimed it at Roger and fired.

With a surge of adrenaline, Roger leapt into the coal car and climbed atop the roof of the engine's cab. From there he continued onto the platform's canopy and over the building's parapet.

Gunshots chased after him.

Head low and knees bent, he raced to the far parapet. Ahead of him, the maze of containers stretched to the edge of the property. After taking time to study the layout, he shimmied down a nearby light pole. Made of wood coated in some kind of oily residue, it smelled of tar and burned his skin. Pushing himself away, he landed on gravel and dashed between two containers.

Roger followed the path in his head and steadily made his way toward a warehouse in the southwest corner. He recalled seeing freight cars parked beside an unlit loading dock. The sound of running feet echoed off the containers, and he drew one of his daggers and pushed harder.

When he turned the last corner, a pool of lamp light illuminated the exit out of the maze. Guarding it, Nate stood with his pistol raised. "Freeze! Charleston Police Department!"

Coming to a halt, Roger broke into a broad smile. "Nate, it's me."

There was a stern set to Nate's jaw, and his eyes held a steely edge. "Why did you do it?"

Roger's smile faded. "Do what?"

"We trusted you. *I* trusted you," Nate replied. His pistol began to shake, and there was a quiver in his voice.

"Don't believe what you've been told," said Roger, taking a step forward. "I didn't do it."

"You killed Lieutenant Bell," Nate responded. He caught sight of the blade in Roger's hand. "Drop the weapon!"

"No, Nate. They want me dead. You and Tee may be in danger, too."

"I said, drop it!" Fear filled the young officer's eyes, but there was also a building determination.

Roger flung his dagger as Nate pulled the trigger.

CHAPTER 18
ONE OF THE HOARD

Friday, April 4, 1969

The bullet grazed Roger's upper arm. He backed around the corner and waited.

Nate came rushing after him, gun raised.

Using his left hand, Roger grabbed the pistol and shoved it out of the way. With the heel of his right palm, he struck Nate in the solar plexus.

Nate doubled over, the wind knocked out of him.

Roger wrapped his arms about Nate's throat and head, cutting off the circulation. "I'm sorry, Nate. I don't want to do this, but I did not kill Lieutenant Bell." Pushing his opponent to the ground, he counted to ten, then slowly let go.

Railmen shouted to one another. They were like baying hounds trying to drive him into the hunters — or in his case, the constabulary. From the exit, footsteps crunched on the gravel.

Frowning, Roger looked down the different pathways of the maze. While running across the station, he had seen portions of it from up high. He had also seen the fence that enclosed the train yard, and the three cabooses next to it. Aiming toward them, Roger ran for a distance before ducking down a shadowed alley.

Double stacked containers loomed on both sides, and he found a pair with vertical lock rods attached to the corrugated doors. Blood dripped onto the gravel as he grabbed hold of a rod, and he realized he was leaving a trail. Pressing his foot against one of the hinges, he pushed with his arms against the rod and walked up the container's jamb. When he came to the top, he stepped on the middle hinge and gripped the upper rim with both hands.

Below, a railman shined his flashlight down the alley. The questing beam skittered over the droplets of blood and up the pair of containers just as Roger disappeared over the edge.

"The trail stops here," said the man with the flashlight.

"How could he just disappear?" asked the railman's partner as he searched around. "Who is this guy?"

"Police said his name was Roger Vaughn. Killed one of their lieutenants," the railman replied.

"Do you think he climbed one of these containers?"

The railman shined his light on the door. "Maybe. He had to go somewhere." He reached out and touched the metal. "It's slicker than owl shit. He'd have to be part lizard to climb that thing."

Lifting his radio, the partner said, "I'm calling it in."

Roger turned his attention to the fence and cabooses. A patrol car sat on the other side with its spotlight blazing through the chain links. *No good.*

He still couldn't believe Nate blamed him for the lieutenant's death. Three bodies and three guns, there was nothing tying him to the cemetery except for his trilby, and that could have been Lieutenant Bell's.

Agent Murray had lied to the police. It explained the manhunt, but Nate... Nate should have known better. He could only imagine what Brie and her family thought. Just thinking about her sent a spike of anxiety through him.

Another pair of railmen passed beneath him, and he moved to the next container. The pain was catching up to him. He clutched his wound and blood seeped through his tunic sleeve. Using his remaining dagger, he cut the cloth away. He probed the wound with his fingers and realized it would need bandaging sooner than later. First things first, he had to escape this trap.

After tying the cut cloth around his wound, he set about crawling toward his new objective. He kept a steady pace and managed to get behind the line of searchers.

Roger climbed down and backtracked toward the freight station. The area was deserted. Mustering all his confidence, he walked inside the back door and entered the locker room. Opening one, he found a set of baggy coveralls and slipped them on over his clothes.

His arm felt wet, and he noticed his makeshift bandage needed changing. Looking around, he found a metal box mounted to the wall with FIRST AID emblazoned on its lid. Inside, he discovered gauze, tape, different sized bandages, and a bottle of something called Mercurochrome. He took the box with him to the washroom and cleaned his wound.

When he applied the antiseptic, it stung like mad. He clenched his jaw and danced about, doing anything to keep from shouting. It left a red stain on his skin, and he felt certain he'd made a mistake. Eventually, the sting subsided to a dull throb, and he reread the bottle. It said it was a general antiseptic. Not being a healer, he decided to go with it and wrapped his arm.

Roger replaced the vile box and made sure he'd left nothing behind, even sticking the soiled sleeve in his pocket. Snatching up a striped cap and flashlight, he strode out the front door.

"Hey! Why aren't you out there searching?" an elderly man asked. He wore metal rimmed glasses and a striped cap that matched Roger's.

"Had to take a leak," answered Roger, mimicking a southern accent.

The radio at the man's belt squawked, "Art, you made it to the station yet? He may try to double back." Raising it, the elderly man answered, "Yeah, I'm here. Stop your bitchin'."

Remembering the name from earlier, Roger said, "Sounds like JD may be on to something. You want me to take a quick look around the perimeter?"

Reclipping the radio on his belt, Art took off his glasses and wiped the sweat from his face with a checkered handkerchief. "Sure, but don't be a hero. You see him, you holler out. Let the police handle him."

It was well past midnight by the time Roger arrived at the corner of Queen and King Streets. He had ditched the coveralls but kept the hat. It was the little things that made disguises effective.

After checking to make sure it was clear, he crossed the street and stepped up to the lime green door. Roger tested the knob. Locked. There wasn't a knocker or anything to alert the owner to his presence. Taking out his picks, he unlocked the door and pushed it open. Its brass bell clanged loudly.

"Scott, it's Roger!"

Hanging from the high ceiling, the bare bulb did its best to illuminate the foyer. Roger closed the door behind him and peered down the pathway between mountains of old newspapers, books, magazines, and whatever else the antiques dealer could find. He relocked the door and sat down on the floor. The tile felt cool beneath him.

All the pains from the night caught up to him. However, the one that hurt the worst was seeing Nate. Roger shook his head to dislodge the vision. He had to find a way to set this right.

"Who steals my purse steals trash; 'tis something, nothing; 'Twas mine, 'tis his, and has been slave to thousands," Scott said. "But he that filches from me my good name robs me of that which not enriches him and makes me poor indeed."

"Evening, Scott," Roger said in a tired voice.

"What have you been up to?" Scott asked, stepping into the light. He aimed a sawed-off, double-barrel shotgun at Roger's head.

"If you're going to shoot me, get it over with, but you'd ruin your door."

"That's not playing fair, Roger, holding my door hostage," Scott said with a smile. "Be glad I like that door." He shouldered his firearm and glanced out the storefront. "Anyone follow you?"

"No," Roger said, rising to his feet. "Guess you heard."

"Tee was here earlier. Said you shot a policeman and two other men. Said if I were to see you, I should turn you in."

"Scott, Lieutenant Bell saved my life. I didn't kill him. Two men ambushed us. Despite being wounded, Bell managed to kill them before he died."

"You need to tell Tee, and Nate, too."

"I doubt they'll believe me." Roger showed Scott his arm. "Nate shot me, and I had to run."

"Betrayal is the only truth that sticks." Scott stepped close and grabbed Roger by the chin. He turned his head one way and then the other, inhaling deeply as he did. "Creosote, marsh, gunpowder, grave dirt, and blood. My, you have been busy."

"Scott, I need a place to stay. The constabulary have my place under surveillance."

Scott stepped back, considering. "What about your lady friend?"

"I couldn't do that to her or her family."

"But you'd do that to me," Scott said. Roger started to reply, but Scott stayed him with a hand. "Nature teaches beasts to know their friends... even their mad ones."

"Thank you." Roger paused as he digested Scott's last words. "I think."

With a sweeping bow, Scott said, "Come, follow me into my lair."

Scott moved quickly through the mountains of paper, glass curio cabinets, and oil paintings. He kept a constant hand on the various items lining the path, and again, Roger was reminded of the minotaur's labyrinth.

"How is it you carry one of their weapons?" asked Roger. "Every time I touch one, it's like touching the face of evil."

"I was here first."

They came to the sales counter, and Scott opened the hinged section to let Roger through.

"You would have found me asleep upstairs, but after Tee stopped by, I had a feeling you'd show up." He motioned toward a pathway partially hidden amongst the clutter and said, "That should suit your purposes."

The entrance was narrow and dark, but as Roger's eyes adjusted, he caught a glimmer of light. He moved down the path a short distance and found where a pile had been pushed against the wall, making room for a cot and a lamp. Centered on the pillow, the ruby Roger had left behind sparkled.

"The washroom is there," Scott said, pointing to the door beside him. "It has a shower and some clothes laid out for you."

"Scott, I don't know what to say," Roger replied.

"You can thank me after you get cleaned up."

When Roger finished, he found Scott sitting beside an oval table and sipping red wine from a half-full bottle. On the opposite side was an empty chair.

"How did you get away from the police?" Scott asked, taking another sip. "Tee seemed at a loss. Everyone thought they had you surrounded."

Roger replied, "They were looking in the wrong place."

"Come now. I am not the fool that's beguiled by modest speech."

"Alright. Let me see if I can be as loquacious as you."

Scott held up his hands to stop him. He entered his office, came out with a second bottle of Italian red and a corkscrew, and set them in front of Roger. "The challenge has been accepted. To the winner goes the spoils."

"Whose judging?" Roger replied.

"No judge. We'll make a gentleman's bet, with only our honor at stake."

Roger removed the cork and let it breathe before taking a long pull. He wasn't sure if this was a trick. When dealing with ancient beings, you could never tell. Deciding to throw caution to the wind, he said, "Agreed, a gentleman's bet it is."

Eyes intense, Scott said, "Tell your tale."

Roger organized his thoughts while he gulped down another swallow. "When you find something that's lost, it's always the last place you look. Well, they should have kept looking. Fences, cargo containers, boxcars, they thought to trap me in the freight yard. The constabulary guarded all the exits, and the railmen served as beaters, driving me towards the waiting hunters. However, they didn't expect their prey to get behind them."

"We were running through this maze of containers when they almost caught me. Cornered, I could have fought them, but I chose a different path. Without them knowing, I climbed above them, backtracked to the station house, and took their clothes."

Scott let out a loud laugh and rocked back in his chair.

"From there, it only took gumption and no small amount of bravado. I aimed for the opposite side of the yard and went out the only open gate that wasn't being watched — the one the train had entered. Following a meandering path, my footsteps brought me here."

"Bravo, sir. Your tale is worthy, if not a little anticlimactic," said Scott. "No worries, though. You are in the presence of a master."

Roger raised his bottle in acceptance of the criticism. The room spun, and he felt lightheaded. He really should have asked for water. "Your turn."

"What tale would you like to hear?" Scott asked, then drank the last swallow of his wine. "A tale of debauchery, or perhaps a tale of woe?"

"What have you found out about John and Lavinia Fisher?"

Placing the empty bottle on the floor, Scott replied, "A tale of woe it is." He stood and pointed to different stacks of newspapers set on the countertop. "They're organized by year. Those go back to 1819. I stopped at 1897, but I haven't finished. I want to make sure there's nothing more current before I give you a complete report of my efforts. The smaller stack over there are the ones with articles about the Fishers.

"As expected, they start in February of 1819 with their capture, and later that year, their sentencing. In September, there was an article that said John Fisher escaped the Charleston Gaol with another prisoner, Joseph Roberts. Then in early 1820, the articles become more abundant. The ones in January speak of the Constitutional Court refusing to grant new trials. The ones in early February discussed a petition and the delay granted by His Excellency John Geddes, Governor and Commander in Chief over the State.

"You might think he did it to appease the public, but the good governor never did anything without a reason. He had a reputation for not letting anything or anyone stand in his way. And if he felt slighted, he'd challenge you to a duel. I remember one in particular. Bastard had his son take his place. Young Geddes was a high-spirited youth, but he didn't know one end of a pistol from the other. Everyone just knew Geddes was a doomed man. Bets were offered two to one that he'd be killed.

"Eight paces apart, young Geddes took a shot through his thigh, severing an artery, but still managed to shoot Mister Edward P. Simmons just below the breastbone, killing him. Oh, and don't get me started about the time Geddes, the elder, tried to buy Key West."

"Scott, focus," Roger said, rubbing at his eyes. "What about the Fishers?"

Stepping to the pile of newspapers, Scott removed a page, and handed it to Roger. Dated February 19, 1820, the article discussed the execution the prior day.

"The Fishers were conveyed to Potter's Field, where they were interred," said Scott. "I also have the letter John Fisher read aloud at his execution. 'May the Redeemer of the World plead for those who have sworn away my life.' Now, you would think that's the end of it, but no. I found a series of letters to the editor from the High Sheriff Colonel Nathaniel Greene Cleary. He was defending the Fishers' arrests and execution. He was the one who John Fisher accused in his letter."

Roger stared at the stacks of newspapers. "Who did you say the sheriff was?"

"Here," Scott replied, handing him the arrest article from February 22, 1819.

Roger read, "The bench warrant was executed by Colonel Cleary, accompanied by a number of gentlemen... We congratulate the citizens that the prisoners were safely lodged in the gaol on Saturday night."

"I took your lady's advice and did a bit of digging at the library. Colonel Cleary was up for reelection in 1820, and he lost by thirty-five votes. He wasn't even the one who presided over the Fishers' execution. Not only that, but he owed money to the state when he left office. He was bankrupt. Seems he used the proceeds of execution sales to pay his daily bills."

"He got paid for the executions?" asked Roger.

"In 1825, he wrote a Memorial to the State. In it he mentioned a Fee Bill, where the fees for certain civic functions were spelled out, including summoning jurors, serving a subpoena, and executions. My guess, he skimmed public monies — money meant for the hangman, the gallows, or whatever else was needed. It was a different time back then."

"And now he's back — or at least his relative is."

Scott replaced the articles, making sure they went back to their proper stack. "What are you talking about?"

"If I'm right, his descendant is the current Sheriff of Charleston County. That's the connection." Roger thought for a moment. "But something's still missing. Packer wasn't working for Cleary when he ran us off the road, Hart was a bank vice-president in Charlotte, and Mister Davis was a hired killer. Who did Cleary work for?"

"He was elected," answered Scott.

"No. I mean who did he answer to," Roger said. "The bench warrant that he executed, that had to come from someone."

Scott replied, "Judge Colcock."

"Have you found anything on him?"

"The judge? No." A confused expression crossed Scott's face. "This may not mean anything, but I found something interesting during my research. In February 1818, Major John Wilson, the same John Wilson on your list of jurors, was appointed to the office of Civil and Military Engineer of the State of South Carolina and entrusted with improving the rivers for navigation. During this time, he served on the Fisher's trial in May of 1819. Three years later, Wilson contracted fever and ague. It so seriously impaired his health that he resigned from his position and moved north. However, he never recovered and died on a ship bringing him back to Charleston. Coincidently, the year after Major Wilson became ill, Doctor Joseph Glover was appointed Surgeon General of South Carolina, with Geddes' recommendation no less."

"You did good work."

Scott got a wide grin on his face. "I guess that means I won."

CHAPTER 19
SIGHT SEEING

Saturday, April 5, 1969

*S*cott held an open book of baby names and leaned against the bathroom doorframe. "You need an alias, a sobriquet, a nom de plume."

"Scott, it's Saturday," Roger replied, feeling frustrated. He faced the mirror and rubbed gel into his hair, slicking it back. "The doctor's office will be closed. I just want to take a quick look at the building. I won't need a name."

"How about Dirk?"

"Dirk?" Roger asked, washing his hands. "No."

"You're good with knives. It's fitting."

"No."

"It needs to be something you'll remember."

"Scott, I know what I'm doing. There's no need—"

"George, then."

"No," Roger said, snatching a paper towel from the roll on the wall. "You're worse than Brie."

Scott's brow furrowed with concentration, then his face lit up. "I got it. Greg V. Haroun."

"What?"

"Greg V. Haroun. It's an anagram. Aren't you glad I'm on your side." Scott had such a smug look, Roger couldn't argue.

"Fine. Greg V..." Roger started.

"Haroun," Scott finished for him. "It's Egyptian for 'warrior lion'."

Roger grinned despite himself. He put on the black framed spectacles and checked the items hidden about his person. He doubted he'd use the cigar-shaped penlight, but the fourteen-piece lockpick set was like an old friend. He felt for the two knives Scott had given him plus the dagger he had carried last night. He raised his arms and twisted around. The glen-plaid three-piece suit and button-up shirt fit snug. He tried not to notice the irregular holes left by silverfish.

"Call the medical college and set me up an appointment

with Doctor Joseph Glover for ten o'clock Monday morning," said Roger, switching off the light.

"Sure, what do you want me to say?"

"Tell them Roger Vaughn wants to meet with Doctor Glover. I heard he's developed an experimental cure for a rare hereditary disease, and it's imperative that I see him. If that doesn't get his attention, tell them that Mister Hart referred me."

"You really want to do that?"

The brass bell clanged, and Tee's voice boomed, "Mistuh Silva, you open fuh bidness?" The door closed, and Roger heard the shuffling of two people.

"Back here," Scott replied as he gestured toward the secluded pathway. Roger ducked inside and helped Scott block the entrance with a stack of cardboard boxes.

Counting in his head, Roger controlled his breathing. Outside, he heard Scott moving the newspapers, followed by the sweep of a broom.

"Twice in two days, Tee. People will begin to talk," Scott said.

"Mawnin', Mistuh Silva," said Tee. "Any word from Vaughn?"

"No, nothing."

There was a scrape of footsteps. "You have a lot of stuff in here," a new voice said. It was a strong voice with a crisp military cadence.

"We haven't met. I'm Scott Silva."

"Special Agent David Murray," the man replied.

More footsteps. It sounded like someone was just on the other side of the stack.

"Corporal Middleton says you're an antiques dealer, and that you've been in business for as long as he can remember."

"Things won are done; joy's soul lies in the doing."

"Shakespeare?" Agent Murray asked.

"Correct," Scott replied. "Are you new to Charleston?"

"Yes. Transferred in from Columbia, yesterday. I'm here to help support the local law enforcement."

"Good luck."

"Middleton mentioned you were acquainted with Roger Vaughn," Agent Murray said. "Have you seen him?"

"No."

"Are you sure?"

"Positive."

"You know he's a cop killer."

"I do.   Corporal Middleton told me yesterday.   Said I should be on the lookout in case he tries to break in."

"How would you know?" asked Agent Murray.

"Excuse me?" replied Scott.

"How would you know if he broke in?"

"Agent Murray, I live a solitary life.   Trust me, I would know if someone else were here."

The certainty in Scott's voice gave Roger pause, calling to mind his conversation with Brie about the antiques dealer's mysterious past and eliciting an involuntary shiver.   He forced his attention back to the shop's visitors.

"Thank you for your time," Agent Murray said.   "We'll stop by from time to time to check on you."

"I'd appreciate that, Officer," Scott replied.

"Boy, come on," Agent Murray said, and then Roger heard someone searching through the maze, heading toward the front door.

"Corporal Middleton," said Scott.

"Tek'care, Mistuh Silva. Vaughn surprised us. Dey's no tellin' warruh he gwine do next."   His Gullah accent had become thick, exposing the emotions hidden behind his professional demeanor.

"Forbear to judge, Tee, for we are sinners all."

After the door closed, Scott shifted the stack aside.   "I bet they're watching the front door, right now.   You may want to hold off on leaving."

"Do you have a back way out of here?" asked Roger.

"Yes, through my office, but they're probably watching that too," Scott replied.   "I do have another way, but it only accesses the roof."

Roger followed Scott through the maze to the party wall where sheets of plywood hid a stick framed ladder.   A scuttle in the ceiling accessed the second floor.

Placing a hand on a rung, Scott said, "There used to be a chimney here, but I had it removed.   This runs all the way to the mechanical well in the roof.   From there you can cross the roofs of the buildings next door.   There's a two story like this one, but smaller, and then a one story."

"What if the constables are watching the roof?" Roger asked.

"Be stealthy."

Roger cast an oblique look at Scott. "When I return, don't shoot me."

"Don't bring the police with you."

Like Scott said, the ladder led to the second floor and roof beyond. The second floor was similar to the first in that it held piles of clutter. Most of them were better organized and seemed newer, but the smell of mildew and rot told a different story.

Roger climbed into the second-floor ceiling and stood on a walkway built between the bottom chords of two timber roof trusses. Sunlight flared when he opened the hatch. Outside was a flat area cut out of the triangular trusses. In front of him, a mechanical box with wires and hoses running from it sat dormant. He closed the hatch behind him and inched toward the roof edge. *Here goes nothing.*

Stepping over the parapet, he crept across the flat roof of the adjacent building and came to a six-foot drop. Roger ducked behind the parapet as a car drove down King Street. At night, he would have felt comfortable, but in broad daylight, there was too much visibility.

A metal vent pipe stuck up from the rear of the building. It ran down to the ground, affixed to the wall with regularly spaced brackets. Testing it, Roger pushed against the pipe. It seemed solid. He looked over the edge of the parapet. Not seeing anyone in the gravel lot below, he grabbed the pipe with both hands and shimmied down it.

Roger stared back up at the pipe. Climbing it was going to be a bloody mess. At least he had avoided the constabulary. Dusting off his suit jacket, he headed south toward Broad Street.

According to their research, the South Carolina Medical College had purchased the Potter's Field five years ago. Roger doubted anyone knew it was a burial ground — at least, not until they uncovered those bodies while digging foundations for the Basic Science Building. He thought back to his discussion with Professor Mike. Building a school on top of a cemetery... It boggled his mind.

His meandering route took him through the heart of Harleston Village and across the grassy lawn surrounding Colonial Lake. Along its banks, several teenagers sat under shade trees, fishing rods in their hands and tackle boxes at their side. Pedestrians taking a leisurely stroll on a pretty day smiled and greeted him. It was a friendly atmosphere, and he remembered the Highlord calling it Southern Hospitality.

Turning up a tree-lined lane, Roger took his time and kept an eye out in case anyone followed him. All total, it was thirty minutes before he passed the county museum.

The medical college was two blocks down on Calhoun Street, but a crowd — most in hospital uniforms — laid siege to the medical college and hospitals.

"We have the right to be treated as human beings!" someone shouted.

People with paper hats marked "Local 1199 Drug and Hospital Union" held picket signs declaring, "Human Dignity for Hospital Workers" and "Hospital Workers Live in Poverty."

Armed constables guarded the college's entrances, preventing the protesters from reaching the buildings.

Having been away from his desk for a few days, Roger hadn't kept up with current affairs. However, he did recall reading an article about the workers' strike, and the governor sending state troopers to Charleston. He had figured most of the protesters would have been young men rattling their sabers, but these were mostly women.

Roger turned his attention toward the two- and three-story brick buildings of the college. Faux columns and pediments adorned each of the main doors, where gold letters declared them to be laboratories, an auditorium, and a library. Moving from island to island of spectators, he noticed people behind the barricade entering a breezeway between the buildings. Following their route, Roger joined a group of students as they approached the guards. No one stopped them, and they passed into an open courtyard.

Roger tapped one of the young men on the shoulder. "Excuse me. Do you know where I can find Doctor Glover's office?"

The student gave him a blank look and said, "No, mister, but most of the professors' offices are in the admin building. He pointed to stone steps leading to a wide entrance. There's a directory in the main lobby."

"Thanks." Roger hurried inside.

Not completely unhelpful, the directory broke the building into departments, but no names. A map posted next to the directory illustrated all the exits with dashed lines showing the shortest routes from the larger rooms. It also showed the elevators and stairs. The one closest to him was at the end of the building.

Looking over his shoulder, Roger spotted the entrance to the stairwell. The corridor was empty, so he took a handkerchief from his pocket and used it to open the door.

Roger dashed up the steps, wondering if this building also hid bodies under its foundations. *How could people want to study here?* The halls seemed so sterile and cold, a front to hide the skeletons in the closet. For all its faults, the Academia de Artes Magicae in Tydway had always felt more honest about its dealings with the dark arts.

At the second floor, he pushed open the door. Careful to keep his hands in his pockets, he nodded to the passing people as he travelled down the hallway. It looped the perimeter with doors on both sides. Based on the frequency and various labels, he gathered that the faculty offices faced outward with windows, while the interior rooms were set aside for research labs and teaching assistants. Not finding the name he was looking for, he moved to the third floor.

Midways down the perimeter hall, he came across a door labeled, 'J. Glover, M.D.' The sidelight window revealed a dark office. He walked past it and entered the men's restroom. Taking off his glasses, he washed and dried his hands. His disguise seemed to be holding up. The corridor was empty. He felt ready.

Moving quickly, he replaced his glasses and crossed the hall. Handkerchief in hand, he knelt and studied the lock. After making sure the hall remained empty, he slipped out a couple of picks and opened Doctor Glover's office.

Acutely aware of the bright sidelight window, he put his back to the door. His vision slowly adjusted, and a dawning horror overtook him. The sheer volume of paper was staggering. Stacks were everywhere, some loose, some in manila folders, others bound by large metal clips.

The longer he stared the more he recognized. He made out the desk, a pair of chairs, shelves overfilled with books and knickknacks, and the various sized certificates covering the back wall. Metal filing cabinets flanked a window overlooking the courtyard. Sunlight filtered around horizontal slats that partially obscured the glass and gave the rear of the office an odd glow.

It wasn't an office where you met patients. It was an office where you intimidated students. It was an office used for research and learning.

Glancing out the sidelight to see if anyone was coming, he relocked the door, then moved behind the desk, careful not to touch anything.

Inside a picture frame propped on the desk was a photo of a large boned man with his arm draped over the shoulders of a younger man. They both wore academic robes. The younger one held up a certificate. Clean shaven and smiling, they looked related, maybe father and son. The older man had a comb over hairdo that looked silver in the meager light.

An open box packed with hardback books rested on the floor beside the desk. Pushing back the flap, he picked one up. The one below it was identical. The cover had a carrot plant illustrated on the front. "The Essential Backpackers Guide to Wild Roots, Tubers, and Rhizomes by Joseph L. B. Glover, M.D." Leaning against the box was a leather courier pouch. Inside, manilla folders with tabs denoting different class times poked out the top.

After replacing the book and closing the box, Roger turned to the file drawers and slid one open using his handkerchief. It was stuffed with a decade worth of class syllabi, schedules, lectures, and teaching planners. None of it seemed pertinent to what he was looking for. *I could spend all day here.*

He was about to stand when a shadow passed in front of the sidelight. Ducking back down, Roger heard someone test the doorknob. He peeked around the desk and noticed a narrow door between the stacks of paper. It looked like it led to a closet.

Hand shading his eyes, a security guard peered through the sidelight. Roger waited, wondering what had possessed him to break into the doctor's office during the middle of the day. He shook his head. No. It was worth it. He now knew what the doctor looked like.

The security guard moved on, and Roger crept to the

closet. It was locked. Using his picks, he unlocked it and pulled open the door.

The closet was a whole other world. Roger's eyes were immediately drawn to the face painted on a huge horseshoe crab shell in bright, garish colors. It hung on the wall with a desiccated rat. On either side were sketches of humanoid figures with animal heads.

Centered like an altar sat a witch's table with various artifacts all jumbled. There were black, human-shaped ceremonial candles, a copper incense boat, a bleached piece of driftwood with a gold chain wrapped around it, a stone disc with ideographic writing, grass dolls and, coiled around a human skull, was a cobra with rhinestone eyes.

Propped in the corner was a gnarled oak staff decorated with bearded moss.

The other items, Roger didn't recognize, but he felt certain they held meaning, if only to the doctor. He really wished he had his glasses — the ones the sheriff had taken from him.

Taking the penlight from his pocket, he studied the skull. Engraved in the eye socket were the letters SCMC. *South Carolina Medical College?*

Roger reached for the skull.

Flaring its hood, the cobra hissed and made to strike.

Jerking back his hand, Roger nearly fell as he retreated. The life in its rhinestone eyes dimmed, and the cobra resumed its coiled position. He experimented a few more times, noting how close he could get his hand before the snake reared.

A smile came to Roger's lips. *Try this, snake.*

Reaching into his pocket, he snatched out his handkerchief. He dropped it over the cobra's head and leapt back.

With its eyes covered, the cobra remained stationary.

He studied the snake while he decided on his next course of action. On one of the bookshelves, he remembered seeing a crystal ball roughly the size of a human skull.

Relocking the doors as he went, Roger fought the urge to rush out of the office. Keeping a steady pace, he retraced his steps, the skull hidden within the courier pouch.

CHAPTER 20
RESURRECTIONISTS

Saturday, April 5, 1969

*T*he sun dipped low in the sky as Roger crossed Calhoun at the crosswalk and made his way to the Charleston Museum. He stopped at the entrance and admired the colonnaded portico. Mounted to the roof, an American flag snapped in the breeze. He was about to move on when the hairs on the back of his neck rose.

Someone was watching him.

Staying calm, he walked behind one of the grand columns. No one was around. The street was empty. Even the houses seemed vacant, waiting for their owners to return home from work.

But he couldn't shake the feeling.

Through the glass doors, he spotted an attractive lady at the front desk reading a magazine. She looked up at him and smiled. Key in hand, she unlocked the door. "Sorry, we're closed. You'll have to come back on Monday," she said and gestured to where the hours were posted beside the door.

Peering past her, Roger said, "But there are people inside." He was half sincere when he said it, and he realized he really did want to tour the museum.

"Yes, we officially close at four-thirty. However, we close the doors to new guests at four. You need at least two hours to see everything unless you're just visiting the gift shop."

"No, I'd want to stay awhile," replied Roger. "Thank you." He stepped away. Behind him, he heard her relock the door.

The feeling came back. He was sure someone was watching him. Then it struck him, and he looked inside the courier pouch. The skull leered back.

Cinching the flap tight, he readjusted the bag so that it rode behind him. He was getting paranoid.

Shadows stretched across the road, and it seemed the neighborhood had turned darker, more sinister. He hastened his steps across the street.

The feeling that someone watched him never subsided. He checked the bag, but it remained closed.

At the periphery of his vision, a dark-haired woman wearing a white gown strode down the sidewalk and turned onto Bull Street. Though her back had been to him, she had an aethereal aura about her that seemed familiar. When he reached the intersection, she was gone. He ran his fingers through his hair, questioning his sanity.

Three blocks ahead, Roger glimpsed her at another corner. Hurrying to keep up, he followed her down Coming and Market Streets. No matter how much he hurried, she stayed ahead of him. It occurred to him that she may be leading him into a trap. His luck thus far hadn't been the best. However, he wanted to know where she was going.

Market Street split at the grand entrance to Market Hall with its high entablature decorated with alternating ram's heads and bucrania. Roger pushed past the tourists gathered at its steps. At the intersection of Meeting and South Market, Roger searched up and down the streets. The woman in white had disappeared into the crowd. An uneasiness settled in his gut.

She reappeared a block south, turning east onto Cumberland. Roger rushed toward her, desperate to glimpse her face. He reached the corner only to find her waiting at the next intersection. Saint Philip's steeple soared ahead. He knew where he was — Church Street — which meant his office was nearby.

He circled, walked a distance, hoping to find her, and came to an unpretentious alley. Sandwiched between two buildings, he would have missed it but for the odd feel it had, like staring down a deep hole, not seeing the bottom, but expecting something to come out at any moment.

Drawn into it, Roger followed the cobblestone path, not knowing what he'd find. An undulating brick wall replaced the building on his right. Behind it, Saint Philip's steeple rose above bearded oak trees. The churchyard had to be on the other side. To his left, wild shrubs had grown through wrought-iron pickets. The alley narrowed as he passed between the churchyard wall and a warehouse with recessed archways. Inside were a pair of wooden doors shaped to fit the arch. Shielded as it was from the sun, a perpetual gloaming shrouded the path.

A man entered the far end of the alley. Tall, with sandy blond hair atop a narrow face, he wore gold tinted sunglasses and a blue leather jacket with three white bands around the sleeves.

Roger ducked into the closest archway and peeked around the jamb.

About midways down the alley, the man slowed and opened a gate in the churchyard wall. "What do you have for me?" he asked.

"A fresh grave outside of town. It's in a small, family cemetery. Real secluded. Should be just right for the doctor," another replied.

Taking off his sunglasses, the man in the leather jacket looked around to see if anyone was about. "Keep your nose clean. This business with Hart and now the lieutenant has the whole town turned upside down."

"Hey, don't sweat it. The boys know what they're doing."

"They better," the man said, replacing his sunglasses. "What else?"

"Take a look at these. We found them on an island in the Broad River. Must have been a Civil War campsite."

"A campsite, huh?" Taking a brown paper bag, the man peered inside. He reached in and pulled out a brass button. "You cleaned them."

"I figured the Judge wouldn't mind. We found a Union army cartridge box plate and a handful of bullets along with a belt buckle."

"Any coins?"

"A few."

"I don't see them in here."

"Come on. Let me keep something."

"Show me." The man in the leather jacket leaned forward. "I'll take this one and this one. Fair?"

"Yeah." From the sullenness of his voice, it sounded like he wanted to argue.

Closing the bag, the man said, "Let's meet this evening at Kelly's Diner."

"Sure."

The woman in white that he'd been following floated past Roger. Hatred marred her features, giving her a demonic expression as she clawed the air. Haggard and emaciated, all humanity had been scoured from her countenance. She reminded Roger of the creature that haunted his nightmares. The creature that had held him captive in the Old City Gaol:

the Executioner, the Jack Ketch.

Drawing his dagger, Roger stepped toward her.

She lashed out at the man in the leather jacket. Staggering back, he dropped the paper bag. Buttons and bullets spilled onto the pavers.

The man on the other side of the wall cried out in terror, and Roger heard his frantic steps fade into the distance.

Finding his voice, Roger called, "Lavinia!"

The apparition turned toward him.

At first, he saw only grey walls and barred windows reflected in her eyes. When her gaze fixed on him, dark velvet replaced the grey. Filled with sorrow, she mouthed, "Help me," before vanishing. The distant crack of a whip and rattle of the paddy wagon echoed down the alley.

Holding his arms across his gut, the man in the leather jacket took a tentative step forward. A smile lit his face.

"These are for you," he said.

Roger gazed up and down the alley, not sure if he should run or stay.

"Here. Take one," the man said, stepping closer.

"Take one what?" Roger asked.

The man stopped and opened his arms. Sliced as if by the sharpest razor, his stomach opened. His guts trailed out and piled on the cobblestone at his feet. Gore splashed the walls and coated the front of Roger's suit.

Shocked, Roger stood frozen while the man reached out with a bloody hand and wrote on the wall.

Two men entered the alley. "The shout came from over here," one said. "Oh Heavens!" a woman gasped, then covered her mouth.

The man fell to his knees and slumped forward. On the wall, he had written, "LEV. 18:25."

Roger ran. He jumped the iron fence, landing in a parking lot, and rushed past the gaping spectators. A woman screamed when he nearly plowed into her. Dodging past, he shot down the alley across State Street.

He had to get out of sight.

Roger exited the alley onto the next street. A car jerked to a stop, almost hitting him. The pilot blew the horn and yelled, "Hey, buddy! Watch where you're going."

Sirens wailed in the distance. Roger knew the

constabulary would canvas the area looking for him, which meant he had to put as much distance between himself and that alley as possible.

Moving east, Roger ran down a cobblestone street. The North Central Wharf blocked the far end. He turned south, skirting the fence. He crossed another street and dashed down Prioleau toward the North Atlantic Wharf. With night moving in, the derelict area was quiet. In fact, it looked like a vast parking lot. A few cars were scattered about, but most of the spaces were empty.

The canopy lights of a filling station snapped on, casting a shadow behind an open bay carwash. *Ding ding.* A car pulled up to one of the gas pumps. An attendant walked out and said, "Evening, Tony. Fill'er up?"

Roger ran behind the carwash and dove inside a metal dumpster. Sitting amongst the refuse, thoughts of his family and friends in Gaia hit him like a heavy weight in his gut. He missed them. He wanted to go home and not have anything to do with this world. He hugged himself and tried to quell the building emotions.

The image of Brie dangling from the Morris Island lighthouse gallery flashed through his mind. A large part of him knew he would never have forgiven himself if she had fallen. However, he couldn't escape the small voice inside his head that kept asking if the price he'd paid — becoming trapped on Terra — had been worth it, and he felt ashamed. *What have I gotten myself into?*

Focusing, he took stock of his situation. He was a mess. He scraped the gore from his suit and wiped it down as best he could. Then he took off his pants, turned them inside out, and put them back on. He did the same with his jacket, also turning it inside out. It looked weird, but it should work for what he wanted. Next, he rummaged around until he found a liquor bottle and brown paper bag.

One good had come from the day's adventures. He knew it was Lavinia doing the killing. More than that, the grey bars he'd seen reflected in her eyes pointed to a darker force controlling her actions, and a deep dread filled his soul.

He lumbered out of the bin, leaned against the side, and urinated, still wearing his pants. The stain blended with where the blood had soaked through, hopefully drawing away suspicion. Keeping up the act, he stumbled away from the wharf. As long as the constabulary didn't catch up to him, he had a plan.

Moving into the residential district south of Broad, Roger made his way west. He followed the laws, mindful of crosswalks and kept his head down, not making eye contact with anyone. The few residents he met looked past him. He was invisible to them, lest he ask for money.

It was late when he stopped at a corner grocery store. Its windows were dark, and the neighborhood was asleep. The building was a converted Charleston Single, which meant the owners were probably upstairs.

Roger peered through the glass front door and saw what he needed. He'd visited the store during his wanderings through the city. The owners had been nice people, which made him feel a little guilty, but it didn't stop him. Within moments, he had the door unlocked. He eased it open, clasping the brass bell mounted over the entry. *Damn things were louder than a dwarf's smithy.*

He waited to make sure no one had noticed before moving deeper into the store. On a shelf at the back, he selected two bottles of wine. Roger laid a ten-dollar bill on the counter and slid out a fresh paper bag.

Moving to the front, he snuck back out and relocked the door. The neighborhood still slept. He stared at the courier pouch, the flap cinched tight, and let out a low sigh. *Yes, I know this is a bad idea.*

He aimed north and crossed Broad Street, apprehension building with every step. Memories of the Old City Gaol became more vivid. He took a slightly different route, hoping it would make it easier.

Heart in his throat, he turned west onto Magazine Street. At the end of the block loomed the dull grey, three-story gaol with its crenelated battlements. Behind rusted bars, dark windows brooded with unconcealed menace. Vertical cracks connected lintels to sills, and portions of the parged skin had peeled away, revealing blood red brick.

Across the street, Roger shivered as he stared up at the towers flanking the arched brownstone entrance and iron gate. After making certain no one was around, he approached it.

"Jack Ketch!" Roger called.

He was met by silence.

"I have a gift for you."

He set the bag with the bottles of wine in front of the dark entrance and backed away.

"They're yours. In return, I ask that you let me talk with Mrs. Fisher."

Roger waited. Nothing happened. Maybe he was being foolish, thinking he could tempt the Executioner with an old vice. It was worth a try.

Car lights flashed down the lane.

Time was up. He dashed across the street, jumped the fence, and raced through the tenement housing.

"You ruined my suit!" Scott stood at the bottom of the ladder with his hands on his hips, watching Roger climb down. "That was my best suit. What happened?"

"Long story," Roger replied as he entered the bathroom.

"Did you wallow in a garbage truck?"

"Something like that."

"You owe me," Scott said. "That suit was expensive."

"Can we talk about it in the morning? All I want to do right now is take a shower and go to bed."

"It'll have to wait. You have a visitor."

Roger stopped. "Who?"

"A young lady," replied Scott. "Very sexy."

Roger's first thought went to Brie, but that couldn't be right. Scott would never describe her that way, at least not sober. Then it occurred to him, to Scott everyone was young.

Standing at the labyrinth's center was a tall woman about the same age as Roger. She wore a simple white gown that touched the floor. Lustrous black hair framed a tan face that was more handsome than pretty. The woman turned toward Roger, and velvety dark eyes drank him in.

Roger knew this was the same person from the alley, and yet, she wasn't. Remembering his manners, he raised his hand and said, "I'm Roger Vaughn."

Taking it with a firm grip, she replied, "Lavinia Fisher."

"I apologize for my appearance," said Roger. "It's been an off day for me."

"Off day," Scott scoffed. "Looks more like it was one of your typical days."

"Mister Vaughn, I've been a prisoner for a very long time," said Lavinia. "You'd be appalled by the conditions I'm used to." She studied the piles surrounding her. "This is a strange place. Does everyone live this way?"

"I'm the one who lives this way," Scott answered. "Everyone else just goes through the motions."

Roger shook his head as he grabbed his old tunic and breeches. "Forgive me, I have to clean the blood off me," he said as he continued toward the bathroom.

"Yours or someone else's?" Scott asked.

"Someone else's," Roger replied and shut the door.

"Guy thinks this is a hotel," Scott griped. "Comes and goes during the day and during the night. Some people work for a living!"

Roger turned on the shower and drowned out Scott's complaints. After a few moments steam filled the room.

"Very interesting," Lavinia said, gazing into the foggy mirror over the sink.

Half dressed, Roger jumped into the tub. His feet slipped out from under him, and he landed on his butt with a splash.

"Jack Ketch accepted your gift." Lavinia slipped the gown from her shoulders, and it puddled around her bare feet. "What did you want to talk about?"

"John Fisher."

Lavinia's velvety eyes flashed. "That man bought me. Traded for me like I was a sack of grain." With that, she vanished.

Surrounded by swirling red water, Roger wiped a hand down his face. He regained his feet and finished washing.

Striding out of the bathroom, Roger took in the pervasive silence with a sigh. Scott slouched behind the sales counter, his good eye fixed on Lavinia, who walked the aisle outside the checkout touching different items. The modern pieces, she picked up, then put back down.

"How did you find me?" asked Roger.

She turned toward him. "I didn't find you. You found me."

"So it is your skull I have, isn't it?"

Hardness contorted her features. "Resurrectionists dug up my body and sold it to the medical college. They chopped me up, studied the pieces, and then discarded me as if I was trash."

Roger asked, "Is that how Doctor Glover came to possess

your skull?"

"Yes." The word, though intelligible, came out with such hate, such ire, it was as if it had been summoned from the pits of hell.

"Where's the rest of you?" Scott asked.

A bleak look overcame her. "Tossed away and forgotten."

Roger had his doubts. Her bones were somewhere. Recalling his conversation with Mister Fisher, he said, "John told me you two met on his uncle's farm."

"You mean Colonel Fisher," Lavinia said. "Did my husband tell you the Colonel was my father? Or mention John and I are cousins?"

"No."

"It wasn't public knowledge."

Roger said, "Probably would have caused a scandal if it had been."

Lavinia shrugged. "We were property. People didn't care."

Roger took her hand. "I care, and I know John cares."

Jerking back, she said, "He wants his property."

"No. You can't believe that. After all you have been through, he has stayed by your side. He could have moved on, but he didn't. He told me to tell you that he'll wait for you. The schooner for Cuba won't leave without you."

Her eyes brimmed with tears.

Roger took her hand again. "You are being used by the Jack Ketch."

"I'm not being used! I'm punishing the people responsible for our execution. I'm punishing the resurrectionists who sold me when I was dead. They all deserve to be punished!"

"Those people died a long time ago. You're punishing their descendants."

"In the alley, you saw. They're still digging people up. They're still doing evil."

Roger looked her in the eyes and saw the grey walls and barred windows of the Charleston Gaol.

"You're punishing the wrong people," he said. "They're pawns. We must go after their king. The one responsible for the attack on Six Mile."

"Sheriff Cleary," Lavinia hissed.

"No, you're not seeing the bigger picture," Roger replied.

"There's a puppet master out there pulling his strings. Find out who he is, and you'll stop the cycle."

Her face clouded over in confusion. "John was sure it was the sheriff," she said. "It never occurred to us there was someone else. We should have known when Colonel Fisher sent David Ross to claim our House. Our House!" She clenched her fists. "He got what he deserved."

"What was inside the trunk?"

She looked up at him. The grey walls had faded.

"The trunk John mentioned in his letter," said Roger. "The one he put in Reverend Furman's care. The one meant for your sister, Sally. There was something inside it; something that cursed the jurors. What was it?"

"The Colonel's book of rootwork and hexes," Lavinia said. She got a faraway look. "I was young when Doctor Glover visited the different plantations and collected the knowledge of the slaves into a journal. It discussed the medicinal use of roots and plants, but it also included some of their darker ceremonies. Being friends, he sent it to Colonel Fisher to help him in his campaign against the natives in Alabama.

"John stole it. That's what we put in the trunk. We wanted it buried so that nobody could ever use it."

CHAPTER 21
POTLUCK

Sunday, April 6, 1969

*R*oger strolled down the sidewalk. It was the final leg of his hour-long journey. The sun had yet to rise, and the morning air held a wet chill. Since his and Brie's visit to the gardens, events had spiraled out of control. Despite being tired, he tried to focus on the good things. He was clean, freshly shaven, and he wore a new bandage, yet his arm still throbbed.

After a bit of convincing, Scott let him pilfer another suit from his hoard. He had chosen a blonde wig and used a jar of skin cream to lighten his tanned skin. He still wasn't sure why Scott had it. His glasses slid down his nose, and he pushed them back. When he did, the side of his finger brushed his fake mustache, tickling his nose. A few more steps and he thrust his hands back inside the pockets of the plaid trousers. It was all part of an effort to not yank the wide paisley tie from his neck and set it aflame.

The trees bordering the sidewalk cleared, and the first of two churches came into view. Behind it would be Brie's home. Quickening his step, he passed in front of a car waiting to turn into the parking lot. Next came the school and parish hall, both owned by Brie's church. Colorful pictures of giant eggs decorated their walls. Underneath, bright banners proclaimed, "He is Risen." A steady stream of ladies carrying covered dishes entered the hall and left empty handed.

Separated by another parking lot, a crowd had begun to gather outside the sanctuary. Above the entrance, a stained-glass window glowed with a brilliant blue, orange, and yellow starburst pattern, a white cross at its center. Roger slowed as he followed a couple up the steps.

The priest, wearing white and gold robes, greeted the guests as they entered. When it was Roger's turn, he said, "Welcome. I'm Father Keating," and held out his hand.

Shaking it, Roger replied, "Greg. Greg V. Haroun."

"Please enjoy the service."

"Thank you."

Armed with his best smile, Roger stepped inside. He followed everyone's example and dipped his fingers in the font of holy water and made the sign of the cross — touching his forehead, heart, left and right shoulders. Before entering his pew, he genuflected and then slid across to the far side. He pulled out the kneeler and began to pray.

His thoughts gravitated to Brie. He still didn't know what had happened to her. Did Sheriff Cleary mistreat her, or did he keep his word and not harm her? As he tried to settle his rising ire, the image of the skull he'd left at Scott's store flashed in his mind. He hadn't mentioned it to Scott last night, but he had a strong feeling the antiques dealer was aware of it. *That's a conversation I'm not looking forward to.*

Preceded by the faint scent of diesel, Mister Tyler led his wife into the church. Behind them came Nate with Cam and Brie. They were all dressed in their best clothes, but none had a smile on their face. Brie bore dark circles under her eyes, and Roger felt as if he'd been punched in the gut.

Once they were seated, he slid out of his pew and sat in the row directly behind them. More parishioners entered, filling the pews, and soon the sanctuary was standing room only.

It was torture being this close. Roger tried to focus on the priest and his sermon, but it was hard to follow. Standing, kneeling, sitting, it reminded him of an old Korellan game, Cicero dicit fac hoc. *Cicero says do this.* Everyone around him knew the songs and prayers by heart, and when it was time for communion, he fell in line.

Father Keating raised his arms and bid everyone go in peace, ending the mass. A zing of fear shot through him when everyone stood and watched the priest walk down the center aisle. Brie glanced at Roger but didn't appear to recognize him.

Two deacons stepped up to the front row. They nodded, and those attendants filed past them. The deacons moved down the aisle, motioning as they went, which gave the crowd at the narthex time to disperse. The Tylers exited, and then his row was selected.

Roger kept his eyes on the back of Brie's head, afraid she'd disappear if he turned away. At the narthex, the priest spoke to each parishioner. When the Tylers approached, he took Brie by the hand and gave her a hug. The others departed, letting the two have a moment.

Roger exited, and Father Keating asked, "Did you enjoy the service?"

"I did. Thank you."

Brie gave him a wan smile and held out her hand. "My name's Brie Tyler."

Roger steadied his breathing and tried not to tremble when he took her hand. "Greg. Greg Haroun."

"Nice to meet you."

The priest seemed to recall something and said, "Vee?"

"Excuse me," Roger said, alarms going off in his head.

"Wasn't that your middle initial?" Father Keating asked. He eyed Roger like he had already added him to his flock. "Greg V. Haroun, the Church Ladies are serving breakfast in the parish hall. I hope you'll join us. It'll give you a chance to meet everyone. Later, we're hosting an Easter egg hunt."

"Sounds interesting," Roger replied, not sure what strange tradition the priest was referencing. He imagined giant eggs sprouting legs, and everyone chasing them with nets. *No, that couldn't be it.*

"Go with God, Mister Haroun."

"Thank you, Father."

Brie remained by the priest's side. The narthex filled with eager parishioners, politely forcing Roger to keep moving. He passed near Nate and Cam. They held hands. For them, it was the biggest display of affection he'd seen.

When Brie didn't come out, Mister Tyler began moving back inside. She appeared at the entrance, and he relaxed. Roger kept his distance, trying to figure out a way to talk with her and not make a scene. He looked back, and the family was already heading toward the parish hall. Family. He watched them for a moment, secretly reveling in their closeness. At least Brie had people to support her. It made him miss home even more.

There were things he wanted her to know, to tell her he was sorry. However, he also wanted to prepare her. She needed to know what was coming.

Then again, it might be better if she didn't know.

Letting out a quiet sigh, he decided to leave and began his hour-long trek toward the Charleston peninsula. He paused under an oak copse and stared east toward the sunrise. *The best thing I can do for her is to leave her alone. Let her start over. Forget all...*

There was a rush, and someone punched him in the arm.

"Vee? Really?" Brie said. "I can't believe you came here. The one place everyone's expecting you to show up."

"I couldn't stay away," Roger replied.

"Dummy, they'll catch you. Greg V. Haroun? How long did it take you to come up with that name?"

"I didn't. Scott did."

A serious look crossed her face, and she said, "You shouldn't have told me that. You need to hide. Take a vacation, something."

"What, you think people will see through my disguise?

She hit his arm again, and he winced.

"You're hurt," Brie said, concern filling her eyes.

Roger looked around, making sure no one noticed them. He removed his jacket, and a thin, red line marred his shirt sleeve. "This is nothing. The Mercurochrome I put on it was a hell of a lot worse."

Brie's look of horror said it all.

"Brie, are you okay?" Nate asked as he approached. "Your parents were worried."

They both turned. Brie grabbed the young officer by the arms and said, "Now don't freak out."

His face clouded over. "Freak out? About what?"

Roger could tell Nate was trying to process what was happening. He stared at Roger, and then recognition blossomed.

"That's... What's he...?"

"Nate, you're freaking out," said Brie. "Take deep breaths."

"He's not supposed to be here." Nate faced Roger. "You're not supposed to be here. I have to arrest you."

Still holding Nate back, Brie said in a calm, steady voice, "He's not the one who killed the lieutenant, and he's not the one who killed that man yesterday. You have to know that."

The tension in Roger's gut evaporated. He kept the smile from his face but hearing her proclaim his innocence was a balm to his aching heart.

Wearing his black shirt with its distinctive white collar, Father Keating walked up and asked, "Is everything all right?"

"Yes, Father," Brie replied, letting Nate go.

"Why don't you join us?" the priest suggested.

Roger put his coat back on and said, "Thank you, Father, but no. I should be leaving."

Grabbing Roger by the elbow, Brie said, "Mr. Haroun hurt his arm and needs a bandage."

"Oh goodness, follow me. We have a first aid kit in the rectory."

Nate frowned at them. It was obvious that uncertainty was at war with his sense of duty.

Father Keating led them beside the parish hall to a door nested inside the crook of an adjoining wing. He took out a ring of keys and opened it. The scent of bacon and sausage rolled over them. Moving down the hall in the opposite direction from the aroma, the priest unlocked his office and invited them inside.

"Here it is," he said pulling out a metal box similar to the one at the freight station. "Sit down, Mr. Haroun."

Nate took the box and said, "Father, let me do it."

"Fine by me," he replied. "I'm sure your police training comes in handy."

"Yes, sir, it does."

"Y'all seem to be in good hands. If you don't mind, I'm going to grab some food while it's hot. Nate and Brie, don't let Greg leave without introducing him to everyone."

"We won't, Father," Brie replied.

Roger took off the jacket and rolled up his sleeve. Blood had seeped out from under the dressing.

Nate removed the bandage and pressed another one against Roger's arm. "Is this where I shot you?"

"What!" Brie exclaimed. "Why did you shoot him?"

"He killed the lieutenant and threw a knife at me."

"Nate, I did *not* kill him. Lieutenant Bell saved my life. It was his last act." Roger looked into the younger man's eyes, imploring him to believe him. "As for the dagger, I never intended to hit you. I only wanted to distract you from shooting me."

"Your fingerprints were all over the weapon."

"Yes, I held it, and yes, I fired it, but I swear to the Eternal Father, I was aiming at Mister Davis. Even then, I still missed."

Nate had a strange look on his face. It was like the facts

added up, but they went in a direction that made him uncomfortable. "Davis. His name was on *your* list, along with Mister Wheelen, the man in the alley." He tied off the bandage and began putting everything back in the box. "They found your dagger beside his body. Eyewitnesses saw you running from the scene. There was no one else in that alley. S.L.E.D. is saying you killed Mister Hart and Mister Packer, too."

Roger gave him a grim smile. "Sherrif Cleary confiscated my knives, and I only own two daggers — the one I have with me, and the one I lost at the train yard. Do you know what happened to it?"

"It's in evidence. I logged it in myself." Nate hesitated. "All the evidence points to you being this mass murderer. Now that Lieutenant Bell is gone, there's no one to defend you."

"Someone is going out of their way to entrap me," Roger said, unrolling his sleeve and rebuttoning the cuff.

"Major Wilson's out there leading a city-wide manhunt. He will find you."

"Maybe."

Nate returned the first aid kit to its shelf. "You need to see a doctor."

"I plan to."

"What's going on?" Mister Tyler asked from the door. "Your mother's worried." Brie's father eyed them with disapproval. Despite his receding hairline that held streaks of grey in otherwise black hair and his medium build, Roger could see traces of Brie and Cam in his features.

"Mister Haroun hurt his arm," Brie answered.

"He looks fine now," Mister Tyler said.

"It's my fault," Nate said. "We started talking shop and lost track of time."

"I see." Mister Tyler studied Roger. An ex-submariner, he had keen eyes that were used to picking out small details. "Your mustache is crooked."

Roger pressed it back in place, smoothing it out in the process.

Mister Tyler interposed himself between Roger and Brie and drew in a deep breath. "You are not welcome here. You are not to see Brie; you are not to come near my family. Do I make myself clear?" He spoke in a low tone that belied the violence in his eyes.

"Father..." Brie cried.

"Brie, don't start." Mister Tyler pointed at Roger. "This man is a killer. You've seen the news." He turned to Nate. "Protect this family. Arrest him."

A helpless expression on his face, Nate went pale as he turned from Mister Tyler to Roger.

Roger stood with his hands to either side. "Mister Tyler, I'm innocent. Please believe me. Ask Nate, ask Brie. Arresting me will not stop the killings. There's something else at work in this city, and it revolves around a one-hundred-fifty-year-old conspiracy and a list of jurors."

"Do you honestly expect me to believe that? It's easier to think you found this list, and you're bent on killing people with the same names. And I'm not the only one." Mister Tyler took a step toward Roger. "As far as I'm concerned, you are trouble. You have been ever since you showed up." Looking Roger in the eyes, he said, "You don't belong in this world."

"You're wrong, Mister Tyler," Nate said. "He's trying to help. You want to protect your family. So do I." Nate took Mister Tyler by the arm and said, "Knowledge is the best protection. A wise man told me I can't bury my head in the sand. We have to keep our eyes open. Yes, his theory sounds crazy, but I'm willing to give him a chance to prove himself. What if he's right? If he's arrested, you know they'll bury him under the jail, and we'll never see him again."

"He saved my life, Father," Brie said. "He's in this world because of me."

Mister Tyler turned his gaze on Nate, then Brie. His eyes softened, though his expression remained stern. "All right, Mister Haroun, prove yourself."

"Yes, sir," Roger said with a nod.

Roger eased around Mister Tyler toward the door.

He had reached the threshold when Brie wrapped him in a tight hug. She whispered, "Mister Haroun, you bring Roger back to me, you hear?"

Handing her one of the two silver reales from his pocket, he said, "I will."

Before she could pull away, he said, "Remember Yorick," and he left her with a confused look on her face.

CHAPTER 22
THE BOTANIST

Monday, April 7, 1969

*I*t was nearing nine o'clock, and the Glover residence still showed no signs of waking. Separated from the harbor by a seawall, it was one of several posh mansions that lined the waterfront, their manicured lawns glistening with dew. To the east, White Point Gardens marked the tip of the peninsula. Car traffic was sparse, but the Battery was already busy with tourists taking pictures.

Since Scott wouldn't loan him more clothes, Roger wore the same suit as yesterday, minus the glasses and wig. However, he had one addition: leather gloves. He had tired of handling everything with a handkerchief. Besides, he had learned a lesson from the dærganfae: people tended to ignore you if you wore a suit and acted with authority.

Roger leaned back against the railing and checked the address on the envelope he had found in Doctor Glover's courier pouch. Unlike its neighbors, this home had a tall brick wall stretching from the corner of the house to surround a second lot. An ornate, wrought-iron gate allowed outsiders a glimpse of the lush garden within, as well as the sprawling piazza.

Crossing the street, Roger peered through the gate. The yard was deserted. The metal gate shifted soundlessly in the soft sea breeze. Surprised by the slipshod security of such a grand home, he studied the garden more intently.   A bluestone walkway led to sweeping brick steps that flanked a porticoed entrance. Gravel paths snaked their way through thick greenery, and a riot of bold flowers fought for space in mounded beds or spilled from hanging pots. Birdsong filled the air.

Fortune favors the bold. He strode through the gate, pausing only long enough to close it.

Roger peered through the sidelight at the grand entrance with its high ceiling. The room was quiet and still. A minute passed, then two with no activity. He briefly wondered why a house so large had no servants. At the very least, he expected a butler and a housekeeper. Brow furrowed as he contemplated the odd situation, he tried the latch. Like the gate, it opened with ease.

Closing the door behind him, he began searching the first floor. He went from the formal dining room into the kitchen. The table with its array of chairs and placemats, the shelf with Lowcountry cookbooks, even the utensils hanging from the cabinets were in their proper place. Everything gleamed as if recently polished. There was no dust, no signs of disturbance. It didn't have the lived-in feel of a home — this was a house for display.

Roger smelled copper as he crossed the hall, and a sinking feeling formed in his gut. Moving through the formal living room, he followed the odor. Hand near his dagger, he crept down an arched passageway, passed a water-closet, and entered a library.

Illuminated by sunlight streaming through the window, Doctor Joseph Glover lay naked in the middle of a blood-soaked area rug. Deep gashes scored his back, legs, and arms; the killer had taken part of the doctor's ear and cropped his nose. He'd suffered Death by a Thousand Cuts. Blood spattered the windows, wood paneled walls, and spines of books, creating odd patterns.

Roger knelt at the edge of the rug and tried to say a prayer, but the words would not come. Doctor Glover wasn't on the list of jurors. His death didn't fit the pattern. Rising, he moved about the room. There was no message here, at least not one written out. Lavinia Fisher hadn't done this.

It appeared that the creature from his nightmare, the Jack Ketch, had found another tool to mete out his twisted punishments.

Roger traced his finger across several botanical books written by various Doctor Glovers. They spanned generations, with the newest being the one from the current doctor's office. He slid out the oldest, written in 1810. Thumbing through the pages, he found a similar flowing script as John Blake White's eyewitness account. Each page held a precise pencil sketch of an herb or root and explained their medicinal value. He replaced the book exactly as it had been.

Roger stared down at the body, the sickening weight of responsibility settling over him. The one man he was certain knew the details of the jurors' curse was dead. Had he led the Jack Ketch to Doctor Glover? Or — worse — by stealing Lavinia's skull from the doctor's office, had he taken away the one talisman protecting the man from the hidden figure at the head of the conspiracy?

A soft click sounded. Roger spun on his heel as a section of bookcase rotated in place, revealing a hidden room. A young man leapt out, a pistol held out in front of him with both hands.

Roger lunged and chopped down on the man's wrists, knocking away the gun, and struck him in the solar plexus. The blow should have driven the air from his opponent's lungs and made drawing his next breath painful.

The gunman just grinned as he tried to headbutt Roger. Dark grey prison bars shone in his eyes.

Swaying to the side, Roger grabbed him by the collar and, using the man's weight against him, threw him across the room. He followed up with a sharp kick to the stomach.

The man collapsed back into the shelves, books spilling down around him. Regaining his feet, he pulled out a knife with a narrow, pointed blade that extended automatically. Bits of dried blood clung to its edge and stained the handle. "You just made the biggest mistake of your life."

Roger unsheathed his own weapon. Longer than a typical knife, the silver dagger flashed in the sunlight. "I doubt it."

The two circled, each feinting and probing the other's defenses. The killer thrust at Roger's belly.

With reflexes honed by years of fighting, Roger spun and unleashed a pommel strike onto the back of his attacker's neck.

The man fell to the floor, losing his knife as he tried to brace himself. A small, blood-soaked bundle landed on the rug beneath him.

Roger bent down and grabbed a fistful of the man's hair with one hand and pressed his blade to his throat with the other. "Unless you're prepared to die right here, you'll do as I say."

The man's fingers crept toward the bundle.

"Uh uh," warned Roger. He increased the pressure with his blade. It nicked the man's skin, and a drop of blood fell to the floor.

If his prisoner felt the cut, he didn't show it. "You cannot stop what's coming."

"And what might that be?" demanded Roger.

"Jack Ketch will rebuild his tower and take his due."

A jolt of fear stabbed through Roger. He drew back his fist and struck his prisoner's temple, felling him. In a matter of moments, he had the man bound to a heavy, ornate chair using curtain tie-back chords. Inside the bloody bundle, he found the missing bits of Dr. Glover's ear and nose.

Roger left the bloody evidence where it lay and turned his attention to the secret room behind the bookcase. Rather than a converted closet like at the medical college, a short flight of stairs led down into the doctor's cellar. The half-basement was larger than Roger expected, almost equal in size to the library.

Against the lefthand masonry wall, a long worktable held crucibles, mortars and pestles in an array of sizes, and an elaborate configuration of glass tubes, flasks, retorts, and vials. Above it, a row of glass-doored cabinets held labeled jars of liquids, herbs, and minerals. Carved into the brickwork on the room's other side were columns of arcane sigils. Between them, shrunken heads, grotesque dolls, and demonic masks leered from hooks.

Centered in the cellar, a copper cauldron and tripod occupied a bronze circle set in the concrete floor. The remnants of a salt ring lay smeared over the metal, rendering both rings useless. Roger crept forward. At the cardinal points, smaller circles were painted on the floor in what appeared to be blood, long dried. Each held strange, twisted symbols, along with a bit of hangman's rope, an empty wine bottle, a pair of manacles, and a coiled whip.

Dreading what he would find, Roger peered inside the cauldron. All that remained of the contents were ashes, soot, and a few small bone fragments.

Making a sign against evil, Roger retreated to an altar with an open binder sitting upon the lectern. Brie had several for her schoolwork, but not like this one. Clear film pockets held ragged-edged, yellowed pages. On the uppermost, spidery script surrounded a diagram of the circle around the cauldron. The few words he managed to decipher led him to believe they were instructions for banishing a spirit. If so, it was a much more complicated spell than the one he'd hoped to have Vie — or perhaps Tee — use on Lavinia if he found her remains, requiring items important to the spirit in life.

Roger reexamined the items around the circle. The ashes in the cauldron could only belong to one person: the Jack Ketch.

Doctor Glover had tried to banish the Executioner. Why didn't the spell work? Roger rubbed his chin. The spell not working meant only one thing — the Executioner was more than your average ghost tied to its mortal remains. He was bound to something else; something larger.

Even more puzzling, how did the doctor acquire his skeleton? Roger shook his head. It defied all logic — unless he'd known the Executioner haunted the Old City Gaol all along.

"Untie me!" The sudden shout from the library pulled Roger from his musings. Flipping through the binder's pages, he discovered a strange mix of alchemy, root-work, and necromantic spells. Of those, the least vile was one for summoning a spirit. He couldn't know for sure, but the pages reminded him of the book Lavinia had described, or at least a part of it. Unsnapping the binder's rings, he removed the summoning spell and slid the pages inside his shirt.

Unwilling to leave the binder for someone else to find and use, he placed it on the concrete floor, doused it with paraffin oil, and lit a match. The film curled and melted. He waited to make sure the pages caught before returning to the library.

He found his prisoner struggling to free himself.

"Don't bother," said Roger, kicking aside the stiletto. "You won't get free without a good, sharp blade."

The man in the chair glared at Roger. The dull grey bars faded from his eyes, revealing irises of a startlingly brilliant shade of green. "You're a dead man, mister."

Roger shrugged. It wasn't the first nor, in all probability, would it be the last time someone made that threat against him. "We all die eventually," he responded. "Now, who are you, and why did you kill Doctor Glover?"

"Bastard! I'm not taking the blame for this." His eyes flicked to the doctor, then to the secret door and the burning pages.

Kneeling beside the chair, Roger studied the young man.

"You didn't know the secret room was there, did you?"

The man tugged against the rope.

"You don't have to answer," Roger said. "I can see it on your face. You have no clue what happened to the doctor."

"You killed him!" he spat.

"And you probably never met the Jack Ketch."

Fear flickered across the young man's face, and he swallowed hard. "It was just a nightmare," he whispered.

For a moment, Roger pitied the fellow. Then, he remembered the murder of Lieutenant Bell. "That's Doctor Glover's blood on your clothes, and there are bits of Doctor Glover in your handkerchief. Do you remember, now?"

The man in the chair glanced down at his clothes. His eyes went wide, and he began to tremble. "I didn't. I wouldn't."

Roger leaned closer. "Tell me. Why were you here?"

"To protect him from you! This is all your fault. You're the one digging into the past. Hart, Packer, Davis, Wheelen, and now the doctor. You're killing us off, one at a time."

"Who's us?" asked Roger.

"Naw, man. I'm not gonna talk."

Roger stood and looked out the window. "I understand. You're a loyal follower, a soldier." Turning back to the man in the chair, Roger said, "But there's no one who can help you, now. You're alone. Lavinia's hunting all of you, and she won't stop until she has her revenge."

The man tied to the chair gasped. "Revenge for what? I didn't do anything to her." He shivered, and patches of red blossomed on his cheeks and forehead.

"You're sick, just like Hart and Packer, just like your father and his father before him."

Nodding miserably, the man responded, "Doctor Glover was supposed to give me a treatment today." Another fit of shaking overtook him.

"Listen... What's your name?"

"W... w... Will Owens."

"Mister Owens, tell me who you work for, and I'll send someone to help you."

"Why would you help me?"

Roger stared into Will's eyes. "Because I'm the only one who can stop Lavinia and stop the curse."

Will's eyes rolled back into his head, and he quivered

uncontrollably. A low moan escaped him.

Roger leapt forward, grabbing Will to steady him. The young man's skin was burning hot. With a muttered oath, Roger lowered the chair onto its side, then ran to the nearby water-closet for a wet towel. He wiped Will's face, then wrung out the towel in the man's hair. Finally, the seizure subsided.

Roger gripped his shoulder and shook it gently. "Come on, Will. I need answers. Who do you work for?"

Taking a ragged breath, he whispered, "Fogartie. Jim Fogartie."

"Where do I find him?" Roger asked.

"They'll... they'll kill me." Waves of heat emanated from Will's skin, and he began to shake again.

Roger tightened his grip. "Will, listen to me. If I don't unravel what's happening, you and your gang of conspirators are going to die — either from the curse or by Lavinia's undead hand. Talk to me."

"Downtown. Ch...Chapel Street. Don't... tell them... I... told... you."

Roger started to assure him, but Will had fallen unconscious. *Damn. The boy really did need help.*

Thinking quickly, he took Will's handkerchief and stiletto down into Doctor Glover's laboratory and placed them in a large ceramic crucible. In one of the cabinets, he found what he needed: oil of vitriol. It bubbled and fizzed in the crucible, dissolving the handkerchief, blood, and tissue. While the acid did its work, he made sure the binder was destroyed, and the fire extinguished. With one last look around to be certain he hadn't missed anything, Roger closed the revolving bookcase and took his leave.

Exiting through the front door, he left both it and the gate wide open, counting on at least one nosey neighbor to notice and investigate. Then, he fell in behind a group of tourists.

A woman with a small, fluffy dog scowled at the group as she passed. Roger surreptitiously watched her stop at the open gate, mutter to the dog, and make her way inside the house. They had just reached White Point Garden two blocks east when he heard approaching sirens.

Zigzagging through the neighborhood, Roger put as

much distance as he could between himself and Doctor Glover's house. As he walked, he twisted and turned the pieces of this strange puzzle in his mind. However, one piece jumped out to the forefront: the Jack Ketch was trying to rebuild his tower, and somehow, he was using Lavinia to do it.

Roger crossed Broad Street, knowing full well he was making a reckless move. He didn't care. He had to discover the truth for himself.

Even in daylight, the Charleston Gaol held a sinister air. He noted the cracks and barred windows. It was what he had seen in Lavinia's eyes Saturday night, and Will Owens' this morning. John Fisher had been right. The Jack Ketch wasn't dead. His memory lived on in each and every one of his victims, and he appeared to be claiming new ones.

Roger's vision swam and grew dark. It was his nightmare from earlier, with one difference. This time, rather than Queen Ambrose, it was Brie he saw.

Hands stretched toward the ceiling and her feet bound, she hung in the middle of an iron plated room. Blood dripped from her ripped skin and ran along the floor into a drain. Roger reached out, yelling her name, but she didn't respond.

"It was you who did this," a voice said.

The floor gave way, and a noose constricted about his neck.

Jerking back to the present, Roger sucked in a deep breath. He swayed on his feet. The gaol's entrance loomed in front of him. Enraged, he charged toward the gate and gripped the bars, rattling the padlock and chain binding them.

"Jack Ketch!"

"Jack Ketch!"

"Jack Ketch!"

Roger stopped cold when he saw the creature reflected in the glass door behind the gate. Haggard and pale, it more closely resembled an articulated skeleton than anything remotely human. Deep black, recessed eyes peered out its skull.

"You're dead!" Roger yelled. "The doctor destroyed you! We destroyed you!"

"Et malus homo de malo thesauro profert malum. Ex

abundantia enim cordis os loquitur. *Evil people do the evil that is in them. For the mouth speaks out of the abundance of the heart.* There's a Jack Ketch in everyone. It's the part of the soul that seeks to punish the wrongdoers, that hungers to drink their blood, and revel in their misery."

"No! You're wrong! You are not a part of me."

The ghost's countenance stretched into a leering grin.

Roger rested his forehead against the gate. He wasn't a holy man who knew the intricacies of the universe. He was a thief and a spy.

"How many have you killed in the Highlord's name?" the creature asked. "Though you deny it, you *are* one of my turnkeys. Culpae poena par esto. *Let the punishment fit the crime.* I demand servitude."

"I will never be one of your gaolers," said Roger as he pushed himself away. "I will not help you rebuild that tower."

The chain and padlock fell to the sidewalk, and the gate swung open.

A chill wind swept past. "Murderer," the sepulchral voice whispered. "Everyone believes you killed those men. Join with me. I am the only one who can save Bryony Tyler. I can save her from finding out who you really are."

Roger shook his head. "I will not deal with the Dark One."

"You already have."

Backing away, Roger noticed people staring at him like he had gone mad. The creature was gone; the gate locked. Only he remained. Maybe he was going mad.

Wild eyed, Roger ran his hands through his hair. *Think! There has to be a way to stop the Jack Ketch.* Vie's face surfaced.

He shoved his way past the crowd and raced down the street.

CHAPTER 23
BESIEGED

Monday, April 7, 1969

*R*oger ran from the Gaol. From the people gathered there. From Jack Ketch. From himself.

He had been such a fool to believe he could face the Jack Ketch alone and unarmed. The Executioner's words were like daggers twisting deep inside Roger's heart, but he refused to believe that his small part in the war against the Dark One had been anything but necessary. Yes, he had killed, but he had also saved lives.

Stranded on Terra, he felt truly alone for the first time. Guilt welled up. Faces of the ones he had killed in the name of the Highlord flashed before him. Had he been doing the Dark One's bidding without even realizing it? He wanted to scream.

The sudden screech of tires and the blare of a horn startled him from his crazed thoughts. Panting, he waved to the driver and hurried onto the sidewalk. The sun beat down, and he felt sweat trickle down his spine. The sensation drove away the last vestiges of panic.

No. His fight was with the Jack Ketch — a ghost with no remains. Fist to heart, he made himself a solemn vow. He had found Lavinia. Now, he would find a way to turn her, stop the curse, and put an end to the Jack Ketch once and for all.

Getting his bearings, he resumed a tourist's pace. Along the way he added the glasses back to his disguise. Roger exited Harleston Village, fear replaced by stoic determination.

Hands at his sides, he passed in front of the shrievalty and crossed the street. He needed to test himself, force himself to calm down. A steady flow of patrol cars passed, but no one paid him any mind. He knew that if you looked like you belonged, no one bothered you. It also helped to be near the one place no one would look for him.

North of the station, the pedestrian traffic thinned. Vacant houses lined the street, some on the verge of collapse.

Seeing them reminded Roger of the Fogartie Construction sign. It had been outside Vie's car when they had stopped for the LTD.

He moved into the commercial district of Upper King Street. Many of the buildings had rotted from the inside out, leaving brick husks. He crossed Meeting Street and turned north. Weathered clapboard residences with dirt yards crowded the narrow lane. They were so close together you could reach out the window and touch your neighbor's house. Outside, children played hide and seek amongst the brick piers within the crawlspace. A heavyset woman stepped onto the front porch and crossed her arms. He kept his eyes straight ahead, avoiding her distrustful glare.

Roger was struck by the disparity between the homes south of Broad and here on the east side. Of course, money played into it, but there was something else. It was as though the city had given up on this neighborhood. Admittedly, the peninsula was in what Brie called a transition phase. Charleston was trying to better itself and attract businesses. You could tell that from the capital improvements along Market Street and around the City Marina. However, the spotlight on that part of the city had cast a shadow over the East Side.

A patrol car drove toward him. Not wanting to look suspicious, Roger kept walking. The car slowed to a stop, and the helmsman rolled down his window. "This is a dangerous part of town, mister," the constable said. "Where you headed?"

Roger stepped closer to the window. Trying to recall the article he had read in the newspaper, he looked over the vehicle at the buildings across the street before turning to the constable. "I work for Fogartie construction," he explained in his best southern accent. "A developer wants to demolish some of the homes near the corner of Columbus and build apartments. The neighbors called the mayor's office to protest and caused a big stink. If you ask me, I don't see what all the hullabaloo was about. The buildings look like they're about to collapse anyways."

The constable gave a short laugh and said, "Well, be careful."

"Yes, sir. I will."

The patrol car moved on, and Roger watched it for a

moment before continuing north. After two blocks, the street ended abruptly at the Cooper River Bridge accesses, and he turned right.

It took him a moment to realize the road connecting Charleston to Mount Pleasant had sundered the neighborhood. He thought back to what Vie had told him about eminent domain. Uprooted by the government and isolated, he began to understand what had happened to the people of Porter Manor.

Long rows of tenant housing abounded on the other side of the crosstown. Patrol cars became more frequent, and Roger found it harder to look like he belonged the farther north and east he went. He stopped when he came to Newmarket Creek and the surrounding marshes. Instead of crossing it at one of the major roads, he fell in behind a group of men heading toward a nearby church. Across the street, a cluster of buildings and a railroad spur fronted the creek bank.

The smell of food grew stronger as he drew closer to a squat building beside the church. A line of men trailed out the door along with a few women and children. All wore threadbare clothes. Some had holes in their shoes; others were barefooted.

"Buckruh, wuffuh oonuh in dese parts?"

Roger spotted RC, the skinny youth from Porter Manor.

Approaching him, Roger replied, "Walking."

The youth smiled. "Hungry?"

Roger's stomach growled at the thought of food.

"Hyuh. Oonuh brek de line in front ub me."

"RC, whatcha doin?" asked the man behind them.

"'E awright. 'E uh fren' ub Miss Violet."

The mere mention of her name was like electricity. The people in line still eyed him warily, but there was a reluctant acceptance. It occurred to Roger that the people here had the church, but they had their root doctor, too.

Once inside, Roger followed the line to a row of servers who handed him a bowl and spoon. Another server dipped a ladle into a steaming pot and emptied it into his dish. Someone handed him a piece of bread and a cup of sweet tea. Balancing the food and drink, he searched for an empty seat at a table. The pastor, who walked the aisles spreading the Word of the Eternal Father, directed him to a place next to

RC.

Hunched over his food, Roger swirled the different vegetables through the red juice with his spoon and asked, "What is it?"

Laughing, RC replied, "Okra soup. Try it. 'E put a tas'e in yo mout'."

RC was right. It was good, and Roger began shoveling it down.

"Chile, that hag almost ride me to death last night," he overheard an elderly lady say to the younger one at her side.

Roger looked over. "A what?"

"A boo hag," the young woman replied.

He remembered Gramma Huger calling Vie a boo hag, and it piqued his interest. He must have had a questioning look on his face because the woman leaned closer and whispered, "It's an evil spirit that turns you inside out."

"Inside out?"

"Not like that. It doesn't ooze all over you. It means you're normal during the day, but at night you're different. Totally different. Your manner is turned inside out."

The elderly woman spoke up. "De boo hag flies t'ru de air en' sneaks inna yo'own house while yuh sleeping, like unda yo do' or t'ru a crack in de flo'boa'd. 'E lights on yo back, steals yo skin, and rides yuh all night. 'E teks a toll on yuh, too. 'Um hurts yuh, ridin' yuh 'til dey's nutt'n' lef', en' if 'e does'um long 'nuf, 'e ride yuh inna duh grave."

Roger looked down at his soup, his appetite gone.

"How do you protect yourself from it?" he asked.

"If my mother caught us sleeping on our stomachs, she'd flip us over," the younger lady answered. "It can't get you if you sleep on your back."

"With the way I sleep, that wouldn't work," Roger mused. "Is there another way?"

"You'd have to ask Miss Violet," she said. "Or Gramma Huger might know — if you can get to her."

Roger caught the concern in her voice. "What happened?"

RC replied, "Attuh oonuh go'way, the rollers quizzit 'bout you, 'bout weh yuh got. Start han'ling Miss Violet real rough. That bex us all. We fought dem all de way to de fence, and dey barricaded de skreets. No one gits in or out ub Porter Manor now. Leastways not b'dout dem leabe."

"And Miss Violet? Gramma Huger?"

"She dey. Hol' hostage. Dey tell'um yuh 'sponsubble fuh warruh happ'n. Tells us tuh find Miss Violet's fren' en' let um know. Dey gwine hu't her mo' if oonuh don't show up."

"Why would the constabulary do that?" Roger asked.

Anger filled RC's voice when he said, "It's luk Malcom say. A hund'ud yeah ago, buckrah usetuh wear a white sheet and use dogs 'gense us. Teday dey hab tek'off dem white sheets and put on police uniforms and traded dey bloodhounds fuh police dogs."

The young woman's face became pinched as if she smelled something rotten. "RC, you hush up. It's not the police. It's dat special agent."

"Yiz all ub dem," RC said. "The Town fuhr'ebbuh hol' us down. Luk warruh dey done wid'em new roads."

Not knowing the history, Roger felt awkward listening to RC. Back home on Gaia, he worked for the Highlord, the ruler of Gallowen. He had no doubt RC would have considered him an authority figure, especially if he knew his family was part of the ruling class. Despite the good intentions, there had always been conflict between progress and the status quo. However, the greater good was little comfort when it was your children who suffered.

Roger pushed those thoughts aside. He looked up from his soup and asked, "RC, can we get to Vie without taking the road?"

A smile stretched across the youth's face. "Me know uh way. Get t'ru wit yo soup, den we go."

The sun dropped below the horizon as Roger followed RC down Huger Street to where it ended at the railroad tracks Roger had been on a few nights before. They crossed them and headed toward the marshy shores of the Cooper River. Roger expected to get wet, or at least muddy. Instead, they entered a grove of stubby trees that jutted into the water and traveled along an abandoned railroad spur. The tracks stopped at the river. RC pushed aside the cordgrass, revealing a johnboat.

Sliding the boat into the black water, Roger jumped in the back with the fishing rod and tackle box, grabbed an oar, and shoved clear of the bank. In front, RC dipped his oar into the water and pointed the nose upriver. Overhead, the last rays of the sun cast a shadow across the city.

"Miss Violet say yuh not from 'round hyuh. Dat yuh from 'cross de ocean," RC said as he paddled.

"Sort of," Roger replied, not sure how to respond.

"I nebbeh bin outside Chaa'stun. Wudduh luk?"

"Similar in some ways, very different in others. Where I'm from, we have a Highlord who rules over us. We have monsters and heroes, same as here. No cars, though. No electricity, either."

"Yuh funnin' me. Not eben de rich fo'ks got 'lectricity?"

"No." Roger considered for a moment. "Well, if you don't count dragons and, perhaps, some mages."

RC laughed. "Now uh know yuh tellin' tales." He was silent for a minute, then said, "Yo accent is skrange. Sound luk'um frum England or sumpin'."

Roger grinned. "If you think my accent is strange, you should listen to yours."

RC's back stiffened. Roger realized he'd said the wrong thing.

"Wuh's wrong wid'um?"

"Nothing," he quickly assured the youth. "It's just different from anything I ever heard before arriving in Charleston."

RC huffed. "Paddle de boat, buckruh."

Resisting the urge to say something more, Roger did as he was told.

The sky darkened and lights dotted the city. RC kept them close to the west bank of the river. He maintained a steady pace that didn't create much of a wake.

Roger found his thoughts drifting as he stared toward the far east bank. For an instant, he thought he saw a large shape glide across the water. He tried to focus on the object, but with no lights on the far shore, it was black on black. "How much farther?"

"Jus' ahead," the teenager replied, pointing. "Dats spiles frum the harbor. Dey's an inlet on de odduh end."

"Will we be near the Navy Base?"

"Nah."

After three-quarters of a mile, the inlet came into view, and beyond it, the lights from Porter Manor silhouetted the manmade island surrounded by a chain link barricade topped with barbed wire. Stubby trees and cordgrass grew along the riverbank; however, the land within the fence was barren and devoid of life.

Once the johnboat touched solid ground, RC jumped out and dragged it ashore with Roger still in it.

"Uh hide it over dey," RC said, lifting the front end.

If RC pointed or nodded, Roger couldn't tell. He was just grateful the lights from Porter Manor were enough to guide him. He hefted the back end and followed RC to a tall patch of grass.

"Keep tuh de fence," RC warned before racing down the perimeter path.

Not able to dispel the feeling he was being watched, Roger looked over his shoulder one last time before chasing after the youth.

As they neared the apartments, Roger caught glimpses of flashing blue lights. RC crouched inside a copse overshadowing the sandy path between the tenant housing and the spoils. The railroad tracks ran directly in front of them.

"De rollers blocked de road," RC said, "but dey not watchin' de maa'sh."

Roger had his misgivings. Stooped next to RC, he studied the well-lit parking lots. There were a few cars, but most of the cover would come from the buildings themselves.

"Where are Gramma Huger and Miss Violet?" Roger asked.

RC pointed to a group of buildings opposite a road ending at a cul-de-sac with a ring of bushes at its center.

"Can we get a message to them?" Roger asked. "Maybe we can meet somewhere closer?"

"If we go t'ru dey," RC said, gesturing to the cul-de-sac, "de rollers won't see'um." Excitement lit the youth's eyes when he nodded toward a path through the grass.

"Stay calm and look like you belong," Roger said.

"Uh do belong, buckruh," RC snapped.

"Not you, me," Roger replied, still watching the parking lot. "It's something I've been telling myself since I got here."

"Oh," RC said.

"Not to worry. One day, you'll be as crazy as me." Roger stood up and gave the teenager a jaunty smile.

"No t'engky," RC replied.

They crept down the path and passed through a gap in

the fencing that surrounded Porter Manor, no doubt cut by RC.

Assuming a guise of purpose, Roger walked a step behind the teenager. It may not have been necessary. Everyone, it seemed, had retired for the evening. However, the feeling of being watched only grew.

They followed the sidewalk as it wound around the cul-de-sac. RC stopped at the intersection and looked both ways. Buildings shielded them from the entrances to the apartment complex so only the reflection of blue lights was visible.

"This way," RC said.

On the other side, more apartments flanked a mostly empty parking lot. Like the others, it was well lit. They aimed for the building on the right and stopped at the last door.

Roger kept an eye over his shoulder. It was nighttime, but it wasn't late. There should have been people about, especially with the police presence. Unless everyone was afraid.

RC knocked.

Vie cracked open the door. Her eyes went wide when she recognized Roger. Opening it the rest of the way, she pulled them both inside and shut the door.

"What are you doing here?" she asked. Light from a tall lamp beside the couch illuminated Vie's swollen lip and the dark bruise marring the side of her face. She wore a long-sleeved pajama shirt that hung below her knees.

Roger took a step toward her. His fists clenched at his sides. "Who did this?" he demanded. "Give me a name." Frustration and anger consumed him. He was weary of this world, and he wanted to lash out at someone.

Vie placed an open hand on his chest. "What are you going to do?"

"I'm going to teach them to not hit a woman."

"Roger, stop. You can't fix this. Let it go."

"You weren't supposed to get hurt," Roger said, pushing against her. "Where's your pilot, Dennis? He should have protected you."

Vie pushed back. "Arrested. Just like you'll be if you go out there. There's a curfew."

"They shouldn't have hurt you," he said through gritted

teeth.

Hand still on his chest, Vie searched his eyes. The cobalt intensified, and he had a hard time meeting her gaze.

"Something's different about you," she said.

"It's been a rough day."

The door crashed open.

"Police!" The constabulary charged inside with guns raised.

Roger reached for his dagger but Vie grabbed his arm. He tried to break her grip, but she held him tight.

"No," she whispered to him. "Live to fight another day."

"Nobody move!" said a stocky commander as he entered the room. He had a close-cropped widow's peak that fed into wide sideburns. Flushed in the face, his skin glistened with an unhealthy sheen. Roger recognized him from the cemetery. He also recognized the voice from Scott's antique store.

"Mister Vaughn, I presume," Special Agent David Murray said. "I've been looking for you." He gestured, and a constable moved toward him. Roger spread his arms while the officer passed his hands over his clothes.

"He's armed, sir." The officer slid the dagger out of Roger's jacket and handed it to the agent.

"Anything else?" Agent Murray asked.

"Just my charm against idiots," Roger answered, "but it doesn't appear to be working."

"Shut your mouth, boy, or I'll shut it for you."

The officer resumed his search. Turning Roger's pockets inside out, he confiscated Roger's money, penlight, the lockpick set Scott loaned him, and the pages from Doctor Glover's laboratory. The officer squinted at the pages, then held them out to Agent Murray. "Take a look at this, sir."

Agent Murray scanned the pages, seeming to have no difficulty with the spidery script. He stabbed Roger with a narrow-eyed glare. "Cuff him. Cuff them all."

RC jerked away from the officer holding him and pulled a pistol from his waistband. "No way, roller!"

"Put it down, RC," Vie warned.

Wide eyed, the teenager looked from her to Agent Murray and back to her.

"Do as she says, boy," Murray ordered.

RC hesitated.

In one smooth motion, Agent Murray drew his revolver and shot RC in the forehead.

"No!" Vie screamed, dropping to her knees beside the fallen teen.

The special agent turned his gun on her. "Mister Vaughn, if you don't do exactly what I say, she'll get the next bullet right between the eyes."

CHAPTER 24
JACK KETCH

Monday, April 7, 1969

*R*oger seethed as a constable cuffed him. With his hands held down in front, he felt impotent. He shouldn't have involved the youth. It had been stupid of him to think he could walk in under their noses and save the damsel in distress.

The constable gripped him just above the elbow. "Come on."

With one last look at RC, Roger was marched out of the apartment. The officer steered him toward a paddy wagon. Another officer stood beside the open door.

Passing them, Special Agent Murray took a pump action shotgun from one of his patrolmen and said, "Call a meat wagon. We got a dead one. And have someone put the evidence bag in the front seat."

"Yes, sir," replied the officer before running off.

Agent Murray hefted the weapon as he entered the back of the transport. A dome light on the ceiling illuminated the armored interior. He moved to the front where a grated partition separated the helm from the prisoners.

"Get in," said the officer gripping Roger's arm.

Roger searched the crowd. Flashing blue lights reflected off grim faces. Old and young, their eyes held a righteous satisfaction. They believed they had caught Lieutenant Bell's killer. He recognized a few, including Thompson and Bradley. Absent among them were the faces of Corporal Middleton and Officer Stone.

The officer at his side gave him a shove. Stepping up into the transport's confines, Roger sat on the metal bench. Another officer pushed Vie inside and directed her to the bench opposite Roger. She glared at Roger, her cobalt eyes filled with blame. Unable to meet her gaze, he bowed his head and stared at the rubber mat under his feet.

An officer took up the end of a chain anchored to the floor, looped it around their restraints, and cinched it tight. After testing it, he gave Agent Murray a nod and exited.

The doors banged shut.

Agent Murray slapped the partition and said, "We're in. Take us to Central."

The paddy wagon began moving.

Eyes fixed on Roger, Agent Murray sat next to Vie with his gun aimed at her head. "Where is it?" he asked.

Roger looked up. He was exhausted and couldn't think straight. "Where's what?"

Agent Murray swayed as they turned a corner. However, the barrel never moved far from Vie's temple.

"Listen, Agent Murray," Roger said. "It's been a long week. You're going to have to speak plain."

"The skull you took from Doctor Glover, where is it?"

Pieces started to fit into place. He now knew why he was still alive. He also knew why they had brought Vie along. Roger leaned back, a tired smile on his face. "It's not on me."

Agent Murray pumped the shotgun and pushed the barrel against Vie's skin. "I know that, moron. Tell me where it is, or I swear I'll blow her head off. And with a shotgun, it won't be pretty. It'll be a closed casket funeral, if you get my meaning."

His dark eyes became ice cold, and Roger knew Murray meant to kill her. He knew his type. He'd seen it before, more than he cared to admit. Once he gave up the skull's location, the agent would kill them both.

Maintaining eye contact, Roger palmed the lockpick from a fold along the seam of his pants leg. He said, "It's safe."

"Go on."

"I've hidden it."

Agent Murray asked, "The antique store?"

Roger tried to dislodge the visions of the agent feeding Scott to the alligators. "No one knows where it is but me."

Agent Murray considered Roger's words before relaxing. He even had a smile. "Tell me."

"I have to show you."

The paddy wagon turned again. When it did, the stench of death filled the compartment. Lavinia appeared next to Roger. Face twisted in an angry snarl, her image flickered a moment then solidified. She reached for the lawman, her fingers hooked like talons.

Agent Murray's eyes went wide. "No!" He swung his shotgun around.

Roger slipped out of the cuffs and launched himself at the agent. Murray twisted as Roger gripped the shotgun. A vision of the forked cross flashed before his eyes. He fought down the rising bile and nausea as he tried to wrestle the gun away.

Roger shoved just as Agent Murray pulled the trigger. A deafening roar filled the interior. Buckshot ripped through the grated partition and the driver, spattering the windshield with blood and gore.

Eyes locked on the agent, Lavinia dug her aethereal fingers into his chest. He blanched as he stared down where she held his beating heart. A red mist coalesced around her arm.

With a screech of metal, the paddy wagon struck a parked car and bounced. Careening one way, then the other, it teetered on two wheels, jumped the curb, and smashed into a tree.

The crash threw Roger back into his seat with Agent Murray sprawled on top of him. Despite the wound oozing at his chest, the agent took in ragged gasps of air. There was no sign of Lavinia. Ears ringing, Roger sat up and rested his head against the hull. His eyes started to slip shut.

"Do something!" Vie cried through clenched teeth. Held tight by her restraints, she had pushed against the vehicle with her arms and legs to absorb the impact. Her wrists were raw and bleeding.

No rest for the weary. Roger leaned over her and unlocked the cuffs. He helped her to her feet, and they turned to the rear doors. Fresh air came through the gap between them. Roger shoved one, and it swung open with a groan.

Vie took up the shotgun and pumped it, ejecting the spent cartridge. Nostrils flared, she pressed the barrel to Agent Murray's forehead. "Bastard," she muttered. "You didn't have to kill RC."

Roger watched the emotions war on her face. Her hand tightened on the grip, but her finger never touched the trigger. He could see her tremble despite her effort to appear in control.

"I can't do it," she whispered and thumbed the safety. Pushing the shotgun toward him, she said, "You wanted to teach him not to hit a woman. You do it."

Even the thought of touching the gun caused the Dark One's forked cross to flare inside his mind. "No. We've no time for a duel, and killing him won't teach him not to abuse those under his dominion. Let your courts mete out justice for his actions tonight. Does your country hang murderers, or behead them?"

Vie stared at him a moment, eyes wide and jaw slack, then she snapped, "The law doesn't care if a white policeman kills a black boy, Roger. All the talk about us being equal is just that: talk."

"Tyranny can only thrive if good people do nothing, Vie. So long as there are people like you, Tee, and Nate standing against the evils in your world, there is hope for a better tomorrow. Have faith."

Tossing the gun aside, she grabbed Roger's hand. "You're a naive fool, Roger, and you're going to get yourself killed. We'd best get out of here." Unsteady, the two stepped away from the paddy wagon.

Roger recognized the street. The Fogartie Construction sign was two houses down. Porch lights were on, and people stared out their windows. Roger went around the side and opened the passenger door. A duffle bag sat on the seat. Inside were the items taken from him, including his dagger and the pages from Doctor Glover's binder.

"Was that Lavinia?" asked Vie. Her voice quivered with adrenaline.

"You saw her?" he asked. He hadn't been hallucinating after all.

"She was there, and then she wasn't."

A patrol car drove toward them. The emergency light lit the dogwoods, creating more shadows than it drove off.

Roger slid his dagger into its sheath.

"I'll say this," Vie said. "It's never boring with you around."

He was about to grab her and run when the car stopped.

"Miss Vie? Mistuh Vaughn?" Tee emerged from the shadows holding a massive handgun. Nate came out from the passenger side, his pistol ready. Tee's eyes went wide at the sight of the wrecked paddy wagon.

"Y'all alright?" Nate asked.

"We'll live," Roger replied. He tilted his head toward the transport. "The pilot's dead, and Agent Murray's wounded."

Nate holstered his gun and motioned for them to hurry. "Come on. Get in. A concerned citizen called Central. Lucky for you, we were just around the corner."

Tee entered the back of the paddy wagon. A loud gunshot echoed, and he came out in a rush. Shotgun blasts chasing after him, he dove behind the door of his patrol car.

Agent Murray stalked out. Slick with blood, his shirt stuck to his chest. The lights from Nate and Tee's patrol car illuminated the image of grey prison bars in the agent's eyes. He raised the shotgun to his shoulder and fired.

With nowhere to run, Tee hunkered down. The shot went above him. It peppered the door and showered Tee's head with glass.

Roger tackled Vie to the street before she could jump into the backseat.

The agent fired again. The shot punched a hole through the front windshield. The next time he pulled the trigger it clicked empty. Dropping the shotgun, he raised his revolver and fired several times pointblank at the car. Bullets ripped through the seats, throwing tufts of cotton.

"Jack Ketch!" Roger called out.

Agent Murray slowed his advance and began moving to the passenger side of the patrol car. A wave of oppressive heat rolled down the street.

"You cannot stop me!" he replied. "David Murray is mine."

"Take him," Roger said. "I don't even like him."

Agent Murray sighted down the side of the car. Roger covered Vie, tensing for the shot.

Nate fired his pistol.

Agent Murray's head snapped back.

Nate fired again and again.

The agent staggered each time, as if punched. Suddenly, his skin stretched and pulled. Something inside was trying to get out. With a loud, wet slurp, his skin sloughed off and puddled on the pavement. In his place stood a ghastly red humanoid. Its black eyes burned with a visceral hate.

"A boo hag," Vie gasped.

"A what?" Nate asked.

"A skin walker," she answered.

Roger jumped up. "Throw the iron filings I gave you!"

The Jack Ketch clenched his hand into a fist. "Tradere

hujusmodi Satanæ in interitum carnis." *Deliver this man to Satan for the destruction of his flesh.*

Roger felt clammy fingers squeeze his neck. The stench of death drowned his senses, and the edges of his vision darkened.

Nate yanked out the leather pouch, emptied the contents into his palm, and tossed them at the creature. A sizzling sound cut through the night.

Roaring, the Jack Ketch released Roger and made to strike Nate.

Nate fell back against the patrol car, emptying his pistol into the creature.

Vie rose. The ghost of her father, Doctor Wampus, whispered in her ear, telling her what to do. Together, they faced the Jack Ketch. She spoke, but the words weren't meant for Roger. The creature flinched and writhed as if each syllable was a knife thrust. Glaring, it leapt into the night air and vanished.

Roger caught Vie when she collapsed.

Sweat dripping down his face, Tee gripped the radio and said, "Dis is 1-Echo-25. Code 10-50 at 32 Chapel. Officers down. Repeat officers down. Request ambulance and wrecker."

Static from the radio preceded the dispatcher's voice. "1-Echo-25. Acknowledged."

"What was that?" Nate asked, reloading. Visibly shaken, he dropped two of his bullets. His eyes kept drifting to the puddle of flesh.

"The Vampire of the Gibbet, the Jack Ketch," Roger answered, holding Vie. "He was the one who held us captive at the Charleston Gaol. I think the High Sheriff paid him with food and clothing, but he mostly did it for the alcohol. The paper I read called him a day laborer of death. He was the one who hung John and Lavinia Fisher."

"I can't do this," Vie said. Tears streamed down her cheeks. She pounded on Roger's chest with the fleshy part of her fists. "You can't make me."

He wrapped his arms around her, trying to calm her.

Vie pushed away, blue eyes blazing. "No. You don't get to be nice."

"Vie, what did you call that thing?" Nate asked.

She sniffled and wiped her eyes with the back of her

hand. "A boo hag, but I've never seen one that's male."

Roger knelt, picked up Nate's bullets, and handed them to him.

Nate stared at them. His eyes saw but didn't see.

Roger had seen that look before: battle shock. "We need to get out of here and regroup," he said.

"Weh duh we go?" Tee asked. Wild eyed, he searched the shadows as if expecting the creature to attack at any moment. "Oonuh cyan' git 'way from uh boo hag."

Roger shook Nate by the shoulders. "Nate, look at me. You need to take Vie and me out of here. If Major Wilson finds us, he'll bury us. Help me stop this."

Nate blinked as if seeing Roger for the first time. "What do you need?"

"A ride out of here," Roger answered, trying to keep his tone even. "We need to stop by my office and collect a few things, then go see Scott, but first I need to leave a message for the devil." Letting Nate go, Roger looked down the street toward the Fogartie Construction sign. "Know this. If you help us, the constabulary will think you've turned on them." He felt a calm he hadn't felt since being in Terra. "But, if we're lucky, it won't be the police that'll come after us."

"You better have a plan," said Nate, some of his color returning.

"I do," Roger said. "You with me?"

"Warruh 'bout Agent Murray?" asked Tee. "Warruh 'bout Gilbert, de driver? We cyan' leave'm dey."

"Yes, we can," Roger said. "We must, if we're to stop that creature. We're the only ones who can."

"What about Lavinia?" Nate asked.

"Somehow, the Jack Ketch is using her," Roger explained. "It's her anger that feeds him. Without it, he dies."

"How is that possible?" Nate demanded.

"I think he's inside her," answered Roger. *He's inside all of us.*

Vie gave Roger a sour look. She knew he wasn't telling them everything. "There's no way out of this, is there?"

"Sure there is," Roger answered. "Go home, lock your door, and pull the sheets over your head, but now that it's seen you..."

"As Doctuh King said, We mus' tek uh stand, eben doh

we risk puhzishun, press-teej... eben our-own life," Tee said in a low voice. "We mus' be uh true neighbuh." There was a quietness about Tee — a resolve. He knew about boo hags and what they were capable of, but it didn't stop him.

Roger acknowledged him with a quick nod.

"Me too," Nate replied. "Vie?"

Vie heaved a loud sigh. She strode up to Roger and poked him in the chest with her finger. "Don't get us killed."

"Need help?" a local resident asked. Two other men walked with him.

Nate eyed the station wagon in front of their house. "We need to borrow your car. Police business."

Tee shifted the car into gear and drove around the paddy wagon. "Weh to?" he asked.

"Stop there at the Fogartie sign." In the back seat, Roger leaned forward and gestured toward the house two doors down. "You have any paper?"

Nate took a notepad and pen from his pocket. "Here."

When Tee stopped the car, Roger jumped out. At the screen door, he slid his message between the decorative metal scrollwork and the screen.

It read, "You want the skull; go to the antique store at the corner of King and Queen. In return, I want to meet the Judge. High Noon."

Roger stopped at the open door to his office. The yellow barricade tape had been cut. Drawing his dagger, he pushed the door open farther and went inside. Nate and Tee were behind him with their guns drawn.

The walnut desk that guarded his office door had been overturned and the leather backing of the secretary's chair slit. On the far wall, the velvet chair, table, and lamp had been broken. The stuffing had been removed from the loveseat. Above it, someone had ripped holes in the encaustic painting.

"What happened?" Nate asked.

"Roger happent," answered Tee.

Moving to his office, sparkling glass littered the floor. All of Roger's alchemy equipment had been destroyed. His eyes went to the broken placard. The people who did this weren't just searching for something. They sent a message, and

Roger received it loud and clear.

He checked his desk. All of the drawers had been opened, and their contents dumped. He knelt and checked the lowest drawer. The bag of gold pieces was gone.

Vie stepped into his office. Tears streamed from her eyes when she saw her father's placard. Wrapping her arms about herself, she fled.

"Vie, wait," Tee said and chased after her.

"I'm sorry, Roger," Nate said. "They destroyed everything."

Sifting through the wreckage of his desk, Roger found the male half of his lodestone. Hung from a string, it swung and spun in lazy circles. He let out a sigh of relief. "Not everything."

CHAPTER 25
YORICK

Tuesday, April 8, 1969

*R*oger waited behind the storefront. He had shifted some of the boxes to see outside. The bare bulb above the foyer illuminated the narrow pathway between mountains of old newspapers, books, and magazines piled atop mildewed furniture. Nestled amongst them, an antique safe guarded the entrance to his bolt hole.

"It's noon," Scott called out from the back of the store. "Any sign of your guests? We're burning daylight. I have things to see, and people to do."

"Not yet," replied Roger.

"You sure you want to give them Lavinia's skull?" Nate asked. He had changed out of his uniform into street clothes. Beside him, Tee looked more ready for a soirée than a gunfight.

"It's the only way to draw the puppet master from behind the curtain," said Roger. He glanced past them to Vie, who retreated deeper into the labyrinth. She hadn't spoken to him since they had visited his office and discovered her father's broken placard amongst the shattered alchemy equipment.

Sure, he worried they'd all be killed, or that the police would arrive instead. A hundred things could go wrong. He just needed one thing to go right.

"Be careful," Nate said, giving him one last look before following Tee to their positions.

Roger's thoughts went to Cerdic, his paladin friend, and Lahar, the pirate captain. He instinctively made sure he still had his dagger. Catching himself, he drew in a deep breath and let it out slowly, willing the tension to go with it. The next few hours were going to be critical. He really could have used their help, but it was all on him, now. Roger glanced toward the narrow ribbon of blue sky over the street. *Well, it wasn't completely on him,* and he offered up a quick prayer.

Half an hour later, a limousine pulled up in front of the

store. The copilot, a short man in a white tee shirt and leather jacket, exited and scanned the neighborhood. A jagged scar ran from his missing ear, along his jaw, and down his neck. Apparently satisfied, he opened the rear door.

The Judge wore an indigo three-piece suit and bow tie. An iridescent duck feather decorated the white band of his fedora. Red hair peeked under the edges. He was younger than Roger expected, with wide shoulders that stretched his jacket. A gold ring encircled the little finger of his right hand. Aided by a cane with a curved handle that ended in a silver-plated boar's head, the Judge ambled across the sidewalk with a slight limp, as if from an old leg injury.

A brawny thug in a turtleneck and suede jacket joined them. He came from around the corner, and Roger could only surmise the Judge had brought reinforcements.

Roger retreated to the aisle.

The bell over the front door jangled when the two guards entered. They kept their jackets open with the butts of their handguns visible.

Stepping past them, the Judge took off his hat and handed it to the short copilot in leather. The door clanged shut behind him. He examined the cramped foyer with a calculating eye. "Mister Vaughn?"

Roger nodded. "Mister Geddes?"

His eyes widened briefly. A cruel smile crossed his face, and he said, "Judge Geddes, retired. How did you know?"

"The limp gives you away," Roger replied. "Figured it was left over from the duel with Mister Simmons."

Geddes waved his hand airily. "Ancient history."

"Isn't history what this is all about?" asked Roger. "Governor Geddes was the head of the conspiracy. The one who tied it all together. Cleary was clueless, and David Ross worked for the Colonel, John Fisher's uncle. Both were, shall we say, unemployed after the Fisher debacle. You wanted their land for Monroe's Navy base. You had your state engineer, Major Wilson, survey it, and Sheriff Cleary remove everyone there. The land was ripe for the taking. Or, at least, that was the plan."

"You talk as if I was there," said Judge Geddes.

"I suspect Nathaniel Heyward was more than you bargained for. It must have struck a nerve when his daughter assumed control and later sold it to Mrs. Lawton who, in turn, sold it to the government. She achieved what your family couldn't. How much money did you lose during that venture?"

"It was no matter. My namesake had moved on to Key West." Judge Geddes stepped forward. His eyes bore into Roger's as if searching his soul. "You've been killing my men. I want to know why."

"You've reckoned this all wrong. I was hired by John Fisher to find his wife."

Judge Geddes' eyes widened again.

Roger continued, "They were released from the Charleston Gaol, but they didn't move on because Lavinia had unfinished business. That business stops when you are dead."

The judge's face hardened. "No one's going to believe a ghost killed a half-dozen men."

"Then why are you afraid?" Roger saw it in his eyes. The question had hit its mark. "You knew the Charleston Gaol was empty. Why else would Doctor Glover try to banish the Jack Ketch?"

"What are you talking about?"

"I found his secret laboratory, his spellwork, and the burned bones. Unfortunately for you and your band of conspirators, the banishment didn't work, and Doctor Glover died for his efforts." Roger paused, giving his words time to sink in. "The only question that remains is, who's going to get you first, Jack Ketch or Lavinia?"

Scarlet crept up Geddes' neck. He thrust out his hand and said, "Lavinia's skull. Give it to me."

His henchmen pulled their handguns.

"Kill me, and you'll never find it," Roger said.

"What do you want, Mister Vaughn? Money?" Geddes asked. "What will it take to make you go away?"

"I want to break the curse," answered Roger. "I want whatever it is you're holding over the jurors' families — the contents of John Fisher's trunk."

"Then expect to be disappointed." An evil smirk tugged at the judge's mouth. "Look outside."

The man in leather opened the door, and Roger's eyes darted to the limo's backseat.

"My men caught your girlfriend snooping around the public library."

Roger went pale, and he took an involuntary step toward the door. "Brie!" he called. Silver tape covered her mouth and bound her wrists. A well-dressed man pressed a knife to her side — the same man he had seen at the county detention center.

"Let her go," Roger demanded.

"The skull, Mister Vaughn."

Roger's mind raced. He'd hoped it wouldn't come to this.

"I have it," Roger said. "Don't hurt her."

"Let me see it."

Roger slowly reached inside the box next to him and drew it forth. Visible in the eye socket were the letters SCMC.

"Here," said Roger.

Judge Geddes snatched the skull. "We won't meet again," he said. Taking back his hat, he exited the store.

As soon as the door closed, the two guards opened fire.

Already on the move, Roger dove behind the gun safe. Bullets ricocheted off the steel, drawing sparks. Dashing down the short aisle, he cut through a tight gap between two curio cabinets and put his back to a brick column.

The report of Scott's shotgun echoed, and the two men chasing after him paused.

The antiques dealer was supposed to remain at the rear of the store with Vie. *The judge must have sent someone to the backdoor.* Roger slid out his remaining dagger. From his position, he could see down the full length of the aisle behind the curios. Nate waited at the other end. The young officer purposely bumped his shoe against a metal storage rack, causing it to shift.

Crouching, the thug in leather and his turtlenecked partner moved down the aisle fronting the curio cabinets. They carried pistols with heavy, angled grips that fed into black barrels.

Tee's cannon boomed and sent Leather crashing into the cabinets. He landed on the floor amongst statuettes, cobalt blue bottles, and glass shards.

Turtleneck laid down cover fire while Leather climbed to his feet.

Tee's cannon roared again. "Stay down!"

This time Leather did — with two large holes punched through his chest.

"Police!" Nate yelled. "Drop your weapon."

Turtleneck fired repeatedly into the clutter, aiming toward Tee, then Nate, then back toward Tee. He stopped long enough to let a box magazine fall and reload.

Roger crept out from behind the column.

Turtleneck kept pulling the trigger. His shots scattered throughout the store. He ejected another magazine and reloaded his gun.

He must have sensed someone behind him. Whipping around, he adjusted his aim even as Roger threw his weapon. The blade caught Turtleneck in the shoulder, and his bullet dug into a box of books, missing Roger by inches.

Charging forward, Roger caught the man's wrist with his left hand, shoved it to the side, and gripped the protruding dagger's hilt with his other. Still using his momentum, Roger forced the brawny man back against a bureau with an angled top.

Sweat and blood mingled as Turtleneck grabbed Roger's face with his free hand.

Releasing the dagger, Roger struck the man in the throat with the inside edge of his hand while twisting and slamming the hand holding the pistol against the bureau's edge. The gun dropped to the floor.

Driven to a frenzy, Turtleneck fought without pain as he threw himself at Roger again and again. Roger countered every kick, punch, or gouge as they moved up and down the aisle, breaking furniture and glass.

Roger caught Turtleneck with a right cross, splitting the skin above his eye. Blood streamed. Blinking it back, he shoved Roger away, removed the dagger from his shoulder and slung it. Roger ducked. The man followed up with a knee to Roger's head.

Shifting so the attack glanced off his ear, Roger tucked his elbows, then struck out with an open right hand. He grabbed Turtleneck's throat and squeezed, cutting off his airflow.

The man's eyes dimmed even as he tried to escape Roger's grip. Grabbing a bronze chamber pot, Roger struck his opponent's head. Once, twice, thrice.

With scant inches between the two, Roger took Turtleneck to the floor and squeezed tighter.

"Roger, let him go. He's done."

Nate's voice cut through Roger's tumult of emotions. He

hadn't even realized Turtleneck had stopped struggling. He released his grip and backed away.

Down a side aisle, Vie knelt beside Tee. He sat in a wicker chair, blood running down his leg. Scott came up from the back, shotgun in hand.

Catching his breath, Roger asked, "Everyone good?"

Nate replied, "How can you ask that? The limo's gone with Brie, and Tee's been shot. No. Everything's not good."

"En' now, dey has de skull," Tee said. His words came out laced with pain.

Roger fingered the Spanish reales in his pocket. "No, they don't."

Everyone stared at him.

Scott gasped and looked as if he had been struck by a thunderbolt. "You gave them Yorick?"

After all that had been going on, Roger couldn't answer. It all came out in a fit of laughter.

"Is he having a nervous breakdown?" Nate asked.

"No," Scott replied, his shock turning to irritation. "He finds it funny that they have *my* skull."

Roger pointed. Lavinia's skull lay nestled amongst antique whiskey bottles and a single-masted jade sampan.

"What happens when they find out they have the wrong one?" Nate asked. "Will they kill Brie?"

"They won't do anything to her," answered Roger. "Brie will know it's a fake, but she doesn't know where the real one is. Lavinia's skull is the only thing keeping her alive."

"You play a dangerous game," Scott said.

Vie took a clean cloth and rod and used it as a makeshift tourniquet. Tightening the windlass, she said, "Scott's right. You shouldn't have involved her."

"After that business with Sheriff Cleary, I stayed away," Roger replied. "Then, when we talked at Easter Mass, I armed her with the only thing I could think of that would keep her alive. Knowledge."

"Yes, but you heard them, they caught her at the library," Nate said. "She was still working the case for you."

Vie studied Tee's leg wound. "It needs stitches."

"I have a surgeon's kit in my office," Scott offered. "Complete with a bone saw."

Panicked, Tee tested his weight on his hurt leg. "I'm awright." The pain must have been excruciating, but he managed to stay on his feet.

Nate looked back toward the front door. "Brie was their insurance."

"What do we do now?" Vie asked.

"Did you kill the one who came in the back?" Roger asked.

Scott gave him a sly grin. "Two barrels to the chest." The grin vanished. "You're going to clean my store, top to bottom. I mean it. I don't want to smell one drop of blood..." He gestured to the broken merchandise. "And you're paying for this damage. All of it."

Roger gave him a tired nod. Eyes resting on the unconscious ruffian, he said, "Help me take Turtleneck to the back. After that, we need to move the bodies."

Tee sat on the sales counter with his leg straight. A towel was spread out under his bare thigh where the bullet sliced his skin. His bloodied pants leg lay on the floor.

Beside him, Vie rummaged through the surgeon's kit. "How old is this thing?" she asked.

"Bought it at the Civil War Centennial." Scott handed Tee a fat bottle of clear liquid. "Drink this. It'll take the edge off." The burning scent of grain alcohol followed it.

Vie checked the tourniquet before dousing the wound with antiseptic.

While Vie stitched, Roger picked up the wallet from the pile he and Nate had collected and opened it. "Hello William Richard Mathews of Rocky Mount, North Carolina." He studied the photo on the driver's license and compared it to the man who sat with his bare feet and wrists tied to a wooden chair.

"Who did you get?" asked Roger.

Nate opened a wallet and said, "Isaac Gespeale of Columbia. He's got a ten-dollar bill and two ones. The man Scott shot was Leroy Grays, a local bruiser. Tee and I have busted him before."

Moving to the suede jacket, Roger removed a half-empty pack of cigarettes and a lighter and laid them next to the pistol with its holster. Farther down the counter, Lavinia's skull stared at him as he worked. He kept seeing her at the edge of his vision.

"Yu's uh purty nyoung gal," Tee said, his words slurred.

"You're drunk, Corporal Middleton," Vie said, finishing the last stitch.

"Don' mean uh ent got no eyes," Tee replied with a wide grin.

Vie gave Tee a quick kiss on the cheek and turned to the man in the chair. "What makes someone like this?" she asked as she cleaned his injured shoulder and bound it with a roll of dressing from the surgeon's kit. Next, she taped the cut over his eye.

"That's what we're here to find out," Roger answered. "Something happened after the Fishers were executed. It cursed the men on that jury, causing them to have this rare form of leprosy. I figure the good Doctor Glover kept them on their feet using a mix of different drugs."

"The Angel Dust," Nate said.

"Yes," answered Roger.

"John en' Lavinia bin heng'd," said Tee. "Hex luk dat iz pussonul. Who bin hate'n dem people 'nough tuh cyas'um?"

"Could it have been a root doctor?" Roger asked Vie.

She thought a moment. "Maybe. It would have taken something personal from each of the jurors such as hair or fingernail clippings. If you're right, the hex would have come at a terrible price. What goes around comes around."

"A price someone was willing to pay," added Roger.

Scott said, "If you prick us, do we not bleed? If you tickle us, do we not laugh? If you poison us, do we not die? And if you wrong us, shall we not revenge?"

"In the Academy, they teach us motive, means, and opportunity," Nate explained. "Who'd be in a position to have all three? And how would we know? It was a hundred and fifty years ago, for crying out loud."

"Lavinia's sister, Sally," Roger answered. "They were Doctor Glover's houseslaves, and he taught them root medicine. However, it wasn't just root medicine, they learned shamanism. I bet Lavinia could have done it, and so could her sister."

"She may have used a variant of hot foot powder," Vie suggested.

"Hot foot what?" Nate asked.

"It's foot-track magic. You sprinkle a special powder in their shoes or have them walk over it or through it. To get the results you're suggesting, it would have taken goofer dust

— but not just any graveyard dirt. It would have to come from the grave of a criminal who died from something viral, like yellow fever.

"These jurors didn't just become sick," Vie continued. Their children did too. If Sally collected their footprints in jars, she could have done this. She could have cast a powerful enough hex on the men that it passed to their descendants, though I've never heard of one outliving the caster. Hexes must be fed. For it to last this long, those jars have to be out there somewhere, and someone has to be feeding them."

"These jars, would they have to be big?" asked Roger.

"Not necessarily," answered Vie. "A pint-sized Mason jar would work."

"Maybe that's what Sally put in the missing trunk that John Fisher left to Reverend Furman," Roger mused. "The one he supposedly hid at the Gardens."

Nate paced across the floor. "Do you think Judge Geddes stole the trunk?" He stopped. "Now you have me doing it — I meant Geddes' ancestor."

"I do," Roger replied. "Did you see the way he limped? Scott, you told me that Geddes was shot in the thigh during a duel."

"I was at the wharf, mingling with the crowd, when their barge arrived from Fort Johnson," Scott said, helping himself to some of the grain alcohol.

"How old *are* you?" Nate exclaimed.

"As old as my tongue, and a little older than my teeth," Scott replied with a grin. "Anyway, Young Geddes had lost a lot of blood, and several surgeons were summoned. They saved his life, but he was forevermore a cripple."

"I think it's part of the curse," Roger said. "He didn't seem to have the same debilitating symptoms as the jurors, but there's only one way for something like that to be passed from generation to generation: the jars."

CHAPTER 26
THE SUMMONING
Wednesday, April 9, 1969

Walking backwards around the ladder-back chair holding William Mathews, Roger drew a white circle. He made sure no dirt obstructed its path and the chalk had an even thickness. Moving clockwise, he drew a smaller circle in each of the cardinal directions. Midways between each one, he drew more circles and colored them in. Again, he was careful to avoid anything that would break his closed loop. It wasn't perfect, but it was close.

"You sure you know what you're doing?" asked Vie. She held the pages Roger had taken from Doctor Glover's lectern, comparing the diagram for a summoning to Roger's work. "Because I've never seen magic like this."

Scott removed four bottles from a box and set them on the concrete floor. "Better not waste my wine."

Still moving clockwise, Roger took the bottles and placed one atop each of the intercardinal circles. Next, he laid one of the old coins he'd cashed inside the east circle. In the south circle, he set a bit of twine tied in a noose.

"Here's the restraints you wanted," Scott said, pulling a set of pinioned shackles from the box. "Had them upstairs."

"Pass them over," Roger said and laid them in the west circle. Last, Vie handed him Lavinia's skull. He carefully placed it inside the north circle, facing the chair. Turning to Nate and Scott, he said, "Stay as quiet as possible, and don't disrupt the circle."

Vie reread the words from the last page of the spell. "Here goes nothing," she said, then extended her right hand toward the circle and spoke the incantation aloud. The chalk took on a silvery glow.

Moving to the circle's south side, Roger sat back on his haunches and closed his eyes, picturing the Charleston Gaol. "Jack Ketch, Jack Ketch, Jack Ketch."

William woke with a feral grin. He tested the ropes tying him to the chair, almost tipping it.

"Whoa," Nate said, starting toward him. Tee stopped him

before he could break the circle.

Roger pulled up another chair and sat down in front of their prisoner. "What's your name?"

An eerie calm came over William. "You know my name." He stared straight at Roger. "I am the Jack Ketch. I am the Executioner."

Sweat beaded on Roger's forehead, and the stench of unwashed bodies threatened to drown him. Panic seized his heart. He was back in the tower. The noose stretched tight about his neck.

"No." Roger shook his head, dislodging the memory. "You are a phantom, a spirit. Nothing more. Your power was taken from you when you were cast out."

Hate contorted the Jack Ketch's features. His skin stretched and Roger thought for a moment he'd reveal his true form like he did with Agent Murray. Instead, the creature turned its attention to the items surrounding him.

Eyes focused on the wine, he licked his lips and swallowed. "What do you want?"

"Free Lavinia. Let her go."

The Jack Ketch shuddered, and an orgasmic expression crossed his face. The wine inside the bottles began to rotate and spiral downward, slowly at first, like sand in an hourglass.

"Someone must take her place. Will it be you?"

Roger paled at the thought. "No one takes her place. It's time for you to go home."

"This is my home!" the Jack Ketch shouted. "I'm not leaving. Ever." His black eyes blazed with anger. He gave each of the five people surrounding him a searching gaze. "Mister Vaughn's lied to you. He's the murderer, the turnkey who's mad."

Scott looked from the Jack Ketch to Roger. "What's he talking about?"

The Jack Ketch laughed. It was a sound devoid of humanity and held only vitriol and rancor.

Roger waited until the laughter ended. "The Jack Ketch and I have a connection. Something it did when we were held prisoner in the tower."

Vie looked at Roger, a mix of fear and sadness in her eyes. "It's been riding you, too."

The vision of Queen Ambrose and Brie in the tower tried

to push its way into Roger's consciousness, and suddenly he understood what the Jack Ketch was trying to do. "No," he said. "He isn't like the boo hag. He needs a willing victim. Someone willing to sacrifice anything to get what they want. Isn't that right, Jack?"

The Jack Ketch shuddered again. The wine bottles were almost empty. Rather than answer the question, he said, "Mister Vaughn is an executioner, an assassin. Like me, he, too, is a Minister of Justice. He has no wife, no child, no kinsfolk to lament his absence. No human tie to this world. He's the one who should take Lavinia's place."

Facing back to Roger, he said, "It takes magic to use a summoning circle. Have you told Mister Silva what you really are? Or that he's not human?" With a smirk, the Jack Ketch proclaimed, "You're all fools. Mister Vaughn uses magic. Can't you see that he's enchanted each and every one of you? You're under his spell."

Only a sip remained in the bottles.

Red in the face, Scott stalked toward Roger. His fists clenched at his sides. "You're a mage? All this time."

Roger backed away from the circle, his hands up, palms out. "He's lying. Yes, I studied for a time, but never graduated. I was expelled, and my magic taken from me. Now, I use items imbued with magic to hunt magic users. I even use alchemy to fight them, but I'm not one of them."

"A half-truth," hissed Scott. "You could have been a mage."

Roger shrugged. "Maybe, but that was a long time ago, and I chose a different path."

Wailing, Scott held his head in his hands. His face became pinched with concentration as though memories were surfacing. Not paying attention, he stepped onto the circle and broke it.

Roger flashed his eyes toward Vie.

Vie snatched up Lavinia's skull and peered into the eye sockets.

Looking over his shoulder, the Jack Ketch asked, "What's she doing?"

"Calling Lavinia," Roger answered.

"She can't do that," he spat.

Vie cast her spell.

Ghostly light illuminated the Jack Ketch. He screamed

and writhed as if it burned him. Slowly, Lavinia's image broke free and traveled along a shimmering path that led to her skull. A red mass followed her. Just as it was about to reach the skull, something caught its attention — the empty wine bottle now sitting at Nate's feet. The aethereal red cloud streaked toward the bottle and flowed inside. The ghostly light winked out.

"Cap it!" Vie shouted, pointing.

Cork in hand, Nate moved to seal the creature inside. With a piercing shriek, the gaseous mass erupted out of the top and vanished.

Nate looked at the cork and the bottle, not a half inch away. "Sorry, y'all. I wasn't fast enough."

William's body slumped forward.

Roger sat back in his chair and tried to exude a relaxed persona despite the knot of anxiety in his gut.

Scott seemed to get control of himself. He stood off to the side with a hand on the countertop and muttered, "Now to 'scape the serpent's tongue, we will make amends ere long..."

With a ragged gasp of air, William bolted upright.

Roger waited for William to catch his breath before he asked, "What's your name?"

Sweat trailed from the thug's hairline. Panic shined in his glazed eyes, replacing the hatred from earlier. "Billy. Billy Mathews."

Roger let out a sigh. It had worked. The boo hag was gone, for now. He leaned forward. There was more he needed to know. "Billy, short for William. Family name?"

"Yeah. What of it?"

"Did you know your name was on the list of jurors who sent John and Lavinia to their execution?"

"Naw, man." Fidgeting in the chair, he cast about for something that might help him. "Untie me. I ain't gonna hurt you." His hands began to shake.

"Who was the short man in the leather jacket?" Roger asked.

Billy reeked with fear. It was understandable. He had seen his compatriots systematically killed, and Roger could only imagine what rumors were being spread. Billy calmed enough to say, "Mister Gespeale. I don't know his first name."

"Next question." Roger leaned closer and asked, "Where did they take Brie?"

Billy looked down at his lap. Red splotches covered his cheeks and hands.

"You're a mess," Vie said from behind Billy. She still held Lavinia's skull. "Chills, fever, sweating, fits of shivering. Your medicine's wearing off. Let me help you before it gets worse."

Billy raised his head, looking as if he had swallowed something bitter. "Are you a root doctor like Doctor Glover?"

The question hung in the air. Roger knew Vie's answer would mean more than anyone could know.

"No," she said. "I'm a root doctor like my father, Doctor Wampus."

Waves of heat spread from Billy, and he began to tremble. Convulsing, he jerked violently back and forth. Nate grabbed him by the shoulders, holding him down.

Roger jumped up from his chair, knocking it back. "Vie?"

Putting down the skull, Vie rushed in front of Billy and grabbed his head. "He's having a fit. I need a root bag."

"Scott?" Roger asked.

"O true apothecary, thy drugs are quick."

"Scott!"

"I don't have any roots, but I do have a bottle of Tilden's Extract," he said. "Would that work?"

Vie gave him a sharp look. "Where do you get this stuff?"

"I know a guy who knows a guy," Scott answered with a wink. "I use it to help me sleep."

"We'll try it."

He raced to his office and came back with a doeskin bandolier around his neck. Faded beads formed a sprawling pattern that resembled tree branches. "It's my medicine bag."

Placing it on the counter, he reached inside, retrieved a bottle, and measured out a small amount into a shot glass, which he sucked up into a needleless syringe. "It's kinda thick," Scott remarked. A sickly-sweet fragrance filled the checkout.

"What is that?" asked Nate.

"Potiguaya," Vie answered. "Extract of marijuana."

Wide-eyed, Nate looked from Vie to Scott. "But that's... illegal," he stammered.

"Hold him while I shove this in his mouth," said Scott, poised with syringe in hand. Syrup beaded at the end.

Vie gripped Billy by the hair and snatched his head back, while Scott leaned in and slipped the syringe between the man's teeth. He depressed the plunger. Syrup ran down Billy's chin, but it looked like more went down his throat than not.

"I have more," Scott said, stepping back to the counter.

The convulsions eased and Nate and Vie let go. Scott prepared another syringe.

"Billy," Roger called out. "Billy, wake up."

After a moment, the man's eyes opened, and he began licking his lips. "I feel funny. What did you do to me?"

"Cannabis Indica." Scott read from the bottle. "Used with success in hysteria, chorea, gout, neuralgia, acute and sub-acute rheumatism, tetanus, hydrophobia and the like."

Roger sat back down in front of Billy. "You feel better?"

"Yeah." A dreamy look appeared in his eyes.

Roger snapped his fingers. "Billy. Over here."

Billy focused on them briefly, then saw the empty bottles of wine. "You have something to drink?"

Roger glanced at Scott and frowned.

"Billy. Tell me about Judge Geddes."

A fearful expression crossed the man's face. "The judge is a *baaad* man."

"We know that, Billy," Roger said, trying to keep the frustration from his voice. "Tell us something we don't know."

"He's everywhere." Billy looked around as if he were following invisible ghosts. "Banking, construction, S.L.E.D., you name it."

"How does he do it?" Roger asked.

Billy answered, "He holds the medicine."

"Medicine? You mean the stuff Doctor Glover gives you."

"Yeah, man. It stops the pain."

"Angel Dust is also very addictive," Vie said. "Tee told me they give this stuff to children. Disgusting."

"It counteracted the effects of the curse," said Roger. "Sort of."

"Iss why we all work for the Judge," slurred Billy. "You know about the curse?"

"Some of it. We know that without your medicine, you

hurt on the inside from the nerve damage." Roger tapped Billy's chest. "We also know your father had it, and his father before him. If you have children, they'll have it, too."

Billy's mouth dropped open.

Roger leaned forward. "We can stop it, but you have to tell us where they took Brie."

"Man, I don't know." Billy shook his head. "I need something to wet my mouth. It feels like cotton."

Vie gave him a drink of water.

"Do you have any idea? One of Fogartie's construction sites? Maybe a lawyer's office?" Roger wanted to reach inside the man's head and yank out the answers.

"Naw, man. I worked for Mister Fogartie. No one told me where the Judge lives, and I didn't ask. Safer that way."

"So, what? You all visited Doctor Glover once a month, maybe?"

"Something like that."

"Have you ever seen the judge before today?" asked Roger.

"A few times."

"Where?"

"In the fall, Mister Fogartie would take the six of us deer hunting at this plantation outside of town. One time, the dogs wouldn't come back. Caleb and I had to chase them down. Found them baying at a racoon on the edge of a fire line. That was the first time I saw the judge. He was walking the line with another man. Caleb knew who he was and told me to steer clear. I did. Except, I saw him again at the office. Last year, he put in a brief visit to our office Christmas party. He remembered seeing me at the plantation."

"You speak like this is a family business," Nate said.

"It kinda is," replied Billy.

Roger wiped a hand down his face. The conspirators were well-organized. They had a tiered arrangement that allowed one division to be completely oblivious to the workings of the other. It had been perfect — except for the juror list that tied them all together.

"Would the judge take Brie to this hunting plantation?" asked Roger.

Billy shrugged. "Sure. If he wanted to hurt her, no one would be around to hear."

"Where is it?"

"South of Charleston off Highway 17, about thirty minutes. There's no sign. Just a gated entry. I remember them calling it Wallace Plantation." Billy gave them a slow blink. "Is there anything to eat? I think I'm getting sleepy."

"Nate, do you know this place?" asked Roger.

"No, but I'll find it."

"What if she's not there?" Vie countered.

"She'll be there," replied Roger, "and so will I."

Nate frowned. "You can't get to her without a car."

Roger held up the Spanish reales from his pocket, letting it catch the light. "Yes, I can, as long as Brie still has this coin's mate."

Scott drew in a sharp breath. "I knew I smelled magic on you."

Vie gave him an encouraging nod. "Go. Save her. We'll be right behind you."

Rising, Roger studied the coin's engravings. He quelled the flood of doubts threatening to drown him. It didn't matter where Judge Geddes took Brie, he'd find her.

In a commanding voice, Roger said, "Assayer, take me to the other coin." There was a flash of light, and he was gone.

CHAPTER 27
WALLACE PLANTATION
Wednesday, April 9, 1969

*R*oger appeared in a formal parlor not two feet from Brie. Spattered with blood and brandishing a cast iron poker, she loomed over the body of the well-dressed man from the limousine who had held a knife to her side. His fancy suit was shredded, and his chest crushed. Another man had fallen back on a chaise lounge. His head lay at an odd angle, and chunks of flesh dangled from his scalp and neck. Gore spattered the fireplace and walls like hellish constellations. The house smelled of death.

Shadowy figures emerged from the two corpses. Different than their once-living forms, they wore linen shirts, open at the collar and faded trousers that fed into the tops of scuffed boots. Each had a short club hanging from his belt. They were the Jack Ketch's new turnkeys.

"Brie!" Roger exclaimed, backing away in shock.

She turned to face him. Barred windows from the Charleston Gaol reflected in her eyes. "Non possum mori. Non possum capi. Ego sum aeternus." *I cannot die. I cannot be caught. I am eternal.*

Footsteps echoed from the hallway outside the parlor.

"Swear loyalty to me," Brie demanded, holding out her hand like royalty. "Kiss my hand. Become one of my turnkeys, and we will start anew."

Two men he didn't recognize entered the parlor with their handguns ready. Faces eager for violence, they waited for Roger's response.

"I do this, you set Brie free," Roger said. It was hard to reconcile the evil smile with the woman he had befriended.

"Of course," she replied. "Do the noble thing. Sacrifice yourself to save her."

Outside the closest pair of windows, the plantation house cast a long shadow. Bearded oaks above the shadow's reach shined with a golden glow from the afternoon sun. Another pair of windows led to the rear porch. Beyond it, marshlands bordered a scintillating creek. His eyes flicked back to the Dark One's minion.

"You leave me no choice." Making as if he were going to kneel, he took Brie's hand. Wrenching it down, Roger shoved her toward the two men. With a leap, he burst through the window onto the porch.

"Get him!" she shouted.

Not stopping, he vaulted over the handrail and landed in a crouch. Quickly taking stock of his options, he kicked in a section of latticework concealing the crawlspace and its grid of brick piers.

Heavy footsteps thudded on the hardwood floor above his head. Someone threw open the backdoor and stalked across the porch. "He's gone underneath the house!" It sounded like Sheriff Cleary.

Not waiting for his eyes to adjust to the dim light, Roger scrambled around the house's foundations. Unlike the rear of the house with its latticework, a brick skirt wrapped the front. Crawling toward it, he aimed for the darkest shadows. The sandy ground sloped toward the front of the house, giving him room to sit up. Hiding behind a cross-shaped pier, Roger peeked around the side.

Daylight silhouetted the sheriff. He knelt at the edge of the porch and said, "Come on out, Mister Vaughn! The Jack Ketch wants you alive."

Roger had seen two men in the parlor. The sheriff made three, not counting Brie. There had been fifteen on the list of jurors, but over half of those were dead — probably serving as ghostly turnkeys.

He wondered what had become of the judge and the rest of his minions. Roger wasn't sure if the curse passed to all the children in a family, or a single male child in each generation. After so many years, the judge could have a small army on hand, ripe for the Jack Ketch to seize and make his own.

Realizing time was getting away from him, he held up the male counterpart to the lodestone he had placed in his coin bag. Attached to a string, it swung until the pointed end settled in a consistent direction. *It must be close.*

Someone opened an access door and light blossomed within the crawlspace. "I see him!"

Roger dropped the lodestone into his pocket and backtracked toward the fireplace's foundations, trying to keep the piers between him and the turnkeys.

A face leered at him from the darkness. Roger smashed the heel of his palm into the man's nose. Not being able to use his whole body, the strike lacked his full strength. It did, however, make the man clench shut his eyes against the pain and welling tears. Roger crabbed toward the nearest edge of the house and broke through the lattice.

The man crawled after him.

Out from under the house, Roger sprinted for the tree line.

"Sunnovabitch, you'll pay for that!" Face streaked with blood, snot, and mud, the man yanked out his pistol and fired. Roger ducked even as he pushed harder.

Men shouted at him from behind. Up ahead, dogs began barking, and he swore he heard horses. Crashing through the underbrush, Roger came upon a trail that led to a barn and stables. The path continued to a kennel attached to a concrete block building with a flat roof. There was an open shed off to one side with several cleaning stations for wild game.

An older gentleman with stark white hair exited the barn. Cigar smoke swirled about his head. Heavyset with drooping jowls, he wore a dark blue suit and tie and carried himself like a military officer. To Roger, it seemed the man would have been more comfortable in jeans and a flannel shirt, maybe working a farm somewhere.

"Don't move."

Roger stopped. Out of the corner of his eye, he watched a man in a camouflaged hunting jacket step from the woods. Deep lines scored his face and gave him a perpetual scowl. Tan skinned and sinewy, he was a man who worked outside for a living. He held a rifle to his shoulder and aimed it straight at Roger.

The older gentleman puffed his thick cigar and exhaled the smoke. Using the two fingers holding the cigar, he pointed at Roger. "Boy, you must be the unluckiest person alive." He spoke with a country accent. It was different from Gullah; it was even different from Captain Walker's drawl. It was like his mouth didn't open wide enough when he talked.

"Major, what do we do with him?" asked the man with the rifle.

"Major. Major Wilson?" Roger asked.

"You, sir, know my name, but I don't think we've been properly introduced," said the older gentleman. "I'm Major John Wilson of S.L.E.D." Gesturing to the man in the hunting jacket, the major said, "That's Mister Fogartie."

Running footsteps crunched on the path behind Roger. "Major, the plantation house, it's changing."

Roger turned toward the newcomers. Two were unfamiliar. Clean shaven and bathed, he almost didn't recognize the third as the man from the boxcar.

"Small world," Roger muttered.

The man's eyes widened in surprise. "You." He drew his pistol. Hand shaking with emotion, his finger closed around the trigger.

"Mister Brisbane!" The major's voice snapped like a whip.

"Major, he killed David and Billy Mathews. He's responsible for what happened at the house. Our men."

"Stand down," ordered the major.

Mister Brisbane looked from Roger to the major.

"If you're going to kill me, do it already. I'm not a patient person," said Roger.

"Mister Vaughn, if I wanted you dead, we wouldn't be talking." Major Wilson locked eyes with Mister Brisbane until the man holstered his weapon, then pointed to the other two men. "Jones, West, you boys watch for trouble coming from the big house. The rest of you, come with me." The major began walking toward the barn.

Fogartie pressed the rifle barrel to Roger's back. "Move."

The major led them down the central aisle. To either side, horses nickered and bumped the stalls.

Outside the feed room, the major motioned to Mister Brisbane and Mister Fogartie. "Stand guard."

"Yes, sir," they replied.

Inside, Judge Geddes rested on a bale of hay with his left arm bound in a makeshift sling. Deep scratches marred his cheek. The boar's-head cane sat beside him like a gavel. His eyes followed Roger as he entered.

Major Wilson closed the door and reported, "The girl has taken over the house. That damned Cleary, he's turned, and so have Joe and Peter."

The judge gave Roger a cold smile. "You appear in the most unlikely places."

"I like your new bench," Roger said.

Red crept up the judge's neck, almost matching the color of his hair. He took a deep breath and the color receded. "Have you heard of Scheherazade?"

"Can't say that I have," replied Roger.

He leaned back and said, "The story goes that a sultan discovered his wife had been unfaithful to him. Deciding all women were the same, he married a new virgin every day and beheaded her the next morning. Of course, news of these events spread far and wide. The vizier, who's duty it was to collect these new brides, had to face the sultan and tell him his sultanate had no more virgins. A death sentence for sure.

"Scheherazade, the vizier's daughter, offered herself to the Sultan. He accepted, and they were married. On her wedding night, Scheherazade told the sultan a wondrous tale that captured his imagination and his heart. It made him want more. She did this for a thousand and one nights and survived.

"Mister Vaughn, what would you do to survive? What story would you tell me?" The judge raised a cautionary finger. "However, choose your next words carefully. Like Scheherazade, it'll be the only thing keeping you alive."

Major Wilson cocked his pistol.

Roger could feel the weight of the major's stare against the back of his head. The thought of using the Spanish reales came to mind, but at this point, he wasn't sure if he wanted to be closer to the trunk or Brie. No matter where he went, people wanted to kill him. It made him wonder what he had done to upset the fates.

"Two weeks ago, Brie and I, along with some friends, were held prisoner at the Charleston Gaol on Magazine Street." Seeing the doubt on the judge's face, Roger added, "It wasn't the prison you see in the daylight. The Jack Ketch had us trapped within some aethereal realm, a realm granted to him by the Dark One.

"Whether he fed off the memories inside that place, or if the Gaol, itself, had absorbed enough misery to become sentient, I don't know, but when I looked into that thing's eyes, I saw the bars and windows of the Gaol.

"There was a revolt, and the Jack Ketch died by his own noose. Those he had imprisoned were freed. Most moved on to be judged by the Eternal Father, but there were a few who remained behind.

"I have since found out the Jack Ketch wasn't destroyed. The evil of that place remains. As near as I can figure, it feeds off the rancor and malice we store inside us. Regardless of the person being alive or a ghost, the dark energy is there, and the Gaol's executioner is drawn to it like a moth to a flame.

"Judge, the Jack Ketch — the same Jack Ketch who presided over John and Lavinia Fisher's hanging a hundred and fifty years ago — has taken over your plantation house. It wants to start over and build a new gaol with an army of turnkeys to do his bidding. But you and Doctor Glover must have already known that. It's why Doctor Glover tried to banish him."

"Who is this Jack Ketch?" Major Wilson asked. "What did it do to the girl up at the house?"

"He's become a boo hag, a skin walker," replied Roger. "Brie, the person Judge Geddes took as a hostage, is possessed by it."

Judge Geddes shifted in his seat.

"When she scratched you, you saw those grey bars didn't you?"

"I don't know what I saw," he replied.

"How do we stop it?" Major Wilson asked. "We barely managed to escape as it is."

"It feeds off hate. It's drawn to it. The curse must be stopped." Roger looked the judge directly in the eyes and said, "Destroy what's inside the trunk."

"No," said Judge Geddes. "It's impossible."

"What's he talking about?" asked Major Wilson. Roger felt the pistol waver.

"Each of the jars inside the trunk, they're what you Terrans call a battery. A battery of dark energy. The Jack Ketch will use them to remake Charleston."

"You don't know that." Judge Geddes approached Roger and gripped him by the shirt with his good hand. "You almost had me. Tale of the Executioner. Very good. Very good indeed."

"You know I'm telling the truth," Roger said.

"I've heard enough," the judge said. His voice held a resonance, like he was proclaiming judgment. "Kill him."

Major Wilson hesitated.

"Kill him!" Judge Geddes shouted.

"Let me show you," Roger said. "I can break the curse. Don't you want yourself and your children to be free of it forever?"

"If you won't do it..." Red in the face, Judge Geddes threw Roger back against the wall and reached for the revolver at his belt. Unsteady without his cane, the pistol drifted, but the judge was too close for Roger to entertain ideas of escape.

"Stop!" Major Wilson aimed his gun at the judge.

"John, what are you doing?" the judge asked.

"Judge, I've known you my whole life, turned a blind eye when I had to, but I've never seen you act this way." Major Wilson glanced at Roger. "What do you know about the curse?"

Roger held up his hands, saying, "I'm going to reach into my pocket and pull out a lodestone."

"Go ahead," Major Wilson said. His gun remained firmly aimed at the judge.

"He's stalling," the judge said. His gun aimed at Roger. "I can see it in his eyes."

It was true. He needed more time. His plan, the one he had hoped he wouldn't need, hinged on one simple thing: whoever took the coin bag kept it with the trunk. A prayer on his lips, he slid out the lodestone and let it dangle on the string. The major gasped when its pointed end moved, causing the string to angle out.

"The door please," Roger said.

Major Wilson slapped his hand on the door and called out, "James."

Mister Fogartie opened the door. Seeing the state of affairs, he snatched his rifle up to his shoulder, but he didn't know where to aim.

"James, kill Mister Vaughn," ordered the judge.

"No," Major Wilson said. "Don't do it."

"You're betraying your brothers, John, and for what?" asked the judge. "The word of a stranger? He killed Lieutenant Bell; he killed Doctor Glover and David Murray. He's the reason we're here."

Doubt clouded the major's brow.

Obviously uncomfortable, Fogartie lowered his rifle. He said, "This man didn't kill Lieutenant Bell. Davis did."

"What?" asked Major Wilson.

"I thought you knew," said Fogartie.

Judge Geddes looked from one to the other when they turned to him for an explanation. "He would have exposed us all."

"He was a policeman! How could you?" Major Wilson asked.

Gesturing with the pistol barrel, Geddes jabbed at the major. "You know damn well we've had to do things that weren't strictly legal. We did it to protect ourselves. We did it to protect our families."

Lowering his weapon, Major Wilson frowned. "I swore an oath. You swore an oath when you became a judge."

"To hell with that. We swore an oath to each other. We come first."

"I didn't kill Agent Murray," Roger said.

He had their attention.

"What's that about David?" the judge asked.

"I suspect you saw the puddle of flesh," said Roger. "The Jack Ketch did that. That's what boo hags do. He'll burn through Brie, then jump to the next person. He'll use all of us until he claims that trunk for his own. He needs those jars to feed. We must destroy them."

"What jars? What's he talking about?" Fogartie asked.

"Nothing. We kill him; we kill the girl. All this goes away," explained the judge.

"You have John Fisher's trunk," Roger said. He didn't know it for sure, but it seemed a reasonable conclusion.

"You have the trunk?" Major Wilson faced the judge, doubt forming a wedge between them. "You told us it was destroyed."

Roger snapped his fingers. "The photo of the ruined tomb. There was no trunk because it had already been removed. You told everyone the earthquake destroyed it, but you had it the whole time."

Judge Geddes backed away, his face devoid of expression.

"Bastard," Fogartie said. "You knew."

"You only have the word of this criminal," Judge Geddes said. "There is no proof."

Major Wilson took a long pull of his cigar and exhaled a perfect smoke ring. "Mister Vaughn, take us to the trunk," he said.

It seemed ironic that Roger didn't consider himself a gambling man. Sure, he'd stopped by the gambling houses of Tydway in keeping with his ne'er-do-well persona, but the games never interested him. However, when it came to gambling with his life, he was an adept fool.

Roger followed the pull of the lodestone to the block building made for processing wild game. He eyed the meat hooks dangling from the ceiling. Various sized saws and knives hung on the wall. In the corner, a bracket and spindle system held a large roll of white paper over a countertop. Under a long wooden table, red stains spread from the center floor drain like the rays of a sunset.

The lodestone pointed toward a steel door.

"You've got to be joking. His magnet found the freezer," the judge said with a laugh. "It's probably the only metal structure out here."

"Open it," Major Wilson said.

Mister Fogartie grabbed the latch's handle and pulled.

Cold air flooded out. The interior was crowded with sides of deer and hogs hanging from hooks.

"You see, there's nothing in there," the judge said.

At first, Roger didn't see it. Nested against the back wall was a chest freezer with ice crusted along the edges. On top of the lid were stacks of meat wrapped in white paper.

"Who has the key?" asked Major Wilson.

"It was lost a goodly while ago," replied Mister Fogartie. "As you can see, we use it for a bench."

Roger didn't like the look of the room. The metal door opened from the outside. Even the switch operating the light was on the outside. It had no lock, only a horizontal chrome latch and a hole to insert the cotter pin dangling from a thin chain attached to the door. From the cool air coming out, he guessed it wouldn't take long for someone to die of exposure.

"Break the latch," Major Wilson said.

"This is ridiculous," protested the judge.

"It'll take time," Mister Fogartie said.

Roger eyed the ice-rimed keyhole. "I can open it."

"No way am I going in there," Judge Geddes said, shaking his head.

The major aimed his gun at the judge. "Yes, you will." He motioned to Mister Fogartie. "Stand guard. We don't want to get trapped."

"Got it," he replied and used his foot to hold the door.

The three entered, pushing aside the slabs of meat.

Ignoring the alarms ringing inside his head, Roger knelt in front of the freezer. Working quickly, he picked the lock and raked the meat off the top. He raised the lid, and there was an antique iron bound trunk with an iron padlock. Yorick and Roger's bag of gold coins were set to the side.

"I swear I didn't put that there," the judge said, gesturing. Roger wasn't sure if he meant the trunk, the skull, or the canvas bag.

"Who else could have done it?" Major Wilson asked, anger creeping into his voice.

"I did," someone said from the door.

Roger turned around.

A man wearing a black frock coat stood outside. Dark haired and lean, a part of his ear was missing. With a sneer, Joseph Roberts shoved the stunned Mister Fogartie inside and shut the freezer door.

The light clicked off.

CHAPTER 28
MESSAGE IN A BOTTLE
Wednesday, April 9, 1969

The freezer erupted into chaos.

"Everyone, stay calm," the major shouted.

Blind, Roger trembled. He couldn't tell if it was from anger or the cold. He reached into the canvas bag and retrieved his lodestone by feel. Fitting the mated pair together, they became one.

"Who the hell was that man?" Fogartie asked.

"Joseph Roberts," replied Roger. "The bastard's been working with the Jack Ketch this whole time."

"Who?"

"The executioner from the Old City Gaol," Roger said. "I need to reach the door."

"This way," Jim Fogartie said. "John, let him through."

Teeth chattering and hands outstretched, Roger pushed aside slabs of meat as he shuffled toward Mister Fogartie's voice. The toe of his boot bumped against something solid, and an unseen hand guided him to a wall. Reaching out, he found the jamb closest to the locking mechanism. He adjusted about six inches and knelt. "Can someone hand me a piece of that wrapping paper?"

He heard scrambling behind him and a quick rip.

"Will this do?" Major Wilson handed him a strip of waxy paper.

"Perfect." Roger flattened it against the wall and held it in place with the lodestone. Sliding it up the door, he pictured the pin in the chrome latch. Focusing on that image, he adjusted the position of the paper and stone until he was sure they were beneath it. He didn't have to be exact. Close would do.

Slow and easy, he moved the magnet upward, rising to his feet as he did. It was probably his mind playing tricks on him, but he thought he could feel the pin shift. Sliding the paper farther, he imagined it pulling from the latch. He was rewarded with the ping of metal against the door. "Got it."

"What good does that do us?" the judge asked.

"Major," Roger said, "I want you to place your gun where I tell you."

Wilson shuffled closer.

Roger reached out and placed his palm against the man's chest. After a moment, he felt the cold steel of a gun barrel touch the back of his hand.

Again picturing the lock, he took the barrel between his thumb and forefinger and placed it against the door. With his other hand, he felt along the surface, locating the rivets that held the latch in place. After sliding the barrel a little to the left of the fasteners, he said, "Shoot here."

"You sure about this?" the major asked.

"Only one way to find out."

"Everyone, cover your ears."

Clamping his hands over his ears, Roger turned away.

The blast was deafening in the confined space.

Rewarded by a sliver of light, warmth caressed his skin, and Roger pushed against the door. Metal ground on metal, and he met resistance.

Mister Fogartie and Major Wilson joined Roger and, together, the three forced the door open. Bits and pieces of metal fell to the concrete. There was a hole dead center of the latch mechanism.

"I heard a gunshot," Mister Brisbane called to someone. It was followed by the sound of people running.

Moving into the sunlight, Roger rubbed his arms, trying to get the blood to flow. Nate, Tee, and Vie crowded around him. "We couldn't find you," Nate said. "We were going to try the plantation house, but that man stopped us." Nate nodded toward Mister Brisbane.

"Have you seen the house?" Vie asked. "It doesn't look right. Not right at all."

They talked over one another, and Roger had a hard time keeping up. He was just glad to be out of the freezer.

"Mister Vaughn, good work," said Major Wilson. He turned to Nate and Tee. "Corporal Middleton, Officer Stone, when did you get here?"

"Just a little while ago, sir," Nate replied. "We would have gotten here sooner but Billy's directions were a bit vague."

"Vague," Vie grouched. "Go thirty miles south of town — you'll find it."

"What are you complaining about?" Roger asked. "You made it."

"Billy's alive?" Mister Fogartie asked.

"Bin so when we lef'um," Tee replied, "though Mistuh Silva had'um trippin'."

"Don't ask," Roger said to head off any further questions. He turned to Vie. "You said the house looked funny. Funny how?"

"It's there, but it's not," she answered. "It's becoming part of the spirit world."

"We have to hurry," Roger said and began walking back toward the freezer.

"Where's the judge?" the major asked.

Everyone looked around. He was nowhere to be seen. The roar of an engine echoed through the trees, then faded into the distance.

"Jones and West are gone, too," Mister Brisbane said. "Why would Judge Geddes run?"

"Come on, I'll show you," replied Roger. "Help me a moment."

Tee guarded the door while Roger and Nate hauled out John Fisher's trunk. They sat it on the floor, and Roger picked the lock.

A cloud of steam escaped when he opened it. Inside were sixteen stoneware jars with a single indigo stripe. Each top had been covered by a piece of tanned hide tied to the rim with sinew. Warm to the touch, each jar bore a juror's name burned into the flesh. One had Sherriff Cleary's name. On the one for William Hart, fresh drops of blood stained the surface. Beside them sat the remnants of a leather-bound book, its torn cover and tattered, yellow pages held together by twine.

"Judge Geddes told me it had been destroyed during the earthquake," Major Wilson said, more to himself.

Vie studied the flesh and sinew on the jars. "This is human skin," she said with a frown.

"That's disgusting," Fogartie said.

"Sally Fisher's?" Roger asked, though he already knew the answer.

"It would make sense," Vie replied. "Geddes must have discovered what she did. He and the doctor twisted the hex on the jurors and used it for their own purposes, taking

Sally's life in the process. She ended up paying the ultimate price for her spell."

"Can you break the curse?" asked Roger.

"Yes," she replied, "but someone has to take care of the Jack Ketch. With Tee hurt, that leaves you."

He gave her a grim smile. "I'll do whatever it takes to save Brie."

"Lavinia and I worked this out," Vie said, handing him a sheet of paper with Psalm 59 written at the top and a short verse beneath. There was an edge to her voice, and her eyes were filled with concern. Next, she handed him a glass bottle. Inside, an inch of wine sloshed around a rolled-up scrap of paper. "You'll have to trick the Jack Ketch into the bottle and trap him there. Then, recite the verse out loud and mean it with all your heart." She fixed him with a stern look. "You cannot doubt, or this will not work."

"I understand."

"As soon as you finish the psalm, smash the bottle — that should sever his bond to this world."

Rubbing the reales between his fingers, Roger read the words, committing them to memory.

While he studied, Vie unpacked a brightly colored cloth from an oversized purse and spread it on the ground beside the open chest. On it, she placed several candles on small plates, two small containers with lids, and her father's root bag. She handed Nate a tightly woven sweetgrass bowl. "Please fetch me some water."

Nate nodded and strode to a nearby spigot and hose.

Satisfied that he could remember the verse, Roger stuck the paper in his pocket. "I'm ready," he announced.

Vie rose from her impromptu altar, murmured a short prayer, and kissed him lightly on each cheek. "Stay strong, Roger."

"Be careful," warned Tee. "'E ain't dumb. 'E knows you'll use de bottle tuh trap'um."

"He's devoted himself to it," Roger replied. "He won't be able to resist the temptation." He gave everyone a quick nod before clutching the reales in his fist. "Assayer, take me to the other coin."

In a flash of light, Roger reappeared in the parlor. Immediately beset by the stench of unwashed bodies, he watched in horror as wispy tendrils of blood red brick wound their way along the walls. The ghost tower had returned.

Laughing, Joseph Roberts shoved John Fisher from behind, and the knock-kneed man fell to the floor. Brie stood over the prostrate form.

"Have you come to join us?" she asked Roger, and then gave a curt nod.

Cleary struck Roger across the back of the knees with a baton. "Kneel, you bastard."

Roger collapsed, catching himself with one hand.

"Do you remember that day on the gallows?" Brie asked John. "Remember swinging from the rope. Desperate for air, your eyes bulged out and your legs thrashed. Did you see your wife with her neck stretched? I wonder. Was she the last thing you saw before you died? No matter, I knew what you were thinking." Brie's voice took on a whiny tone. "It's finally over. I'm free. Heavenly Father, take my soul. Hah! What nonsense. He didn't care about you. He left you at my mercy."

"I'll go back to your prison," John pleaded. "Just release Lavinia. I beg you."

"You see, Mister Vaughn, everyone makes a deal with me sooner or later. It only takes a little nudge."

"John, she's not here," Roger said.

"What's this?" Cleary asked and reached for the bottle of wine.

Roger shrugged him away and held it out for Brie. "It's an offering."

Brie eyed the bottle warily, even as she licked her lips.

"I offer myself for Brie and give this to you as a gift."

Suspicion flared in her eyes but so did triumph. She took a step toward him. "Her soul for yours?"

"Yes."

"Oh, glorious day! Let it be known that Roger Vaughn has given himself to me."

Brie and Roger held the neck of the bottle together, fingers touching. A red nimbus limned her body. It concentrated over her heart and traveled down her arm. Her eyes flicked to the bottle and its scrap of paper. Brow furrowed, she asked, "What's in the bottle?"

"A message from Lavinia."

She tried to jerk away but Roger gripped her hand. Using

all the strength he could muster, he didn't allow her to let go.

"No!" she screamed.

Cleary and Roberts rushed forward but stopped when the aethereal red cloud encircled the bottle, then moved up Roger's arm.

Roger felt it crawling over his skin. He wanted to vomit, fighting the urge to release the bottle. Doubt gnawed at him. He wasn't a cleric, he was a thief. What made him think the Eternal Father would answer his prayer — especially one in borrowed Terran words? Panic coursed through him as he watched his fingers slowly relax.

Have faith, the memory of Cerdic's voice whispered to him. *The Eternal Father is always with you, even in your darkest hours.*

Roger's fear receded, and his grip tightened.

Moments away from triumph, the last of the red nimbus left Brie, and surged toward Roger. However, there was a single tentacle that lingered at the mouth of the bottle. It held the red nimbus like an anchor. Unable to escape its own vices, the Jack Ketch plunged inside.

Sweat dripping from his hairline, Roger plugged the bottle with a cork.

Using the baton, Cleary jabbed him in the kidney.

Pain lancing his lower back, Roger staggered even as he whipped around and struck the sheriff's temple with the bottle. He followed up with a punch to the middle of his chest. Air knocked out of him, the sheriff doubled over, losing the baton.

Joseph Roberts clutched a stunned Brie about the waist, yanking her off her feet. "Give it to us," he demanded, holding out his hand.

Assuming a fighting stance with his fists up, Cleary said, "You're dead."

Hefting the bottle, Roger shouted, "Defend me against the workers of evil, my God, and rescue me from bloody men. For, look, they want to take my soul. Do not have pity on any master of the dark arts. Consume them in violent anger, devour them completely!" and he slung it into the fireplace.

The bottle shattered against the brick. Green fire engulfed the hearth and spiraled up the flue. Hot flames swirled out, lashing the walls. Furniture caught fire even as the paint bubbled and peeled.

Out of the fire, spectral hands reached for Joseph Roberts and Sheriff Cleary and dragged the two men toward the raging conflagration. Their screams filled the parlor. Flesh blackened where the fingers touched them.

"Brie!" yelled Roger.

Coming to her senses, she wrestled out of Joseph's grip.

Roger grabbed her away, and they leapt through the broken window onto the porch. They ran down the stairs and staggered to an old well where they fell to the ground. Above their heads, green flames geysered out of the chimney. Like a fountain, it rained down on the roof, igniting everything in its path.

"I had the most horrible dream. You were there and so was the Jack Ketch," Brie said. Her sapphire-colored eyes searched for something familiar.

Roger touched her cheek and gently directed her gaze toward his. "I've got you. You're safe now. The ghost tower is gone."

Holding each other, they didn't hear the roar of flames consuming the house.

Tee and Nate crept to the well. "Come on," Tee said, crouching. Nate pointed to the path through the bearded oaks.

"Tee, I thought you were hurt," Roger remarked.

"Jis' a scratch. Scott's med'cine tek de edge off," he replied. "T'odduhs ain't far. Can oonuh mek it?"

"I'm certainly not going to stay here," Brie replied, getting to her feet. Roger hurried to keep up, and together they raced back to the barn.

John Fisher stared down at the empty trunk. He seemed lost when he turned to Roger and asked, "Mister Vaughn, where is my wife?"

Afraid to let go, Roger still held Brie. Brie must have felt the same way. She gripped him just as tight, with her head laid against his chest.

"Aren't you supposed to move on?" Vie asked, wiping a tear from her eye. All around her were empty stoneware jars.

Roger searched but there was no light. Nothing to indicate John was going home.

"Not without my wife," replied John. "Please, tell me

where she is."

Reading the expression on Vie's face, Roger said, "We don't know."

"But I hired you to find her," John said, frustration fueling the strain in his voice.

A breeze swept through the trees and with it came the smell of spring. A look of wonder came over Major Wilson's face. "I can feel the wind," he said. He reached out and touched a leaf, then a twig.

"I can too," Fogartie said.

"So can I," added Brisbane.

"The curse is broken," Roger said. Releasing Brie, he moved to where the ground had been disturbed.

"I buried the root," Vie answered his unspoken question.

"What about John and Lavinia?" Nate asked. There was a tenseness about him, and Roger was reminded that ghosts weren't supposed to be real. At least, not in Nate's world. "We need to help them."

"What can we do?" Brie asked. "We're not Saint Peter guarding the gate to heaven. We're people."

"We need to get His attention," Roger said with a smile.

"How do we do that?" Brie asked, taking him seriously.

He looked around. They all expected him to have an answer.

"I'll help anyway I can," Major Wilson said.

"Do we get to keep our jobs?" asked Tee.

"Yes," he replied. "So does Mister Vaughn. After what I've seen and what y'all did, I'll do whatever it takes to keep you on the force."

Brie looked into Roger's eyes. Thankful he didn't see any traces of the Charleston Gaol, he hugged her again. Suddenly, she stiffened and pushed away from him.

"Roger, I'm sorry. Geddes took it from me when they nabbed me at the library."

"Took what?" he asked.

"A copy of a newspaper article I found from August 8, 1922. Titled, 'Skeleton on Display,' it stated that Mrs. Lavinia Fisher had been exhibited at the Charleston Museum some time ago and removed because her skeleton was out of order. It went on to say the museum decided to repair her skeleton and bring her out of her hiding place."

Roger couldn't believe it. *I found her. She didn't find me.*

He looked at the others and said, "This is it. Vie, Tee, go back to Scott's and collect Lavinia's skull. Bring the pages from Doctor Glover's book, too. We're going to the museum."

CHAPTER 29
NIGHT AT THE MUSEUM
Wednesday, April 9, 1969

*A*pproaching the Charleston Museum from the north through a grove of live oaks, Roger paused in the shadows. Behind him, Nate pulled Brie to a stop before she stepped into the glow of streetlamps bathing the colonnaded portico.

Again, the hairs on the back of Roger's neck rose. *Someone was watching him.* Resisting the urge to look around, Roger remained behind one of the grand columns and motioned for the others to do the same. There was no one around. The street was empty. Even the houses seemed asleep. However, he couldn't shake the feeling.

Careful to avoid the bands of light lying between columns, he crept to the front door. It was unlocked. Waving Nate and Brie over, they slipped inside and paused beside the front desk. A hint of smoke hung in the air. He closed his eyes and sniffed, trying to identify what was burning. It wasn't a cigarette or cigar, but something more pungent — herbs, perhaps.

"The main exhibition hall is through there," Nate said, pointing to a pair of twelve-foot-high doors. Intricate bronze lion heads with rope-loop handles in their mouths glinted in the dim lighting. One door was slightly ajar.

Roger whispered, "I can't believe she's been here, right under our noses, the entire time."

"There must have been a connection between the medical college and the museum," Brie said.

"Do you recall seeing anything that could be her?" asked Roger.

"There was one exhibit," Brie replied. "It had mammal skeletons arranged from the lowest to the highest forms. It culminated with the skeletons of a man and a woman. However, there were no labels or anything that said who they were or where they came from. I never thought to ask."

"Let's investigate," Roger said.

They moved from the front desk and down the short hall.

To the north and south, carpeted stairs led to galleries on the second floor.

"Do we split up?" Nate asked.

Roger didn't give the suggestion even a moment's consideration. "No. We stick together."

Nate drew his revolver. "You know, until I met you and your friends, I'd never had to shoot anyone."

Brie grabbed the rope handle and pulled the door open farther.

The main exhibition hall's diffused lighting teased them with glimpses of the artifacts and relics held within its display cabinets. Near the northwest end of the vast room, a flickering glow reflected off the rib cage of a whale skeleton suspended from shadowy bow trusses that arched overhead.

Roger crept inside. Gunfire erupted from the galleries.

Retreating, Roger pushed Brie and Nate back toward the entrance. He charged past the southern stairs and through a heavy door into a corner classroom with windows on two walls. Light from outside pooled around a security guard's sprawled corpse.

A second door opened into a conservation laboratory. Roger beamed with delight. More than fifty feet long, light from the windows glinted off tools, beakers, jars, glass tubes in racks, and burners. Organized and sorted, the room was an alchemist's dream.

"Do you need a moment?" Brie asked, arching an eyebrow.

There were two doors on the right-hand wall and one at the far end. Nate rushed to the nearest one and peered through the sidelight. "It leads to a service hallway." He ducked down. "I don't know where it goes. Probably back out to the main exhibit room."

"Find something to block the classroom door," Roger said as he collected ingredients.

Looking around, Brie asked, "What should I do?"

"I need something to put this stuff in," replied Roger, setting his stash on the lab table.

"Like what?"

"Anything that burns."

She set off, and Roger began mixing. "Did you block the door?" he asked when Nate returned.

"Yeah. No one's getting in that way unless they have a

battering ram," Nate answered. "Who do you think is out there?"

"Judge Geddes and his remaining henchmen. The judge wanted Lavinia's skull, and he wasn't happy about losing his position of authority with Major Wilson."

"What do you think he's trying to do?"

"I don't know, but I aim to find out."

Nate nodded and took up a lookout position at the door with the sidelight.

Brie came back with a bag of toilet paper rolls. He was about to shake his head and tell her they were too flimsy when he noticed that someone had handwritten "Fire Starters" on the bag. Inside the paperboard rolls were wads of soft, grey fuzz.

"Dryer lint," Brie explained. "I didn't know if you could use it."

"Perfect."

Selecting six rolls, Roger portioned out his ingredients and filled them.

"You two stay here," he said.

"What are you going to do?" Brie asked.

"I want to even the odds."

"Even the odds?"

Roger gave her a look, and she gripped his wrist. "Don't kill all of them," she said with a wry smile.

"I'll try," replied Roger. It wasn't until after he answered that he realized she had been joking. The weight of his remaining dagger pulled at him, a reminder of what he needed to do.

Nate eased open the door, and Roger crept down the service corridor. He passed the second entrance to the lab and stopped at two sets of double doors opposite each other. The one on his left was labeled, Preparation Room. On his right, the other pair led back to the exhibit hall. Straight ahead, the corridor opened into a large assembly area. Like the laboratory, light from outside filtered through the windows. Facing a podium and short stage along the south wall, rows of chairs filled the room.

Counting to three, Roger charged through the double doors leading to the exhibits, yelled, and slung two of his fire starters. Purple fumes spewed out one end. Heavier than normal smoke, it pooled close to the floor.

Several men began coughing.

Roger retreated and ran down the aisle behind the chairs. At the far end of the room, a single door accessed the southwest end of the exhibits. He threw it open, yelled again, and hurled two more of his smoke bombs. Not knowing how many people he was dealing with, he wanted it nice and thick.

Moving back into the assembly room, he looked toward the laboratory, trying to decide what to do next. The service corridor was empty. Hopefully, he could lead the gunmen away from Brie and Nate.

Someone tried the knob at the southwest door.

Crouching with his dagger ready, he noticed a narrow opening through the west wall. It led to another corner classroom, which in turn led into a carpenter's shop. Shelves lined the walls holding an assortment of tools. With the smell of fresh pine assailing his senses, he moved past the long tables and stacks of lumber. The pyromaniac in him wanted to burn it all.

He quelled the notion and peeked around a sliding barndoor at the opposite corner. Huge double doors barred either end of a wide hallway. Straight across from him was a single door labeled, 'STAIRS.'

The exhibit hall door eased open. One of the men from the plantation — he wasn't sure if it was Jones or West — crept across the threshold. He held his pistol out in front of him with both hands and swept the corridor.

Roger lit a fire starter and rolled it toward him.

The man shot at the toilet paper roll even as smoke filled the hallway. Wracked by coughing, he retreated. "Back here!" he croaked out.

Another voice ordered, "Take some men and search the west end. Find him!" It sounded like the judge.

Roger raced up the stairs. Hastening through the various workrooms, he steadily aimed toward the north gallery.

Light flared at a doorway, and Roger came face to face with the judge's other man from Wallace Plantation. Surprised at first, the young man quickly recovered and brought up his gun.

Closing, Roger jabbed his dagger through the

mercenary's lower jaw, severing his trachea. The act was pure reflex. He snatched out his weapon and moved to the next room. The door at the opposite end opened onto the gallery.

He could see down into the main exhibit hall, hazy with purple smoke. Directly below him, the judge knelt inside a thick, black circle, studying several yellowed pages spread on the floor. A large, multicolored chalk circle spread before the judge. On its northern point, a single red candle flickered, while black candles burned at the other cardinal points. At the cross-quarters, smoke curled up from small brass bowls. A second, inner circle of pure white crystals held carefully stacked bones with Yorick perched on top. Nearby, an exhibit case held only broken glass.

Roger leapt atop the nearest display case and down to the main floor. The judge twisted around, saw Roger, and yelled for his lackeys.

Two men charged forward, guns ready.

Leaving behind his last fire starter, Roger dove down the aisle between exhibits. He rolled and came up at a glass cabinet holding a massive elk.

Thick smoke billowed. Roger held his breath and moved into it. From the coughing, it sounded like the two men were ahead. Coming up behind them, he grabbed one by the neck and head.

The other turned and fired, hitting his comrade.

Dropping his body shield, Roger moved toward the noise, chopped down on the hand holding the pistol, and struck the man in the throat. The man gasped, sucking down a lungful of smoke.

Two more men rushed toward Roger. He ducked low to the floor, took a quick breath, and climbed to the top of a display cabinet. Lying flat, he heard the two men walk past.

The smoke partially cleared, and Roger jumped down. A third man saw him and yelled, "He's there!"

All three turned and fired.

With glass shattering all around him, Roger hunkered at the base of a cabinet, his arms over his head.

A loud boom resonated through the main hall — Tee's hand-cannon.

"Police! Everyone, drop your weapons!" It was Nate.

Roger heard a man fall, but the other two had fled.

The smoke cleared a little more. Eyes alert, Tee and Nate walked toward him.

"Vaughn, you awright?" Tee asked, looking over the barrel of his large pistol.

"Just covered in glass," he replied. "Brie?"

"I'm here," she said.

"So am I," Vie added.

Roger stood and tried to shake away the bits of glass embedded in his clothes. It made them stiff, but he didn't want to rub at it.

"Are you bleeding?" Nate asked.

Roger double checked himself. "No."

"I see a blood trail," said Nate.

Roger joined them. The red smear went past the smoldering ritual circle and around the westernmost exhibit.

Vie barely glanced at the black salt circle, now broken and vacant. She gathered the loose pages from the floor and studied them for several long minutes. Nose wrinkled in disgust, she knelt at the north point of the spell circle, chanted a short incantation, then blew out the candles one by one before running a finger through the chalk lines to break them.

"Does that mean Lavinia's gone?" asked Nate.

"No. This wasn't a banishing spell. It was a binding. From the looks of it, I think it's a page from Doctor Glover's book of spells, but it wouldn't have worked anyway. Not without a complete skeleton." Vie pulled Lavinia's skull from the courier pouch draped over her shoulder.

"That belongs to me," the judge said. He gestured toward the skull with his gun. The other two men came out from behind display cases.

"What are you going to do with it?" Vie asked. "The power of the jars is destroyed."

"I want Lavinia," he replied. Madness shone in his eyes.

"You found her," Lavinia said. Her ghostly form appeared directly in front of him. She reached inside his chest and squeezed. "You did this to us. You took away everything and gave us to that monster at the Gaol."

The judge's mouth opened, and a low moan escaped.

"You will die," Lavinia said bringing him closer, "knowing that Six Mile will never be yours."

The two mercenaries bolted.

Another ghostly figure appeared. "Lavinia, let him go."

"John, this was the fiend behind our land being taken away from us, our imprisonment, our deaths. My sister..." Lavinia's face took on a malicious snarl, and the judge cried out.

"The man you're after died long ago," John said.

"Can't you see? He stands before us," Lavinia replied. "The same vile blood flows in this man's veins."

John laid a hand on her arm. "Is it worth your soul?"

She looked from the judge to her husband. "What? Do you expect me to forgive him?"

"I want you to leave judgment to the Redeemer," replied John. "That is what the Jack Ketch took from us; that is what has been given back to us. You need only accept it."

She stared into his eyes with a mix of fear and hope.

"Lord help me, I know you can't forgive him because *I* can't forgive him, but I tell you this: my last act on this world will not be born out of hate."

Her arm relaxed. "You sound like the good reverend." She backed away, and the judge fell to his knees with a gasp.

John took her by the hand. Tentative at first, he seemed uncertain. Lavinia moved into his arms, and the two held each other. For the first time in a long, long while, it wasn't out of mutual fear but out of love.

"What do we do now?" Brie asked.

"Hand Judge Geddes over to me," Major Wilson said. He approached them, holding a pair of handcuffs. There was no one else with him.

Nate and Tee moved to collect Geddes.

"You can't touch me," said the judge. He pointed at Nate and Tee. "You can try, but by sunrise tomorrow, I'll be a free man, and you two will be out of a job. And you—" He turned to Major Wilson. "—you'll wish the curse killed you by the time I'm finished." He reached into a pocket, yanked out a miniature handgun with over-under barrels, and aimed it at Roger. "Prepare to meet your maker, Mister Vaugn."

Brie gasped. Wide-eyed and with her hands over her mouth, she stood rooted to the spot.

Tee grabbed the judge's wrist and squeezed. The gun dropped from the judge's hand, and Tee deftly caught it. "Leh we go fuh a walk," he said. "Dey's uh nice room waitin' fuh you at de five-bar hotel."

Nate pushed Judge Geddes' shoulder from behind, and they marched him to the major, who cuffed him.

Brie trembled, and tears welled.

Roger wanted to put his arm around her, but the sparkle from his clothes reminded him of the cut glass covering him.

"I don't think I'm ever going to get used to the danger," she whispered, taking his hand.

Brow furrowed, Roger watched Major Wilson hold open the door for Tee and Nate to escort Judge Geddes out of the main hall.

"What's wrong?" Brie asked.

"I don't know. It just doesn't feel right," he replied, his eyes following them. "I don't think this is over," he said. The four exited, and the double door with the bronze lions closed with an ominous boom.

Brie let go his hand and asked, "What about Lavinia?"

Shaking off his worry for the moment, Roger turned to the ghost. "Are those yours?" he asked, gesturing to the stacked bones.

"No," Vie answered. She held Lavinia's skull in front of her like a divining rod. "But they're here."

Lavinia and John huddled around her. It was like they were lost in the woods and Vie was their guide.

Skull held out in front of her, Vie crossed the exhibit hall. Roger and Brie hurried to keep up with her. She took them under the north side gallery and through the museum library.

Turning west, she entered a storage room. The room was longer than it was wide. Brie flicked a wall switch, and overhead lights buzzed to life. Boxes, stacked to the ceiling, created narrow aisles and skittering shadows.

They aimed for a single door in the far wall. It was locked. Roger knelt and had it open before Vie could ask.

The northwest corner room held more boxes and crates. Fragile from age, the contents seemed to have been tucked away and forgotten.

Vie didn't hesitate. She pointed and said, "That one."

Roger reached up and slid out a wooden crate. Dust billowed, and he fought against the sneeze threatening to send him to another dimension.

With Brie's help, they set it down on the floor and opened the lid. Inside, a woman's skeleton lay nestled amongst

packing cotton. The head was missing.
"Lavinia," Roger said. "We found you."
Aethereal light filled the room.

CHAPTER 30
A SCHOONER TO CUBA
Thursday, April 10, 1969

Sea breezes swept across the bustling docks of Charleston Harbor, carrying the promise of adventure in distant lands. Stevedores crowded the pier. A single tall ship was at port — a schooner bound for Cuba. Its bell rang out, the first of three alerts to passengers that the time to embark approached.

John took Lavinia's hand in his. A large smile spread across his face, and he wrapped her in a tight hug. She pushed him away. Fear and worry made her handsome features harsh and bitter.

Lavinia said, "I don't have a ticket."

"I booked passage a long time ago." John pointed. "See, they're loading our luggage now."

She looked down the dock. It seemed to stretch before her, getting longer and longer. "I can't do it."

"Yes, you can," he said.

"What if something goes wrong? Maybe I'll get seasick."

"You won't get seasick."

"What if we sink? Or get attacked by a sea monster?" She was getting worked up. Heart racing, visions of writhing tentacles took her breath away. She raised a hand to her chest. "I need to sit down."

John gripped her arms and stared into her eyes. "None of those things are going to happen. And if they did, at least we'd be together."

"I'm scared," she said.

"I know."

"Will there be another ship? Maybe we can stay for a while."

"No," replied John. His tone was firm and held a note of finality. "This is the one. This is our ship."

The ship's bell rang out again. She chewed at her lip, and her dark hair spilled across her face.

John stepped aside and gestured with his hand. "You have to take the first step. I can't make it for you."

Lavinia looked around her. She recognized the expectant faces; some she had only recently met. The one called Violet, or Vie, carried on her father's legacy. Doctor Wampus watched over her and supported her. Full of energy, Brie Tyler was a gypsy soul. She, too, had a power she was not even aware of. Lastly, she gazed at Roger Vaughn, son of Earl Wolverton. Stranded in Terra, he was like the sea breeze, promising adventure but also fraught with disaster.

The last bell rang. It was time. She turned back toward the long dock. It seemed to stretch forever. The sun beat down, illuminating the path she must take. After one last look around, she stepped toward the light.

Standing in the corner storage room, Roger watched the aethereal image fade. Slowly, the boxes and crates took shape and became solid once more. Brie held his hand, tears streaming down her face. Vie sniffled and tried to hide her tears behind her hand. Roger sighed as he brought up his hand and touched his face. It was nice to know that he still felt something.

Then he heard the gunshot.

"Come on," he urged.

"What about Lavinia?" asked Vie, gesturing with the skull. "We can't leave her here."

Lifting the crate, he replied, "We'll bring her with us."

They rushed out of the museum. Patrol cars and fire trucks were just arriving. Their emergency sirens pierced the night air. Lights in windows snapped on as the sleeping neighborhood awoke.

North of the museum, Nate and Tee waited under the sprawling canopy of an oak tree. Mister Brisbane knelt at their feet, his hands behind his head. Off to the side, a body lay on the ground.

Major Wilson approached from the shadows. "The judge is dead," he said. "John and Lavinia?"

"They're gone," replied Roger. "It's just a box of bones, now."

"Not just," Brie said.

"Of course, Miss Tyler," Major Wilson said.

"What happened?" Roger asked. Suspicion flared in his mind, but he wanted to hear the official answer.

"Mister Brisbane ambushed us outside the museum.

Shot the judge in the head," Major Wilson replied. "It was quicker than what I wanted."

"I guess it was for the best," Roger admitted.

Everyone turned to him.

He nodded toward the body and said, "If this had gone to trial..."

The major gave him a sharp look. "I'll be staying on for a while until a replacement can be found for Lieutenant Bell. If you need anything, anything at all, you only need to ask."

"We need a place to bury Lavinia," said Vie.

"Assuming Mister Fisher's body wasn't disturbed, I'd like to see her interred at the Potter's Field with her husband," said Brie.

"How would we know?" Roger asked.

"The Potter's Field? I've never heard of it," said Major Wilson.

"It's the burial ground near Saint Luke's Chapel," replied Brie.

"Still never heard of it," he said.

"It's owned by the Medical College," added Roger. "Where the buildings are under construction on Ashley Avenue."

"The old Military Academy?" The major's eyes went wide. "The remains they found under the Basic Science Building."

Roger nodded. "That's the one."

"I'll see what I can do."

It rained the day of the funeral. Dressed in his best suit and wearing his trilby, Roger waited in the narthex with Tee, Nate, Major Wilson, James Fogartie, and Scott Silva. According to the sign on the wall, the small chapel had a bit of history, having originally been a federal arsenal then, later, a school for orphaned boys.

Father Keating gave them a subtle nod, and the six men approached the altar where Lavinia's remains had been placed inside a plain pine box.

Having not advertised the event, the chapel was nearly empty. Brie and Vie were there. Roger was surprised to see Brie's parents and her sister, Cam. He wasn't surprised by their aloofness toward him. He had a feeling they didn't understand the funeral's importance, though Nate and Brie had surely tried to explain it.

Mister Owens and Mister Mathews sat on the opposite

side of the aisle. Roger had greeted them, but they, too, remained standoffish. Mister Brisbane was there as well. He wore a plain suit, but there was an officer on either side of him. Roger had overheard he'd be out of gaol in a few years, with good behavior. It seemed to Roger that he and the major had cut a deal.

Roger took up his position beside the casket and grabbed hold of the huckle. Lighter than expected, he lifted the casket with the other pall bearers, and they marched out into the yard, where a six-foot deep hole waited for them.

Father Keating spoke a few words to the gathered audience. Raising his hand, he blessed everyone and said, "Go in peace."

A gravedigger slid straps around the coffin and lowered it into the grave using a portable winch. Beside the grave, a shovel protruded from the pile of dirt. Each of the men there took hold of it and dropped a shovel-load on top of the box. Brie stood in line and Vie followed her lead.

For Roger, the service seemed cold — a mere formality. Father Keating gave an encouraging eulogy, but it was clear he maintained a moral distance, not knowing if Lavinia was even baptized.

The gravediggers finished filling the hole. Major Wilson stood off to the side, talking with Mister Brisbane. Roger didn't know what favors the major had cashed in, but he was glad. All things considered, Lavinia's remains were where they were supposed to be — hopefully, never to be disturbed again.

"Mister Vaughn," Mister Tyler said as he approached.

"Sir," Roger replied.

"Major Wilson speaks highly of you. He told me the police had officially apologized for suspecting you of murdering those men."

"Yes, sir, they did."

"I'm not sure what went on, but I'm glad you returned our daughter back to us. Thank you."

"You're more than welcome," replied Roger.

"This may be an inappropriate place, but I have to know. What are your intentions with Brie?"

"Keep her safe," he replied.

"Anything else?"

Roger swallowed. He remembered Nate telling him to be

direct. Turning to face Mister Tyler, he said, "Sir, I know you don't see me as an acceptable suitor. I'm not Catholic. You don't know my parents, or where I come from. But know that, even though I've only known her a short time, Brie means the world to me. I'll do anything it takes to be by her side, for as long as she'll let me."

Mister Tyler made a noise, somewhere between a cough and a clearing of the throat.

They both glanced at Brie, who stood talking with her mother outside the chapel. By the look of it, she was having a similar conversation with Mrs. Tyler.

Yes, he wanted to be with Brie, but there was more to it. Traditional people, Roger couldn't tell her parents that Brie was able to cast magic. He didn't know how or why. He didn't know what would happen if they left it alone: would it die of its own accord — or grow? On Gaia, if magic-users couldn't control their power, it consumed them.

Mister Tyler straightened, as if he had come to a decision. "I'll have Nate pick you up tomorrow morning."

"Sir?" Roger asked.

"You're going to help me fix Brie's car."

"Yes, sir."

Mister Tyler shook his hand and headed toward his family.

Brie smiled at him brightly and gave him a thumbs up.

Roger returned it, not knowing what he had committed himself to.

"Journeys end in lovers meeting — every wise man's son doth know," quoted Scott.

Roger said, "Come on, Scott, let's go home."

The End — for now.

Thank You for Reading!

We hope you've enjoyed our latest adventure as much as we enjoyed bringing it to you! No author would be where they are without readers, so please accept a HUGE thank you for taking a chance on our endeavor. Whether you loved it, hated it, or landed somewhere in between, it would be of immense help to us, as well as other readers, if you would take a moment to leave a review on Amazon and/or Goodreads. Even a single sentence will mean a lot.

We love to hear from readers! Feel free to drop us a line at mcdonald.isom@gmail.com Let us know what you loved (or what you hated). If you have questions about the story, we'll do our best to answer them. For more information about cultures, countries, creatures, and races of Gaia, visit the glossary on our website, www.mcdonald-isom.com. You can also find us on Facebook, @McDonald.Isom.author.

There are more adventures yet to come!

Please keep reading for a behind the scenes dive into the fact vs. fiction in our story, as well as sources for a little sleuthing of your own!

Behind the Scenes

If you had not already guessed, writers are rather like magpies. We collect bits of interesting information and hoard it away for later use as the occasion arises. Several years ago, a contractor invited Jason to tour the Old City Jail in downtown Charleston with him. About the same time, Stormy was reading <u>Six Miles to Charleston (SC): the True Story of John and Lavinia Fisher</u>. Jason's intriguing visit, his numerous photos, and Bruce Orr's book inspired us to research the jail's long and sordid history and to dig further into the legend of Lavinia Fisher. That research led us to the South Carolina Historical Society archives, where we read John Blake White's description of John and Lavinia's hanging and the executioner employed for the task. Newspaper articles, old maps, and the few available court records proved to contain conflicting information regarding Six Mile House and its infamous caretakers. We asked ourselves, what if the Fishers really were innocent as they claimed? Would their spirits move on to whatever lies beyond, or would they linger to seek revenge against those who wronged them?

Because so much history informed and inspired *Message for the Devil*, we wanted to give you a bit of "Fact from Fiction." If you find you have questions about places or events in our tales not covered in the following pages, please reach out to us via email (mcdonald.isom@gmail.com) or through our Facebook page:
(https://www.facebook.com/McDonald.Isom.Author).

Facts:

The 1908 Police Station: R. Thomas Short, architect, designed the facility located on the corner of St. Philip and Vanderhorst streets.   The building had a castle-like appearance, including the corner tower and turret. Charleston's central police station remained at this location until 1974, when operations moved to Lockwood Drive Extension.

Antonio de Erqueta: Assayer for Spain, he ran the mint from 1651 to 1679. His mark "E" can be found on many of the silver reales — "Pieces of 8" — with their distinctive Pillars of Hercules over the waves of the Atlantic Ocean design.

Charleston History Museum: "America's First Museum" founded in 1773 by the Charleston Library Society, the museum occupied the Thompson Auditorium at the corner of Calhoun and Rutledge avenues from 1907 to 1979. On October 18th, 1981, the vacant building burned under mysterious circumstances.   Today, the grand entrance columns (pictured on this book's cover) stand vigil in Charleston's 2.7-acre Cannon Park.

Gullah: The language spoken by Tee, RC, and Gramma Huger. Although use waned for many years (as of 2021, there were an estimated 5,000 people semi-fluent and only 300 fluent speakers), the creation of the Gullah-Geechee heritage corridor has sparked renewed interest in both the language and culture. We've tried our best to be true to the language, and hope readers will forgive any errors we have committed.

Hoodoo: Equal parts belief system, magic, and shamanic medicine native to the Gullah and Geechee cultures of the Carolinas and Georgia. Goofer Dust is but one of many "tools" in a Root Doctor's repertoire. There are many great books on the subject, written by members of the Gullah/Geechee community, anthropologists, and botanists. We strongly encourage you to research and explore the fascinating history of this culture.

Lavinia Fisher: Touted as South Carolina's (possibly the United States in general) first female serial killer. In 1819, she and her husband, John Fisher, were arrested for assault. In 1820, the couple were convicted and hanged for the crime of highway robbery. It was not until many years after the fact that articles and stories begin to claim she was a witch who poisoned her victims with oleander tea.

Magnolia Cemetery: Still in operation today, the expansive cemetery contains a wide array of funerary monuments and markers dating from the mid 1800s to modern times. The pyramid tomb is a real building on the property.

Magnolia Gardens: Founded in 1676 by the Drayton family, the property was originally a rice plantation. Reverend John Drayton created the gardens for his wife in the 1840s. The grounds were opened to the public in the 1870s and remain a popular botanical garden, education center, and wedding venue to this day. (www.magnoliaplantation.com)

The Old City Jail: Built in 1802 and decommissioned in 1939, the jail originally consisted of four stories, topped with a two-story octagonal tower. It lay vacant under the ownership of the Charleston Housing Authority. Later, the American College of the Building Arts purchased the property and taught aspiring historic preservationists joinery and other "lost" arts. In more recent years, the property was purchased by a development company with plans to convert it into offices and an event center.

Roger's Office: The building on Church Street which Roger calls home and office is a real building with an art gallery on its first floor.

Sandborn Map Company: Founded in 1866, this company created lithographic maps of towns and cities in the United States (roughly 12,000 total) for use by fire insurance companies to assess liability. Although the last maps were published in the late 1970s, they are still available in various historic archives and through your local library.

Fiction:

The Conspiracists: Although we used the actual juror list from John and Lavinia's trial, the "descendants" who appear in this tale, the curse, and the conspiracy are complete fictions. We hope the true descendants of those jurors will forgive our tall tale.

Doctor Wampus: to our knowledge, there is not, nor has there ever been, a root doctor who called himself by this name.

Roger's Office: We loved the look of a real building on Church Street so much we placed Dr. Wampus (*Thief on King Street*) and now our favorite Gaian spy on its second floor. We've never actually visited the upper floors, so the layout and décor are pure fiction.

Wallace Plantation: Although https://south-carolina-plantations.com lists a "Wallace Place Plantation" in Beaufort County, there were none in Charleston County (to the best of our knowledge) by that name. The name of our fictional property came from a local waterway named Wallace Creek. The house and grounds portrayed here are not based on any single real-world location.

Acknowledgements

The authors would like to recognize the language, culture, traditional medicine, and beliefs of the Gullah community of the South Carolina sea islands. We offer our deepest respect to the ancestors and keepers of the language and heritage of this rich community.

We would also like to give recognition to the following authors and organizations whose work informed and inspired this story:

Bailey, Cornelia Walker with Christina Bledsoe. *God, Dr. Buzzard, and the Bolito Man – A Saltwater Geechee Talks about Life on Sapelo Island, Georgia.* Anchor Books, 2000

Geraty, Virginia Mixson. *Gullah Fuh Oonuh/ Gullah for You: A Guide to the Gullah Language (English and Gullah Edition).* Sandlapper Publishing Company, 1998

Gulf States Historical Magazine, Vol 1 (July 1902 - May 1903)

Gullah Geechee Cultural Heritage Corridor. https://gullahgeecheecorridor.org http://visitgullahgeechee.com/

Martin, Margaret Rhett. *Charleston Ghosts.* Columbia: University of South Carolina Press, 1963

McTeer, J.E. *Fifty Years as a Low Country Witch Doctor.* iUniverse, 2013

Montgomery, Jack. *American Shamans: Journeys with Traditional Healers.* Busca Inc, 2008

Neilson, Peter. *Recollections of a Six Years Residence in the United States of America.* 1890

Orr, Bruce. *Six Miles to Charleston (SC): The True Story of John and Lavinia Fisher.* The History Press, 2010

South Carolina Historical Society. The Fireproof Building, 100 Meeting Street, Charleston, SC 29401. (843) 723.3225 www.schistory.org

SCHS Archives. 205 Calhoun Street, Room 340, Charleston, SC 29401

Trinkley, Michael, Hacker, Debi, & Southerland Nicole. *The Silence of the Dead: Giving Charleston Cemeteries a Voice.* Chicora Foundation, 2010

White, John Blake. *Essays on Capital Punishment.* South Carolina Historical Society, Charleston, SC, 1834

Zamba (edited by Neilson, Peter). *The Life and Adventures of Zamba, an African Negro King; and his Experience of Slavery in South Carolina,* 1847

There are so many friends who have helped us hone this story. Foremost, we'd like to express our appreciation to our editor, Dana Isaacson, who never hesitates to ask the tough questions that unfailingly improve our stories. A huge thank you as well to our Beta Readers, who helped pick apart and polish our story: David B., Lacy B., Leslie B., Alan, I., Jimmy R., John R. Last, but not least, for critical analysis and five decades of friendship, Ray W.

About the Authors

Jason McDonald: An engineer by day and world builder by night, Jason is an advocate for using both sides of the brain. With his stepfather as a guide, Jason traveled the worlds of Edgar Rice Burroughs, Robert E. Howard, and J. R. R. Tolkien at an early age. As he grew older, he discovered Dungeons and Dragons and the joys of creating his own campaigns.

During all this, Jason graduated from Clemson University and embarked on a career in structural engineering. Now, he owns a successful engineering firm, where he continues to design a wide range of projects. His attention to detail and vivid imagination help shape the various adventures that challenge his characters.

Stormy McDonald: Coming from a family of storytellers — traditional, oral storytellers, that is — it's little wonder that Stormy is driven to weave words as well. She can't remember a time when she didn't love books — from the feel and smell of the pages, to the information they hold, to the tales that they tell — but storytelling is a labor of love, which doesn't always pay the bills. A ridiculous variety of side jobs have supported her writing habit, including waitress, security guard, library minion, salesperson, hairdresser, handyman, engineering drafter, and small business owner.

www.ingramcontent.com/pod-product-compliance
Lightning Source LLC
Chambersburg PA
CBHW060810190726
48285CB00002B/616